MW00908560

To my two angels who have been with me the whole time while writing *Black Switch*. You put words in my mind I could never have imaged. You put inspiration in my heart to compose with feverish passion. And you gave me the confidence to know that the story I put forth on paper is truly special. Because of you, for the first time in my life, I have been able to do something extraordinary and incredibly proud to have written. For that, I am internally grateful.

D. Van Bui

Black Switch

Austin Macauley Publishers™
London * Cambridge * New York * Sharjah

Ordering Information
Quantity sales: Special discounts are available on quantity purchases by corporations, associations, and others. For details, contact the publisher at the address below.

Publisher's Cataloging-in-Publication data
Bui, D. Van
Black Switch

ISBN 9781647505974 (Paperback)
ISBN 9781638293682 (Hardback)
ISBN 9781638293699 (Audiobook)
ISBN 9781647505981 (ePub e-book)

Library of Congress Control Number: 2022907868

www.austinmacauley.com/us

First Published 2022
Austin Macauley Publishers LLC
40 Wall Street, 33rd Floor, Suite 3302
New York, NY 10005
USA

mail-usa@austinmacauley.com
+1 (646) 5125767

No words can describe the incredible support, my family has given me. To my children, Adriana, Ceci, and Sebastian you guys are my love and my life always and forever. Nothing ever means anything without you all in it. Thank you for always being there for me!

And a special shout out to my husband, Wayne. I want you to know that this book is a love note to you… my darling. You will never stop being my muse. I could never have written it without you in mind. After all these years, I love you more than I could ever imagine. Thank you for giving me such a great family and life with you!

Prologue
Roots

Louisville, Kentucky

Sebastian Sinclair was typing away on his computer, excited about some brand-new project he was working on. This assignment would give him the promotion he needed to move up in the company, he thought.

Currently, he was a junior director at the Brown-Forman Corporation. Widely known for their massive empire in the liquor business. He loved his job. Maybe a little too much. It was close to the end of the day when he looked at his phone. He had gotten a text from his wife:

When you get home, we need to talk.

"Christ, what is she upset about now?" When he got home from work, she started harping on him about spending more time with her. She was growing tired of being neglected. "Come on, Sebastian, let's go away together for once."

"Alexia, I can't; with all the work they are shoving at me, there's just no way I can take time off."

"But it will be on the weekend, Sebastian."

"Alexia, I have a deadline to finish this project, and I need the weekend to fine-tune whatever the executives tell me to polish up."

"How many times are you going to keep putting your work ahead of me?"

"What do you mean? I have to work...you can't penalize me for that?"

Alexia let out a deep sigh. "Okay Sebastian, don't say I didn't try."

"So now you are saying that I'm not trying?"

"Sebastian...when was the last time we even went out together?"

He started to get defensive. "Two weeks ago, we went out with Charles and Stephanie."

"That's the problem...if we do go out, it's always with other people. I'm just trying to get us back on track. I can't remember the last time we went out by ourselves. Don't you miss just the two of us?"

He was so annoyed that she was even having this conversation with him. "How can you think that I don't?"

Alexia rolled her eyes. "This conversation is going nowhere, Sebastian. Just forget it."

Thank God, he thought to himself. *Dodged another one with her*. "Listen, I can't go away, but I'll make sure to carve out some time for you on Saturday."

Internally, she was infuriated with him...*he'll just never get it*, she realized.

He got up for work the next morning, ready to start the day. He picked up his phone and took off. On the way there, he was thinking about the specs to the new design layout project he was working on last night. If the executives approved of his plans, he would have to travel back and forth to Bordeaux, France, for a year to watch over the development. Alexia would not be happy to hear that news. But he didn't care, he loved traveling to Europe. This would be his third project overseas.

"Shit...I left the design layout on the counter." But they don't need to be shown to the executives until later on in the afternoon. He'd just go home at lunch to get them, he decided.

When he got to work, he noticed Charles standing by his office. He was one of his best friends. "Hey bro, what's up?"

"Nothing man, just came by to chat for a minute."

"Oh yeah, about what?"

"Nothing really, just wanted to see how things are going with you?"

"Well, Alexia is driving me crazy."

"Why?"

"I'm trying to move up in the company, and she doesn't get it. She keeps complaining that I don't give her enough attention."

"Oh, man, sorry. But may I offer you some advice from a friend to a friend?"

"What's that?"

"Sometimes you got to weigh in what is more important...it's either her...or it's your ranking in life."

"Charles, my ranking is for her!"

"Really Sebastian? You're not even buying that, I can see it on your face."

"Aw Charles…you're such a better person than me. Why are you not married already?"

Charles looked somber for a minute. "I am in love with someone, but she is married."

"I thought you were seeing Stephanie. Man, she's hot."

"Yes well, although she is hot, she is not the one."

"So this girl who you are in love with, what makes you think she will leave her husband for you?"

"We talk every day and meet up often. We have become very…close."

"I see." Sebastian glanced at his watch. "Oh God Charles, you are going to kill me right now, but I need to cut our talk short. I have to finish something that I promised would be done this morning."

"Hey sure, no problem buddy. I'll see you later." Charles walked out of his office and closed the door.

He continued to work. Hours went by and he noticed it was already 12:20 pm. *Time flies*, he said to himself. As he was driving home, he realized that maybe he was being too hard on Alexia. He knew she didn't have to work today, so he thought he would surprise her by bringing home some lunch.

He ordered her favorite Stromboli, but it took forever to get the order. It was almost 1:30 pm before he arrived. When he came through the door, she was surprised to see him. "Hey there…what are you doing home?"

"Well, I forgot my spec designs so I thought I would come home and surprise you with some lunch." He held up the food.

"Oh Sebastian, that was nice of you, but I already ate. I'll save it for dinner though."

When he went to look at the counter for his project, he noticed it wasn't there anymore. It had been replaced by two sets of plating on the table. *What the hell is going on here?* He thought about any other explanation he could think of that would give him a different conclusion. He blew out a deep breath and moved his hand through his hair. "Um, Alexia…" His face directed her to the plating. "Is there something you're not telling me?"

She just looked at him…determination in her eyes. *This was it*, she thought. "Yes…Sebastian, there is. I'm actually glad you found out this way. It makes it easier."

"Alexia, how could you do this to me, I love you!"

There was no way she was taking that…practically screaming at him, she said, "No…you don't, Sebastian! You don't treat me with love! You don't talk to me with love! And you certainly don't show me your love!…It's over with! I've decided to see someone else!"

Sebastian just sat there. Jealousy starting to seep through his veins. "Who is the guy?" He was getting angrier by the second. "Who is this person you…" And then he stopped for a moment because a previous conversation started replaying over in his head. *We talk every day and meet up often. We have become very…close.* "Alexia…please don't tell me it's Charles."

She just stood there and said with no emotion, "What if it was?"

"Goddammit Alexia!"

Without even thinking, he grabbed his keys and went to work. When he got there, he was on the hunt for Charles. Going down the hallway, he asked anybody he saw if they knew where he was. But nobody knew. Finally, ten minutes later, he spotted him.

Sebastian went up to him. "What the fuck, Charles? You're supposed to be one of my best friends!"

Charles stood at a strong stance. "I'm sorry, Sebastian. But I love her. I'm able to give her what you are not. Initially, I felt horrible about doing this to you. However, you said it yourself today…the rank you hold in life is more important than the love you have for her. That is your choice, not mine.

"Before I could go through with it, I had to give you one more shot at keeping her. That is why I had that conversation with you this morning. I tried to provide you with one last opportunity to keep her. If you had shown one ounce of the love I have for her, I would have bailed out.

"I made my decision with a clear conscience, and you can believe me when I say this, so did she. We decided we were going to tell you this weekend. But she obviously had the burden of informing you on her own."

Sebastian lost it. In his fury…he began to pulverize him. Screaming at him. Punching him. It wasn't till security came in and pulled Sebastian off Charles that he started to realize how bad he was beating him up.

The next thing he knew…he was in Human Resources getting fired, of course. "Sebastian…it's not okay what you did. We unfortunately have to terminate our contract with you. You need to leave now."

He left the office. While he was leaving…all he could think about was how bad he was going to make Alexia pay for it in the divorce.

Chapter 1
Good Riddance

It had almost been a whole year since they had started the divorce proceedings. It had given Sebastian time to think. How his marriage had ended with Alexia in such a short amount of time. But what was worse was the regret of how he handled Charles. Finding a new job was painful. No one would hire him on that level ever again. He had to settle with anyone who would take him. He landed up getting a job as an appliance technician for a company called 'We Do It Right Appliances'.

His boss Henry hired Sebastian because he fit the profile. When he first walked in for the interview, Henry immediately took notice of his appearance. He thought, *Why would a guy like this, very well-groomed and dressed up in a sharp suit, be knocking on my door for a job? Let's see what this is all about*, he thought.

He sat down at his desk and picked up his resume. "Just give me a moment to look this over." He squinted his eyes to view it. After a minute, he laid the paper back down on his desk. "So Mr. Sinclair, do you have any experience repairing appliances?"

"No, actually I don't, but I'm willing to train for whatever you need me to fix."

"Oh, that's good. I do occasionally take on new trainees." Sebastian couldn't believe he was sinking this low.

Henry took another look at his resume. "I see your last job title was a junior director; it looks a little weird that you are now seeking employment as a repair technician."

"Yes well, let's just say things didn't pan out the way I had hoped."

"That's all you have to say about the subject matter?"

Sebastian hated explaining his circumstances. "Well, the short version is my soon to be ex-wife had an affair with a friend of mine at work, and that didn't sit well with me. Unfortunately, my former employer did not like the way I handled it."

"Oh, I see, that is quite unfortunate."

Most employers would not find Sebastian's plate so enticing. But Henry saw a different version of his story. Here was a guy who didn't get fired because he can't perform. He got canned for personal reasons, completely unrelated to his work abilities. So to him, he saw Sebastian as a smart, hardworking man, young and could handle physical labor if necessary. But more importantly, he would be unlikely to ever quit given how desperate he was for a job…any job.

In Henry's line of work, employees came and went all the time. If you invested in all the training needed for the job, it could cost him a great deal of money if they quit early on. That was why he sought out people like Sebastian. Longevity was more important than personal flaws.

"Okay, Sebastian, I'll give you a shot. You can start tomorrow. Of course, wearing a suit will no longer be necessary for this line of work." Henry got up and started roaming his hands through a box. He pulled out five shirts with his company logo on it and tossed them over to Sebastian. "Just wear one of these with a pair of clean jeans that have no holes in them."

When Sebastian left the interview, he thought about Alexia. If he had only given her more attention. That was all she was asking for. All that hard work of trying to move up in the company and gaining status in life was for nothing. Karma was definitely having its way with him. That was the first time, perspective of what should be important to him started to surface.

But that interview happened over ten and half months ago. He had plenty of time to gain much more perspective since then. So as he was sitting in his lawyer's office waiting for him to walk in and give another way of how to screw his ex over again, a new thought began to sink in.

He could either continue to keep her in divorce hell or cut his losses and just move on with his life. What was he getting out of holding her hostage anyway? She had clearly moved on with Charles. It was at this moment he decided to end the game.

Just then, his lawyer, Robert, walked in. "Hey Sebastian, sorry I kept you waiting. I had to grab copies of something else I found out about Alexia. Apparently, she—"

However, Sebastian didn't want to hear about any more dirt he had on her. "Excuse me, Robert…sorry to interrupt. And please don't kill me, but I'm reversing my decision on the divorce agreement. Just…give it all to her."

"Give it all to her…are you nuts?" Robert did not like what he was hearing. "Look, she doesn't have a leg to stand on. She is the one who cheated on you. You lost your job because of her, for Christ's sake, and now look at where you work! Please Sebastian, as your lawyer and your friend, listen to me. I can win this for you. You are making a mistake!"

Sebastian thought about it for a second…but decided to stick with his gut. "Robert…I know you mean well." He had been a good friend to Sebastian for as long as he could remember. They grew up down the street from each other and always had each other's back. Robert was a bulldog in life. He succeeded at everything he sought. It was why he got along with Sebastian so well. They were both go-getters in their aspirations. It killed him to watch his friend go down like this.

But Sebastian had slowly been changing in a different direction for quite some time now. That was why he was able to look at his friend with a stoic face and say, "It's time to let it go. Nothing good came from this marriage, including me. I was an asshole to her. It is why she cheated on me in the first place. Now, she is pregnant with Charles's baby. I caused my own demise with my current employment situation. We all make choices. I'm trying to make the right one now."

"Sebastian…you sound like your mind's been made up."

"It is Robert. I can't do this anymore."

Losing a divorce case was not someSthing Robert took lightly. "Are you sure, Sebastian? Because there is no going back on this. Have you thought about everything you are giving up? Are you just going to let go of all your investments? The house alone, if sold in the market today, would be worth almost double of what you already put into it. Why would you give that up?"

"That's just it, Robert. I don't look at it that way anymore. Karma has made sure of that. You mentioned my work. The job I have now can't keep up with the status I once was able to pay for. Even if I am rewarded a good amount of money, how long will that money last to keep up with that lifestyle?"

"Then sell the house and keep the money for yourself. Use it for whatever you like down the road. But don't just give it all to her. Let's wait this out!"

"And for how long, Robert! This is never going to end. I have thought about this decision. It's been weighing on my shoulders for a while now. I just didn't have the guts to do it till now."

Robert could see his friend's conviction was set. There was no turning him back. So, with a heavy heart, he conceded. "Okay, Sebastian, I'll send you the revised paperwork next week for you to sign."

"Thank you. I know this is hard for you to digest. However, there is something in my gut telling me that this is how it needs to end for me." Then he got up and gave his longtime friend a hug. "Thanks for always being there for me."

"Anytime, man."

With that, he turned around and left.

Sebastian quietly moved on with his life after the divorce. He felt this deep need to work on his personal life. He continued to think about his relationship with himself and others. How he could mistreat someone so severely that it would cause her to cheat on him with one of his best friends. Going through something like that changes you.

Doing the right thing with Alexia made him feel good about himself. Something he was unfamiliar with for a very long time. It gave him a new platform to live off. He even decided to write Alexia a letter of apology.

This will be a new beginning to a horrible ending, he thought to himself. He went to his computer and started to type:

From: Sebastians@yahoo.com
To: alexiab@gmail.com
Alexia,

I'm sure you will be surprised to read this email. Especially after everything that I put you through in the divorce. But I've had some time to reflect on my behavior with you. Let's just say, I didn't come out on top. You were right all along, you know.

I never treated you with the love you deserved. In my own way, I thought I was giving you a good life. But in retrospect, I wish I would have taken a step back and paid more attention to you. I was wrong on so many levels. I want you to know that I never meant to hurt you.

Thank you for the years you gave me. I may not have appreciated it back then. However, it has taught me so much more than you will ever know. I took your love for granted, and now the lesson has been learned.

I wish you and Charles all the best. In fact, I heard you two were expecting a child. I'm glad it was with him. I know his love is strong with you. I regret very much how I treated him when I found out about your relationship. I'm truly sorry for all the pain I caused both of you.

As for me, I'm not sure where my road will lead, but I feel good about starting fresh. These words I am writing to you today is the foundation of my new beginning.

Take care of yourself, friend!
Sincerely yours,
Sebastian.

His eyes began to tear a little as he pressed the send button. *That was long overdue*, he thought. *Time to move on with my life now.*

Sometime later, after he wrote that letter, things in his life really did start to alter. Only, not at all the way he ever expected it to. Out of nowhere, strange phenomena started to occur. He was experiencing premonitions and high levels of foresight like something you would only see in movies.

It all started one day when he was doing his regular weekly grocery shopping. When he was done getting everything he needed, he got in line to check out. The clerk grabbed his attention right away. He had this incredible overwhelming feeling inside that she was heartbroken over something. Yet on the outside, she greeted her customers with a happy smile and even joked around with one. The despairing emotion he felt internally from her was so intense he had to ask her.

"Excuse me…I'm sorry, I hate to ask you this, but I just have to know. Is everything alright with you? I mean, you don't look visibly upset. Still, I have this sense that something has made you exceptionally heartbroken."

She just stared at him for a second, her eyes started to water. But he could tell there was no way she was going to cry. She held it back in and barely whispered the next words. "Do you see that guy over there bagging groceries at the next counter?"

Sebastian looked over and quickly turned back around. "What about him?"

"We were supposed to get married last week. Only...I saw a text. It was a very explicit one with another woman. We're now broken up."

"I see, I'm sorry to hear that. Obviously, it's his loss."

She looked at him curiously. "I thought I was pulling off a pretty good performance?"

Sebastian smiled. "As I told you...you are putting on a good show. You do look incredibly happy from the outside. You can rest assured of that. I'm sorry to have intruded."

"It's okay, it was actually kind of nice knowing someone got me today." With that, he grabbed his groceries and walked away.

Weeks later, he was taking a walk at Brown Park when suddenly, he stopped in his tracks. A deep heaviness began to take over his chest. No matter how much pressure he put on it, it would not go away. Then without any warning, he began to hear voices in his head. Screaming loud sounds. "Oh, my God!...Tony come here!...I love you...Help!...Help!...This isn't happening!"

It was hundreds of voices all together with the same kind of terrifying expressions. When the noise finally stopped, he caught his breath. *Wow, what the heck was that?*

When he got home from his walk, he turned on the TV...there was breaking news that a bridge had collapsed into the water; understanding took over Sebastian. It must have been the exact same time it was occurring. He knew what he had been hearing. The cries of people falling off that bridge.

What was happening to him? It was so confusing. He was just a normal human guy. How could this be? But it didn't stop there. Oh no, in fact, his intuitive abilities seemed to expand into other areas as well.

Monday morning, he got up to go to work. He grabbed his keys and took off in his car. As he was driving, he noticed something unusual happening. No...unusual didn't describe it. It was just simply unbelievable. His body began to feel distinct pockets of energy. Some of the pockets felt light and connected to a feeling of happiness. Some of the pockets felt dark and connected to a sense of heaviness, almost like in a despondent state. It was exhausting for him to feel it really.

He had just pulled into the parking lot of his work. Depression suddenly took over his thoughts. Turning off his car, he reflected on his job. *God, I hate this place!* He remembered the first time he came in for an interview. He had opened the front door only to find stuff...everywhere! The place was not just filthy, but filled with wall to wall junk. It was as if they never threw a single thing away since they had opened their doors in 1991.

Even so, tolerating the garbage was nothing compared to putting up with his boss. He was the most condescending person he had ever met. Constantly yelling and degrading everyone around him. Including his wife, who also worked for him.

Still, at the end of the day, Henry knew all too well that Sebastian needed this job. So much so, he knew he would put up with whatever crap he dealt out to him or anyone else for that matter. It was the way he rolled with his employees and they simply learned to accept it.

Just then, he looked down at his watch and realized it was time to go in. *There's only so much reflection I can take anyway.* When he walked through the office door, he saw his friend, John, wondering the hallway. "Hey man, what's up…how's Henry today?" Sadly, this was a common question most employees asked when they first stepped foot into work.

"Well…if you must know. I just went by his office to drop off some documents. When I gave it to him, he proceeded to ask me why I filled out all the forms. I said, remember you asked me to do it last week. He said, 'No, I didn't.' I said, yes, you did.

"So then, he decided to look through the paperwork. He told me that all the documentation had been filled out wrong and asked me what I was going to do about it. I told him I did the best I could, and that I was surprised he had even asked me to fill it out in the first place. Of course, the old fool denied ever telling me to do such a thing. At that point, he was so irritated with me he threw all the forms in the air and kicked me out of his office."

"Oh…wow…you would think by now I would have expected that story coming a mile away."

"I know, right!" They both laughed.

"Well, thanks for the heads up."

"No problem, bud, anytime." After that, they walked away and carried on with their day.

He walked over to his desk and sat down to work on some order forms he needed to push through this week. A couple moments later, he overheard his boss's wife Margaret talking with the carrier from UPS. He couldn't help but overhear the conversation.

The guy sounded like he was giving Margaret a hard time. "Ever think of throwing anything away here?" Margaret looked at him, upset with his comment but nevertheless tried to defend herself.

"Oh, it's not what you think. You see, we keep these items around in case we need to use them down the road."

The carrier looked at her. "Lady…if it looks like a duck and quacks like a duck…it's a duck."

Internally, Sebastian started to laugh. Not at Margaret specifically. It was Henry who made her save everything. It was just nice to finally hear someone else say what he couldn't.

When the UPS man left, Margaret came up to Sebastian. "The nerve of that guy thinking we're hoarders, he just…" but before she could finish the conversation, Sebastian began feeling something coming from the stairs. He couldn't believe it. It was a large patch of darkness, and it was attached to his boss. How did he know what Henry's energy felt like anyway? He could not even physically see his boss at this point. In spite of that, he was absolutely positive he was right.

Sure enough, seconds later, Henry appeared running down the stairs. "Margaret…why did you send out those orders without my approval?" Sadly, this scene was nothing new for her. She knew her place in his life, and it was under the bottom of his shoe.

"I'm so sorry…I didn't realize you needed to know."

"How is it that you never get it right, Margaret?"

"You're right, Henry, again I'm sorry. I need to work on that."

Immediately after their conversation, he proceeded to walk towards Sebastian's area. "Did you get those parts I asked you to order?" At first, he was struggling to tell him that they hadn't arrived yet. But quickly, he realized Henry's energy had faded into a more neutral zone. How peculiar.

After work, while he was driving home, he got to thinking about his new abilities he was acquiring. They were really starting to come at him full blast. Although it was all fascinating and exciting for Sebastian to have these…these…well, he wasn't even sure what to really call them. He realized at that moment, he had absolutely no understanding on how to control them. If this got any stronger, he worried it might become more of a problem than he could handle.

The next day he woke up, made some breakfast, and left for work. Of course, the same light and dark pockets came back. However, this time, something additional occurred. He heard a voice in his ear, a slight whisper really…

"…Tell her I'm still around."

"What the hell?" He had heard voices before, but never one singular voice directed specifically to him. Sebastian immediately pulled his car over to the side of the road.

"Okay, who's doing that?" He waited for somebody to answer. But nothing came. After about five minutes, he got back on the road.

When he arrived at the office, he went straight to his desk. Once again, he began to feel his boss's energy. Oh crap…here we go. He could feel Henry directly behind him at this point. He put a fake smile on his face and turned around.

"Can I help you with something, Henry?"

"Yes actually, let's do a conference call with Metro Compute. They have a new product I'm interested in purchasing." He nodded his head in agreement and followed him over to his office.

Everything went fine in the first part of the conversation. But then Henry's energy began to change. He was growing more agitated with Sebastian by the minute. The pressure of his darkness was rising and rising.

All of a sudden, Henry burst, "Just SHUT UP, Sebastian! You don't know what you are talking about!"

The vendor was taken back by how he spoke to his own employee. He was almost going to say something, but then stopped himself. At the end of the day, he wanted the sell more than helping out Sebastian.

When they finished the conference call, his boss simply got up and walked away. Which would have been fine as far as Sebastian was concerned. The problem was, Henry's darkness never left his space, and slowly, it started connecting with Sebastian's body. As much as he tried, the ugliness latched on to him.

Later that night, he went to the grocery store. Everyone there seemed to bother him. There was no reason for him to be so annoyed. But no matter how much he attempted to amend his behavior, he just couldn't shake it. Thank God he got out of there without telling anyone off. The energy of his boss was bringing out this new angry alter ego.

This was exactly what he was worried about…how was he going to tame what he didn't understand?

Chapter 2
Untethered

Weeks went by, and still nothing changed. He couldn't get rid of the negative energy if his life depended on it. He became more and more distraught with the situation. One night he met up with his friend, John, at a placed called, Bourbon Bistro. They both loved to debate the different flavors and aging processes of bourbon. But not this night, tonight Sebastian was hoping to unleash his troubles.

"So what's up man…you don't seem yourself tonight?"

"Ah, yeah, I've been wanting to talk to you about something, but it's not your typical everyday conversation. I need to prep you for what I'm about to say."

"Okay…"

"All right, here it goes…have you ever had that feeling when you know something bad is going to happen, but you can't quite put your finger on why that is? And then inevitably, something terrible really does occur."

"Yeah, I can think of a few times that has happened to me."

"Good, so you get what I'm saying. Now here is the kicker…take that statement and amp it up about 100 times over and you will begin to scratch the surface of where I'm going with this conversation."

"Jesus, Sebastian, what are you saying?"

He leaned in a little closer to John. "Lately, for some unknown reason …I've been experiencing certain unnatural things that most humans are not privy to encounter."

"Like what?"

He took another swig of his drink before letting the rest of his thoughts come out. "…While I was at work today, minding my own business…out of the blue, I felt Henry's need to come and talk to me. I could sense him walking towards me before he physically showed up by my side. And it's not just his energy for that matter. It's everyone around me, including yours."

"Okay …so you're telling me that you can hear my thoughts?"

"Not exactly… It's more like I feel the energy connected to your thoughts."

"So what is going on in my head right now?"

"That's easy, your mind is on me at the present moment. But just for laughs I can divulge something you were thinking about earlier." *Huh, all right …let's see where he goes with this.* He nodded his head in agreeance.

"Okay…before we got into this conversation your thoughts were directed towards the girl located at my nine o'clock with the pretty blonde hair and pink lips. Though…there was also a nervous introspection going on inside you at the same time. I'm guessing maybe you thought she might be out of your league. Even so, the chase of possibly getting her number supersedes your apprehension for rejection."

"Damn, Sebastian. That was unbelievable. How are you able to do that?"

"Well, that is the problem right there…I don't know how? This ability of feeling energy seems to come and go at its choosing. For instance, right now, my ability just left me. I cannot hear or sense anything whatsoever."

"Still Sebastian, when it is turned on, you are dead on balls accurate. Frankly, that's pretty freaking amazing!"

"Well…yes and no. I mean, think about it. How far are these abilities going to take me? And what about the negative energy that I'm taking in? It's not all positive, man. Just think about what it would feel like to be imprisoned with Henry's energy.

"And it's not just that. There are other aptitudes materializing within me as well."

"Damn, bro. This is some juicy shit you are telling me."

Sebastian, took another sip of his drink and let it slowly flow down his throat. "…There are voices. They just randomly pop into my head."

"Voices?" *Jesus.* "Where do you think they are coming from?"

"That's the thing. They're coming from everywhere. For example, not long ago, there was a bridge that collapsed straight into the river. Do you remember hearing about that in the news?"

"Yeah, of course I did. Something like 63 people died."

"Yes, it was a tragic ending for many. And while I wasn't there personally to witness it, I believe I heard it all unfold in my head as it was happening."

"Holy crap, man, I don't know what to say! I mean, I've heard of a sixth sense, but I've never known anyone who has actually proven it to be true." He picked up his phone and googled it. "It says…ESP is when you receive information not through your five regular senses but through your mind, which some people call the sixth sense."

He looked back up at him. "Do you think this might be what you are using?"

"I wish I knew. However, my main concern right now is not about where it is coming from, but rather how to control it."

"Yeah, okay… I see the dilemma." John lifted up his bourbon and was about to take another sip, when his phone began to buzz.

He viewed the caller ID as he picked up the phone. "It's my mother. She's been sick with the flu. I told her to text me if she needs me to come over. So unfortunately, I have to go. I'm sorry to just leave you like this."

"It's okay, man, I understand. Go take care of her. And thanks for giving me an ear."

He grabbed his drink and took his last swig. "I wish I knew more about this stuff so I could help you out."

"No, worries. I didn't expect you to solve my problems. It just felt good to finally be able to tell someone."

He picked up his phone as he was getting ready to leave. "Listen, I do have a little piece of advice if you want to hear it."

"Lay it on me, bro."

"My grandmother used to tell me…*Nada ocurre nunca al azar*. It means…Nothing ever occurs at random." Then he patted him on the back and started to get up out of his seat. "Hope that helps, my friend."

"Ah, not really." They both got a chuckle from that.

"Sorry man, that's all I have for you." Then he smiled and walked away.

Sebastian was left with his own thoughts to stew over for a while. Eventually, he grabbed the bartender's attention again and ordered another Eagle Rare. That's when the girl next to him caught his eye. Although he could not currently feel her energy, he noticed her glance at him. He moved his head in her direction.

"Can I help with something?"

She looked at him with a peculiar expression. "Sorry, I'm not quite sure how to bring this up, but given your circumstances, I guess I couldn't say anything more weird than what has already come out of your mouth."

"Excuse me?"

"I'm sorry…it's just sitting right next to you; I inadvertently heard everything you said to your friend. You're very lucky, though."

"Lucky?"

"Yes, I happen to have a friend who I believe you will very much want to meet." She brought her head in a little closer to him and whispered, "She has 'abilities' too."

He wasn't exactly sure how to take her directness about the subject matter. "Is that so?"

"Yes, it is."

"Okay then…tell me more about this friend of yours."

"Her name is Clarissa. I'm not really sure how to categorize her gifts. However, I can tell you this. She understands quite a bit about this energy issue you are having."

"And how is that?"

"I went to her years ago for an issue I was having, and she was very helpful. We remained friends ever since."

"I see."

She shrugged her shoulders. "You should at least give her a shot. What do you have to lose?"

He thought about it for a second. How odd was it that he would be sitting right next to a person who could actually help him with such a problem. He was so struck with curiosity over meeting this woman; he couldn't help but continue with wherever the conversation was leading.

"I'm sorry, what was your name again?"

"Oh, well, I never actually told you…it's Sophie Freemont. Yours?"

"Sebastian Sinclair."

Sophia had an instant attraction to him. He had wavy black hair and crystal blue eyes that most woman would have a hard time looking away from. But it was not just because of his good looks. The whole energy thing he had going on was also an enticement. She had recently found out in a letter that her father passed away. She hadn't spoken to him in over 5 years. Being around someone who may or may not have access to the dead realm was oddly appealing to her.

"I can text Clarissa and see if she can fit you in tomorrow evening?"

"Wow, tomorrow, that quick?"

"Sorry, I just assumed based on your situation that you would want to see her as soon as possible."

"No…I mean…yes, you are right. I am just surprised you are willing to do this so soon for me."

"Well…frankly, I'm curious myself to see if she can help you."

He was surprised by her openness. If there was one moment he really wished he could use his ability on someone, it would be right now. He wanted to know what made her tick. Yet, as much as he desired it, nothing opened up for him. He was as blind as the next person to her thoughts.

"Hold on a sec, let me just text her real quick." After a few seconds passed, she finished and put her phone back down. "Let's wait and see what she says." She looked back up at him and gave out a small grin. He suddenly found himself feeling so grateful for her help in the matter.

"Sophia, are you like this with everyone?"

"What do you mean?"

"It's just that you barely know me. For you to go out of your way to help me like this, it's…well, it's refreshing and kind."

"Thank you, I think." She wasn't quite sure if he felt she was being too forward or if he genuinely thought she was just being helpful. "But to answer your question…no, I don't normally talk to strangers at bars and ask them to come with me to visit a total stranger who may or may not have answers about the supernatural domain."

All he could do was laugh at that comment. He was rather enjoying her sarcastic approach.

"Yes, well, I guess it was a rather obtuse question to ask. I think I need to up my game a little with you."

"Game, Sebastian? I didn't know we were playing one."

He paused for a second to think if he should continue to be so outspoken with her. But he couldn't help himself. "Yes, I definitely need to up it with you. You're a bit too clever for my own good."

He couldn't believe how flirtatious he had become with her. She was the first woman who was able to make him laugh since the divorce. It as a welcoming encounter he was having with her.

In the middle of his thoughts, Sophia's phone started to buzz. "Oh good, looks like she can meet with us tomorrow. How does 7 pm sound to you?"

"Yeah, I can do that."

"Okay, let me just confirm with her." She quickly texted her back, then glanced back at him.

"I can give you the address now if you want?"

"Yeah um…that would be great." He hesitated for a slight second more then went on with asking her the inevitable. "If you don't mind, can I have your phone number as well? You know, in case I'm running late or something."

"Yes, of course." She told him her number, and then gave out Clarissa's address. "It might be good if I have yours as well. You know, just in case." He was all too eager to share his number with her.

After the exchange, he put his phone down, then lifted his glass, and gave it a tilt for a toast. "Until tomorrow, Sophia."

She followed suit with her own words. "Yes, let's see what tomorrow brings you, shall we?" She took the last sip of her wine and started to get off the barstool. He waited for her to look back at him, and then locked eyes with hers.

"It was nice meeting you, Ms. Freemont."

"Yes, you too, Sebastian." Then she grabbed her purse and left.

He watched her leave and decided it was time for him to head out as well. The drive home was great. He reflected on his luck with Sophia. He was hopeful that her friend might be able to give him at least a better understanding of his new found abilities.

The next day played out much like the ones before. Hearing voices and feeling energy. Unfortunately, Margaret only had one appointment for him in the morning, so work went by extremely slow. He was thankful when five o'clock finally approached.

When he got off, he went home and made some dinner. Except as soon as he took a bite of his meal, he abruptly felt extremely full. "Damn, I'm not even hungry." His nerves for this evening were catching up with him. He didn't know if he was more excited to meet Clarissa or to see Sophia again. There was just something about her he found so intriguing.

When he looked at his cell phone, the time read 6:16pm. He went to his bedroom to take a shower and change clothes. Twenty minutes later, he was ready and out the door. As he drove to Clarissa's house, reflections of his past started racing through his mind. In a very short period of time, he realized how different things were becoming for him. *What an odd turn of events*, he thought.

When he arrived at the address—10502 Frankfort Avenue—he got out and waited for Sophia to pull up. While standing on the curb, he took a glance around the outside of the house. Floral vines covered both sides of the wooden fence. And the top half of the double front doors were designed with blue and gold stained glass windows. You could tell the house was very old yet somehow still kept up in pristine condition.

After about five minutes passed and she still hadn't arrived, he decided to message her. However, as soon as he grabbed his phone, it started to buzz.

Sophia: Running late. I'm not going to make it for the introduction. So sorry. But I'll see you soon.

Huh, guess I'll just go in then. He walked up to the porch and was about to ring the bell when a woman suddenly opened the door. "Ah…you must be Sebastian?"

"…Yeah. Sebastian Sinclair actually. Sophia is—"

"Yes, I'm aware that our friend is running a little behind. No worries, though. There's lots to divulge before she gets here anyway."

"I'm Clarissa by the way. Please, do come in. The only thing Sophia has told me about you is that you hold some very interesting…talents. I'm inquisitive to see what we are dealing with here."

This should be interesting, he thought.

He had to admit though; her demeanor was welcoming in and of itself. Right off the bat without even having a single conversation with her, he could tell she was wise beyond her years. There was also a certain attractive quality about her but not in the way most people would perceive someone's beauty. There was simply an essence about her that made her glow from the inside out.

As he walked through her living room, he was drawn back to one of the walls. It was covered with exquisite portraits of her. *What kind of life has this woman led?* One of the pictures was of her standing in the middle of a jungle watching a herd of elephants pass her way. Then there was another of her walking along the Great Wall of China. Clarissa walked up behind him as he was viewing a painting of her standing outside some sort of Renaissant looking cathedral. "I felt compelled to remind myself of why I'm in this line of work. It's not necessarily about the travel as one might think." That was all she said as she walked away without another word.

When he was done observing the other various pictures of her life he walked over and sat down on one of the couches. It gave him a moment to really observe the rest of the place. The furniture was a mix with both traditional and bohemian style traits. Very European, he thought.

Clarissa came back in not long after and asked him to follow her. She walked him down a corridor passing by several more rooms. Then made a left into one of the most peculiar spaces he had ever laid eyes on. The actual room had nothing in it, except chairs. Two chairs to be exact and they were placed in a very specific way. One chair was facing diagonal while the other was facing straight forward. It was very odd indeed.

"Please take a seat." She gestured for him to sit down in the chair facing straight forward. After they both got comfortable, they sat in silence for a while as he watched Clarissa appear to put herself in some sort of a meditative mode. When she finally opened up her eyes, he took that as his cue to start the discussion.

"I'm here because..."

Clarissa held up one of her hands, "No dear. It's okay, I already know. You're here to learn how to manage it, right? Whatever 'THIS' is...yes?"

He nodded in agreeance.

"We all have gifts if we are meant to see them. And let me tell you, my friend, you have many...gifts! Your eye is very bright...very bright! Now let's see what spectrum you are in right now. I'm going to let something in, and you tell me what you see, okay?"

"All right."

Clarissa closed her eyes again for a while and then reopened them. "It looks like you are all over the place with your abilities. Sometimes you have it open, and sometimes it's closed. There is no order to the madness in your head. So the first thing I need to do is teach you is how to control your portal.

"Now just relax...I want you to clear your mind. Don't think about anything. There should be nothingness in your head. Try that for me?"

"Okay." He closed his eyes and made his thoughts turn black. That was his version of nothingness. It took a while, but eventually, all the light and dark energy started running back through him slowly at first. But not long after, he was suddenly struck with hundreds of voices in his mind.

He opened his eyes back up only to see Clarissa subtlety change her body posture. Then her head slowly moved to the right of him. Without any warning, he unexpectedly felt the energy of an abnormal presence standing beside him. "…What is that? Do you feel it too?" He waited for a response from her. But quickly realized he wasn't going to get one as he watched her sit silently in her chair.

Soon after, he began to hear the faint voice of a little girl. "Hello Sir, can I play with you? Father has been very sick lately and I've been really lonely with no one to keep me company."

He looked at Clarissa… startled by what he just heard. "Is that what I think it is?"

"Yes, it's exactly what you think it is."

Immediately he felt tingles gush rapidly throughout his body. "How in the world can you be so calm about this?"

"Don't worry, Sebastian, she can't hurt you. She's dead, remember."

"It's just…the voices I have heard up to this point have always been in my head. Never have I felt the presence of a ghost, let alone one that is standing right beside me. Why can't I see her?"

"Oh my dear, don't worry about that right now…let's focus on what is in front of us." Clarissa gave a mischievous smirk and then swiftly turned her face to the left. "Ah…here comes the other one."

This time, a little boy's voice spoke up, "Um…Mr., can you help me get my ball down from that tree over there?" Sebastian looked all around the room for God knows what reason. He had no idea where the boy's ball was at.

"My brother tried to get it down, but he didn't make it." Sebastian turned his head back towards the sound of the boy's voice.

"It would be helpful if I could see you?"

The boy simply looked at him with a straight face. "I'm right here, Mr." He was about to respond back to him when out of nowhere his attention instantly shifted to something else. Their energy. It was so incredibly, potently, dark. Yet, shockingly enough, he found absolutely zero danger attached to it. *Huh…maybe Clarissa was right about them.* He decided to study what was going on inside their internal thoughts. And once again, he found them to be harmless.

He sat there for a while longer in silence, continuing to analyze them, when Clarissa eventually spoke up. "Okay, Sebastian, I see where you are at on the spectrum. Here is how you turn it off. Close your eyes and just breathe in and out slowly. Then go back to the nothingness you originally started within your mind."

After a long while, the voices in his head gradually began to dissipate. But not without a great deal of concentration on getting into the meditative state.

"So, does this mean I'm going to eventually see these ghosts?"

"I can't say for sure where your gifts will flourish, Sebastian. But your light is very intense. Most likely, there is a very good chance you will. I haven't seen one this bright in a very long time, even mine does not come close to yours."

"Wherever your gifts take you…just know, you were meant to have them."

"What do you mean?"

"Some people have these…abilities because they want to help mankind in some way. Others have them because they need it for their own path. I'm not allowed to know why you have your gifts. However, I can promise you this…there will be more to follow."

Just then, she looked towards the door. "Oh, I see Sophia has finally arrived." She smiled and left the room to open the door for her. He heard Clarissa tell her where he was at. She walked into the room with a little bit of apprehension showing on her face.

"Sorry I couldn't get here any earlier. My boss needed me to do something before I left and then the traffic was not on my side tonight."

"It's okay, Sophia. The fact that you even set this up with Clarissa and I was kind of you. No worries, please." His calming words set her at ease.

"Okay…so tell me. How did it go?"

"Ah, very interesting, actually. Clarissa and I just had a pleasant conversation with two little children. They just happen to be dead."

Sophia's eyes popped out. "Wow…what was that like? I wish I would have been here to witness it."

"Well, to be honest, I couldn't actually see them. But I could hear them."

"Still though, that's pretty amazing."

"Yeah, I guess it is."

Walking out of the room, they looked for Clarissa. She was sitting on her couch with her eyes closed. They both glanced at each other. Sophia whispered in his ear, "Let's give her a second."

He agreed and nodded his head.

After a minute, Clarissa spoke up even though her eyes were still closed. "Anything else I can help you with, Sebastian?"

"Um, I do actually have one more question, if you don't mind."

"Go ahead."

"How do I get rid of the bad energy?"

"Everyone is different." She paused for a moment as a pained look flashed across her face. A look of loss, perhaps? They did not know and certainly were not about to ask.

She slowly opened her eyes and asked them to take a seat. "Okay, I want to warn you though…sometimes things just aren't meant to be at the moment. It doesn't mean it's permanent. Do you understand what I'm saying to you?"

He thought it was strange how she was carefully going about the subject matter. "Yes, Clarissa, I get it."

"All right then, let's get on with it. Now…do you feel all that negative energy in your body."

"Yes."

"Try to grab it in your head and push it down to the ground. If you are able to move it, the universe will eventually take it from you."

He stood there for a good while trying to move it along.

Unfortunately, as hard as he tried, he could not release it. Frustrated, he opened his eyes. "I take it that means I'm a late bloomer?"

"As I said, we shall see where your gifts take you. You are so new to all this. It will come if it is supposed to come. Things will be better now that you know how to turn it on and off. And sleep will also greatly help release the negativity."

"Now you need to go, my friends, I've become…tired. As you will soon find out, these abilities can be quite difficult on your mind as well."

So they left, with a new understanding that his gifts may take him a lot further into the abyss than he expected. As he walked Sophia to her car, she asked him how he felt about tonight's experience. He let out a little chuckle. "Well, I'm going to be known as a freak. So that's something I never thought I'd be identified as."

She knew he was only trying to make light over his new circumstances. "Listen Sebastian, it's going to be okay. You'll just have to be patient to see how it all plays out." She gave him a reassuring smile. "But I'm glad Clarissa was able to give you a better sense of what you are dealing with."

"Yes, I am too. Thanks to you, Sophia." She was about to turn to open her car door, but he wasn't going to let her go that easily.

"So, when do I get to see you again? Obviously, you need to give me a chance to return the favor that you have so kindly given me."

She was taken by surprise with his comment. "Oh, well, what did you have in mind?"

"I was thinking of maybe taking you out on a date? If that is something you would be willing to venture into with me?"

That brought a smile to her face. "Okay…that could be fun."

She opened her car door and got inside. Before she could say anything else, he told her he would call her and thanked her again for helping him tonight with Clarissa. "Glad I could help." Then she started up her car and left.

Driving home that night, he thought about his job. Going to work after everything he learned with Clarissa seemed ridiculous. Everything had changed about who he was as a human being. He had gifts, perhaps enormous gifts that he was going to receive in the future. How would he use these abilities, he did not know. But he knew, in his soul, that his life would never be the same again.

Chapter 3
A Shift

It had been a couple of days since his fortunate encounter with Clarissa…thanks to Sophia. When he arrived at work, he sat in his car for a moment. Out of nowhere, he started to feel his boss's energy even though he wasn't in the building yet. Great…he's already at it with his wife. It was one thing to treat him that way. But to see how he tore her down all the time, it was increasingly bothering Sebastian.

Perhaps it was his own life's hypocrisy that got him so vexed over Margaret these days. After all, he had spent five years of his life treating the woman he loved horribly. Learning that lesson was difficult for him. Now he found himself trapped having to watch an even worse version of himself over and over again, through Henry.

He glanced down at his phone to see the time. It read eight o'clock…time to go in. He let out a deep breath as he walked into the office and made his way through the hallway.

"Margaret, hurry up and answer the damn phone will ya!" Not wanting to make him even more angry she moved hurriedly to her desk.

Sebastian could hear her scheduling something for him this morning. *Thank goodness*, he thought. He had no idea what the rest of his day would look like; nevertheless, he was happy just to be out of the office for at least a little while.

She came up to him as soon as she got off the phone and gave him his appointment schedule for the day. "Looks like you have a pretty full day set up. Your first appointment begins in half an hour."

He couldn't help but think about how low of bar he had set for himself. He went from managing multi-million dollar projects to being excited about working outside of his office compounds…fixing…stuff.

Still, that was his life now…for better or worse. He was about ready to head on out when he heard Henry's wrath once again. "Margaret!"

She looked at Sebastian with the saddest eyes. "His back is killing him today. Sounds like he is going to struggle a little with his temperament."

He was having a hard time swallowing her ability to put up with his bullshit day after day. Normally, he was able to keep his opinions to himself, yet he couldn't hold it back this time. "Funny…there's always something that gets him all charged up, isn't there?"

She didn't quite know how to handle his comment. It was the first time he had ever spoken distastefully of Henry. Seeing that she was a little taken back by his words, he decided to rephrase the message. There was no need to get her all upset.

"That is…I meant to say, I feel bad that his health causes so much discomfort to his body. It seems to bring so much hardship as to how he lives out his life."

"Oh, um, yes Sebastian. I'm grateful you understand where he is coming from."

Still, he could tell, even without having it open, that she was not happy living out her life with him. It was more as if she forced herself to co-exist with the madness he bestowed upon her.

After he left the office, he put his unpleasant thoughts of Henry behind him and focused on something that actually made him happy. He planned on asking Sophia out tonight if she was free. He thought about where he should take her, and then the perfect idea came to mind. There was one place in particular he felt would really set the tone for the evening. That said, none of his planning mattered if she wasn't available. So he quickly picked up his phone and texted her.

Sebastian: Are you available to go out tonight?

Almost instantly, she answered back.

Sophia: What do you have in mind?
Sebastian: You know…a little of this and a little of that.
Sophia: That's rather vague.

Sebastian: Okay then, Ms. Freemont, here it goes...I would love it if you would accompany me out on a date tonight. I promise it will be worth your while.

Sophia: Since you put it that way, how can I refuse?

Sebastian: Great. Is 6:30 okay with you?

Sophia: Sounds like a plan.

Sebastian: Address?

Sophia: 5424 N. Hampton Road, #6.

Sebastian: Thanks.

Sebastian: Forgot to tell you one more thing. Don't eat anything for dinner tonight. I'll be taking care of that.

Sophia: Yes sir.

Sebastian: Sorry. <u>Please</u> don't eat anything for dinner =).

Sophia: =)

Sebastian: See you tonight!

He put his phone down, excited for the evening. The rest of the day went by fast on account of the back to back appointments Margaret set up for him.

As he drove home, he thought about what it was that made him so attracted to Sophia. Of course, her physical attributes were beautiful in and of itself with her golden brown hair and gorgeous deep green eyes. Yet when he thought about it...what really set her apart was the way she walked through life. She was good inside. There's not enough of that in this world. In the past he had been so selfish when it came to taking care of a woman. However, Sophia was changing all that. She made him want to be a better human being.

When he finally got home, he went straight to his bedroom to get ready. As soon as he finished, he looked at his watch and saw that it was already 6 pm. *Man, where did the time go?* He grabbed his keys and took off. As he was driving along Brownsboro Road, he abruptly had to reduce his speed for traffic.

Slowly, he kept driving down the road heading towards the Watterson Hwy. But for no apparent reason, his eyes began to unexpectedly wander over to the opposite side of the street. Then...out of nowhere, a man suddenly appeared.

Huh, were his eyes playing tricks on him? He didn't recall seeing a man there a second ago. What was even more strange was what he was wearing. He looked like he was dressed for a costume party. He had long wavy blond hair and was decked out in bell-bottoms and a bohemian top that said, 'Peace Equals Rock-N-Roll.' *Okay.*

He wondered why the guy was just standing there. But his thoughts got immediately interrupted as he watched the man go from standing on the sidewalk to marching directly into traffic. *Oh God, please let that car see him. Please let the…Oh shit!* Sebastian had to look away.

When he glanced back up a second later, he saw that the man was still alive and not only that, it appeared he was now heading in Sebastian's direction. He watched as car after car drove right through him. His heart began to speed up when he realized what was really going on.

He had to quickly come to terms with the fact that a ghost was seeking him out. However, he wasn't interested in finding out what the dead man wanted. So he swiftly changed lanes and turned left to a side road where he could get more speed. Moments later, he turned his head around and saw that he had not followed him. *Thank God!*

After finding another direction, he arrived at her house twenty minutes later. He walked up to her porch and rang the bell. A couple of seconds later, she opened the door. "Hey, come on in. I need to change out my purse and then we can go."

He couldn't believe how stunning she looked. Though he didn't want to say it out loud to her. Not yet, anyway. He was afraid that he would be giving too much away and scare her off. No, he would wait to see where the night would lead.

When she finished changing out her purse, they left. As they were walking to his car, she asked him where they were going. "I'm taking you to a restaurant called Bistro Le Relais, it's French. However, now that I think about it, I should have asked you if you even like French cuisine."

"Well, you are in luck again, Mr. Sinclair, because I happen to love escargot."

He smiled at her comment. "That is very lucky of me, isn't it?" He opened her door and gestured for her to get in. As they were driving to the restaurant, he told her about his unexpected ghost exchange.

"Remember how I told you at Clarissa's that I could hear spirits but I couldn't see them?"

"Yeah."

"Well, that's not true anymore. I just saw my first one on the way over to your house."

"Seriously? I can't believe I missed that, tell me everything!"

"Okay, so I was driving in my car when I noticed a man standing on the sidewalk. Oddly enough, he was dressed in an outfit from the 70s. I kept thinking maybe he was going to a costume party or something.

"To be honest, other than his dress attire, his features were exactly the same as any other normal human being. I couldn't distinguish him apart from anyone else."

"Huh, that's wild that there is no distinction between the two."

"I know."

"Anyway, continue on…what happened after you realized he wasn't alive?"

"Right…so next thing I know, I catch him just blatantly staring at me. This goes on for only a little while, until suddenly, he started chasing after me.

"Of course, I totally freaked out and made my way down a different road till eventually I lost sight of him."

"Wow, that's insane!"

"I know right! Anyway…that was my fun experience before I came to pick you up."

"Good lord, Sebastian, that was quite the encounter."

"Yes, I would definitely have to agree with you on that one."

They arrived at the restaurant right as he finished his story. It was located at an old historic building surrounded by a small airport. Sophia was surprised by the setting. It gave her an idea.

"This building looks like it has been here since the early 1900s. Wonder what kind of mischief we could get ourselves into here?" He knew what she was getting at; however, he wasn't sure about opening it up in such a crowded environment. Maybe later on tonight would be a better option.

"There is definitely a good chance of finding old spirits here but I'm not sure how my reaction would be welcomed at a public place like this. I very well might completely freak out like I did earlier today."

"Oh well, we can't have that now, can we."

"Believe me when I say, nobody wants that." He gave her a playful grin then got out of the car to open her door.

"Can we see the planes land from the restaurant?"

"Yeah, if we sit outside on the deck. Let me see if they have anything available."

When they walked into the restaurant, the owner came up to greet them. "Only the two of you today?"

"Yes, actually, do you have anything outside?"

He took a brief look at his seating chart and gazed up at them with a smile. "I have one table left, please, follow me."

After he got them situated at their table, he put down a cocktail menu. "Your waiter will be with you shortly…enjoy."

Sophia took her time looking over the listing.

"Last time I saw you drink, I believe you were having wine, right?"

"Yes."

"So is that your drink of choice?"

"You could say that. Mostly, I like to dabble in pairing wine and food. It has become sort of a hobby of mine ever since…" But before she finished her words, another thought came to mind that stopped her in the middle of her exchange.

"Ever since what, Sophia?"

"Oh, um…nothing." Out of nowhere, she started to look unsettled. "Sorry, what was I talking about again?"

Huh, something's off with her. He didn't want to make her feel more uncomfortable so he swiftly put the conversation back on track. "You were telling me that you like to pair food and beverage."

"Oh yes, thank you…sorry about that."

"No worries."

"Yes, well, it's an art really that I'm still trying to master."

The waiter came over right as she was finishing her sentence. "Hello, my name is Lafayette, here is your menu for tonight. Please take your time looking it over. In the meantime, what can I get you to drink?"

"Sophia, what would you like?"

"I'll take a glass of Sauvignon Blanc, Le Hameau. Sorry I probably butchered how you are really supposed to say it."

"Not at all, you said it perfectly. And for you sir?"

"Buffalo Trace, neat, please."

"Very good. Please take a look at our menu and I'll be back shortly with your drinks."

Sebastian brought his head in a little closer to hers. “You think Lafayette is his real name?”

She laughed. “Stop Sebastian, this place is giving me the full French experience.” Just then, she glanced to the right and saw a plane beginning to take off. “Look, how cool is that.”

He nodded his head in agreement. Pleased that she took so much of a liking to the place.

After they spent a moment looking over the menu, he glanced back up at her. “So…escargot and what else would you like?”

“Um, I think I might not be able to forgive myself if I don’t try the scallops.”

He smiled. “Okay, anything else?”

“No, I’m good with that.”

Not long after, the waiter came by with drinks and some freshly baked bread. “Are you guys ready to order?”

“Yes actually. She’ll start off with the Escargots de Bourgogne and I’ll have the Mushroom Vol au vent. Then we would like the Saint-Jacques and Côtelettes d’agneau.”

“Excellent choice, sir. I’ll be back soon with your hors d’oeuvres.”

She looked at him, thrown off guard. “That was pretty impressive.”

“What?” A grin slowly flaunted his lips.

“So, do you speak French fluidly or do you only know the cuisine?”

“*Je parle un francais fluide*.”

“I take it that means fluidly.”

“*Laissez-moi vous raconter l’histoire derrière le fait de savoir tant de français*.”

“That one is a little harder for me to translate.”

“It means, let me tell you the story behind knowing so much French.”

“Oh yes, please do so.”

“Okay, well, everyone has to learn a foreign language in high school. I chose French. I really don’t know why, I guess at the time it seemed more interesting than learning Spanish. But once I got into it, I took a real liking to it. It came very easy to me.

“So when I went to college, I majored in business and I minored in French. I know it’s a rather odd thing to minor in. Even so…it was a good thing that I did because it was one of the reasons I got hired at my old job with Brown-

Forman. They needed someone who could travel to Europe and handle the communication difficulties of starting new projects. French is one of the more popular languages spoken there."

The waiter soon came back with their appetizers right as the sun was starting to set. Sebastian couldn't have planned a more desirable scene. They spent the next hour and a half eating, drinking and getting to know each other a little better. "Obviously, I don't need my foreign language skills for work anymore." She noticed his face turn a little sour as he said those words.

"True…however, it's definitely earning some points with me. I mean, come on, you know how…um, that is I mean…" *Damn, why did I go and say that out loud?*

A small smile started to spread across his lips. "What is it you mean, Sophia?"

"You're going to make me say it aren't you?" He simply sat there staring at her with his mischievous grin. "Okay, fine…I was merely saying that you sound rather sexy when you speak French."

"Oh, well, now that you have said that little bit of information, I think it's the perfect time to leave."

"What?"

He looked down at her hand and gently cupped his fingers in hers.

"May I?" She was stunned by his candor. "You may." He gently picked up her hand and gave it a kiss. "After what you just so boldly said, there is no way this date is going to get any better than it is right now at this moment." She smiled at his words. "Besides, I have other things planned for the night."

"You do?"

"Yes, so come on. Let's get out of here."

After he paid the bill, they got up and walked out of the restaurant. She thanked him for taking her there. "*Au fait, tu es superbe ce soir*, Sophia."

"I take it that means you're welcome?"

"Something like that." Really, he was commenting again on how beautiful she looked tonight.

"Now…are you ready for dessert?"

"You're kidding me, right?" Not reacting to her comment, he grabbed the keys out of his pocket and held them out to her. "What…you want me to drive?"

"Yes, I want you to drive me around town so I can do what you wanted when we first started our date."

"What's that?"

"…Ghost hunt."

"Oh, I didn't expect you to say that."

"Yes, well, neither did I before I came to pick you up. But I aim to please, Ms. Freemont." He opened the door for her to get into the driver side of his car. She wasn't use to a man paying so much attention to the detail of her wants. It was a welcoming quality she was surprised to experience from him.

She drove him down Baxter Avenue, where there was far less traffic this time of night. A cold front was also starting to come in so it meant fewer humans on the street. "There"…he pointed his finger to the right. "I see a blonde-haired lady who looks like she is in her late fifties. She's sporting a purple jumpsuit."

Sophia laughed. "Oh yeah, sorry, she's not dead. I see her too."

"Huh, well, you see this is why I need you with me. If you weren't here, I wouldn't be able to differentiate between human and spirit. Which apparently has become an important need in my life."

She smiled. "Glad I can be of assistance to you."

Soon after, he pointed to a guy standing by a tree. "Yep, I see him too."

"Wow, I'm batting zero tonight!"

"Relax, we're not on a timer." However, as soon as she said that, he saw a woman with a stroller looking like she was about to cross the street. "Oh Jesus, I hope this one's not alive!"

"Why…do you see someone?"

All of a sudden, he held his hands up to cover his eyes. "What's going on?"

He took a couple of seconds to calm himself down. "Well, to put it bluntly, you just drove over a woman with a stroller. Sorry, correction…that would be a dead woman with stroller."

Seconds later, he saw another one. He pointed his finger to the left as he watched a man fall to his death. "Jesus."

"I take it you saw another one?"

"Yes, though the scene was a little too depressive for my taste. A man unfortunately killed himself jumping from the rooftop."

"Oh God…did you see him, you know, land on the ground?"

"No, thank God. Apparently, I'm not privy to that information."

"So let me get this straight. You see dead people, yet you don't have to witness the actual moment they die?"

"Yes, that's pretty much the situation."

"Well, not a bad gift, I have to say."

"I hadn't looked at it that way, but now that you mention…it is rather fortunate."

That night they drove around town for hours, stumbling upon all kinds of phenomena. On one occasion, he saw two little children riding bikes with their mother. Another time, he caught sight of a man barbequing on his front porch. When she turned right down another road, he spotted countless joggers strolling the streets. He even caught glimpses of energy footprints displaying scenes from where people had gotten into car accidents.

Still, the kicker that caught them off guard was seeing all the animals on the streets. He observed all kinds of deceased wildlife. Everything from deer, dogs, and cats…to coyotes, raccoons, flying squirrels, and bats.

Throughout the night, he must have observed over a hundred ghost encounters. Sophia thought it was endearing how much Sebastian was embracing his gift. She was also touched by how in tune he was with her during the whole experience. Making sure he explained all the details of what he witnessed.

As he drove up to her apartment, he turned to face her before she got out of his car. "Tonight was an insane experience. Sometimes I can't believe this is actually happening to me. Even so, I want you to know that I'm so glad I'm not doing it alone. I'm glad I'm doing it with you." He opened up his gift for a second to feel her energy. However, he was taken back by what he received from her thought.

Misunderstanding paraded over his mind. "Sophia, why are you scared?"

She waited a second before she could get the words out.

"Sebastian…will you promise me something?"

His brows came up worried with anticipation of what she might say. "What is it?"

"It's just that although you have this wonderful, amazing gift of knowing what people are feeling inside, that doesn't mean it's always welcomed whenever you desire to open it. More importantly, that awareness you have is only going to grow, and soon, you will have an enormous amount of power over every person you meet. It's an incredible responsibility to not take advantage of it at your leisure."

He looked into her eyes. "Tell me what you want me to do?"

"Promise me from this moment on that you won't ever look into my soul unless I give you permission first." He could completely understand where she was coming from.

"You ask so little, Sophia. Of course, I can promise you that."

"Thank you." Relief passed over her eyes.

"Frankly, I'm surprised you didn't listen to my thoughts earlier in the evening."

"Yeah, well…on that note, let me explain something. When I do have it open, it's extremely difficult to concentrate on one thing. Focusing on having a meaningful conversation with you while rummaging through your feelings would have been too difficult to do."

"Huh, interesting to know." She was thankful for his candidness.

Satisfied with his answer, she moved on with other thoughts. "By the way, to answer your question. I'm not scared of you, specifically. I'm only afraid that we have grown close, so quickly. That's not usual for me." He was grateful for the explanation. She started to open the car door. "I'll see you soon, K."

"Okay…I'll call you. Goodnight, Sophia." Looking back, she smiled at him before closing the door and leaving.

That night, he went to bed exhausted from everything that had occurred. Clarissa was right; these abilities can take up a lot of human energy. He could have slept for days. However, time was money. Which meant going to work was still a necessity for him.

He made it two steps into work when he felt Henry's rage. Three…two…one. "Sebastian! Where is that goddamn guy?"

Seconds later, he ran into him in the reception area. "I told you to not throw anything away without my approval!" He wondered what in the world could he have thrown away that would have made him so angry.

He held out a power cord in the air. "This should never be tossed out."

"I tested it out personally, Henry. It's definitely broken."

"I don't care…you never know what we could use this for!"

Usually, Sebastian was mentally able to handle his craziness. However, today was extremely difficult. It took all his strength not to just quit on the spot. Nevertheless, he held it together, and eventually responded to him in his normal way. "Sorry…Henry, I'll make sure to check in with you next time, okay?" But without so much as another word, he simply got up and walked away.

After that encounter, it set the tone for the rest of the day. He was yelling at everyone, especially Margaret. The day went by slowly because Sebastian had no outside appointments to fulfill. It was an agonizing eight hours.

When he finally got off work, he drove home and went directly to bed. Originally, he had made plans to meet up with John, but he had to cancel because he was so tired from the night before with Sophia. The next day, he woke up at three in the afternoon. He felt so much more lighter getting all that sleep in.

Not long after he started his day, he got a phone call from Clarissa. "Sebastian dear…I'm having a little get-together tonight with some friends, and I thought you might be interested in meeting them. Shall I add you to my list?"

"Yes, thanks for the invite."

"Great, you'll know the time to come." Then she hung up the phone.

What the heck does that mean…I'll know the time to come?

Fortunately that thought was quickly answered minutes later after he got into the shower. As soon as he felt relaxed and began to let his mind wander, something came to him. The word…*seven* suddenly popped into his head.

"It can't be." Then it happened again, *seven*. But this time it didn't stop and got louder and louder by the second. *Seven …SEven … SEVen …SEVEn …SEVEN*. Ironically, after the 7th time it finally stopped. *How is she doing that?* He laughed at how ridiculous his life was becoming. Thank God Sophia was around to remind him that he wasn't completely nuts.

Soon after he finished getting ready, he grabbed some lunch. While eating he started reflecting on Sophia's concern about his abilities. She was right to put boundaries between her and his gifts. The more he thought about it, the more he wondered…why him, and why now? For Christ sake, he was a 28-year-old man with a not so moral past history. What merit did he have to receive such gifts? He thought about a handful of people who would be far more deserving than him. Sophia, for instance, would have been a better choice.

But his thought got disrupted by the buzz of his phone. He picked it up and saw that Sophia was texting him.

Sophia: Hey there…are you up for Clarissa's tonight?
Sebastian: Yes.
Sebastian: By the way, did she happen to mention what time to come?
Sophia: No actually…she said that you would know.
Sebastian: Yep, I know all right, I found out while I was taking a shower.
Sophia: What! You were talking to her in the shower?

He gave out a little chuckle…

Sebastian: Sorry, let me rephrase. While I was in the shower, I heard a voice in my head utter the word 'seven'. Pretty sure it was somehow connected to her.

Sophia: Well, I got to admit, you are definitely not shorthanded when it comes to entertaining me.

Sebastian: It suits me well to know that my life provides you with so much amusement at your leisure.

Sophia: That you do, Mr. Sinclair.
Sophia: See you tonight
Sebastian: Yes, looking forward to it!

Chapter 4

The Dinner

He had just arrived at her house to pick her up. When she opened the door, he couldn't help himself. "Wow, you look…I mean…that is to say."

"Yes?"

He wanted to say, *you look even more beautiful than the last time I saw you, if that is possible.* But courage was not his strong suit at the moment. So he stuck with his French skills. "*Tu es encore plus renversant que la dernière fois que je t'ai vu, si c'est possible.*"

"That's not fair, you can't just hide behind the language."

"And why not? Besides, I thought you liked it when I speak French?"

"I do when you also translate the message."

"I see, Ms. Freemont. But I'm not sure you are ready for what I have to say in English. I don't want to scare you away."

"Oh." That stumped her for a second, but she recovered quickly. "In that case, I won't comment on how you look tonight either."

"Well, that seems like a very fair response." He smiled. "Let's go to the party, shall we?"

"Yes, let's go."

They arrived at Clarissa's house right at seven o'clock. She opened the door before they had a chance to ring the bell. "Ah, my two favorites and just in time…how good of you to be…punctual."

"Come on in, my guests will want to meet you." As she let them in, she started to sense commotion in the kitchen. "Excuse me for a minute, let me make sure everything is okay with the chef. Make yourselves comfortable and I'll be right back."

It was then Sebastian noticed something unusual about the guests. "Strange."

"What is it?"

"I can't feel anyone's energy. Oh, wait a sec…I stand corrected. I can feel the chef's energy in the kitchen. He seems to be ecstatic about creating tonight's dinner, and surprising…he is also a little nervous."

"Why?"

"Apparently, he feels that the people he is serving tonight are not his typical run-of-the-mill clientele. He wants to make sure he puts on a good show."

"Huh…"

"Yes, that's about where I am at too."

"Well, we are talking about Clarissa's friends. Who knows what to expect."

"I guess you're right."

Just then, Clarissa walked back over to them. "Sorry about leaving you like that, are you ready for introductions?" They both nodded in agreement. "Okay, come with me."

Without further ado, she walked them towards a woman dressed in a black tight fitted jumpsuit. It was showy in all the right places. Funnily enough, the rest of her wardrobe grabbed just as much attention as her outfit.

"Josephine, love…this is Sebastian and Sophia."

He couldn't help but comment on her appearance. "I see you are wearing a turban."

"Yes Sebastian, I acquired it from an old friend in Morocco, do you like it?"

"Yes, it's very…worldly." Josephine gently brushed her long jet black hair in front of her shoulder.

She gave them both a quick look up and down. Then without any hesitation, she asked them the most outlandish question. "So…are the two of you together?"

How very intrusive, he thought. Sophia didn't quite know how to respond to that. This provoked Sebastian to quickly speak up. "Um yes, well, we haven't really discussed that subject matter, Josephine, but we have become very…fond of one another." He wanted to say more, but he did not want to push his luck with her. So, he just stuck with what came out.

"Huh. Well, that doesn't exactly scream out the deal is sealed between the two of you."

Clarissa stared at Josephine. "My goodness Josie…no need to rock the boat here."

"Yes…yes…Clarissa…calm down, I was just having a little fun with your friend here." She gave out a mischievous grin towards Sebastian then laughed it off. "Let me start over with you guys. My name is Josephine, but as you can see, sometimes people like to call me Josie…pick whichever one you like." They made small talk with her for a minute or so, but soon Josephine excused herself to go grab a cocktail.

Sophia leaned in closer to Sebastian and lightly touched his arm. "I'll be right back, I need to use the ladies room."

"Okay." He smiled at her and watched her leave. Not long afterwords, Josephine came back up to Sebastian and snatched his attention. He turned around and found her eyes wandering directly into his.

"I see you have it open, Sebastian?"

"Yes, and I see that you have it closed. Is there a reason for that?"

She gestured for him to follow her. Out of curiosity, he went along with her lead. She found a quiet corner to talk.

"Is it necessary to be so far away from the others?"

"It was just too loud over there. Anyway, I believe you asked me a question. Why are you not able to read me, right?"

"Yes."

"It's because Clarissa asked all of us to turn it off. She didn't want to put your mind on overload with what we have to share with you tonight. You are still kind of a virgin around all this."

…Okay?

"Is it possible for you to elaborate just a little bit more into what you're talking about?"

"Ah …I get the feeling you really don't like to be in the dark about things."

Who in the hell would?

"I'm just saying Sebastian, that sometimes surprises can be a gift. Speaking of which …I hope your gifts haven't been giving you too much trouble? It can be quite difficult to control them at first."

Damn, how much has Clarissa told her?

"Well, Josephine, I gotta say …I'm a bit taken back that you know these little intricate details about my life. But to answer your question, she has given me some helpful pointers. I'm very thankful for that."

"Looks like you have help all around." She nodded her head toward Sophia. Who at the moment, was conversing with another gentleman. *Hmm,* Josephine could have sworn she saw him slightly flinch at the sight of them.

"Does it make you uncomfortable watching her talk to another man?"

Surprised by her candor, he retorted. "Why do you seem to be taking such a strong interest in my personal affairs? You barely know me."

"I was just being inquisitive, Sebastian, that's all. You must be receiving my directness as a negative. When really I was just trying to be friendly."

"Friendly, you say?"

"Yes, don't friends take interest into each other's lives?"

"Not when you first meet, you don't."

"Well, you do if you are as direct as me." She chuckled a little. "Come on, Sebastian, lighten up a little." He thought about it for second and realized that maybe he was overreacting just a tad.

"Okay, Josie, maybe I misunderstood your very direct personality, for something else. Sorry if I offended you."

She gave him a sharp-witted smile and accepted his apology. "You're forgiven."

"Good, now…to answer your question about the man over there with Sophia. The answer is no, it doesn't bother me in the least. As you can see I'm here doing the same with you. Having a very innocent, friendly chit chat. Besides, I trust in what we have."

"And what is that?"

"It's how you put it earlier, actually. She has been quite a wonderful partner when it comes to helping me with my newfound abilities." He glanced back over to her once again. "Truth be told, I have grown very attached to her."

"Yeah, I got the memo on that." She took another sip of her martini and then carried on with the conversation.

"So listen, other than the lovely support system you have already made for yourself. If you ever come across the need for a stronger management service …I may be able to assist in that department." She handed him over a card. "Just call that number." He glanced down at her business card and saw that there was literally only a phone number on it. "Guess you are not a fan of giving out too much information." She rumbled out a small chuckle. "I don't think remembering my name is going to be too much of a problem for you." After that, she gave him a wink of the eye and walked away.

He stood there alone for a second thinking over her words. *Wow ...what a bizarre conversation.* He had never met anyone like her. *She is definitely eccentric*, he thought. But than his mind quickly turned back to Sophia. He saw that she was still talking with the gentleman. So he made his way over to them. "Hey Sophia." She gave him a warm smile. "Sorry, I didn't mean to interrupt you guys."

"It's okay, Sebastian, no worries. By the way, this is Landon Palmer."

Without delay, he put his arm out to shake his hand. "Hello, Landon, I'm Sebastian Sinclair. It's nice to meet you."

"Yes, likewise."

"Landon is visiting from the UK."

"Yes, I noticed the accent. If I had to take a guess, it sounds like you are from England."

"Yes, that's right, I grew up in London. Have you ever been?"

"Just a couple times, but it was a while back." He glanced around the room and saw Clarissa speaking with Josephine.

"So, how do you know our wonderful hostess?"

"Well, as I was telling Sophia, every time I travel to the States, I always make sure to pay a visit to her. She is a very dear friend of mine. We also happen to work really well together. Obviously, you know how she is able to help people."

"Yes, in fact, if it weren't for her I'm not sure how I would be able to deal with my gifts right now. She is a very kind soul."

"That she is, my friend."

Landon looked down at his beer and saw that it was empty. "Do you guys want a drink?"

Good God, after my last conversation with Josephine, I could really use one.

He gave a nod over to Sophia. "I wouldn't mind a glass of wine myself."

They all headed towards the bartender and got their drinks. Then settled down on the couches in the living room. Sebastian couldn't help but ask Landon a question that was lingering in his head.

"I hope I'm not intruding but you mentioned something about working with Clarissa. Does that mean you have abilities as well?"

"Ha …now that is a giant can of worms you are stepping into."

"Oh, man, I'm sorry. I…"

"No, no, don't worry about it. I was the one who made the comment in the first place. It's just, if you have not figured it out alrea…"

"Um… excuse me." A tall man sporting a stubble beard interrupted their conversation.

"Sorry to break up this wonderful exchange you were all having. But Clarissa asked me to come over and introduce myself to our guest of honor." He held his hand out to Sebastian. "My name is Benjamin McAlister." Sebastian thought he was joking at first. But then realized nobody else was laughing.

"I'm sorry, you're saying that I'm the guest of honor?"

Without answering his question. He held his hand out to Sophia. "And you must be Ms. Freemont. Clarissa told me she's known you for years."

"Ah, yeah… I have known her for quite some time now."

"She also told me that you were the one who introduced him to her."

"Yes, that's true as well."

He turned his attention back over to Sebastian. "So I guess you're wondering why she is throwing you such a gathering?"

"Yes…"

"Well, as it turns out, she thinks there is something very special about you. Now after meeting you in person. I rather concur with her assessment. You're quite the gem, actually. What do you think, Landon?"

"I think it's been a long time since we've seen one like this."

Just then Clarissa and Josephine came up to them. "My dear guests…dinner is ready to be served."

As they all sat down, a server came over to take additional drink orders. When he left, Clarissa spoke up, "Sebastian, as you may have realized by now, my friends came here today to give you perhaps a hand of wisdom if you desire to take it. As you will find out, we all have some unique abilities that you may or may not possess…yet. Gifts you cannot even imagine, but we are all different, and none of us have all of them. I believe, however, you may be the exception to that. It's that light of yours…it's brighter than ever."

The server quietly stepped back in with the drinks, followed by the chef who carried in a cart of food. "Ah, perfect timing. Everyone, this is Chef Anthony Guy. His food is going to blow you away tonight." He was surprised by her compliment, but thankful that she set the tone. "Chef, why don't you take it from here?"

"Yes, of course, Ms. Clarissa." He looked over to his server as a signal to pass out tonight's menu. They all looked down to view it.

First Course
Little Gem Salad with Canal House Vinaigrette
Second Course
Vegetable Root Soup with Goat Cheese, Cranberry Relish and Orange-Zest Toast
Third Course
Garlic Butter Bucatini with Tiger Prawns, Roasted Cherry Tomatoes and Parsley Dust
Fourth Course
Chilean Sea Bass with Lemon-Caper Gremolata and Stuffed Tomato with Herbed Rice
Fifth Course
Cinnamon Mascarpone Napoleon with Chocolate Drizzle and Fresh Berries

"As you can see, your first course will be a Little Gem Salad with a light Canal House Vinaigrette. The Little Gem lettuce is a smaller, sweeter version of romaine. Please enjoy."

"Thank you, Chef Anthony." He finished helping the server hand out the first course and left.

Clarissa then lifted up her glass to make a toast. They all followed suit. "May we keep an open eye to things we don't always understand and trust in the wings we were always meant to fly…Saluti!" Everyone took a sip of their drink and started making small talk with the people around them.

Sebastian leaned in closer to Sophia, and whispered. "What do you make of this menu?"

"It's over the top…just like her." He smiled. "She really is isn't she." He moved his hand under the table and gently laid it over her hand. "…If I haven't said it already. I'm so glad you are hear with me tonight. It wouldn't be the same without you." She looked at him with endearing eyes. "You say the sweetest things to me." That prompted him to tenderly embrace her hand just a little bit more. He looked around the table and saw the other guests eating and mingling with one another. "Let's feast, shall we?"

"Yes, I can't wait to dive in." He casually moved his hand back onto the table and began to eat.

After he got through half of his little gem salad, he realized that he hadn't even thanked Clarissa yet for all that she had prepared for him. He glanced over in her direction. "Clarissa, I can't believe you would do this for me. I mean, gathering your friends to come here and setting up this elaborate dinner party. It was incredibly thoughtful of you. And Josephine …you were right. I am new to all this. Any knowledge you guys can give me is valuable. I want to thank you all for coming here tonight. I appreciate it more than you know and I look forward to hearing from all of you."

"You're quite welcome, Sebastian. We all remember what it was like when we first learned of our gifts. It can be overwhelming to say the least. As far as dinner goes, I asked Chef Anthony to manage the timeline of delivering our courses to his discretion. I thought it would help keep our conversation flowing. There is a lot to say tonight and I didn't want there to be any interruptions.

"So, with that said, shall we begin? Let us tell you just how far the rabbit hole can really go. Benjamin, would you mind starting us off?"

"Yes, of course. Well, I believe I was a little older than you, Sebastian, when I first received my abilities. You look like you are in your late 20s, right?"

"Yes, I'm 28."

"I was 32 at the time when I learned that there are other dimensions you can travel through. You see…your body is just a vessel to help you function through life. But your soul is actually who you really are inside. One day, when I was meditating I felt my soul come out of my body. I was just floating in the air almost in a ghostlike state observing my physical human vessel.

"After the astonishment of learning what I was capable of doing began to wear off, I wondered what else I could do with my newfound gift. Curiosity pushed me forward to seek the unknown. Obviously, I could use my sense of sight, but was that it? I floated down to see if I could actually feel my vessel. As it turns out, I discovered that I could use all my senses, not just sight and touch. I began living my life through my soul while my physical body just sat there.

"Of course, I would always have to come back and make sure it was taken care of. I fed it on a regular basis and well…you know, took care of its other needs. But for the most part, I preferred to stay in my soul.

"Eventually, I acquired the ability to travel outside of my home. At some point, after connecting all the dots, I realized that I was not even traveling in the same human dimension that we are in right now. Apparently, there are many different realms connected to the planet."

Sebastian was stunned by what Benjamin disclosed to him. "Wow …I mean, I'm trying to wrap my mind around what you are capable of doing."

"I know, it might be a little difficult to comprehend what I am saying to you, but once you receive the gift, it will become easier to understand."

"How do you know I'm going to have this gift?"

"You have…certain qualities about you that stand out to me."

"Like what?"

"It's hard to explain, Sebastian. But I guess we shall see where your future leads." Then he gestured for someone else to go.

Landon spoke up next. "I have the gift of seeing the past of any human on earth."

Sebastian again, was taken aback. "You mean, you can see my entire life history?"

"If I wanted to, yes."

"My God! How can that be?"

"Well, for starters, let me begin with the fact that there is a Heaven, or whatever you like to call it. I prefer to name it the Other Side, and it's every bit majestic as you think.

"That particular dimension sits a little above the human realm. When you die, you visit the Great Library Dome to see how your life turned out. Did you fulfill the plan you laid out for yourself as a human the way you thought it would be?"

He explained that the Library holds the archives of our life's footprints. "After you pass away, you can simply view moments of your life upon your choosing. This is how I am able to see the past. Because I too have access to all the video footprints of the Dome. I can see the history of any human on this earth provided the information that I give out does not alter anyone's current path choices.

"People come to me from all over the world to seek the truth from the archives. I have to be careful because lives need to be interpreted as fact, not an opinion from reviewing a scene. If you do receive my gift, you will understand the great importance of this matter."

He stopped talking at that moment and looked towards, Josephine. "I believe it is your turn now. I've said, all that needs to be told tonight."

"Thank you, Landon."

"My abilities align with the dead. The forgotten. They come to me when they want to conclude something they didn't get to do when they were alive. When we are human, we sometimes lead a messy life. So when we leave this earth, and there is unfinished business, I help them resolve whatever problems they left behind." Then, she said with a straight, almost daunting face. "It's universal law to always finish what you started in your life.

"Sometimes, their negative energy…is difficult to bear. You have to refuel yourself regularly, and you can never let your guard down when you're dealing with dark entities. Be sure of that…their energy most likely can't kill you, but it can definitely fuck with your mind."

Clarissa politely interrupted, "As you can see, Josephine is my most colorful friend. Isn't that right, Josie?"

She gave a smirk-smile. "I guess I can be a little too dramatic sometimes. Forgive me, Sebastian." Then she turned her head towards Clarissa. "The floor is all yours."

"Thank you, my dear."

"Sebastian, the universe as you know it is more than what you ever thought it could be. It is limitless. Infinity could not describe the timelessness of it. Except, time does not really exist either. In truth…we live in a continuum that never stops. How do I know that? Like my lovely friend Josephine here who speaks to the dead. I, on the other hand, speak to the spirit world. The realm that helps keep order to humankind.

"The miracles that take place on our planet happen because this other realm of souls watch over us. Fixing the accidental universal mistakes. I am able to speak to these souls. Let's call them what humans call them, angels. And there are all different types of them. Some are here to aid us during the passing of our life. You could call them the angels of death, if you'd like. Then there are others that help keep you alive when we are not supposed to die. To put it mildly, there are angels around for practically every faucet of our existence. At least, that is what they have told me."

Sebastian curiously spoke up. "What about guardian angels. Are those real as well?"

"Yes, in sense. I guess you could call them your personal angels. Every human gets assigned to at least one. But you can have more if need be. It just depends on what you feel you need when you are charting out your life. By the way, my angels spoke to you earlier today in the shower. I wanted to give you a little taste of what was to come of tonight… In case you were wondering.

"Oh, and there is the matter of God. He does exist. But not in the matter of how most people perceive him to be on planet earth. God… is actually an 'it'. And 'it' represents both male and female species. There are other things you should know, as well. Like the fact that we all live multiple lives. Each of us who decide to come down on earth and live another life knows there will be pitfalls. The point of incarnating is for us to learn and grow from those difficult experiences.

"As far as you are concerned, Sebastian, your light shocked me when we first met. I've only met one other that comes close to such magnitude. I knew if I told you everything we are unloading on you today, it would be too much for you to take in at the time. I felt I needed to give you space to ease into your new…awareness.

"So, now that you have been more informed of what you could possible evolve into, what do you think?"

"What do I think? Well…to be honest, I feel like I just took a crash course on learning the greatest mysteries of our existence. I'm both terrified and ecstatic, at the same time. And I have so many questions boiling through my brain right now."

"Then ask us, Sebastian, that is why we are here tonight."

"Okay, let's start with this one… Recently, I received the gift of seeing ghosts. One day, Sophia and I decided it would be fun to go out on a hunt for them. Now this might sound strange to you, but we did it in my car because I didn't know what to expect from them. And I was glad that I did. Because they seem to be very drawn to me."

"Yes, Sebastian…" Josephine took this one on. "They are most definitely drawn to people like us. It's because they can feel our frequency. They know we can see and hear them."

"Okay, but what if I don't want to hang out with them? Is there a method to get them to go away?"

"Yes, there is. And you will be happy to know that it's actually quite simple. You just need to show them 'who's the boss'. You can tell them what you want, but more importantly, you need to mean it."

"So you're saying all I have to do is to tell them to leave?"

"Exactly, they will leave on your command."

"But that's so easy."

"I know, as I already said…it's simple."

That prompted Sebastian to ask Clarissa a question. "I believe you can see the dead world as well, right?"

"Yes and no. Much of my abilities align with the spirit world. Although I do have the gift of hearing and feeling the dead, I cannot see or interact with them the way you and Josephine can. As I said at the beginning of this dinner. No one here at this table has all the gifts. Tonight, we each shared with you our main ones."

"And why do you think I might be the exception? You are all extraordinary people. To think I might have even an ounce of your collective abilities is simply just too hard to believe."

"And why is it you say that, Sebastian?" It was Landon who responded to that. "You have recognized for yourself the beginning of your capabilities. Were they not just as extraordinary to you before you met us? Based on what we've felt from your inner light, more gifts are bound to emerge, my friend. To what degree…it does not matter. What you need to do now is accept what is to come."

Those words were still too hard for him to digest at the moment. So he put it in the back burner of his mind and went onto another impending question. "Clarissa, the last time I visited you, I learned how to open and close my abilities. Yet for some reason, every once in a while, a voice comes through beyond my control. Why is that?"

"Ah, you are speaking of the time, for instance, when my angels spoke to you. You did not have it open then, did you?"

"No, I was completely shut."

"Those voices or occurrences that you encounter happen because they are not coming through your third eye. They are coming from a different realm all together. I was able to push the message into your mind by tapping in though my angels from their dimension. Ghosts also live in their own realm. You might want to keep that in mind as well."

He was about to respond, but as she finished her sentence, she could physically see how tired he was becoming. They had given him so much to process, it was beginning to wear on him. So she decided it was time to end the night.

"Listen Sebastian, just take some time to digest everything we said. It's a lot to accept, I get it. But in time, you will begin to feel more comfortable with your gifts." *At least she hopped anyway.* "Now I'm afraid it is time for our evening to end." She lifted up her drink glass one last time. "Too the guest of honor, we wish you the best of luck to whatever comes your way." They all concurred and clinked their glasses together.

After that, Sebastian and Sophia got up and said goodbye to everyone at the table. Then Clarissa walked them to the door.

"I don't know how to express how grateful I am for all that you have given me tonight. I will never forget this dinner."

Sophia chimed in as well. "Really, it was an amazing experience. Thank you so much."

"It was nothing, guys. You know me...I throw parties all the time. Sebastian just gave me a good excuse to have another one." They both smiled at that and began to walk out the door.

"Good night, Clarissa."

"Good night, my friends."

Closing the door behind them, she reminisced about the last time she witnessed someone with a light like his. It was quite the journey that person had to endure. *I guess now we shall see where his road leads.*

Chapter 5
The Dead Get It

The drive home from dinner was quiet for the most part. Both of them were caught up in their own reflections of what was revealed tonight. Sebastian could not help but feel humbled by Clarissa's words. The abilities he had already acquired up to this point were quite astonishing by itself. But to know that someday he may also receive the other gifts as well. He was beside himself on what may become of his future.

Towards the end of the drive home, Sophia asked him what he was thinking about. "Oh, you know…the normal things like being able to talk to angels and viewing archives from the other side."

She laughed. "I know, I get your point. I'm sure it's definitely different then the life you expected to have."

"You could say that."

"Are you going to be okay?"

"I think so…I'll just have to wait and see how it all turns out, you know."

"Yeah, I hear you."

He slowly pulled up to her driveway. "Can I walk you up to your door?"

"Sebastian, you're exhausted." She started to open the door to get out.

"Wait, Sophia, um…I was thinking after talking to Josie, I might be able to handle visiting a cemetery now. I thought you might like to experience that with me."

"Really…yes, I would love to do that. When are you going?"

"I'm not doing anything tomorrow night, after work." After everything he had heard at the dinner, a sense of urgency to explore the unknown came rushing through him.

"Okay, I'm in."

"Good, I'll pick you up around 6ish."

"I'll be ready, see you tomorrow." She closed the door and waved him goodbye. He didn't drive away till he saw her reach the front door.

That night, it took a while for him to fall asleep. So many things were going through his head. He was thankful when he felt his eyes start to grow heavier. Eventually, sleep welcomed him.

Eight hours later, he woke up to his alarm. He got out of bed feeling refreshed and ready to start the day. The first thing he thought about was going to the cemetery. He was excited to see what would come of the experience. But until then, he would have to endure going to work. Something that was becoming inherently insignificant in the wake of the extraordinary changes taking place in his life.

When he arrived at the office, he walked up to Margaret to see if she had any appointments for him today. But when he asked her, she seemed offish. It wasn't what she said, it was the tone in which she said it. *Strange?* He wondered if Henry did something to her? He couldn't help but ask her if something was wrong.

It took her a moment to respond. "Um, actually, yes there was something that happened. Last night…" She lowered her head down and gave herself another moment to breathe. "Last night…my father…died."

"Oh God, Margaret, I'm so sorry to hear that." He felt so bad for her. But he didn't know the first thing on how to console her. He did however wonder why she was working right now. During a time like this, she should be with family. *Maybe she needs a distraction to get away from dealing with the sorrow.* He thought about bringing it up to her in a gentle way. Last thing he wanted to do was upset her.

"Margaret, listen, if you are concerned about keeping things up here, don't worry, I've got everything covered. You've showed me how to manage all the scheduling in the past."

"Sebastian, that is kind of you and I will take you up on that this afternoon. But I didn't come into work for myself. Henry wanted me to drive him to the office today because his back went out on him again. He said he would only be a couple of hours."

Sebastian knew that was such bullshit. He had gotten to know the business pretty well since he started working there. And there was not one pressing thing that needed to be done that would take preference over a family death. Even during a time like this, Henry was the most selfish bastard he had ever met.

She was barely holding her emotions together. He could tell that work was the last place she wanted to be right now. Her eyes were starting to water up. "Listen, if you would like to leave, I don't mind taking Henry home when he is finished."

"No, Sebastian, it's okay." She paused for a moment and moved in a little closer to him. "He is very temperamental today. I wouldn't want to put you in an uneasy position."

"Margaret, your father just passed away last night, for God's sake. I think I could handle Henry and his antics for one drive home. Won't you consider it?"

"No, Sebastian. I'm good. He shouldn't be much longer anyway." They both knew that was not true. But he could tell she was not going to budge, so he made that his cue to leave and give her space to mourn her father's death.

He walked back to his desk and grabbed some paperwork he needed to finish up. When all of a sudden, he heard a familiar voice in his head. *"Flower...Flower."* It was the same voice he had heard when he was driving in his car a while back. He recalled the message was "*...Tell her I'm still around."*

He spoke to the entity through his mind. "*What about this Flower?"*

The voice whispered back, "*Petunia was her name."*

"I see. So you use to know someone named Petunia?"

After a couple minutes went by, he realized he was not going to get a response. So he moved on with his day. As it turned out, Margaret landed up having three appointments lined up for him by early noon.

It was 5:05 by the time he finished his last job. Perfect, that meant he still had time to go home and change. He gave a quick peek in the mirror before he left. It was vain of him, he thought. But he didn't care, he wanted to make sure he looked good for her.

As he drove over to pick her up, he noticed an old graveyard called Harrods Creek Cemetery. For whatever reason, he was immediately drawn to it. *Maybe this is the one we should go to*. A tiny piece of him was still a little trepid over the fact that he may not be able to manage the situation. But then he reminded himself of what Josephine had said. *I just need to be in charge, that's it. If I can do that, they will do as I wish.*

Shortly after he got himself in the right mind frame, he was at her house. He was about to get out and walk to her door, but she had beat him to it. She was already walking halfway to his car when he noticed the giant smile on her face. *Good, she is just as enthusiastic about this as I am*. She opened the door and got in. "Ready to do this?"

"I've been waiting for it all day."

"Okay then, I have one question. On the drive over here, I noticed a cemetery right next to a small church."

"Oh, yeah, Harrods Creek, right?"

"That's the one. Are you alright with us going there?"

"Sebastian, this is your show, if you feel comfortable going there, then I think we should do it."

He started the car back up as a grin grew on his lips. "Let's go see what awaits us then."

They were on the road for maybe 10 minutes when they arrived at the cemetery. He parked his car next to the church. They both got out and he instantaneously felt a presence. He lifted his arm and pointed his finger to the right. "Do you see a man in that direction?"

"As far as I can see, we are completely alone."

"Good, let's go then." He gently grabbed her hand and lead them in the direction of the man. She was a little surprised by his gesture, but she liked that he did.

As he got closer to the man, he noticed that he was wearing silver soldier tags. *He must have served our country at some point*. They found him standing over someone's grave. He whispered over to Sophia, "Guess I'll just greet him."

"Yes, let's give it a try."

"Hello."

The man slowly turned to look at him. "Hello."

He pointed his finger to the gravestone. "Do you know the person who was buried here?"

"Yes, this is my father's grave. He died before I was able to make it home." Sebastian felt the energy of his pain. It was deep-rooted. He suddenly felt a strong urge to help him. Then something extraordinary happened. As soon as the impulse to help entered his thought process, he immediately knew exactly what to do. It was as if someone or something planted the answer in his brain.

He decided he needed to get a little more personal with him if he was going to pull this off. But first, he wanted to clarify something with Sophia. He whispered into her ear. "I'll tell you everything that's going on as soon as I finish what I need to do with him." She nodded and motioned for him to carry on.

He looked back over to the man. "What is your name?"

"It's Tristan."

"Mine is Sebastian and this is Sophia. I see that you are wearing soldier tags."

The man brought his arm up to his tags and wrapped his hands around them. "I fought in the Iraq war. When my deployment was over, I came back home only to find out that my father had passed away from a massive stroke." His mouth began to slightly frown. "I never got a chance to make things right between us before he passed away."

"I'm sorry to hear that, Tristan. But you know what…there might be another way for you to see your father again. So you can make things right." He looked interested to hear what Sebastian had to say. "What if I told you there is a place where people go after they die? Some people may call it heaven; others may identify it as the promised land. I like to refer to it as the other side. There are all kinds of names for it." He paused for a moment to make sure Tristan was in tune with what he was saying.

"You see, when your father died, he went through one of the portals to get to that place where I was telling you about."

He looked at Sebastian, curiously. "Portals?"

"Yes, they are all around you actually."

"And where do you find these portals you speak of?"

"Oh, it's easy to see if you are open. I believe all you need to do is seek the light and you will be able to find one."

"Is that right?"

"Yes, it is. Now…close your eyes and try to feel the light within you." Tristan closed his eyes and then opened them after a short period of time. "Do you see the portals now?"

"Yes, I believe I do. Strange, I never noticed them before."

"None of that matters now, Tristan. What counts is that you go through one today."

"I suppose you are right." He slowly started to head towards the closest portal. As he was walking, he thanked Sebastian for all his help. "No worries, my friend…I'll see you when it's my turn to go to the light." Sebastian could feel his energy fade away as he watched Tristan vanish into thin air.

"Wow, he just left earth."

"That's casually putting it. You realize what you just did?" Sophia was spellbound with his ability to literally help a lost soul find its way back into the system. "I have a million questions."

"Ask away."

"Okay, how did you know what to do?"

"Well, it was the strangest thing. Suddenly knowledge of how it all works just came to me. I knew instantly without question that he should simply seek the light. But not in the same sense as what you might think."

"What do you mean?"

"It's difficult to describe but I'll give it a try."

"I can say this for sure…it's definitely not like how Hollywood portrays it to be in the movies. There is no bright light that appears before you when you die and sweeps you off to heaven."

"Okay, then how does it happen?"

"From what I saw, the universe is filled with these light energy portals. They are circular in shape and there are millions upon millions of them spread throughout the entire planet.

"When you die you are naturally attracted to the portal closest to you. As soon as you walk through it, it leads you to the other side. However, his soul was different. When he died, he didn't realize he was dead, so he couldn't see the portals."

"That's fascinating."

"It is actually. What else do you want to know about?"

"I'm curious about the portals. How are you so sure where they take you?"

"Right now, I don't have access to see the other side. But I can feel it. And it is the most pure form of joy I have ever felt."

"Wow…that's just…I mean, I don't even know what to say."

"I know I'm still trying to wrap my mind around… Oh, hold on a second, Sophia."

Out of nowhere, right in the middle of their conversation…another ghost appeared before Sebastian. He was dressed in a red suit and white tie, with a black fedora hat. *Well, that's an interesting look.* He had his hand out to introduce himself when Sebastian suddenly felt an enormous amount of pressure coming from his chest.

Without warning, ghosts started emerging in droves. They were trying to talk to him all at the same time. There must have been over 50 spirits surrounding him at this point. "Where are they all coming from?"

"What do you mean, Sebastian?"

"They are everywhere!" He quickly grabbed her hand and headed towards the car.

Looking back, he shouted, "Stay away from me, there's too many of you!"

"Sebastian, what is going on?"

"They just keep coming!"

"You mean ghosts? Are they trying to hurt you?" She started to get worried for his safety. He was so distraught with the situation that he stumbled and fell over a tombstone on the way to the car. Sophia quickly helped pick him back up and continued on their way.

"Please…leave me alone! I don't want to help you anymore!" They were close to the car at this point. He pulled out his key and clicked the button for his car to unlock. They both plunged themselves into the car and locked the doors. The ghosts then started hovering over the outside of the car. He had to remind himself that they were not humans he was about to run over. He turned on his car and drove right through them.

As he looked in his rearview mirror, he saw that no ghost had followed them. *Thank God!*

"Okay…what…in the world…just happened back there, Sebastian? Were they trying to kill you? I'm totally freaked out right now!"

"I'm sorry, Sophia, please give me a moment to catch my breath." After he drove about 5 miles away from the cemetery, he pulled over to the side of the road and got out of the car. Sophia followed suit. He looked back down the road just to reassure himself that they did not follow him. After a couple more deep breaths, he finally calmed himself down and had time to digest exactly what occurred.

Oddly enough, humility is what took over his mind next. A grin grew on his lips as he realized what kind of scene he just played out for her. "I must have looked like an absolute idiot to you." He started laughing at himself even more.

"So I take it from the mood change that they were not trying to kill you?"

"Okay, promise me you won't judge."

"Maybe just a little," she started to laugh.

He rolled with her banter. "That's it…forget it." He started walking to his car.

She playfully pulled him back away from the door handle. "Alright…alright…you know I'm just kidding. Tell me what really happened."

He looked at her with a grin on his face. "You're going to think I'm ridiculous, but here it goes. In the middle of our conversation, out of nowhere a new ghost appeared in front of me. He was asking me to give someone a message or something like that. I couldn't really understand what he was saying because seconds later, more ghosts emerged around me. And then more and more. Before I knew it, there were so many spirits surrounding me I couldn't count them all.

"They were all talking simultaneously. When I asked them to go away, they simply wouldn't leave. They were very persistent. All I could think to do was to get out of there as quickly as possible. I was freaking out because I was worried they would follow us home. And then what would I do? Maintain a residence hosting hundreds of ghosts?"

She started to laugh. "Well…I have to say, that was an unexpected story."

"It always is with me, isn't it?"

"I suppose it is."

She got quiet for a moment reminiscing over the words Sebastian kept shouting at them.

"What are you thinking about?"

"I was just wondering why they didn't back off when you initially told them to leave you alone."

"Now that I have gone through the whole encounter, I understand where I went wrong. When it was all happening, I lost control over the situation. If they don't feel you are in charge, they will do what they want."

"How do you know that?"

"Because as I was leaving, I got the control back as I drove right through them. Suddenly, my emotions showed them I had the conviction to leave instead of the fear I was pushing out prior."

"Oh, that makes sense."

"Yes, well, I only needed to embarrass myself profusely to figure that out." They both laughed. "Come on, let me take you home. Enough drama for the day, don't you think?" She smiled and walked back to the car with him.

After he drove her home, he realized how exhausted he had become. That took a lot out of him. When he finally got home, he didn't even eat. He just went to bed for a much needed sleep.

The next morning, he woke up and went to work. As he walked into the office, he observed the mood to be much lighter. Now that Henry was going to be out for the next couple of days, it would be a pleasant change in the workspace.

He went to his desk and started to work on some order forms when he heard a voice whisper his name. Except, the voice was not coming from his head. It was coming from the back of his chair. *Jesus Christ...* He blew out a long deep breath. *So this is what it is going to be like.* He turned around to find a short stocky man starring at him.

"Hello, Sebastian, I'm Stephan, Margaret's father."

"I see...and what is it that you want from me?"

"I loved my daughter very much. But I had trouble showing her that until my recent diagnosis with stage 4 cancer. It changed my way of thinking. But that is inconsequential for you to know at this time.

"What I need from you is a favor. I have something for her...something of great value. I was meant to give it to her when I was still alive. But, as you can see, I died before that could happen. I was hoping you could tell her where to find it?"

He thought it over for a moment, images of Margaret's sad face flashed through his head. *Maybe this will help heal her*, he reflected. He glanced back over to Stephan. "Yes, I will do that for you. Tell me where it is?"

Without delay, he explained the details of where to find it. When he finished talking, he put one of his hands on Sebastian's shoulder. "She saw me die, you know. I was about to go to the portal, but then I saw her watching me in the hospital room as they tried to resuscitate me one last time. I realized that I couldn't go yet. I needed to make sure that she found what I left for her."

"I promise to make sure she does. You have my word."

"Thank you for doing this for me."

"It's no problem, Stephan. You can go to the light now if you wish, and watch her from the other side." He gave Sebastian a quick nod goodbye. Then seconds later, he vanished away. *This will be tricky,* he thought. He just committed to something he had no idea how to do.

Chapter 6
Wonders Never Cease

Three days later, Margaret and Henry arrived back at work. He contemplated over how he was going to bring her father up to her. He definitely was not ready to explain to her that he had certain…abilities. That was when a thought occurred to him. Maybe he could angle the conversation to be more of an intuition thing.

He continued to mold the idea over in his head when suddenly, he felt Margaret's energy coming closer to him. At first, he started to panic a little. *I'm not ready for this!*

But then her father's words came rushing back to him. *I saw her watching me in the hospital room as they tried to resuscitate me one last time.* It was the prompt he needed to move forward with his promise. *Everything's going to be fine,* he told himself.

"Hey Sebastian, how did everything hold up while we were gone?"

"Oh, um, good actually. Everyone did what they needed to do to keep things flowing. We have been surprisingly busy this week. Did you see the appointment book?"

"Yes, in fact, that's why I came to see you. I have you scheduled with back-to-back appointments all day. I just wanted to make sure it wasn't too much for you to handle." She passed the schedule over to him.

It showed that his first assignment was in half an hour. *This might work out as a blessing*, he thought. *It won't give her much time to ask me a lot of questions*.

"As you can see, you don't need to come back to the office today. You can just go home after your last one."

"Okay, sounds good, thank you."

"No problem."

She smiled and started to walk away. "Ah Margaret…I need to leave soon, but I was hoping to have a word with you about something not related to work?"

"Yes, of course, Sebastian."

"Hold on a second, let me get you a chair." He quickly grabbed the first one he could find and placed it down beside his desk. "Please, have a seat."

She sat down hesitantly. "I'm going to say something to you that might not make sense right now. But I'm hoping this information might offer you some peace of mind."

She looked at him with her sad eyes. "Okay, Sebastian, what is it you have to say?"

"Well…I have this feeling, if you go to your dad's house and look under his bed, you may find something of great value with your name on it. Also…my gut tells me that whatever you find should be kept as yours and yours alone. I don't believe it was meant to be shared with the rest of your family members." Her father had never specially told him that fact, but he could feel it in his soul that it was only meant for her.

She was surprised, to say the least, of what was coming out of his mouth. "What do you mean, something of great value; how do you know this?"

"I don't really know. It just came to me while you were gone. Let's just call it a hunch, if you will." She looked at him, perplexed.

"Listen, please don't kill me, but my first appointment is in twenty minutes. I have to go. Just promise me that you will look for it…and the sooner the better?"

"What's the rush?"

"If my hunch is correct, I think it will bring some much needed joy back into your life." He looked at his watch. "I'm sorry, Margaret, I really do have to go or I'll be late. You know how Henry can be."

That did the trick. He knew if he just mentioned his name…it would be enough for her to let him go. "Okay, Sebastian, you're right, better go before it gets too late."

As she watched him walk away, she couldn't help but ponder over what in the world could be waiting for her underneath her father's bed. She felt strange following his request over a hunch. But she promised him she would, so the next thing she knew, she was making arrangements with Henry to go to his house after work.

"Why do you have to go over to there tonight, Margaret?"

She made up a lie. "I'm anxious to go through his belongings." He thought about it for a moment. She knew he was trying to come up with an excuse not to go. So she beat him to the punch. "Don't worry, Henry, it's not a big deal. I'll drop you off first. You'll be bored anyway just watching me go through his stuff."

"Oh, well, in that case, that would be great."

Truth be told, she didn't want him to be there anyway. If there was something waiting for her, she wanted to experience it on her own.

Throughout the rest of the day, lots of things came to mind. Yes, she was of course, curious about what might be underneath the bed. But she also thought about her father and how their relationship ended. It made her sad to reminisce about their past history.

When 5:30 finally rolled around, she walked up to Henry's office to get him. "You ready?"

"Yes, let's go." They didn't talk the whole drive home. However, this was pretty normal for them. He was busy doing his own thing. He spent the entire time on his tablet watching college football on YouTube.

Not wanting to waste any time, she dropped him off and quickly got back on the road. Before she knew it, she was at her father's house.

She made her way up to the front door, opened it, and turned on all the lights. It was a big house. You might even call it a mini-mansion. She made her way up the stairs and walked down the hallway. His bedroom was the third one down on the left.

She paused as she stood over his side of the bed. *Come on, Margaret, just do this.* She slowly bent down and looked underneath the bed. The first thing she saw was a wrapped gift. She grabbed it out from underneath the bed and noticed there was an envelope on top of it. She lightly brushed her fingertips over the top of the envelope. It was addressed to her.

She was beside herself on how in the world Sebastian could have known about this. But that was abruptly discarded as she imagined what her dad could have possibly written to her. She quickly opened the envelope and read the letter inside.

Dear Margaret,

First and foremost, I want to make sure you know that I love you so very much. I'm not really good at saying stuff like that out loud. So I'm glad I got the courage to write these words to you on paper.

I find myself filled with many regrets in life, especially towards you, Margaret. How I've treated you all these years, I should have stuck up for you more. I should have been there for you. However, I know I was not.

I understand why you chose to marry Henry. I didn't give you the tools to make better decisions. I've known for a long time how he has treated you and yet I've said nothing. As your father, I'm ashamed.

I remember a week before your wedding, you had come up to me looking very sad. I asked you what was wrong. You said that you were not sure if you should marry him. I should have told you my true feelings then. I just knew he was going to be a son of a bitch. But I didn't say a damn word. I put it back on your shoulders to bear. For that, I am truly sorry.

As to why I haven't been there for you... I am a man who grew up in the '40s. I had all boys and one girl. The way I was taught to live was that the men held all the cards. They are the breadwinners. Since your mother passed away...I felt at the time I needed to raise them to be the best, and that was where my attention went.

Your mother, if she had been around, would have made sure to balance everything better. Throughout most of my life, I really thought I was doing the right thing. But, recently, I was diagnosed with stage 4 prostate cancer. It caused me to have a chance to reflect on my life, including my accomplishments and failures.

Unfortunately, they have not lined up well with each other. I helped your brothers go off to the best colleges, open the best law firm and become a great doctor. Well...you know how they ended up. Sadly, I did not teach them how to be decent human beings toward one another. They treat each other horribly and I especially don't like the way they treated you all these years. Much like how I did not get along with my own siblings, it seemed like a normal way to live. It's all that I knew at the time.

This is why I wanted to write you this letter. I wanted you to know that I am living my best life right now, at this moment.

So...let me say what I should have told you a long time ago. You are beautiful, and you are bright. You could run any business yourself if you wanted to. Henry got you doing most of the work there anyway. It's never too late to start your own thing.

Besides this letter, I also wanted to give you something else you've needed for a long time. Something I'd like to call...hope. Hope that you can believe in yourself enough to have a future of your own, if you so desire. And it is perfect timing really...as it is your birthday. Probably the best present I have ever given to anyone. Use it for whatever will make you happy in life. It warms my heart that I can do this for you. I also hope that it is not too late for you to forgive an old man like me.

Happy Birthday, my darling!
Sincerely,
Dad.

Margaret sat there for a while, tears rolling down her face. She couldn't believe he had finally said the words she always wanted him to say. Their relationship had been strained for years. He had planned on giving this gift to her on her birthday, which was tomorrow. However, he passed away too early.

She waited a moment to open it. This was all so overwhelming for her. *Just breathe, Margaret...*

After she finally got her wits together, she unwrapped the present. It was a beautiful jewel box with a hand-painted picture of a ballerina on the top of it. There was a key on top of the box as well.

"Okay dad, let's see what you left for me." When she opened the box, her eyes had to take a second glance. It was filled with what looked like all his precious belongings. There was pictures of mom and dad when they were a young couple, love letters he wrote to her when she was alive, a gold locket that she used to wear around her neck and her wedding ring. There was also monetary items in it as well including small blocks of gold, an envelope filled with cash and a bunch of bonds from all kinds of companies. It was his life's worth all packaged up in a beautiful box. As her eyes peered back down, she noticed something else. It was a small black journal. When she opened it up, there was a note inside.

Here's to making it count, Margaret! If you do decide to free yourself from him. This journal contains a list of all my close business contacts that I have ever made throughout the years. I trust this short list of people with my life. I know they will help you through your journey if you should ever need them.

My God…this was all beyond what she could have ever imagined. When it finally hit her…the magnitude of his words, *Use it for whatever will make you happy in life*. She had never been in this position. No one had ever believed in her this much before…it meant the world to her.

Tears began to roll down her face as she thought about all those times Henry degraded and humiliated her. It was incredibly painful to reflect on the torture and abuse he inflicted on her. However in time, that pain eventually turned into anger. *All those God Damn wasted years with him! Come on Margaret, just say it out loud for once… Just say it!*

She started to shake as the words came rushing through her mouth. "YOU ARE A GOD DAMN LOSER HENRY!!! I HOPE YOU ROT IN HELL FOR EVERYTHING YOU PUT ME THROUGH!!!" *My God, that felt so good!* Suddenly a feeling of freedom overtook her. *"But no more, Henry… no more."*

It will feel good to have control back in to my life.

With that, she picked up the jewel box and letter and went home. It was late by the time she got back. Henry was already asleep. *Thank the Lord*! She didn't want to sleep in the same bed as him. But doing anything out of the ordinary was out of the question for now. So she sucked it up and fell asleep with him.

The next day she woke up in the best mood. Reminiscing over a dream she had right before she woke up. *I need to get up*, she told herself. *Today is the first day of the rest of my life. No need to waste it on spending time here with shitass.*

She got dressed and went downstairs. Henry was already up. "Hey, I've got to go to the office today."

"Oh, okay, I guess I'll just see you tonight."

"What, you are not coming with me?"

"No, I have other plans for the day."

"But you always come with me."

Obviously, she did not want to upset him… yet. "Oh, sorry Henry, unfortunately, I'm still dealing with my father's affairs. But, it won't be much longer, I'm almost finished."

"Yes, I certainly hope so, Margaret! He looked down at an empty table, frustrated as all hell. Can you at least make me some breakfast before you take off?"

"Yes, of course I can." *I CAN'T BELIEVE I HAVE BEEN LIVING LIKE THIS!* "Two eggs with sausage and bacon okay with you?"

"I guess." *I'm sure his heart will love this.*

After she made him his food, she quickly left and drove back over to her father's house. The first thing she did was review the black journal. She noticed the name Paul Turner in it. She had remembered meeting him at the funeral, but they had really only exchanged names with each other. Both had been too grief-stricken to have any meaningful conversation. She decided to call him first.

"Hello…Mr. Turner, this is Margaret Harrington."

"Oh, yes, I was waiting for you to call." She did not expect him to say that. "You know, your father and I go way back. He was a very close friend of mine."

"Really, I did not know that. Although, I guess you could say we had somewhat of a strained relationship. I didn't know much about his life or business for that matter."

"Yes, Margaret, I hope you don't mind, but he mentioned that to me. We had a long conversation about you before he passed away. He felt terrible about how things ended up between the two of you." He paused for a moment, not knowing how to approach his next words.

"Did he by chance…leave you with anything? He said he made plans to give you something on your birthday. However, I wasn't sure if he was able to do that before he…unfortunately left us."

"As a matter of fact, he did, Mr. Turner."

"Oh please, Margaret, call me Paul. And, I'm sorry if I'm asking too many personal questions. The last thing I would want to do is upset you at a time like this."

"No, it's okay, Mr. Tur…I mean, Paul. Sorry, I'm just a little taken aback by how much detail he put into my care. I'm just not use to it."

"I know, Margaret, near the end of his life, he lived with deep regret with his behavior towards you. However, I will say that he had hoped to make it up to you. He asked me to take good care of you if you should ever call. And that is exactly what I intend to do. That is, if you should need my assistance."

"Well, actually, I really could use your help. It says in the journal he left me that you are a business lawyer?"

"Yes, I am. Whatever aid you need in that spectrum of the law, I can help. I also have contacts with lawyers who practice other types of law as well."

"Oh…" He gave out a slight cough before saying his next words. "Again, I don't want to overstep my words. But Stephan mentioned that things might be…sticky in other areas of your life, as well."

"Yes…he was right. At the end of the day, I'm looking to rip off a horrific band-aid. Are you sure you are up for the challenge?"

"Let me explain something to you, Margaret. Your father and I did a lot of business together throughout the years. But he was more to me than just that. He helped me get through some deep personal hardships. I will miss him very much. And I promised him before he passed, that I would help you with whatever you needed in life, for as long as you needed it."

Huh…she was beginning to realize that these contacts might possibly be worth more value to her, than all the other assets he left her.

"So, I know it is a Saturday, but I am at the office today. Why don't you swing on by in a couple of hours and we can sort through your immediate issues. I think you will be surprised how short of time it will take to…clean up the wound."

"That would be great, Paul. You don't know how much this means to me."

"Anytime, Margaret. I'll text you my address."

"Thanks."

She hung up the phone, astonished by his sincerity. Why did it take her father's cancer diagnosis for him to become this kind of man to her? But then she thought about his untimely death and how quickly he passed away.

"Life is too short," she reflected. It was at that moment she made a decision not to waste another single breath on the past. From this moment on, she was only going to move forward. Happy with her new-found situation.

Chapter 7
The Visitor

Sebastian woke up Saturday morning feeling unusual from a dream that had emerged in his sleep. He remembered the details specifically. He was sitting on the couch in his living room, staring at nothing. Suddenly, he burst out the word. "strange." Then, a picture appeared outside his head. It was about 12 inches from the center of his forehead.

The image eventually morphed into a video clip. It was of him when he was a little boy. He was outside writing something in a notebook. When he finished, Sebastian was able to observe what he wrote.

January 6th, 1999, Sebastian Sinclair made this paper airplane.

Then he gently ripped the paper out of the notebook and turned it around. He glanced up to the sky for a moment as if pondering over something. Then looked back down at the paper and started to write. When he finished, Sebastian glanced down at the paper to view the message. But as he continued to watch the video, he became aware that he was not allowed to see the message. For whatever reason, the words were all blurred out. *How peculiar*, he thought.

The scene continued to play out and he watched as he began to construct the paper into an airplane. Not bad, he reflected. He took his time and played with the plane for a while. Until he heard his mom outside, calling him to come in for dinner. He quickly grabbed a cylinder-shaped time capsule next to him and stuffed the plane in it. "I'll come back to get you someday when it's time." Then he buried it in his front yard.

That's when the scene stopped and he abruptly woke up. *Hmm... that was the most unusual dream.* But then he realized why that was. He remembered that scene had played out before. Only it was in his own real life. *Holy shit...* he thought. Although it was a long time ago, he still maintained a faint recollection of that day. Could it be that he was watching an actual archive in his sleep?

That would mean he was in the beginning stage of receiving Landon's gift. He was astonished by that possibility. He felt a strong urge to hunt down that time capsule. Immediately, he began to text Sophia. He can't experience this without her.

Sebastian: Interested in going on another weird adventure with me? Promise, no ghosts will be allowed this time.

Moments later, she messaged back.

Sophia: You just love shocking me with weird, don't you?
Sebastian: I thought that's what you like about me?
Sophia: Hum…thinking…
Sophia: JK…You definitely know how to grab my attention, Sebastian. ☺
Sebastian: Do I now…Good to know…I shall like to catch your attention today then around 3 pm. Will that work?
Sophia: I'll be waiting.
Sebastian: K. See you then.

He spent the rest of the day, doing his normal take care of thyself routine. He had to admit. Ever since he had acquired his gifts, his typical life schedule had been taking a backseat.

He had just finished his laundry when the phone rang. He looked at his cell. It was Clarissa. "Ah perfect. Caught you in time. I'm checking up on you. I thought you might have some new questions for me?"

"Yes, I do, actually. I'm glad you called. A lot has happened since I've seen you."

"Good, my dear…I thought so. Would you like to come over tonight?"

"Yes, though it won't be until later in the evening, and obviously, I know you will not mind, but I will have Sophia with me as well."

"Oh yes. Yes. Yes. About our lovely Sophia. May I ask what you are waiting for?"

"No, you may not."

She just chuckled and said, "I'll see you tonight then."

When he ended the call, he noticed the time was already 2:45 pm. "Man, I better go." As he was getting into his car, a strong floral scent plunged through his nose. He looked all around the area, but there was not a single flower to be found. *It must be that spirit who's been lurking around me lately.*

"Why don't you just present yourself?"

"Not without her permission."

"Whose permission?"

"That is for her to say."

Okay, this is going nowhere. "Listen, buddy, I'm sorry but I have to go. I'm late to see someone."

"I see," was all he said. He drove off after that, wondering what that poor spirit wanted from him.

When he arrived at her house, he got out to greet her at the door. When she opened it, he raised an eyebrow. "I see you look as stunning as ever, Ms. Freemont."

"Well, you certainly know how to charm a woman."

"Not just any woman, Sophia."

"Are you like this with everyone you take an interest to?"

"Non ma douce, seulement toi."

She stared at him with a smirk, waiting for him to translate.

"The answer is no, Sophia, only you." *Just ask any one of my exes.*

That made her feel good.

"So, what eccentric activity do you have planned for us today?"

"Oh, yes, we are going to go track down a time capsule that I buried a long time ago in my front yard."

"Okay…" She chuckled. "I can't wait to hear where this is leading too."

"Right…so, this morning while I was sleeping, I had what I thought was a dream at first. But then I realized it's possible that I might have been mistaking it for an archive."

"Wow…that would be amazing if it's true."

"Yes, it would. That's why I want to recover it so badly. There was also a message in it that I couldn't make out."

"Do you remember where you buried it?"

"Yeah, I think it's between these two pine trees in front of my house."

"Well, let's go find out then."

"Yes, let's go."

When they arrived at his childhood house, he suddenly felt very anxious. "What if someone comes outside?"

"We'll just have to wing it, Sebastian." They got out of the car and walked towards the pine trees. "How far do you think you buried it down?"

"Well I was really young, so probably not too deep." He pointed his finger to the center of the two trees. "I'm going to try there."

"Okay then…I'll be on the lookout while you dig."

"Sounds good."

He started to plow into the ground for a couple of minutes, but did not find anything. "Huh, maybe this isn't the right location after all?"

"Try digging a little while longer. Your first instincts are usually correct." Sure enough, after another minute, he began to feel the tip of the cylinder. "Found it!"

After scooping out the rest of the dirt, he tossed the garden shovel to the side and pulled out the capsule. "Wow…after all these years." He held it up in his hands and took a moment to admire it.

"Ah, Sebastian."

"Yeah?"

"I think we should wrap this up. I see people rummaging around the windows."

"Oh, roger that! Just let me put everything back in its place." He finished up quickly, and then they headed back toward the car.

As they drove away, Sophia picked up the capsule and made a comment. "Man, that's such a cute thing to do as a little kid. You must have quite an imagination."

"Yes well, I also ate grass as a kid…so…there's that."

She giggled. "There is a lot of information you are giving out today, Sebastian."

He smiled. "Yes, and lots more to come."

He drove them to Brown Park and they found a place to sit. Wasting no time in opening it, he put his hand through the cylinder and pulled out a paper airplane. Gliding his finger over the top of it he said, "I remember how much I loved making these when I was a little kid."

He closed his eyes and took a deep breath before unraveling the paper. "Here goes nothing." He opened up his eyes and read the message out loud.

January 6th, 1999, Sebastian Sinclair made this paper airplane.

"So ...is it what you saw in the video?" Goose bumps ran up and down his spine. "It is."

"Ah, wow ...so that means you really were watching an archive."

"Yup."

"That's Landon's gift!"

"Yup."

"Do you want to see what was written on the other side of the paper?"

"Oh, that's right?" He had completely forgotten about the other message given everything he just discovered about himself.

He quickly turned it over. This time Sophia was the one who read it out loud.

I don't know why, but when I see this message someday in the future. It will remind me that I needed to see this plane at this moment and at this exact time. Sleep will lead me to it.

"Good Lord, Sebastian. Even back then you had the foresight to know what message to put on this plane."

"I guess I did."

"You know, this is really turning into a pretty big day for you."

"Yeah ...it really is."

"I'm curious, if you can view someone's entire history how do you know how to find the different various parts of their life?"

"That's a good question. But I haven't the slightest clue." *Hmm...* She got quiet for a moment thinking something over in her head.

"You okay, Sophia?" She glanced over at him. "Yeah, um, I was just thinking if it would help you. I'd be willing to give you permission to view my archives, but only if I can choose which ones I want you to watch."

He was so taken aback by her consent. However, there was no way in hell he would ever concede to it.

"Sophia, I can't let you be my guinea pig for the sole purpose of learning my craft. Besides, I have no guarantee that I can even do what you're asking. What if I can't just pick which archives you want me to see?"

"Well, Landon indicated that when you die, you can simply view the moments of your life upon your choosing. So it sounds like there is probably some way of controlling all the videos in the library."

Where is this coming from? He knew how private her life was to her. She had made that abundantly clear when they first went out. Then again, judging by her character, he could also say that she had a natural instinct to want to help people. He thought about the first time they met. Without even knowing him, she was more than happy to set up a meeting with Clarissa. Still, he just didn't feel comfortable prying into her life without understanding a little bit more how it operates.

"Listen, Sophia" …he picked up her hand and put his other hand on top of it. "What you are offering to me is a very kind gesture. But I am not in any rush to learn how to manage the archives the way you need me to. Secondly, I quite like getting educated about what makes you tick by spending actual time with you. Not by what I could learn from your archives. At least not during this particular journey we are in right now." *Well damn,* she thought. *How do I go against that?* "All right, Sebastian. I was just wanting to support you in any way I can. Your life is pretty fascinating, you know?" He gave out a small chuckle. "Yes, that's one way to put it."

He looked at his watch. It read 7:00pm. "If it's okay with you, we can hang out at my place for a while and then head on over to Clarissa's later on this evening?"

"Yeah, sounds like fun."

When they got home, he could instantly sense a presence in the air. *There he is again*. Sebastian rolled his eyes. *"As I said already...please present yourself or leave. As you can see, I'm in the middle of something."*

The voice abruptly replied back to Sebastian. *"Not until she gives me permission."*

And then it hit him. *Oh my God...* He had to pause for a moment to take in the situation.

Sophia could literally see he was struggling with something in his head. "You want to tell me what's going on?" *Jesus, how do I go about this?*

"Um, well… funny enough. I think our night is about to get a whole lot more interesting." Given the day they just had, she wondered how in the world that could possibly be.

"Okay, keep going."

“All right…” Again, he fidgeted with his hair while thinking about how to handle the situation.

“…You see …there’s this spirit that’s been following me around for a while now. I’ve been asking and asking for him to state his business. But up until this point, he just kept sending me cryptic messages.

“However, it is at this moment that he has decided to come out with it.”

“Oh, well… I guess I will just sit back and let you do your thing then.”

“Ah, that’s the thing you see. You are the business he wants to discuss.” She started to feel tingles on the back of her neck.

“When did you say your father passed away?”

“Oh shit!” She started to look frantically in every direction of the room. “Are you telling me that he’s here!”

“Sophia, it’s going to be okay.” He went over and gently held her hands. “Nothing is going to happen that you don’t want to happen. I promise you that.”

She took a moment and glanced around the room again.

“Where is he?”

“Well, he is somewhere in this room. But he won’t come forward unless you give him permission to do so first. He says that he wants to respect your space.”

That was a lot for Sophia to believe. It had been over 5 years since they had last spoken to each other. And now he was asking for her permission? It was very unlikely for him to do that when he was living. *Guess the afterlife has changed him.* But it didn’t matter. She was going to get on with it regardless.

“Fine Dad… you have my permission.”

Just like that, he instantaneously appeared, along with two others. Sebastian was surprised to see all of who showed up. “Huh…I see you come with friends.”

He wasn’t quite sure what to think of the extra company he brought with him. They looked and felt differently than the other spirits he had come across. He started to become a little overwhelmed at the scene that was unfolding. Nevertheless, he knew for Sophia’s sake, that he needed to hold it together.

He looked over at her. “What was your dad’s name?”

“It was Ray.”

"Okay… Ray, who are these interesting friends you brought with you? I believe they are from a different realm, That much I can tell."

"Yes, they are my angels. They are here to help me get through the journey of my afterlife."

"I see. Can I talk to them?"

"Yes."

He glanced over to one on his right. "What is your name?"

The two angels spoke simultaneously, "We don't have names. That is more of a human trait."

"Then, how do you call for each other?"

Again, they both spoke. "Where we reside, we don't call…we just do."

"Fascinating. Sounds very 10th dimensional." *Maybe I'll ask a question that is a little easier to understand.* "You are both so beautiful…yet you look human. There is not a single imperfection on you. Why are you so perfect-looking?"

This time, only the angel to the right of her father answered, "That's just how we choose to look with you. We cannot say why. It just is."

"Well, I suspect there are deeper answers than this, but perhaps for another time. Sophia…it's your turn. Do you have a question for your father?"

"Ye…yes…I have so many questions. The first one is, why you are here?"

Sebastian waited for his response then repeated it back to her.

"He said he didn't want to leave earth without knowing why you abandoned him."

She was astonished that he stayed back because of her. She couldn't believe it. "So to be clear…you are saying that you became a ghost because you have unfinished business with me?"

"He says he's not sure what to call himself. But if you are asking if you are his unfinished business, the answer is, yes."

"I see." She didn't feel it at first because it was so small. But at that moment…a tiny piece of her heartache began to slowly chip away. "I was also wondering how you died. The letter I received from Mom never explained the details."

"He says he was in the hospital. The doctors were doing minor surgery on his shoulder. It was expected to go smoothly. But with his cancer, it complicated the situation. His body simply started dying.

"He could tell it was his time to go when memories of his whole life came flashing before him. It was like he was watching a homemade movie made especially for him. But then he paused the movie when he started to see memories of you.

"He began to wonder what happened to his Sophia. Suddenly, he was filled with the need to have answers. He just couldn't leave this earth without taking in your side of the story. The experience of being a human is worth nothing without being able to take in both the joy and the heartache."

"It kills me that you didn't try to fix the situation while you were still alive. Instead, we both had to suffer years of anguish."

"Yes, Sophia. He says you are right, that would have been better. But he is here today…at your mercy."

She didn't have a response for that.

"He says it was by chance that you happen to know someone that can translate his words. Otherwise, he would have wandered the earth, following you around until he was able to understand all the pain that caused you to leave him."

It was so much for her to take in, she almost started to cry. Still, she held it together. Sebastian felt her burden. "Are you okay? We can take a break if you need to."

"No…please don't." Her voice started to crackle from all the emotion. "I'm okay. Just go ahead and continue."

"He says he does not wish to see you in anymore anguish on his account. If it will make it better for you, he will leave and do what he needs to do quietly in the background of your life."

The kindness of his offer was uncharacteristic of the person she had known while he was alive.

"If there was one thing I am sure of, Dad, it is that I do not want you to leave. I'm glad that I have an opportunity to tell you how I feel. It's just that you came out of nowhere. You are dead, yet I'm talking to you as if you are still alive. It's a bit overwhelming as you can image. I've had no time to prepare for what you need to hear from me. So my emotions might be running a little thick right now."

"Understandably, he says."

She took a deep breath before she spoke her next words. "So you want to know why I left the family? The answer is not so simple really. It wasn't just one thing that created our demise. The best way I can describe my world with you is to say that more times than not, I felt isolated and alone. You were not around a lot, but when you were, it's like being with who you are right now…a ghost. You allowed Mom to make very poor decisions on my life. Decisions that affected me deeply as a child. Things I cannot change even now as I have spent so much time away from you all.

"The way Mom structured the family was extremely strict. When I did something wrong, I was repeatedly made to feel guilty for it. Problems rarely got resolved. And everyone was constantly fighting with one another. Yet, we were made to look like the perfect family on the outside. As I got older, I was able to break away from what I knew. I realized that not everyone lived like that.

"Changes needed to be made for my own well-being. I knew if I didn't break it off, I would end up exactly like you. An angry and bitter old soul. At least, that is how I felt you became towards the end. And that was not something that sat well with me.

"So I stopped all communication. It wasn't easy, you know. I still struggle with the fact that I don't have a family. But if I had to go back and do it all over again, I wouldn't change a thing. I'm a better person because of it." She stopped talking after that.

Sebastian waited for a response.

"He says to tell you that his chosen life path was to learn how to support a family financially with minimal means. Unfortunately, he left most of the other decisions to your mother."

Sophia became infuriated inside!

"Knowing the kind of person she is…you still left life-altering decisions to her?"

"Yes, in retrospect, he agrees with you. He should not have done that. When he got married and started to live life with your mother, his ego became very pleased.

"When he would come home after a long day of work, he didn't have to deal with any of the family issues. At the time, he liked that it was her job. He can see now that it was selfish and lazy of him.

"For what it is worth, Sophia, I can feel his soul taking accountability for his actions. Even at this very moment, it is filled with a deep regret.

"He says to tell you that he is profoundly sorry for not being there for you when you needed him the most."

"When you were alive, you never offered me an apology."

"He knows. His arrogance got the best of him in all aspects of his life. You could say he treated himself like a king. Though, he did not deserve the title. He says that now that his ego has left his body, he can apologize as much as you need him to do. In fact, it brings him joy to make amends with you. He is grateful for this moment." She just sat there and continued to listen.

"He says, despite his behavior while he was alive, he wishes you could understand how much he has always loved you. When you are in the process of living your life and there's nobody out there pushing you to be better, your mind can go crazy with self-importance and vanity. That is what happened to him. He says it is the downfall of the human race.

"Except for you, Sophia. No, you came down more evolved than most. He says, he can remember so clearly now, how much you tried to get him to understand. You wrote him a heartfelt letter, asking…no, begging him to alter the way he treated you.

"As a human, he took it as an insult that something might actually be wrong with him. He would not accept that possibility. In fact, he only put you down more for it and dismissed your words. It was at that point you realized there was no hope in mending your relationship. He never heard from you again."

Sophia was beside herself at his admissions. It was a conversation long overdue. But she would take it any way she could get it. Hearing those words coming out after all these years was bittersweet.

She started to think about their life together. Suddenly, she felt her heart begin to open up just a little bit more for him. There was an innate yearning to embrace his light. They must have shared some good memories during the existence of their relationship, she reflected. However, she could not recall a single one. "Dad…please…remind me of a happy memory that only you and I shared together."

"Oh…yes, that's easy, Sophia. I have the perfect one. Do you remember when we used to dance together? It was our special thing." Sebastian started uttering, "Oh yes…I think I have that one…" Out of the blue, he got up and left the room. A minute later, he came back with a record in hand. "Your dad said that this was your favorite music to dance to." He put the record on the player and blasted out the sound. Before she knew it, 'What a Wonderful

World' by Louis Armstrong, was playing throughout the entire apartment. He let her sit there and just take in the whole experience.

When the song finished, Sebastian came up to her and put his hands on her shoulders. "I want you to know that I could feel the joy he had inside his soul when he was dancing with you all those years ago. He was able to share those memories with me. All I can say is that his energy was filled with the brightest of light."

She was full of happiness when he said those words. "I'm overcome with joy myself, Dad. Thank you for bringing that memory back into my life."

"He says you are very welcome and that he has one more to share with you." Sebastian paused for a second to hear what he had to say.

"...Okay, got it."

"He says to ask you if you remember what he used to call you as a child?" A smile rose from her mouth. "He called me Ms. Petunia." Her eyes got a little teary from that remembrance. She rather liked when he called her that. "I was the only child in the family that got a nickname. It made me feel special."

"He said to tell you one of his fondest memories of you as a child was when he played refrigerator. He would call you Ms. Petunia over and over while whooshing you up and down the fridge. He said it made you laugh and laugh."

Sebastian gave out a little chuckle. "That explains all the cryptic messaging I got from you about flowers."

"Yes, I tried very hard to push that through." In the middle of that exchange, the angels spoke telepathically to Sebastian.

"His energy is starting to get too low to stay any longer. So we will have to go now. Tell her he will be back at some point. Unfortunately, we cannot tell you any more than that."

He glanced back over to her. "Sophia, listen... the angels say he needs to go now."

"What? Why?" She cried out. "We've only just started, and now you are leaving me!"

"It will be alright, Sophia. They said, he will be back to visit you at some point." Her father started to fade away. Sebastian seemed strained, trying to hear him as he was leaving. But eventually, he understood the message. "He says ...thank you for all the joy you gave to him while he was still alive and that he will love you…always."

She couldn't take it anymore. Tears began to burst out of her eyes. Sebastian quickly came over to her. "It's okay, Sophia, just let it all out." She cried for a long time until eventually, there were no more tears left. After that, she just sat there staring out the window as the time past, who knows how long. But he knew she needed to process it all. That was a lot for anyone to handle. Out of the blue, Sebastian remembered they were supposed to go over to Clarissa's tonight. He got out his phone and sent her a text.

Sebastian: So sorry about tonight. A lot happened in which I will fill you in on. Can we come visit tomorrow?

As the night began to run its course, she slowly started to fall asleep. He watched the beautiful contours of her face slide in and out of grief. *It will take her some time to heal*, he thought. But this was a good beginning.

He had trouble falling asleep that night. Unfortunately, that was something he desperately needed to have in his life. Finally, when midnight rolled around, his eyes felt profoundly heavier. It was at that point his mind was relaxed enough to fall asleep. *What a remarkable night*, was the last thought he had before falling into a deep slumber.

Chapter 8
Admissions and the Other Side

The next morning he woke up around ten o'clock. First thing that popped into his head was last night's event. Being a part of that whole experience made him feel even closer to her than he already was. He still couldn't believe what had all transpired. He looked at Sophia resting her head on the pillow of his couch. Her eyes were still puffy from all the crying she had done the night before. He had to remind himself that most of those tears were relinquishing years of pain from her father. Her soul became much lighter after the release.

Shortly after he finished reflecting, he heard his stomach start to rumble. He went to go see what he could make from the fridge. However, when he opened the door, there was practically nothing in it. *Groceries man... now that's just a simple basic need I shouldn't forget to do.* He pushed his hand through his hair in annoyance with himself.

Better just go get something quick for now, he thought. He grabbed his keys and took off to a local bagel joint not far from his place. After twenty minutes, he was back. And just in time as he saw Sophia stretching her arms on the couch. *She must have just woken up.*

She came into the kitchen with a surprised look, "Whatcha got there?"

He smiled at her. "Breakfast. I didn't know what you liked so I just got a variety for you to choose from."

"Oh, wow…thank you." She grabbed an everything bagel and smeared a layer of cream cheese on it. "What kind do you like?"

He pulled out an asiago one and held it up. "It's my favorite."

"Ah…that's a good one as well."

She watched him as he spread cream cheese on his bagel. "So, last night was pretty…um."

Sebastian understood her vibe. “Yes, it was intense. How do you feel about everything that happened?”

“I feel like I just met someone who can walk on water.” They both laughed at her banter. But soon after, she took a moment to really think about what she wanted to say to him.

“What you were able to do for me last night. I mean…it’s almost mind-blowing. I still feel like I’m dreaming. There is no amount of therapy that could have ever healed the pain I suffered through with my father. Yet, you were able to do so in one night. And here you are…sitting in front of me, casually eating a bagel as if last night did not just completely rock my world. I’m absolutely in awe of you right now.”

Suddenly, that provoked Sebastian to say something he had been holding inside for quite some time now. “Then we are finally on the same playing field, Sophia. Do you not know by now how much you light up my world as well? Not a day goes by that I do not think of you.” He lifted up her chin to look into her eyes. “That is why I am not afraid to tell you what I’m about to say.

“If you told me right now, that this is as far as you ever want our relationship to go, I would take it, if that is all I can have of you. I would go on with my life just being grateful that you are in it. Whatever form that you may come in. But if you desire something more, Sophia? I am not reluctant to tell you that this is something I have been wanting from the moment we first met.

“What is even more important for you to know…is that I am in love with you. Completely and utterly in love with you. And I don’t know why, but I feel as if I’ve known you my whole life. It’s not just that I can fully be myself around you. No…it is so much more than that. It is a connection like I’ve never known before.

“So that is where I am at with you. Tell me what you want, Sophia, and I will give it to you.” He got quiet for a moment and brought his head down. Bracing himself just in case she did not reciprocate her love for him.

“Sebastian, please look at me.” She matched her eyes with his as he slowly brought his face back up. “Listen…I’m surprised you have not already picked up on how I feel about you. Not because you felt my energy or anything like that. It’s just… what we have shared together has been pretty extraordinary. And I truly am in awe with who are and what you’re becoming. But it’s not just about your precious gifts. I’m in agreeance with you about the connection we share. I feel closer to you than anyone I've ever met in my entire life as well. Yet, we have not known each other for more than a half-second. That being said, let me be clear to you now.

"I want our relationship to mature every bit as much as you do. I'm in love with you too, Sebastian. There is no denying that. I cannot understand it myself though. With all the pain that I have gone through in the past, I closed myself off from the idea of love a long time ago. Yet, when I am with you, I cannot help myself.

"These words that I am saying to you do not come out lightly. At this very moment, I feel so vulnerable, but like I said…I cannot help myself. You just bring it out in me."

He couldn't help but want to embrace her. He came closer to her face and softly kissed her lips. Then he whispered in her ear, "*Mon amour*." Looking back at her, he said, "From now on, you will always be that to me. You will always be… my love."

Then he kissed her lips again and again until they both had to stop and catch their breath. He thought about how badly he wanted this to happen. How unexpected it was that it happened today.

"I got to admit, Sophia, I didn't anticipate the morning to end up like this."

She smiled. "But I'm glad that it did." They spent the rest of their morning kissing and holding one another. Giving themselves permission to explore what they had both been craving.

It was 12:15 when they finally took a break. "Are you hungry?"

"Starved…we never got a chance to finish our breakfast."

"Yes, I remember the distraction very well, Ms. Freemont. You wanna go out for lunch?"

"I would love to, actually."

He took her to a little bistro called the Village Anchor. She looked around at the surroundings and then back over to him. "This place has a lot of character to it."

"It does indeed; it's why I took you here. I thought you might like it."

"I do, very much." The host showed them to their seats and gave them their menus.

"By the way, we are supposed to go see Clarissa today, if that's okay with you?"

"Oh…um, actually I was hoping to go home this afternoon. Not that I want to be away from you. It's just, well, I need to get clean clothes, brush my teeth, and do normal everyday living stuff."

He chuckled. "You know what, I completely understand. I guess I've kept you with me as long as I could."

She smiled. "I loved every minute of it. Although I got to say if I didn't feel the need to take care of myself so badly, I would have loved to have come with you. I mean, there is so much that has happened since we saw her last. There will be lots to divulge to her."

He looked at her and gave a seductive grin. "There definitely is, Sophia."

An hour and a half later, he paid the bill and handed it back to the waiter. "Ready to go home?"

"Yeah, let's go before I change my mind."

On the way out, she thanked him for lunch. "You're very welcome, Ms. Freemont." Then he tenderly grabbed her hand as they walked to his car.

When he pulled up to her place, he got out of the car and opened her door. They walked up to her porch together. "Sophia…" She turned around to respond. But he didn't give her a chance to say a word. He swiftly leaned in closer to her and gently cupped his hand around the line of her jaw. Before kissing her, he said, "*Ma belle amour*."

When they finally stopped, he moved his head down so he could connect his forehead with hers. "I'll see you soon love." He ended the exchange with a smile and then walked away. She watched him get into his car and drive away. Wow…was all she could think.

Once he had dropped her off, he didn't know what to do with himself. So he headed over to Clarissa's house. Surprisingly, she looked tired as she opened the door, but she put on a good show. "Well, hello, my dear friend, come in and have a seat." She gestured her hand over to the couch.

"So…tell me, how have you been?"

A smile grew on his lips before he even said a single word.

"Ah… I see you have some happy details to spill. Would they have anything to do with our lovely Sophia?" His mind lingered for a second, reminiscing over how his morning went with her.

"Truth is, Clarissa… I'm in love with her. And I had an opportunity to make that known to her this morning in fact."

An affectionate smile beamed on her face. “Well that is wonderful news indeed. What did she say back?”

“She said she loves me too.”

“Good for you guys. What was it that allowed you to finally say it to her?”

“Her father actually. He appeared to me in the form of a ghost. Apparently, he had too much unfinished business with her. So he came to reconcile with her.”

“Wow, that must have been a scene.”

“It was, actually. That whole experience of helping her heal with him, brought us closer together. It gave us the courage to say what we have both been keeping inside for a while now.”

“Well, you already know how much I love Sophia. She is very special to me. How did she handle the reconciliation with him?”

“You should feel her, Clarissa. She is so much lighter now. It was what she needed from him.” That reminded Sebastian of something he wanted to bring up with her.

“By the way, I meant to tell you…her father also brought two angels with him. I did not know what they were at first because I could not recognize the realm that they came from.”

“Oh, my goodness, Sebastian, you have the ability to communicate with the angels. What do you think about your new-found ability?”

“Actually, within the last 48 hours, I have received more than just one gift.”

“Really, what else have you acquired?”

“Well, it’s kind of a long story, so I’ll just cut to the chase. I have received Landon’s gift as well.”

“Wow… so that means you now have access to the library archives?” He nodded his head yes. “Jesus, Sebastian, that’s a lot to take in.”

“To be honest, I do have one concern.” He hesitated for a moment as he brushed his hand through his hair.

“It is something that has been lurking in the back of my mind. I don’t understand why, but I still have not received the ability to release the dark energy. I mean…you said it yourself. I just obtained two large gifts in a very short time frame. And while sleep and having the skill to turn it on and off at my leisure does help, I’m worried that those aids will not be enough to get rid of the energy.”

Clarissa put on a serious tone. "Has the darkness started to reveal itself to you yet?"

"I've only felt an ounce of its strength and that was before I even met you. In fact, it was one of the reasons why I came to see you in the first place.

"It revealed itself as an unnerving irritation to my soul. I remember one time I was getting groceries and I couldn't unleash the frustration I had towards every single person I encountered in that store. No matter how hard I tried to break the mood, I could not do it. I was lucky to have left without screaming someone's head off.

"But then after I visited you, and got some tools on how to cope with the darkness. I was totally fine. Until now, that is. Although, nothing has happened yet, I fear I will need something more powerful to aid in the balance of these new gifts."

"Well, Sebastian, I'm afraid I share your concern. Although I'm glad up to this point you have been able to manage it. But you make a valid argument about the balance of it all.

"Let us bring your angels into the picture…maybe they will have some insight for you. Come with me."

He followed Clarissa to the same room she took him to the first time he visited her. Once again, he wondered how she came up with the layout of the space. "This room, Clarissa, I'm intrigued by the detail of it. What's the story behind the setup?"

"Oh, so you are curious about the setup, huh? What exactly are you inquisitive about?"

"I mean the lighting is so…um…dark. And there are only 2 chairs in this entire room, which are positioned in quite an unusual way."

Clarissa gave out a small chuckle. "Well…to your second question…I only have two chairs because I don't usually have a big human audience in this room. You'll see what I mean when we bring in the other side. To your third question…I position them in this way because the reception is better when the chair is angled. And as to why the room is so dark? Well, I wouldn't call it dark, but rather dim."

She pointed to the wall. "See over there, I installed a dimmer on the light switch years ago. I quite like it…I think it sets the tone. But if my dear friend doesn't like the ambiance of the room, we can easily turn it up to normal. So what shall it be? Normal or interesting tone, Sebastian?"

They both laughed. “I wouldn’t have it any other way. Let’s keep it interesting, shall we.”

“Okay then.” She was about to get started, but then realized he was not finished. “Go ahead, Sebastian…I see there is something else on your mind.”

“Oh, thank you…I was just wondering what you meant when you said that you get better reception when the chair is angled a certain way.”

“Well…feeling energy varies for everyone. For me, sitting at an angle from the person I am reading gives me a stronger frequency of their energy. It’s kind of like an old-fashioned radio. When you start turning the switch to get the best sound frequency for a particular radio station.”

“Oh, yeah, I get it. That makes complete sense.”

“Once you get more comfortable with your new abilities, you will naturally fine-tune yourself as well. You’ll see.

“So, are you ready to start?”

“Yes.”

“Then let us consult with the angels.” Clarissa closed her eyes, and Sebastian quickly followed suit. Within seconds…they came. “Ah, we have a colorful room today, don’t we, Sebastian?”

There were so many of them, he almost fell out of his seat.

“Welcome, everyone! Let’s see here…” She started counting. “1,2,3,4,5,6,7,8,9,10,11. Oops, missed one…that makes 12 of you. Wow, heavy crowd.

“Now, some of you I know and some of you I don’t. Sebastian, the three spirits behind you are your angels.”

He looked at them with complete captivation. “Hello,” was all he could say at first. The scene that had unfolded in front of him was extraordinary. Twelve of the most spellbindingly beautiful souls he had ever seen were all nonchalantly hanging out in this one room. And there outfits were just as riveting. One of them was wearing a dress dated back to the 1930’s. Another had on a perfectly tailored modern day business suite. He wondered why they all dressed the way they did. But that topic of conversation was not something he was going to bring up today.

Clarissa started the conversation. “May I ask why so many came forward today?”

One of the angels in the back of the room spoke up. While he was talking, he began to move in closer to the middle of the room. He stopped when he reached the exact center. "Yes, we came for Sebastian. He wrote in his chart that he would need extra support at this point in his life. Especially from me. I come from a different perspective because I have so much experience. I have lived through hundreds of different lives on earth. So remembering what it was like to be human comes easier to me than others."

He looked directly at Sebastian. "Before your journey ends here on planet earth, you will have accomplished many great things. Things that will help advance the human race to a new way of co-existing with one another. There is a revolution going on right now to evolve humanity to a more natural balanced state; and you are one of the first souls to lead its transformation."

My God, he thought. The magnitude of what he contracted himself out to do was shocking.

"And how exactly am I supposed to pull this evolution off?"

The angel could feel his trepidation. "It's okay, Sebastian; you are not going to be alone. There are other souls out there leading the way with you. Sophia is one of them in fact. We will discuss her role in a minute. The important thing for you to know right now is that this meeting is a big moment for you. It puts you into alignment for your life's purpose."

Sebastian began to get confused about the rules of their engagement. "I'm sorry but I'm puzzled as to why you are sharing my future with me. Clarissa had mentioned to me in passing that it was forbidden? Not that I don't appreciate the information you are giving me. I'm just trying to understand how this whole process works."

"Yes, Sebastian, you are forbidden to know of anything that can alter your path in any way. But what I'm telling you is not something that will muddy your course. In fact, it's quite the opposite in your case. You were meant to know certain future information as part of your journey to fulfillment. It is why I am here today. This is the exact time period you chose for me to meet you. With your life circumstances, you felt you could not take any chances."

"So you're saying that I needed to have this meeting and receive the information you're telling me today, in order to fulfill some part of my destiny."

"Yes, exactly."

"I see."

It was hard for Sebastian to take it all in. He had so many questions. "When you say that I will have accomplished many things that will help the human race. What do you mean by that?"

"I mean these immense gifts you have been given are intended for a higher purpose. They will help evolve mankind in a big way."

"You make it sound like I'm supposed to become some sort of Superman."

"On the contrary…superheroes are fictional while you, my comrade, are a fact. However, don't get caught up with the labels right now, Sebastian. Labels are unimportant to this conversation. Let's get back to the initial reason why you invited us all here. I believe you are concerned about the darkness in your life?"

"Yes, I have apprehensions." All of a sudden, every single spirit in the room simultaneously said the word, "Sophia."

Clarissa chimed in. "It appears that even a couple of Sophia's angels have shown up today. I have to say, you certainly can bring in a gathering."

One of Sophia's angels started to speak. "We can't disclose too much information. But what we can say is that you cannot serve your purpose on earth, if you do not fulfill a significant undertaking with Sophia. You will have to bear enormous obstacles with her." Then she moved in closer to him, now standing face to face. "Things you could never imagine will take place between the two of you." She backed off a little as the other angel took her spot.

"It will require you to have…blind faith."

"You are making it sound like it will be nearly impossible to live my life out with her successfully." Suddenly, he felt sick to his stomach. "No, it's definitely possible to achieve. But you cannot achieve great things unless you go through great obstacles. I believe that is a phrase you humans are familiar with on earth."

"But let's say I'm not able to fulfill my charted plan."

They both said simultaneously, "Do not trouble yourself with that question today. We cannot tell what you will do yet."

Then one of the angels said, "Just know that the stumbling blocks you put forth onto yourself is what you needed to learn in order to become what you are supposed to be."

A great sense of fear was beginning to smother him with the realization that he created such a regrettable life chart. "Why couldn't I have just come down here to learn what it feels like to be rich?"

The angel in the center spoke up again. “Ah…but you are not understanding life’s purpose, Sebastian. Every soul that decides to come down is equally brave in and of itself. It all depends on the mission you are wanting to achieve.” He gave him a moment to let the understanding of his words sink in.

“I can also tell you this, you and Sophia were both very eager to come down and play this life out together. She is your kindred spirit on the other side.”

“What does that mean?”

“It means she is someone you connect with very closely to, in your spirit form. You are so close, in fact, that you can feel that deep connection even while you are living out your lives here on earth.”

He was stunned by what he was hearing because it made sense why they felt so bonded towards each other. “I would do anything for her.”

“Yes, we understand that you would, Sebastian. But please remember to keep in mind the whole reason you choose to come down and live out another life. That is all I am allowed to say for now.”

“And what about the gift to release the darkness? Did I not grant myself the ability to cleanse myself of it?”

“I cannot say when or even if you will ever receive that gift.”

“Then how will I get—”

The angel interrupted, “You will just have to live this one out and see what happens. The fact that we informed you of the possible speed bumps that lie ahead of you gives you a leg up, don’t you think? Now there is no more any of us can say about this particular subject matter at this time.”

“Okay…well, I’ll say this, you have given me a lot to reflect on.”

“Yes, we have. As was meant to be.” He started to feel some of the angels’ energy fade away.

“Please, wait…I have another question.”

“Ask away, Sebastian.”

“How can I get a hold of you again?”

The angel looked around the room. “As you can see, you have many that can help you here. But if you want me specifically…you will have to look for me in the tunnel.”

“What tunnel are you referring to?”

"It is an outer realm that is connected to earth. It allows us to travel from one destination to the next."

"How do I find this realm?"

"That is something you have chosen to find out for yourself."

"I see, well, that's just perfect."

"Don't take it personally, Sebastian. Look at it this way. You must have needed the journey to learn about the tunnel on your own in order to connect another dot in your path."

He was starting to feel worn-out. "Okay, just one more question then…since I am on earth, we tend to give people a name."

"You and your labels, Sebastian. All right, if you must…you can call me Thomas. It was one of my favorite names when I lived out one of my past lives on earth. I recall I was some sort of an inventor during that existence."

As soon as he finished those words, they all vanished. Clarissa looked at him with a concerned face. "Are you going to be okay? There was a lot they revealed to you today. In all the times that I have brought the other side forward, they have never divulged so much information. It was kind of epic what they said about your future."

"Yes, I'm aware now of what I got myself into. Though, what they insinuated about me and Sophia's life journey together is overwhelming. But I can't even think about it right now, I'm just too tired."

"Me too, actually. Listen, go home and get some sleep, we will talk soon." She gave him a hug. "Please make sure to give Sophia my love."

"I will. And for what it is worth, although I did not like everything that came out of this meeting, I am thankful to have these angels in my life. It brings me comfort to know that they are there."

"I know exactly how you feel, Sebastian." He gave her a smile, then turned around, and closed the door.

His eyes were so heavy as he drove, he almost pulled over to the side of the road. But he was so close to home, he opted to continue. Three minutes later, he was home. "Thank God!"

The next morning, Sebastian woke up to his alarm clock. He rubbed his eyes and got out of bed. That's funny, he didn't recall setting his alarm. In fact, he didn't even remember how he got into bed. And then a new thought came to him. *Damn…I didn't call Sophia last night.* He quickly picked up his phone from the nightstand.

Sebastian: So sorry I did not call you last night. A lot happened at Clarissa's house. I'll tell you everything when I see you next. Hope you had a good night sleep =)

After he sent the message, he got ready for work and left. As he was driving to the office, he kept thinking about his angel, Thomas. He couldn't have been talking about the famous, Thomas Edison? That would be crazy! Then again, what wasn't crazy these days?

When he got to work, he immediately felt Margaret's energy. "Huh…where is Henry?" As he got closer to the door, her energy became even more outspoken. He was so surprised because he had never felt this on her before. It was a feeling of…optimism? *Huh?*

When he opened the door, she immediately turned around. "There you are…I've been waiting for you to come in."

"Okay…"

She didn't seem to care about his expression. "Listen, Sebastian, we need to talk, let's go to the coffee shop across the street."

"Oh, that's fine but where is Henry? Who is going to manage the phone?"

"Yes…I guess you would notice that Henry wasn't here, wouldn't you? But don't worry about that right now. I can get John to do that for me. Let me just go get him." She walked away in a joyous manner.

Good for her, he thought. It was nice seeing her happy for once.

Chapter 9

A Change in the Air

When they got into the coffee shop, she immediately looked for the most secluded place she could find. There was a spot in the corner that would be perfect. She glanced back at Sebastian and pointed. "Let's go over there." Without saying anything, he just followed her lead and sat down.

"Nobody should bother us here." She looked at him and gave the most endearing smile. "Sebastian…in a matter of just a few days, something very significant has happened to me. Your one act or hunch as you like to call it has given me something I've never had before."

"And what is that?"

"…I have the ability to dream again."

A smile began to form on his face. "I see. So what is it that you are dreaming about?"

"I would love to answer that question. But first I'd like to know more about this gut feeling you had. How did you know something would be waiting for me underneath my father's bed?"

This was a road he did not want to go down with her.

"I don't really think you want to know how I received that knowledge, Margaret. It might open a door you don't want to visit."

She looked at him straight in the face. "As it turned out, what my father left me was something of great value. But even more importantly was the joy that you predicted would come with it. This kind of awareness does not come from just a hunch, Sebastian." She waited for him to reconsider his words.

However, what he was feeling inside was far from moving in her direction. His mind was filled with apprehension. If he told her what really happened, the identity of how she viewed him would be altered forever. Up to this point, he only shared his abilities with people inside his own private circle. Although he cared deeply for Margaret, he was not sure if he was ready for her to look at him so differently.

But then another argument came forward. It was a reminder of what Thomas revealed to him the other day. *These immense gifts you have been given are intended for a higher purpose. They will help evolve mankind in a big way.* And just like that, he suddenly grasped what he had started without even realizing it. The second he had made that promise to her father, was the moment he began his part in the movement of the revolution. There was no turning back now.

As the resolution of the truth began to sink in, he decided to give her what she wanted. "Okay, Margaret. I'll tell you what you want to hear. But please, remember we are in a public place. Are you going to be able to show discretion?"

"Yes, I can do that."

He brushed his hand through his hair and took a deep breath.

"While I was at the office last week, you father paid me a visit." Her fingers immediately came up to her mouth and hovered over her lips. "His name is Stephan, right?"

"Yes," was all she could say.

"He appeared to me in a ghost-like state, which means he still had something to fulfill in this present life before he could move on to the other side…or heaven whichever way you prefer to call it.

"He asked me to help show you the way of finding what he left for you. I promised him I would make sure you received it. I felt the instant relief in his soul as soon as I made that promise. So I told him he could now return to the other side if he wanted and watch over you from there. He thanked me for my help and moments later, he vanished."

She was about to ask him a question, but she got interrupted.

"Hold on a second, Margaret. A voice is trying to come through." *"Tell her that I was with her."*

He looked back at her. "So…um, it appears that your father has been listening in on our conversation. He asked me to give you a message."

She sat there stunned by what was transpiring. "What is it?"

"He says to tell you that the night he died, he saw you in the hospital room watching his death unfold before you. He wanted to let you know that you were not alone. Though you could not see or feel him there, he was with you…holding your hand while they tried to resuscitate his body one last time."

She sat there, numb to the bone. Thoughts of him dying right in front of her came barreling back. She needed time to process it all. Sebastian waited patiently, giving her the time she needed.

Eventually, she came back to consciousness. Her eyes began to open. "So, I wasn't alone after all."

"No, you were never alone."

"I didn't expect to receive this message from him. I believe the nightmares of watching him die can now be replaced with a much more calming version of his passing. You have no idea how much peace you have just provided me, Sebastian."

"I'm happy to be able to give you what you needed, Margaret. Really."

She looked at him with a gracious smile. "Thank you for all that you have given me. Now, I'm ready to give something to you."

"What do you mean?"

"You asked me, what am I dreaming of doing?"

"Ah…yes, but…" That was when he began to feel the wheels turning in Margaret's head. It was some kind of plan that involved him in the making of her dream. The drive that she had to pursue her aspirations was like none he had ever sensed before.

"You see, my father left me an enormous amount of money to use at my leisure. However, none of that wealth holds a candle up to the most beautiful letter I have ever received. After all these years, he was finally able to explain why he treated me the way he did. He also shared his regrets and gave his apologies. But what struck me to the core was what he had wished most for me. Do you know what that was, Sebastian?"

He did not even need to think of the answer. It came to him in his mind as soon as she started speaking. "Yes, I believe I do. He gave you hope, Margaret. Hope to dream big, I see." Nonetheless, he didn't want to say the idea she was projecting out loud because that would make his life forecast all that more real. So he tried to explain where his feelings lay in the subject matter.

"Margaret, what you are proposing is so overwhelming. I'm not sure I'm ready for change on that kind of magnitude."

At this point, she knew she needed to plea her case with him. "Sebastian, this hope that you speak of is something we have been needing as a species for a very long time now. Just look at what you did for me. Imagine how many countless of others could use your gifts to heal."

"I'm only one man, Margaret. I can't—"

She gently interrupted him, holding up her hand. "This will be a gradual movement, Sebastian. We will start off small and eventually grow into what it will become."

"How can you be so certain of this journey you want to take with me? You've only had a few days to mill this over." Then suddenly he saw her thoughts evolve. *Oh sweet Jesus… It can't be…* he was stunned to see Thomas, his own personal angel popping up in Margaret's head. *What is he doing there?* Of course, she had no idea what Sebastian was marveling over, so she kept moving on with the conversation.

"I'm going to tell you something, Sebastian, that I think you of all people will understand… I had a dream the same night I found my father's present. An angel appeared to me. He told me that I was to pay forward all that I have received. I asked the angel, 'do you mean all the money?' He said 'yes.' But even more significant is the hope. I am to spread it to as many people as possible. I questioned him on how I was supposed to do that. He told me to use the person who helped me receive so much treasure. Then he reached in closer to me and said, 'After the day ends tomorrow, we believe he will be ready to serve you.'

"Next thing I know, he started filling my mind with visions of possibility. It was on such a grand scale, I couldn't understand it all. But there was something specific that is worth mentioning. I saw a massive spiritual center being developed. It was like nothing I've ever seen before. I believe that is where this journey is heading."

Upon hearing her words, Sebastian started to connect the dots. She was going to become his platform for what he was meant to do in this lifetime. Chills began to run through this body as to how this whole scene was unraveling in front of him. He whispered underneath his breath, "I didn't expect to stand out so quickly."

But she could still hear him. "What do you mean by that, Sebastian?"

He moved his head down. "Nothing…just something I need to come to terms with."

Obviously, he was in deep thought over the matter. So she halted the conversation and gave him his space. Eventually, he spoke up again, but only to divert the subject matter at hand. Even if for just a short while. He needed to take the pressure off of having to contemplate this new altering shift in his life.

So he asked her where Henry stood in all this.

"Oh, that's right. Of course you would be curious about that. What happened is we had a meeting of the minds over the weekend. In which I told him that he was no longer going to be a part of my life anymore."

"What do you mean, no longer in your life?" He was surprised by her level of confidence. "How in the world did you pull that off?"

"Poor fool didn't even see it coming." She gave out a halfhearted laugh. "You see, my father didn't just leave me his fortune. He also left me a list of people who could help me find a clever way out of my situation, if I desired."

"Really?"

"Yes. So, the first thing I did was call a man by the name of Paul Turner. As it turns out, he was my father's long-time business lawyer. And he was more than happy to help me with anything I needed. He drafted up an iron-clad agreement to get me out of doing business with Henry and made it possible for me to keep all of my new-found assets.

"In the meantime, he called a well-known divorce lawyer named Hershey Wyndate to start the initial process of separation. Then I called a real estate agent recommended by my father. She knew a landlord that would rent me a place to live in on the spot. Eventually she will help me find a more permanent place to live."

"Wow...impressive. How did he take it when you told him you wanted a divorce?"

"Oh, that's the best part. After I spent the day getting my plan in order, I went home that night to tell him I was leaving. Paul came with me too. He said he knew how to handle men like him. As soon as we came through the door, he started yelling, 'Where the hell have you been! I've been calling you for hours!' And then he notices that I had someone with me. 'Who the hell are you?' he asked.

"I told him he's my attorney. He came with me today to help handle a sticky situation. Naturally, he was caught off guard. I have never been so smug with him before. That was Paul's cue to step in. He revealed to Henry that he has been working with me all day on an exit plan.

"An exit plan from what, he asked. Paul then spelled it out for him. And let me tell you Sebastian. He couldn't have been more clever with his words. He says to him…'An exit plan from you, Henry… Unfortunately, she doesn't have a desire to be with you anymore. Therefore, we took action on how to get her out of your life…today, in fact.'

"Oh my gosh… Henry was so dumbfounded by what Paul was suggesting he had to take a step back. He couldn't believe what he was hearing. But when clarity began to resonate with him, he looked like he was going to wring Paul's neck. Pointing his finger at him, but shouting at me, 'Did he put you up to this, Margaret?' I said, 'No, he didn't! I am the one who initiated the whole thing.' And I was all too satisfied to make that known to him.

"Anyway, Paul could tell he was about to blow a gasket, so he took over the conversation. He told Henry to bring his attention back to him. He quickly opened his briefcase and pushed a thick document over in Henry's direction.

"Naturally out of curiosity, he picked it up and read the top ledger. He was surprised to see that it was a business contract. As he was starting to digest everything that was put into the agreement; Paul says to him, 'As you can see, Henry, today is your lucky day. Margaret was feeling rather generous with you. She is handing the company completely over to you 100%. There is only one stipulation. You need to sign the contract tonight. Otherwise, it will be null and void within the next couple of hours. And we will take this whole thing to court. Course, as her friend, I will personally be handling all of her business affairs at no charge. I'm prepared to stay in court as long as it takes to win her case successfully.'

"Oh Lord, that's when Henry went to town. He looked at me and screamed out, 'You wouldn't survive five seconds without me. How are you going to be able to live without the money that I provide for you?' But Paul stepped in again, this time he said with a more aggressive voice, 'She is leaving you, Henry, get it through your head. Her welfare is no longer your concern. Now, read this agreement, sign it, and the company is yours. Otherwise, prepare yourself for a long, nasty divorce.'"

She paused the story for a second to give Sebastian her own two cents. "You want to know what was really sad about this whole thing."

"What?"

"I could tell all he was thinking about was the bottom dollar. There was no care in the fact that he was losing me." But then she stopped herself for a moment. She had promised she would not get caught up in the emotions of what happened to her. So she moved on, telling him that part of the story wasn't worth talking about anymore.

"Now, where did I leave off… Oh yes, I remember. He continued to read over the contract. But when he got about halfway through, he abruptly stopped and put it down. He looked up to me and asked, 'Why are you just giving me the business, Margaret? For Christ's sakes, I don't even understand why you are leaving me.'

"That's when I lost it. I told him 'Men like you will never get it. You think you are actually a good person. But you are not. Everything and everyone revolves around your selfish way of living. And I can't live that way for one more second!'"

"Margaret! I can't believe you were able to stand up to him like that. So what happened, did he sign the agreement?"

"After I went upstairs and started packing my suitcase, he finally realized that this was really happening. Eventually, he signed it. On my way out, Paul told him that his people will be back again later to pick up the rest of my belongings.

"And that was how I departed from Henry's life."

"Unbelievable!"

"I know. It's funny how cowards show their true colors when they know they cannot get away with something anymore. He knows his place now. And I'm ready to leave him behind.

"So, now that his chapter is over in my life, it leads me back to my new journey."

He started to feel anxiety creep up on him again. "Margaret, there is a lot going on in my mind right now. I have some questions—"

"Yes, that would be understandable. Please go ahead with them."

"Well, to begin with, you mentioned you wanted to start off small. What are you envisioning?"

"For one, I'm getting a place for us to conduct business. Nothing too big or extravagant. I'll work out the logistics of how we will operate. But since we are just starting off small, there shouldn't be too much detail to uncover. Once I get it up and running, I can start bringing in customers."

"Where do you think you will find my kind of customers? I mean, it's not exactly a normal way to handle mental health issues."

"Honestly, I haven't exactly figured that out yet, but I know it will come to me when the time is right."

"How are you so sure?"

"I can't explain it, Sebastian. Nor can I explain the drive that I have to get this project up and running. What I do know is that I've never felt so passionate about anything in my whole life."

He knew exactly where the drive was coming from. It was her calling in life. And the other side was getting her on board to pursue it. Except he was still trying to resist what he knew was going to be. So he continued to ask questions.

"How do you plan on making any money?"

She walked through that question treading very lightly. "I think you would agree with me that charging people for your kind of services would be unimaginable. Healing people the way you can should be free. But I'll say this, Sebastian, people will want to give back. They won't be able to help themselves. Just like how I'm not able to help myself right now."

She grabbed her purse and pulled out an envelope. He opened it up and saw there was a check with a ridiculous amount of money written on it. He was so taken aback by the amount he nearly fell off his seat. "Margaret, no! I can't accept this."

"It's called a donation for your services, Sebastian. And you will take it. You can't very well continue to work for Henry after all that has transpired."

"Margaret, if you knew how uncomfortable I feel about accepting donation money for something I have been given for free. It doesn't sit well with me."

"Sebastian, I have no intension on exploiting your gifts to make a profit out of greed. As you already know, I have plenty of money to last me the rest of my life. However, you don't. So, a small portion of the donations will be used to financially support yours means. But the rest of the money will be sourced to building this venture into what it's meant to be. It is without question that we will need donations to do that.

"And one more thing to be clear, what we are starting is meant to help people. I will not be advertising that the only way they will have access to you is through a donation. There will be people who can't or won't want to give and that is okay. It will be understood that anyone who wants your help will be given an opportunity to see you."

Sebastian had to stop her for a moment. He was at a point where he needed to begin accepting what was being laid out to him. He also knew darn well that she was being genuine with her intensions. It was time to become resigned with his fate.

So that meant there was just one last thing detaining him from moving forward. That had to do with Sophia. How would she fit into all this? It may start off small as Margaret suggested, but if she is right, eventually it could transform the way he lives his life. It seemed important to include her in the conversation.

He looked back at Margaret. "Did I ever tell you that I have a girlfriend?"

"No, you never mentioned it."

"Her name is Sophia. She has become very important in my life."

"That's great, Sebastian. I take it then she knows of your abilities?"

"Yes, in fact, she has been with me almost from the beginning of when I started to receive them."

"Really, it must have been wonderful having her be there through this whole experience."

"Yes, it has. I think we've grown even closer because of it. That is why I think we need to bring her into the picture of your vision."

"Of course, Sebastian. Anyone you want to bring on board, I would fully support. When will I get a chance to meet her?"

"Well, I need to bring her up to speed with everything and see what she says, first. But I know you are enthusiastic to get this thing going as soon as possible, so I promise I won't take too long."

"No worries, rushing you to have that conversation with her will do neither of us any good. I want you both to be excited and ready for what is to come of our venture."

Her thoughtful words put a smile on his face. "So you have given me a lot to discuss with her."

"Yes, I have, Sebastian. And when you are all set to move forward, call me at this number." She ripped out a piece of paper from a small notepad she kept in her purse and wrote a number on it. "This is my new cell. I gave my old phone back to Henry."

"Okay…I will call you soon."

Margaret then grabbed her purse and got up. She gave him a huge hug and said, "The angel told me you would feel apprehensive, but please try not to worry yourself, I will take good care of you. I promise." With that, she turned around and walked away.

He sat there for a second, thinking over everything that had occurred within the last week of his life. The gathering of the angels at Clarissa's house alone had been a lot for him to handle. But now this enormous proposal from Margaret. He wondered what else could possibly be coming his way! His life was suddenly changing at an astronomical speed and he hoped he would be up for the challenge.

He took a deep breath over the matter and glanced down at this phone. Sophia had texted him back. This put his mind a little more at ease.

Sophia: It's all good. I was busy with my own stuff anyway. Ready to be with you again =).

Sebastian: Are you now?

He put his cell back down and waited for a response. Seconds later, his phone buzzed.

Sophia: I'm off early today at 2 pm. Do you want me to meet you after you get off work?

Sebastian: Actually, I'm already off.

Sophia: Really. I thought you work till five every day?

Sebastian: Normally, I do. But it was not a normal day for me.

Sophia: Of course, it was not.

Sebastian: I know...I'm always full of drama.

Sophia: You are indeed. Now, what's on the docket today? Ghouls, goblins, or witches?

Sebastian: No goblins I hope...heard they smell dreadful.

Sophia: LOL...guess you would know!

Sebastian: ☺How would you feel if you had the opportunity to free a ghost from being earthbound today?

Sophia: Sounds very normal and boring.

Sebastian: Well, I must say, Ms. Freemont, you really are difficult to please these days.

Sophia: That I am, Mr. Sinclair.

Sophia: Okay, seriously though…to be responsible for returning a ghost back to the other side. I can't think of anything more awesome!

Sebastian: Glad you approve, I'll see you soon then.

Sophia: Yes, you will!

He put his phone down on the table with a giant grin showing on his face. However, the mood didn't last long as the conversation he had with the angels came floating back to memory. How in the world was he supposed to break the news to Sophia of their future obstacles that lay ahead of them. It was the last thing he wanted to do. In fact, the more he thought about it, the more he wanted Clarissa's input. He decided to send her a quick text.

Sebastian: Do you have time to talk this week?

When he finished messaging, he got up and put his phone back into his pocket. On his way out, he realized he finally had time to take a much-needed trip to the grocery store. So he went, and by the time he made it home, it was already noon.

He put everything away. Then shortly afterwards, he took a break and lay down on his couch. Unexpectedly, he began to feel his eyes become heavy. He gave out a yawn and let his eyelids start to fall. All these new revelations coming at him must be taking a toll on his energy level. Before he knew it, he was out like a light.

As he slept, the room stayed completely silent for nearly two and a half hours… Then, out of nowhere, Sebastian's voice screamed out, "*No… Please NO! I told you…I can't do this! Do you hear me! I CAN'T DO THIS!*"

Seconds later, he woke up with sweat covering his face. *Why the hell am I all wet?* Suddenly a horrible recollection of a dream struck his mind. A very intense dream. However, when he tried recalling the details of the nightmare, nothing came to mind.

He went over to the faucet and splashed water over his face. *So strange*, he thought. He took another moment to try and remember something about the dream. Still, not a single memory popped up into his head. *Damn*…he glanced at his watch, and saw that it was 2:15 pm already. It was time to get ready for his date with Sophia. So he opted to let it go…for now.

He had just finished getting dressed when she arrived. He opened the door and the first thing he thought about was how much he needed her. "Sophia, it's so good to see you." He gestured for her to come in. "How have you been?"

"Good, actually. I feel like—"

But suddenly she stopped short mid-sentence. There was something about the way in which his eyes were looking at her.

He came over to her and lightly kissed her lips. "I've missed you, Sophia." He reached over and gave her a long warming embrace. He didn't know why, but after experiencing that dream… holding her made him feel so much better. Eventually he let go of his hold and moved his way back over to her lips and neck. "Like I said… I missed you love." She kissed him back with the same passion and desire. "I missed you too, Sebastian."

That prompted him to take things to a different level. He took off his shirt. Then gently started to take hers off as well. She helped him push it over her head. Letting him know she wanted the same as well. Still a little voice in the back of his head was telling him he was going too far. It caused him to abruptly stop where he was going with his intensions.

"I'm sorry Sophia, I think we should take a little breather. I'm not trying to be an asshole. Obviously, I see that you want this too. However, my gut is telling me we should take this a lot more slowly." They both continued to breathe heavily as they were trying to calm down.

"Please tell me you are not upset with me, Sophia?"

"No, I'm not." She got lost in her own mind for a second and then quickly concurred with him.

"You're right. No need to rush things."

He gave her a smile. "Good, then are you ready to go on our little adventure to the spirit world?"

"More than you know," she said with a beam in her eye. She had been looking forward to this ghost quest since the moment he told her about it.

"Okay then." He went and grabbed his keys then handed them over to her. "I wish I could drive you around, but that might prove to be hazardous on both our ends."

She started to laugh. "Yes, we definitely don't want that." They got in the car. "Where to, Sinclair?"

"Let's drive towards Brownstone Road. That will eventually take us to Hwy 349."

"Oh, yes, I've been down that Hwy before, it's a really beautiful drive this time of year."

"Yeah, I think it will be."

"Okay, then let's go." She turned on the ignition and off they went.

Chapter 10
Tighter Bonds

Sophia was taking in the scene. "It really is beautiful out here."

"I know and very little traffic, which is perfect for us."

"Do you see anything yet?"

"Well, since we've been on this road, I've passed three joggers and countless of wildlife."

"It's so crazy that you can witness all that yet all I see is land and trees. You live such an extraordinary life, Sebastian."

"And I would love for you to see it all with me. However, since that is not the case, let me demonstrate what I can give you."

He pointed his finger towards a small white cottage-style home. "Let's park where that house resides."

"What if someone is home?"

"The only person I feel attached to that house is the teenage girl sitting right on that porch."

Sophia took a second look. "There is no girl sitting on that porch."

"Good, then I was right. But before we go talk to her, I wanted to say a few words to you."

"Okay." She turned off the car and looked at him.

"I feel this girl is in a very fragile state of mind. The good news is she already knows she is dead. A lot of ghosts are not aware that they have even died.

"Give me a second to find out why she won't go to the light." He closed his eyes to get a sense of what her soul had gone through. A couple of minutes later, he returned to consciousness.

"Alright, here is what is going on with her. She feels the world has not been fair to her. Cruel is the notion that comes to her mind when she thinks of humanity. She took it out on herself but especially on her body. That was the root of her demise. She died by starving herself to death. Not like a suicide. She lived with a mental illness called anorexia. It was the only way she felt people would accept her."

Sophia was a little worried about what he uncovered. "Will she be insulted if I bring that up to her?"

"I don't believe she will feel offended if you do. However, I would take caution with your choice of words. She is really broken inside."

"Also, please try to understand, if you can't help this one, we will just move on to the next spirit who is willing to see the light. Trust me, I'm feeling a lot of energy on this road, there will be plenty more to choose from."

"All right, thanks for giving me the heads up. I'm ready to go."

They both got out of the car. Sebastian held her hand as they walked towards the girl. "I believe she will be able to see and hear everything you have to say. So, as soon as I get her response, I will translate it back to you."

"Okay." When they reached the porch, he moved behind her so he could position her body in the exact direction of the girl. "Go ahead, Sophia."

Surprisingly enough, she got right into it. "Hello, my name is Sophia and the person behind me is Sebastian." She waited to hear her response.

"She says her name is Violet. She wants to know why we have come to visit her today."

"We are here to help stop the pain you have been enduring." Again, she waited to hear back.

"She says…she is not sure about talking to us. Everyone is always constantly judging her, why would you be any different?"

"Because, Violet, I have nothing to gain by it. You have already passed away and are living in a completely different dimension. No human can harm you anymore."

The girl looked at them curiously.

"She says she could never please anyone in the human world. They drove her crazy, especially her mother! People treated her best when she was thin…when she was thin…when she was thin…" He stopped for a second and whispered in her ear, "She just keeps repeating that phrase over and over again."

“Violet, I understand your point of view about humanity. People can be very cruel. But there is another place you can go where cruelty does not exist. You just have to let your mind find the light.”

“She’s asking…how do you know this?”

Sophia looked back at Sebastian for a brief second. “Because I have witnessed this man behind me lead others to that place before.”

Again, he whispered into her ear. “Keep going, Sophia, this may be her day.”

“Think about it, Violet. Have you ever met another human who can communicate with you the way he can?”

“She says she hasn’t.”

“See…he’s special. I think you should follow his lead.”

The girl took in what Sophia was saying…

“She’s wondering if she goes to this other place, will her mind erase all the judgement or does it have to come with her?”

“That’s the best part, Violet. The place you will be going to is entirely egoless. I promise you will only experience happiness in that realm.”

She thought it over for a moment and decided that anything would be better than where she currently resided. Slowly, she raised up her long frail body and told Sebastian her decision. “She says she will go but she wants me to take her there myself.”

“Yes, of course, he can take you but only to the edge of the realm. He is not allowed to step through it until he passes away himself.”

“She says she is okay with those terms.” So she held out her hand and he led her to one of the white portals.

“I don’t see the light yet.”

This time, Sebastian had to take over the conversation. “I know, Violet. You need to do something first.”

“What is it?”

“Close your eyes and comfort yourself in knowing that the place you are going will release all the pain you have been holding. Believe this place exists as if you can’t get there fast enough. Let your mind accept that you no longer wish to stay in this realm for one more second.”

After a while, he felt her body start to transition its energy from dark to light.

“Huh…I feel almost weightless now.”

"That is because you are floating through the portal even as we speak."

She opened up her eyes and let go of his hand. "Oh, Sophia was right…I've never felt so much joy." A smile grew on her face. "Please tell Sophia I said thank you!" Seconds later, she was gone.

He looked at Sophia. "You did it! Her soul is now on the other side."

"Oh my God, Sebastian, it's such an amazing feeling to be able to send someone back like that. Thank you so much!"

"Actually, she asked me to thank you for all your help."

"Really?"

"Yes, and I felt her soul as she was leaving earth. She is finally at peace with herself."

"I can't tell you how happy that makes me."

He was so overjoyed that she relished the experience so much. He gently grabbed her hand as they walked back to the car.

"So you have successfully sent an earthbound back to where she belongs, what would you like to do next?"

She laughed. "I don't know; as long as I'm with you I don't care what we do." She was falling more in love with him every day.

Without even feeling her soul, he could since her attachment was getting deeper for him. He couldn't help but love that it was.

They got in the car and he started to drive back to his apartment. It was still early on in the day. He didn't expect to be done so quickly. It was good though, he was thinking it would give him time to have a much needed talk with her.

When they got home, they both sat down on the couch together. "So listen…um…I need to speak to you about some things." She was caught off guard by his serious tone. "The last day or so, while you were gone, a lot has happened."

"Oh, does this have anything to do with Clarissa's visit?"

"You can say that…and then some."

She looked at him oddly. "Okay…keep going."

"…So when I went to her house, we took a trip to her special room. You know which one I'm talking about. Unexpectedly, my angels, along with yours, hers and about a half of dozen others came to visit us."

One of her eyebrows rose up. "That's quite the caravan you had."

"Yes…it was.

"They all came down to see me, specifically. They said, I ordered this meeting to occur at this moment in my life. Not to be dramatic, but some of what I'm about to tell you might shock you. Including the fact that you were also a topic of their discussion."

"Jesus… What was the meeting about?"

"…Okay, given everything you know about the planet and all the energy it consumes. It shouldn't be too far of a stretch to understand that it can create lifecycles of its own."

"Wait a second…what you're telling me is that the universe itself has its own existence within our human existence?"

"Sort of speak." He knew how outlandish this was sounding. "Listen, I don't have a clue as to who or what is in charge of the universal energy. All I was made aware of is that there is a change happening to the planet even as we speak and we are meant to play a role in its massive transformation."

"We?"

"Yes…apparently, there was a small group of souls that decided to join in this evolution. Before you and I came down on earth to live out another life, we agreed to be a part of that alliance."

"Oh my God, Sebastian!"

"I know, Sophia. I know how you're feeling, believe me I do. But let me finish with everything I have to disclose with you. Besides, I think you will like the outcome. It's right down the alley of who you are as a person."

Huh…

"So as I said, we came down together to start the beginning of a revolution. Our objective is to restore more light back to the planet. The purpose of that is to evolve humanity's way of thinking. At the end of the revolution, many years from now. The universe will have reinstated its way back into a more balanced nature."

If it had been anyone else saying those words, she would have thought him crazy. But this was Sebastian, no ordinary man by any stretch of her imagination. She took a long deep breath before sharing her next thoughts.

"So this is why you have been given all these gifts."

"Yes…I am to use them to heal as many souls as I can. At least that is the beginning blueprint of what we are to do."

"You've already been given a plan of action?"

"Yes, and by the oddest person you could think of."

"Person? You mean it wasn't the angels who told you?"

"No, actually. What happened was this morning, I had another very significant discussion but this time it was with my boss's wife, Margaret."

She gave out a confused look. "Whenever you have mentioned her in the past, it has always been about how awful your boss treats her. I believe selfish prick is how you described him."

"And that is still how I think of him, but not of her. She has changed, Sophia.

"In a small way I played a role in that. However, that bears no relevance to the conversation we are having right now. There is so much to tell you, I have to stick with what is most important first. What you need to know is that she recently received an enormous amount of wealth from her father. And she wants to use that money to provide me the platform I need to fulfill my purpose in life."

"How in the world did she know you needed that? And what about her husband?"

"Long story short with Henry, he is no longer in the picture. And to answer your first question…how did she know what I needed? My angel came to her several nights ago in a dream. He expressed to her that she was to use the money to start a new venture with me. The main focus of our new enterprise will be to spread hope.

"She went onto say that there were other bigger visions she has lined up for us in our future. Ones that even she could not comprehend right now. But that we will start off small in the beginning."

"I see." Sophia got quiet for a second, thinking over everything he had just divulged to her. Something else was also stirring in her mind that became important to say.

"You mentioned that we both came down to lead this revolution. What role am I expected to play in all this?"

"Well, for one, I want you to come on board this venture with me."

"To do what, Sebastian? I don't have anything to offer."

"Sophia, trust me when I say this…you don't need to offer anything. I'm merely asking you to come and support this journey with me…for now. Eventually, your role in time will reveal itself."

"Sebastian, what you are asking me to do is to just drop everything with no specific plan as to how I will help the cause, in the blind faith that something will turn up?"

Those two words sent chills down Sebastian's spine. He knew sooner or later, he would need to bring up a different conversation with her about the obstacles they will be facing together.

But he wasn't prepared to voice it to her yet. It scared him to death to think of what they would have to go through. He needed Clarissa to walk him through on how he should approach the subject matter. Speaking of which he realized she still has not texted him back. He wondered if everything was okay with her.

He was completely lost in his own thought until he felt his body start to shake. Suddenly, he broke out of his daze and heard Sophia's alarmed voice. "Sebastian… Sebastian…" She saw that he was finally coming around. "What happened? One minute I was talking to you and the next, you were totally shut down."

"I'm sorry, Sophia, I just have so much going on I guess I got lost in my own reflections."

"It's okay, I was just worried for you, that's all."

Her concerns of not being helpful to the cause came rushing back to him. "Listen, love…" He gently put his hand around the back of her neck while his thumb brushed her check. "I understand your apprehensions over not having anything to offer to the cause. Don't think I'm not listening to you. Please understand that this entire thing is unfolding so quickly. I myself only know one small piece of what I will be contributing to this whole conversion. The rest I am in the dark…just like you."

She was taking all his words into account but she was not quite over the hump. "What does Margaret have to say about bringing me on board?"

"I told her that it was important to me that you do this with us. She knows how much I love you and that you are a big part of my life."

"And what did she say to that?"

"Of course, she said yes. She wants to know when she can meet you. I asked her to let me catch you up to speed with everything and then see what you have to say." He waited a moment to see if his words were having any effect on her. But she was still not ready to commit.

He found himself feeling a deep seated fear if she decided not to be involved. It caused his words to become more frantic. "All I know, Sophia, is that I cannot travel this road without you. I need you desperately to walk through this with me. Please…"

That was when she saw the trepidation in his eyes. He was genuinely afraid of doing this without her. That was the final straw she needed to push her decision to his side. Though she did not feel comfortable with the fact that she had no specific role in place. She trusted him enough to take their leaps together.

"Okay, Sebastian. If this is the road we need to take, then I'll run its course with you."

A smile formed on his lips as she told him her decision. "That is why I love you, Ms. Freemont." He put his arms around her and embraced her with his lips.

They stayed locked together for a while. Just kissing and touching one another. In the heat of everything, Sebastian rolled on top of her. He was about to give her another passionate kiss. When all of a sudden, Sophia froze up. She laid there, stiff with a blank look on her face. Of course, he became alarmed at her demeanor.

"Sophia? What's wrong?" He immediately got off her. That was when she curled up into a ball on the couch. Her head slouched down into her knees.

He was beside himself on what just happened. Obviously, she was deeply troubled by something. He went back over to the couch to try and console her. "What's wrong, my love. Did I go too far? Please tell me, Sophia." She said nothing…she just sat there in that same position. It took everything for Sebastian not to look into her soul. But he had promised her he would never look without her consent. In time, she slowly rolled her head up with a grim look on her face.

Thank God, he thought. "Please tell me what is going on with you? I'm so sorry if it was something that I did."

"I don't have words, Sebastian."

"You don't have words? How can that be. I obviously triggered something in you to react in the way that you are."

"I just can't go there right now."

"Sophia, I do not have it open with you right now. But I know something terrible must have physically happened to you. Please…" Still she said nothing. *Damn it… this must be why my gut was telling me to take things slowly with her.*

He knew not to push her too far with his probing. Whatever occurred must have been a nightmare in order for her to react this traumatized. He got up to give her some space and went to his closet to grab her a blanket. He pulled one out and gently laid it over her body. He sat back down on the couch in silence, giving her the time she needed to work through the trauma.

Hours went by when she finally turned her head up to speak to him. Her voice sounding very monotone. "I love you, Sebastian. But I just can't get into this with you. It's too painful to discuss."

"If you let it out, you might find that the pain will go away. Just like it did with your father."

"What happened to me wasn't even close to the same situation as my dad."

He could see that she was starting to get worked up, which was not the direction he wanted to see her go in. "Okay, Sophia…I'm sorry…you're right. It wasn't my intention to upset you more than you already are. What can I do to help?"

"Pretend I never reacted that way in front of you?"

No…no…she can't be asking me to do that. It was the last thing he wanted to do. This was going to kill him inside conceding to act as if nothing ever happened. But he felt he had no choice. It was how she wanted to handle it and he would abide by her wishes. So with a heavy heart, he answered her request.

"If that is what you need from me, Sophia, then yes. I will do that. I only want you to be happy." Instantly, he could sense her relief. So as uncomfortable as he felt, he went right into pretend mode. Putting a smile on his face, he asked her if she wanted to go outside and catch some fresh air.

"Yes, that sounds good actually."

They spent the rest of their night in that same manner. Days went by and still no change. This left him more and more distraught each passing day. But he just didn't know what else to do.

She too had mixed feelings over how she chose to handle the situation. He was the love of her life. If anyone could understand what she went through, it would be him. Yet, having her share that part of her past out loud with him filled her with fear and anxiety. Not that he would leave her, but that he would know her ugly story. Something that mortified her to no bounds. So she continued on with that charade.

Thursday morning they got up and ate breakfast together. A thought occurred him out of the blue. He had never told Sophia about them being kindred spirits. He couldn't believe he forgot to tell her such a special piece of news.

"Sophia, something just came to mind that I neglected to tell you about. The angels revealed something else to me during our meeting with them."

"What is it?"

"Well…they spoke of how we are very close souls on the other side. I believe the term they used was kindred spirits. It means when we live life on the other side our spirits are tightly bonded to one another. That is why we have such a deep connection here on earth. Our souls somehow can make that distinction."

That hit her hard…because she knew exactly what he was talking about. She did not need his explanation as to the bond they shared together. It was at that moment when clarity over what Sebastian must be going through struck her soul. He was in the middle of being passionately intimate with her when out of nowhere, she had a complete mental break down. He must be freaking out inside. Still, he had done what she had asked without question.

Understandably, he must be worried where her boundaries were at this point. He hadn't so much as even held her hand since the whole unpleasant scene occurred. She was beginning to realize that this was starting to tear at their relationship.

It was for this reason she felt she could no longer hold her nightmare back from him. It was time for her to let this go and face her darkest demons…this time with him.

They had both just finished their plates. He asked if there was something she wanted to do today. She didn't answer him. Nor did he ask the question again. Obviously, he knew she was within her own thoughts at that moment. So he got up to take their dishes away.

"Sebastian…" He turned around surprised that she called out his name. "I'm sorry," was all she said at first.

He came to her side, careful not to touch her. "Why are you sorry?" And then she let it out.

"I was afraid that putting my story on the table so openly in front of you would be too mortifying for me to bear. But I can see now that all it has done was keep us more distant from each other. So I'm changing my mind." She gave herself another second before releasing her next words.

"…I'm ready to share my story with you. You can look into my archives."

He was taken aback. "Sophia?" His face engulfed with uncertainty.

"Listen Sebastian, I realize what my secret has been doing to us, and more specifically to you. You must be a train wreck inside. I'm sorry I put you through that."

"You've got to be kidding that you feel compelled to apologize to me. You owe me nothing. Yes, I admit, these past days have been difficult to get through. But that is only because I love you so much and I hate seeing you in such horrific pain. Pain that I myself triggered back into your mind. The last thing that I want is for you to do this for me. Please…promise me you won't."

She appreciated his thoughtful sentiment, but she knew this was not just about him. She was tired of holding onto to the affliction. "I'm not, Sebastian. I swear to you. I'm ready to take the suffering away."

He looked at her lovingly.

"Okay, then give me some time to get into the right mind frame." He closed his eyes and tried meditating for a while before an unexpected voice telepathically spoke in his head. *"I see you are anxious, Sebastian. But you won't even get into her archives unless you relax."*

"Thomas…?"

"Yes, it's me."

"*Thank you for coming. As you can see, I'm having trouble tracking down a specific footprint?" "You need to concentrate on the timeline she gives you. Then find her darkest emotion. You will be able to track down her footprint from there."* That was the last thing he heard before his voice went away.

After a long time passed, he finally unwound his mind enough to get into her archives. It was absolutely mind-blowing, he thought. To see her whole life appear before him.

"Okay Sophia, around what time-frame did this event occur in your life?"

"It was my first year in college. I was 18 years old."

His arm raced back and forth, as he flipped through the archives of that time period. After about ten minutes passed, he believed he found something. "Was there a teacher involved in all this?"

With trepidation in her voice, she forced herself to answer him. "Yes, there was."

He started to watch the videos of that timespan. Twenty minutes later he spoke up.

"I see often times he asked you to stay after class and talk. He acted as if he was your friend. Except he wanted more than that with you. You didn't know this at the time, but he was sizing you up to see how he could have his way with you.

"I see him asking you personal questions on purpose so he could find out your weaknesses and fears. This was so he could use them against you later when he had a game plan figured out.

"One day instead of staying behind in class and talking, he asked if you were hungry. You thought it was weird at first, but then eventually you told yourself that maybe it's not that uncommon for teachers and students to have an outside friendship." He briefly got quiet for a moment to watch another specific archive.

A couple of minutes later, he revealed more. "He seems to be very passive aggressive with you. Being friendly with you one moment then giving you a backhanded jive the next. One time I saw you guys eating at a restaurant. He says to you, 'I see you decided to pull your hair up today. That's a good look for you.' The next moment, he commented on how you were not the prettiest student he ever took out to lunch before. Your answer back to him was, 'I know.' For whatever reason, you didn't seem to get the putdown.

"Hold on for a second, Sophia. Let me look into why." Ten minutes went by and then he came back with an answer. "The whole point of you being friendly with him in the first place was the sale of goods he sold you. He wanted you to idolize his success so he could get you to need him. Many times over, he told you that he was going to introduce you to the people of his inner circle. That you would gain lots of contacts from him for your career."

Then he saw another thread to her storyline. "Sorry…I don't mean to keep breaking like this. It's just there seems to be another side narrative to your story that I feel I need to view."

She was becoming more anxious by the minute as he was unwrapping more pieces of her life. This time he took a longer period of time to come back to her. Thirty minutes later, he stopped and looked at her.

"Sophia, your mother…well…to put it mildly, I can see that she caused you a large amount of grief. I see that she really didn't want you to go to school for the degree you were seeking. It was in culinary arts, right?"

"Yes."

"You had many fights over that career choice but especially over the student loans. There were so many arguments in fact that going to school and enjoying what you were learning came secondary to this desperate need to become successful in your profession.

"Somehow, your teacher, Bradley, dragged that storyline out of you. That is how he kept you under his wing. He kept dangling the successful road in front of you.

"You had what you thought was an odd relationship. There was never any plans for you to become sexual with him. Yet, he flirted the idea around with you all the time. Like when he commented on your hair, for instance.

"Too be honest, you were so understandably naïve at that time period of your life, you really didn't have a clue as to what he was plotting…But he did."

He hesitated for a moment to think about how he was going to say his next words… "Sophia, I'm about to view the video of the incident. I know this because I feel it is the darkest one of them all. Are you sure you're alright with this?"

"Let's just get through this, Sebastian."

"Okay."

He closed his eyes and began streaming the footage. "Looks like you are driving to his office. But before you arrived, he was there with his buddy pounding out a couple of drinks." Sebastian's breath abruptly halted. "He has a plan in mind for you tonight. My God…Sophia!" He had to stop himself from watching for a second. *I hope it does not play out the way he has it calculated.* He was thankful he did not say that comment out loud.

He went back and continued on with the archive. "When you finally arrived, he went over to open the door for you. Immediately, you noticed another man with him. He's introducing you to him right now. He tells you that this man produces a very highly rated food show, but you can't recall ever hearing the name of it before. You're thinking that's strange, but then it appears he is distracting your thoughts with something else. He's suggesting that you be a contestant on the show. You seem intrigued and excited for the opportunity…of course, as anyone would.

"I see that you are about to ask him a question. But he is interjecting. 'You know, Sophia, all this help I'm giving you for your career…most woman would be overjoyed to give back something in return.' You're shocked. Just plain shocked right now! Not wanting to believe what he is insinuating, you say back to him, 'What is it you are wanting exactly?' 'No Sophia, not just me…' He looks over to his buddy…'Us.' I can feel your heart pounding as we speak.

"You're so pissed at this moment you told them to go fuck themselves. But they are so drunk right now. They are not taking that comment very well. Oh shit! …Your teacher…he just slammed you against the wall and you've fallen to the floor. His friend is starting to unbutton his pants. Oh my God, Sophia…" *Their fucking tearing her apart.*

"Your teacher is now on top of you. He's got his hand jarred up against your mouth while his other hand is busy ripping off your shirt.

"At this point he wants to do things that require both hands so he tells you that if you scream out so much as an ounce of sound, things will get way worse for you. 'Remember there's two of us here, Sophia.' You were so terrified, you believed him. His friend has now joined you guys. His hand is crawling underneath your skirt.

"Sophia…I can't watch this anymore!"

Suddenly, it becomes apparent to her that her story needs to be heard. "Finish it, Sebastian…please! You don't have to say anything more out loud. I know my own ending. But somebody should know what happened to me that night. Please do this for me!" she shouted with tears rolling down her eyes.

He just stared at her. Traumatized by what he had already seen them do to her. Wondering how he was going to stomach the rest. But he did as she requested. He could not deny her frantic need to expose her two attackers.

He spent the next hour watching them do unimaginable things to her. Sometimes, they took turns having their way with her while the other seized the moment to have another drink. Other times, they both used her at the same time. When he was finished, he stumbled to the bathroom and threw up.

He couldn't help himself. It was just too much for him to witness. When he was done, he looked at himself in the mirror as a thought began to fill his mind. Maybe he could find a way to put some new perspective on her tragedy. He walked back out to see her and got on his knees. Still making sure not to embrace her with his touch. "Sophia, what happened to you was shocking and horrifying and straight up heartbreaking. But let me see what I can do to mend you back together again."

Chapter 11
Unbroken

He got up and sat back down on the couch next to her. “Can we talk about how you escaped?” She could only nod her head yes. He took a breath before he said his next words.

“They were incredibly drunk towards the end. His friend got off you and mentioned to Bradley that they ran out of booze. So he took off to get more.

“That left just you and him. He hoisted you up on his desk and pushed your chest down so hard you nearly passed out from the impact. He started to have his way with you but this time, he got more aggressive. He tightly wrapped his hand around your throat.

“When you looked into his eyes, you saw that they were completely bloodshot. It was at that moment you realized he was too out of his mind to know that he could very well kill you if he continues.

“That gave you the courage to do what you needed to do. It was do or die, you thought. And you were right to think that way. He would have killed you without question. You started to fight him off, moving your body around as hard as you could. That caused him to want to hang onto you more. But you continued to fight him off. Somehow, your legs got the strength to push him away.

“He lost his balance from being so intoxicated and fell to the ground. That was your cue to get out of there. Your shoes and ripped clothing were scattered all over the place. But you saw his shirt laying on the floor next to you. So you grabbed it and threw it on. You saw your purse laying close to the door. Before you went over to pick it up, I saw you take a second look behind. Bradley was still trying to recover from his fall.

“Frantic to make sure he would not follow you, you ran over and kicked him as hard as you could. That gave you a second to push him down. If he was sober, that push may not have done much in your favor. But that was not the case. He fell down to the ground and you felt it was enough to keep him occupied.

"So you quickly went running back towards your purse. You grabbed it from the ground and ran out of his office as fast as you could. Since you didn't know where his buddy went, you were terrified that you might run into him. Fortunately, he never returned.

"When you got into your car, you immediately locked the door and took off. Driving home was a mess. You could not think clearly. People were honking their horns at you for driving so reckless. But that didn't bother you. You were finally out of their hands. You were safe.

"By the time you got home, you were done for. However, you refused to close your eyes before taking a shower and wiping all their filth off your body. That's when I started to see you cry. You sat down in the corner of your shower letting the water drip over your body and cried for God knows how long."

He moved back down on the ground and looked into her eyes. "I'm sorry, Sophia…I'm so sorry that happened to you! No human being deserves to go through what you went through. You were so brave, though." He wanted to embrace her badly, but he knew that was not what she needed right now.

He moved his head up for a brief second. "Your angels are here now. They have come to bring you answers. Tell me what you want to know, Sophia?"

Her face naturally wandered the room for a visual. "They are to your left love." She took comfort in knowing that. "I want to know whatever came of their lives?"

"Okay, hold on…let me see what they say."

Ten minutes went by before he started to speak again. "…His buddy, Malcom, never made it back to the office that night. He was busy getting arrested. The police pulled him over because he was swerving. When he got out of the car, he had an altercation with one of the policeman. They booked him for a DUI, with assault and battery.

"The angels said that they were watching over you that night. They tried to help whenever they could. They made sure the police took notice of him." Somehow, knowing they were there in the background of her life, trying to help, brought a bit of comfort to her soul.

“He landed up passing away a few years ago from cancer of the liver. No one attended his funeral. As you already know, he did not live a very pleasant life.

“As far as Bradley is concerned. Several years after your attack, he moved to Sacramento and took another teaching position. Not long after, a girl came forward with an incredible allegation of being sexually assaulted by him. It was for doing some of the very same things he had done to you. He was charged and prosecuted.

“But before his case had even made it to trial, he was charged with several other sexual assaults. It seems once the word got out to the general public, it gave others the courage to step forward as well.

“In the end, he was charged with multiple crimes and found guilty on all accounts. He now resides in prison and will be there for the next 55 years without parole.”

She couldn’t believe what she was hearing. He finally got caught. Although this could not take back what they did to her, karma had finally seemed to play its role in the matter.

Sebastian looked into her soul to see if any of this was helping. What he found was a light that came back on through that thread of her life. Knowing that she was not the only one he did this to. Knowing he got caught and would have to pay for it in prison brought her so much vindication. It was enough to tame some of the heartache she went through all those years ago. He could feel only one other emotion that wasn’t being attended to.

“Sophia, how in the world could you feel guilty over what happened to you?”

She put her head down in shame, not wanting to look at him. “…I think I was just so desperate to succeed. Because of that, I did not see him coming. I didn’t recognize his manipulation tactics.”

“But isn’t that the point? Believe me when I tell you this, Sophia. None of this was your fault. From the moment he met you, he started conjuring up ideas on how he was going to have his way with you. You didn’t even stand a chance.

“Although, yes…I could sense how desperate you felt because of how your mother made you feel. But that doesn’t mean another human being is supposed to use that to his liking. No, Sophia…this has and will always be solely on him.”

He could tell that she was slowly starting to come around. “Well, I’ll say this… It does make me feel better knowing that he got caught. I didn’t expect to hear that.” A small smile began to form on her lips.

“Your angels have gone now. But I can bring them back if you still need them.”

“No, I don’t think I do anymore.” She looked at him with the deepest love. “If you knew how much it meant to me that you watched what they did to me. It gave me so much relief to know that somebody else knows my story.

“Yet, you took it to a whole other level by bringing in my angels. Finding out that they are both out of my life forever, brings me the kind of relief you can’t imagine. You didn’t know this, but I quit school. I just couldn’t go back.

“But what made it worse was the harassment that followed. I think he was worried that I would tell the authorities. So he kept calling, leaving threatening messages for what seemed like a very long time. Eventually, he stopped. But always in the back of my mind, I have been living in this invisible bubble that he could strike again at any moment. That is…until now, Sebastian. I can let go of that fear now…thanks to you.”

She got quiet again, putting her head down. There was something else brewing in her head. “…I want to address a different need with you.”

“What is it?”

“It’s just that I know you, Sebastian. Now that you know what happened to me. You won’t feel comfortable being intimate with me.” The thought did cross his mind. “But I’m asking you to please not let that stop you from touching me again. That will just make what they did to me all that much worse. It will mean that they took a piece of my happiness away from me.” He had words to say as well. But she kept on going.

“I just want to be free from of all this for once in my life. And I would love it if you could just continue to be who you have always been with me. That is to say…please don’t change how you show your affection towards me. If something you do in the future prompts me to remember a particular touch, I promise I will stop and let you know what is going on. Trust me when I say this. I’ve never felt more safe with anyone in my entire life.”

“Sophia, whatever you want I will give you. It’s your life and your body. You know what is best. I want you to be unburdened from all this as well.” He gently pulled her hair away from her face and rested his hand against the back of her neck. Pulling his body in closer to her lips, his other hand wandered around her back and gently drew her in for a tighter embrace. "Is this what you want, love?"

"Yes."

He slowly laid his back down on the couch all the while still kissing her lips. He only stopped for a brief second to whisper to her… "If you only knew what you do to me, Sophia." Then he kissed her neck and shoulder line over and over, until he brought his lips back up to her mouth.

They stayed caressing each other for what seemed like hours. At some point, they stopped because they were getting closer to doing other things they had not yet explored before. "Do you realize that we haven't eaten a thing since breakfast? It's almost four o'clock."

She smiled, "Okay, maybe we should eat something. Let me just go to the bathroom and freshen myself up a bit."

It gave him a chance to ponder over everything that had transpired throughout the day. A lot of healing took place. But then a new thought started formulating in his head. Something that he felt would really do wonders for her.

He got up to go take a second glance at the envelope Margaret had given him. *Good lord…* It really was an extraordinary amount of money.

When she came out of the bathroom, he had a huge smile on his face. "What are you so happy about?"

"Well, something good has come up that I think will give you a reboot from all that has happened."

"Sebastian, you have already done so much. I don't need anything else."

"He softly touched her cheek with his hand. "You don't even know what I have planned yet, love. Just give me a minute to figure everything out and I'll get right back to you. In the meantime, if you are hungry, I finally had time to go to the grocery store. So eat or make whatever you like. I need to call Margaret to catch her up to speed on everything."

He looked so endearing she couldn't help but let him continue on with whatever he was putting together. "Okay, then…I'll just go make us some dinner."

"Thank you, love."

He quickly moved on with things. He picked up his cell and dialed Margaret's number. "Hello there, how have you been?"

"Oh, Sebastian, it's so good to hear back from you. I've been great."

"That's good to hear. So listen, I had a chance to talk everything over with Sophia. She says she is on board with us."

"That's wonderful, Sebastian, I'm so glad to hear the news!"

He had to smile over hearing her excited voice. "So where do we go from here?"

"Well, I'll need about a week to line up rentals for us to view. How about we plan to meet on the 23rd? That's next Tuesday. It should give me plenty of time to have showings lined up for us. Will that work for you guys?"

"Yes, that's perfect." He needed about a week to pull off what he was planning for Sophia. "Just text me the first address that you want to check out around 9 am, Tuesday morning. We will meet you there an hour later."

"Will do, see you in a week then."

"Yes, until then, Margaret, bye."

When he got off the phone, he noticed she had already started to make something. *Perfect, I'll tell her while eating dinner*. He went over to help her with whatever he could. Putting his arms around her waist, he uttered in her ear, "Could you use a sous-chef, Madame?"

She smiled, "Yes, actually. I'm making chili and cornbread."

"Is that right…sounds delish." He went over to lift up the box of cornmeal. "I didn't even know I had this in my pantry."

"Yeah, I noticed it has never been opened."

He laughed. "I really do mean well. It's just when I go to make something like cornbread for instance, the directions get lost in translation for me."

She gave out a little chuckle.

"Well, I promise to not lead you astray in my directions, Mr. Sinclair."

They spent the next half hour prepping and cooking in sync with one another. Oddly enough, he had never made a meal with a woman before. In his prior relationship, his wife had always done all the cooking. He had never realized how much you could bond over making a meal together. Something his ex had asked him to do repeatedly, but he had been too selfish at the time.

When the cornbread was taken out of the oven, they sat down and started to eat. "So love, before I divulge my plan to you, I should probably tell you that Margaret gave me a rather sizable amount of money as a donation for helping her reconnect with her father."

She looked at him peculiarly. "She gave you a donation?"

"Yes…a pretty big one. I told her it was too much. But she refused to take it back."

"Wow…that was generous of her."

"It was…and now I know the perfect way to spend some of it."

"How?"

"Let's go be free for a while. We have until the 22nd of next week to go anywhere you want."

She was taken by surprise with his suggestion. "Where were you thinking about going?"

He brought his index finger up—

"I said anywhere you want to go, Sophia. This trip is for your benefit, love. Remember your request…'you just want to be free from all this for once.' Well, this is your chance for a reboot. Let's go and do whatever we can to give you that."

"My God, Sebastian. That's…that's…just about the kindest thing anyone has ever done for me." She embraced him with her arms and started to kiss his lips. After a while, they stopped.

Sebastian gently pulled her chin up to his. "So, think of something you've always want to do or a place you've always wanted to go and I'll make it happen." She sat there and thought over his words.

…And then it hit her. She had a list she had created in her head a long time ago. "I just remembered that I have a small bucket list. One of the items is related to the culinary life that I never got to pursue. After I graduated, as a gift to myself, I had planned on taking a trip to wine country in Napa Valley.

"While in school, I was looking forward to learning how to pair wines with different cuisines. By the time I would have received my degree, I figured I would be educated enough to really enjoy a true wine and culinary experience. But as you know, that never happened."

"Alright, that sounds amazing. What was the second item on your list?"

"Well, I always wanted to go do something adventurous and daring from the sky. But the idea of parachuting was too extreme for me. That's when hang gliding came to mind. I wanted to feel the rush of floating freely in the sky."

I can definitely pull that off. "Okay…one hang gliding encounter coming up. What's next on your list?"

"Um…honestly, the last item is kind of funny really because I could have done it a long time ago. But maybe I was just waiting to share the experience with someone special."

"What is it?"

"Watch the sunrise and sunset on the same day. I know the idea of this is incredibly bland. But when was the last time you watched how the universe begins and ends its day. There is just something poetic about it. Don't you think?"

"I do, and I'm very much thankful that I get to be the special person to do this with you." Her lips began to grow into a smile. "Now, is there anything else on your bucket list?"

"No, that's it."

"Alright then, let me take you home so you can go pack and do whatever else you need to do. After I drop you off, I'll take care of all the arrangements."

"Are you sure you don't want me to help you?"

"Then it wouldn't be a gift, Sophia. Please, I want to do this for you. You just relax and live in the moment. Okay?" She could hear the deep sincerity in his voice. "Alright, Sebastian. You win. Let me just get my things and we can go."

After he dropped her off, he went home and started right away on the preparations. It was kind of fun to do something so endearing for her. It took him the better part of four hours to get it all planned out. When he finished, he texted her what time the trip will begin.

Sebastian: I'm ready to start your adventure. I will pick you up tomorrow early. 7 am. Are you all packed?

She texted him back as soon as she received his message.

Sophia: Yes, I can't believe you planned all of that so quickly.
Sebastian: I was happy to do this for you.
Sophia: So sweet ☺
Sophia: I'm packed and ready for tomorrow. See you then.
Sebastian: Goodnight, Sophia.
Sophia: Goodnight.

That night, he quickly packed his clothes for the trip then went straight to bed. He was going to need his sleep.

The next morning, he woke up jazzed. He arrived at her house at 7:05 am. When she opened the door, she had on a smile as big as the sunshine. "I still can't believe we are doing my bucket list, I'm so excited."

"Good, love. Let's keep it that way." He went over to grab her suitcase and they took off.

"So where are we going?"

"Well, first we are heading to the airport to rent a car for the road. Then we will be traveling south through Tennessee and onto the tip of Georgia. Where you will get to do one of the items on your list…hang gliding.

"However, we won't be able to work all that in today as we will be driving for a good while. But I have us booked to rent a tandem flight tomorrow."

"Tell me that you will be the one gliding us."

"Of course, I used to do it all the time when I was a teenager. It's like riding a bike."

"So how does it all work? Are we gliding off a mountain together?"

"God, no…I'm not that brave." They both laughed. "Actually, what they will do is lift us up using some sort of cord attached to a small plane. Then at some point when they feel we are at a safe level, it will detach itself from our glider."

"It seems much safer than I originally thought."

"Trust me, you'll definitely feel the adventure…but without all the worry of having to run off a cliff."

She nodded her head. "Sounds amazing."

They finally made it to the airport and rented a car. When the guy at the counter asked them if they wanted a convertible Ford Mustang or a Toyota Corolla, they both looked at each other. *No-brainer*, they thought. "Convertible, please."

They were so thrilled to get that option, they couldn't believe their luck. But when they walked up to the car and saw the color of it, they broke out in hysterical laughter. "Guess we are going to stand out a little."

"Yes, it would appear so."

When they got in the car, they rolled down the convertible top and off they went in the most brightest electric blue car you've ever seen. The drive was beautiful this time of year. They talked almost the whole time. "By the way, I wanted to tell you about the update with Margaret. I told her that you were on board. Naturally, she was happy. She said she needed a week to get things together."

"That's great news. What does she need help with first?"

"When we get back from our trip, we are all going to go look for office space together."

"It's kind that she wants our input on the location."

"I thought so too. When you meet her, you'll see that it's in her nature to be that way."

"I'm sure I will."

He picked up her hand and gave it sweet kiss. "Oh look, we are almost here. We are staying in a little town called Chattanooga. I've been here once. It's very quaint. I think you will like it."

They pulled up to a hotel called The Read House. The building architecture on the outside was stunning. When they walked inside, it was just as picturesque as the outside. "Sebastian, it's so…"

"I know…it really is."

After they checked into their room, they decided to take a walk in the city to grab a bite to eat. By the time nightfall hit, they became exhausted from their travels. So they went to sleep early that evening.

The next morning, Sebastian woke up and gave Sophia a light kiss on her forehead. Her eyes began to flutter open. "Good morning. Sorry to wake you up, but I need to order room service soon. I don't want to be late for our adventure today."

"Oh, no worries…do they have eggs benedict on the menu?"

"Yes, I believe they do."

"Okay, I'll take that with some hot tea, please."

He moved over to grab the hotel phone to order the food. When he was done, he laid back down on the bed. "So, Sophia, what should we do to occupy our time until the food arrives?" He gave her a mischievous smile.

That look always made her heart start to pound. "I'm sure we can come up with something interesting."

He had to remind himself that she wanted intimacy in this way. Because he was contemplating on doing something that deeply affected her the last time, he touched her in that way. So he moved forward with caution. He began kissing her lightly as he slowly shifted his body over hers. "Are you okay with this?"

"Yes," she told him.

He put his left arm underneath her shoulder, leaving his other hand free to wander. He started to kiss her shoulder and then her neck. That led to other areas of her body. This went on for a while…until they heard the door knock. They both abruptly stopped and gave each other a smile. "Guess it's time to eat."

They got out of bed and put on their robes. He opened the door for service to come in. The waiter placed their food down and left. "This looks delicious."

"Yes, indeed it does."

After they ate, they got ready and drove off to knock the first item off her bucket list. Once they arrived, Sebastian began to pick up on her vibe. "Don't worry, love, you have nothing to be nervous about. I'll take good care of you." She gave him a smile to reassure him she was okay.

He finished putting her in her harness and then did his own. When he was done, the flight attendant came over to make sure everything was secured. "Okay, you are both cleared to go." With that, he signaled the plane for take-off.

It was remarkable; as soon as they began to fly, all of her emotion drifted away. She felt like a kite being lifted up into the air. It was exhilarating. When the plane finally let go of its hold over the glider they were left to control it themselves. No words could describe the liberation she felt.

They flew up through a small opening within the cloudbank…What they were witnessing was something not many get to encounter in a lifetime. Above them was clear blue sky as far as the eye could see. Below them looked like an ocean of pillowy white clouds that appeared so beautiful it felt as if they were flying on top of heaven itself. She was truly living in the present moment. Taking in all the magnificence of the journey.

The entire experience lasted only a half hour, but it felt like forever. When they started to leave, she looked back one more time at the sky. She noticed the small opening that once existed for them in order to glide above the clouds was no longer there. *Very rare moment indeed*, she thought.

They held hands walking back to the car. "Well, Sophia…I would ask about your flying encounter, but I felt it all as we were up there in the sky. I see it did wonders for your soul. And don't worry I wasn't prying into your life, I promise you. It's just you were so open up there. I didn't need to use any of my gifts."

"I wouldn't care even if you did, Sebastian. That was the most breathtaking experiences of my life. Thank you for giving it to me." He was so elated that she had enjoyed it as much as she did.

They were ready to head to their next destination. So they drove to the Chattanooga Airport, where they parted ways with their electric blue Mustang. Then they boarded a flight to San Francisco.

Upon arrival, they took an Uber to a nearby hotel to stay for the evening. When morning hit, they got up rented another car and drove two hours before finally hitting their destination spot, Napa Valley. Sebastian had them booked at a quaint inn called 1801 First. It was for a three-day, two-night excursion.

While there, they toured many of the countryside's most celebrated wineries like Pine Ridge Vineyards, Stags' Leap, and Domaine Carneros. They dined at places like Harvest Table and The Grove at Copia.

However, even after all of that, her favorite event took place the last night they were there. Sebastian planned a special culinary experience for her. They pulled up to The French Laundry.

"So have you heard of this place?"

She couldn't believe what he was asking. "Yes…of course, everyone has. It's widely known in Napa for its three-Michelin-starred awards. It's one of the most sought after titles you can receive in the industry." She looked at him confused. "Is this where we are dining tonight?"

"As a matter of fact, it is."

"Sebastian, this vacation has already cost you so much money. We can't possibly eat here."

"Sophia, are you telling me that your mental health is not worth the therapy that this experience will give you? This trip is supposed to be about new encounters and liberating the past.

"Besides…as I said, Margaret gave me a sizable contribution to my wallet. The cost of this whole dinner affair means nothing to me, but it will be worth everything to you. It signifies that despite the fact that you quit school, it does not mean all is lost. You can still enjoy your passion without inviting all the pain you inflicted back in."

“Good lord, Sebastian…how do you do it?” She nearly had tears in her eyes. “How do you come up with the most perfect words to say?”

“Because I love you, Sophia. Now…what do you say? Can we go live this one up?”

Her smile widened. “Okay…obviously, you know how much this means to me. Thank you for setting it up.”

He lifted up her hand and gave it a tender kiss. “You’re welcome, my love.”

Then they both got out of the car and walked into one of the most incredible nights of their lives. The chef paired wines from all over Napa Valley with each of their tastings. From savory to sweet, they ate the best you could buy for three full hours.

Afterwards, they found themselves walking around town, just laughing and talking about what the future might hold for them. Sebastian was so thankful he could provide Sophia with this rare venture.

Tomorrow, they were to fly off to Southern California where she would fulfill the last item on her bucket list. “Are you ready to go back? We have an early flight to catch in the morning.”

“Yeah…I’m getting a little tired anyways.”

They made their way back to the inn. “So are you going to tell me where we are flying to?” He just gave her a mischievous look. “I see, so you are not going to tell me.”

“I just want to keep this one a surprise.”

“Yes, I noticed you are full of surprises lately.” She gave him a kiss on the lips. Then whispered in his ear, “Thank you for all your sweet surprises.”

When they got off the plane at LAX, she was so thrilled to see what he had in store for her. He rented a car yet again to take them to their next destination. Thirty minutes into their drive, they arrived. He pulled into the driveway of a gorgeous beach house and told her this was where they were staying for the next couple of days.

Sophia’s eyes grew wider. “You’ve got to be kidding. It’s so huge.”

His lips grew into a grin. “I’m glad you approve.” He got out of the car and grabbed the luggage from the trunk. Hauling it up to the porch, he pulled out a piece of paper from his pocket. It was the code to unlock the door. “Okay, let’s see what it looks like on the inside.”

She followed him into the house and started to explore. After a few minutes, she shouted for him to come upstairs. He found her standing outside in a privately spaced patio overlooking the ocean front. It was exactly what the renter had said it would be like.

Coming up behind her, he wrapped his arms around her waist. “Looks like you approve of the setting as well?”

“That’s putting it mildly, Sebastian. I mean, it feels like we are living in a dream right now.” They stood there for a while taking in the ocean breeze.

“So tomorrow, the sun will rise at approximately 5:39 am in the morning. Then towards the later part of the afternoon, it will set at around 7:48 pm.

“I have everything planned out including today. There is a restaurant I want to take you to called the Paradise Cove Beach Café in Malibu. It looks like a fun environment, nothing too fancy. But for dinner, that’s different. There might be some fanciness involved in that.”

“Of course there would be with you.” She smiled. “Just give me a minute to freshen up.”

“Take your time, there’s no rush.”

They took off a half hour later. It was a gorgeous day outside, they enjoyed eating lunch outside on the terrace. Following that, they spent their day walking down the Santa Monica Pier. Then later, they dined at a restaurant called 71 Above. They are known for their cuisine, but also for their 360-degree views.

That night, they didn’t get back to the house until sometime after 11 pm. Needless to say they were exhausted. “If it’s okay with you, I’ll wake us up around 4:45 am tomorrow.”

“Yeah, sounds good.” Shortly after, when they hit their pillows they fell sound asleep.

The next morning, Sebastian woke her up and drove to a nearby coffee shop. “Hopefully, this will give us a jolt.” They sat down and she took a sip.

“Good lord, Sebastian, this is really good.”

“I know…it’s as if they put MSG in it.” She laughed.

By the time they arrived back at the house, it was close to sunrise. He gently grabbed her hand. “Come on, Sophia. It’s almost time.”

They stood together in their private balcony watching as the sun began to rise. He wanted to remember the moment. She was wearing a white sun dress with a blue shawl hanging over one of her shoulders. She looked breathtaking. He put his arm around her back as they both took in the view.

When the moment was over, she turned to look at him. "Life won't get any better than this exact moment here with you." He responded back to her with a kiss. Shortly after, he picked her up and laid her down on the outdoor bed lounger.

"What do you want Sophia? Do you want me to go further then we already have?" She nodded her head in agreeance. He softly touched her cheek. "Then let's move forward with your journey to live freely again."

It was in that decision, he was able to give her back what she'd been longing for ever since that one dark night. He made things feel normal again as he made passionate love to her all morning long. It was what she needed to come full circle with her past. This just made her love him all that much more.

They spent the rest of the day staying intimate with each other. As it was getting closer to sunset, they decided to take a walk along the beach. After a while, they stopped and held each other letting the waves splash against their feet.

He whispered in her ear, "*Le coucher de soleil est presque sur nous…* Look, Sophia." He pointed his hand up to the sky. She turned around and laid her back against his chest. Then wrapped his arms around her waist.

"The end of my bucket list is about to happen."

They stayed quiet for a while as the sun began to set. When it was over, Sebastian turned Sophia around and put one of his hands around the back of her neck, embracing her lips with a kiss.

When they finally stopped, he looked into her eyes. At first, all he could feel was the love he had for her. But then, suddenly another emotion crept in …FEAR! Fear like he had never experienced before. Ever since he had that meeting with the angels, he worried about what Sophia and him were going to have to face in the future. Yet, up until this point, he was able to keep that anxiety in check. Hidden away in his brain somewhere with a do not disturb sign on it. However, for whatever reason, that fear could not be shut away any longer.

"Sophia, I can't imagine my life without you." He brought his head down so he could connect with her eyes. "Promise me something."

"Yes, of course, Sebastian…whatever you want."

"Promise me you will never leave me." She found that to be such a strange request given all that they have gone through together. But maybe he felt she needed to say it out loud to him.

"Sebastian…I promise that I will never leave you. I'm yours forever." She had no idea how much he needed to hear those words.

He let out a deep breath. "Thank you, Sophia. Now let's go back and live out the rest of our night." As tomorrow marked the beginning of their new journey with Margaret and her future plans for them.

Chapter 12
Contribution

Sebastian had just finished brewing coffee when he got a text.

Margaret: Good morning! Looking forward to our first listing. It will be at 6158 Dickerson Road. See you guys in an hour.

Sebastian: Yes, we are too! See you then!

He put his phone down and walked into his bedroom to tell Sophia it was time to get up. "Oh, you're already awake?"

"Yeah, I was just about to climb out of bed to see if you got the text yet."

"I did actually. She just sent it to me. So, if you want, we can get something to eat on the way?"

"Sounds good, let me just get ready real quick."

"We have an hour before we meet so no rush, there's plenty of time."

"Okay, thanks."

But it didn't take her long to get ready at all. They were on the road within ten minutes and got breakfast at a local bakery. "Let's go see what Ms. Margaret has lined up for us."

"Yes, I'm very excited."

She turned her head towards the window. Last week's memories were still rolling through her head. Now they were off doing this new venture together. She couldn't have been happier.

"What are you thinking about, love?"

"Oh, you know…casual stuff like how my boyfriend lifted me off my feet last week."

He gently lifted her hand up to his lips. "I'm glad I could do that for you, Sophia. You mean everything to me, you know that, right?"

She smiled at his loving words. "Yes, I do."

Looking back towards the window, she noticed they were going through a residential part of town. *Huh.* "Where is our first location?"

"Actually, it's right here." He started to slow down. Then turned left into a driveway.

"It's a home?"

"Yeah, I didn't expect that either, let's see what she has cooking."

The house itself was gorgeous. It was an old Victorian home, colored white, and had four beautiful pillars around the front of the porch. There were flowers landscaped throughout the entire front yard. And a majestic green steel fence with the symbol of an angel on the top center of the opening. Perfect for the kind of visitors they were expecting.

"Hello, Sebastian."

He turned around. "Margaret…so good to see you." They gave each other a hug. "I'm happy to finally be able to introduce my girlfriend to you. This is Sophia Freemont."

Forget the typical friendly handshake you do when you meet somebody for the first time. Oh no…Margaret went in for the hug. Sophia couldn't help but giggle inside…*very welcoming*, she thought.

"It's good to meet you too." She pointed her hands out to all the flowers. "I have to say, Margaret, the outside of this house is appealing. I wonder if the inside matches its beauty?"

"Well, let's go take a peek." They followed her up the stairs and waited as she looked for the key. "Oh, here it is."

When they stepped inside, the first thing they noticed was its fairly sizable entryway. It had a uniquely shaped crystal chandelier that hung high from the ceiling. There were rooms connected to both the right and left side of the foyer. So they decided to hang a left. It led them to a small den that opens to a formal dining room. It came fully embellished with floral printed wallpaper, dado railing and another small but stunning chandelier.

On the opposite side of the wall, it had double doors that gave way to the kitchen. Continuing to circle around they found a quaint little bathroom, and generous size closet. And to the right of the hallway was a large bedroom. It was centered directly in the middle of the house. *Interesting layout*, Sebastian thought.

The last area they viewed on the first floor was the living room. It was hard not to take your eyes off the silvery marbled fireplace and decorative mahogany wooden mantelpiece just above it.

"Oh look, Margaret, the same classic Victorian features seem to play out throughout the entire floor with all this wooden paneling and crown molding. It just takes your breath away how much detail was put into this house."

"I agree, Sophia. I mean, the cabinetry alone in the kitchen looks completely restored from its original state."

Making their way up to the second floor, they found that it too carried the same characteristics as the first. Right away, they took noticed to a small but charming loft along the rail of the stairs. Eventually, they made their way through three additional bedrooms and two baths.

"So what do you guys think?"

Sophia and Sebastian looked at each other. "Um, Margaret, this place is impressive, to say the very least. But how much are they asking for rent?"

"Oh, yes, about that. The rent is $1,500/month."

"$1,500…that's it? How is that possible?"

"Well, I think we got fortunate really. You see, yesterday I met with Paul…you know, my lawyer friend I told you about. Anyway, we ate dinner at Cunningham's. The place was jam packed with people so we landed up just eating around the bar.

"I was catching him up to speed with the new venture we are all doing. But when I got to the point of telling him that we were looking for office space, the man next to me grabbed my attention.

"He said he didn't mean to be rude but he had overheard a part of our conversation. I was shocked by his casual tone because I had just finished explaining to Paul some of the things you could do. You know…things like being able to speak to the dead and angels. Most people would have thought our exchange was on the slightly nutty side; however, he reacted on the contrary.

"Then he proceeded to tell me that he was a property owner and landlord. He said he had one particular location that would be perfect for us." Her face swayed around the room as her arms lifted in the air. "This is it, guys.

"And I have to admit, when he told me the price, originally, I figured it would be much…much smaller and definitely not in this kind of mint condition."

"I see…" He was about to say something else, but she continued to talk.

"Course, now that I have seen the place, I'm curious myself as to why the rent is so low."

She looked at her phone for the time. "Perfect, he'll be here shortly so we can ask him our pending question in person." Just then, there was a knock at the door. "Ah…speak of the devil, I'll go let him in." She went down the hallway towards the front entrance.

"Mr. Church, good to see you again."

"Yes, you too, Margaret."

"Come with me, the others want to meet you."

"Sure, I'll just follow you."

She wasted no time in introducing everybody. "Christopher, this is Sebastian Sinclair and Sophia Freemont."

"Well, hello there, it's a pleasure meeting the both of you." *Huh…*Sebastian was taken aback. For the life of him, he could not read his energy!

"So what do you think of the space, Sebastian?"

"Honestly, I have to say, your home is exquisite. We were just wondering about the price of rent."

"What, you think the price is too high?"

Sebastian and Sophia looked at each other. "No…actually, we thought it was little too low."

Christopher started to laugh excessively. "Well, that's a new one. I've never had anyone complain that the price was too low before."

His banter caught him off guard. He was about to explain himself except, Christopher continued to carry on with the conversation. "Okay…okay, in all seriousness, I did give a bit of a discount in the cost of doing business with you guys. But only because I really want you as tenants. You see, I'm a fan of your industry."

"What do you mean, our industry?"

"Let me explain. You see, by day I am a hard-working landlord and property owner. But by night, I practice a different trade…ghost hunting. I'm fascinated with the paranormal. One might even suggest I'm obsessed with it.

And from what I overheard from Margaret, your supernatural abilities are like no one's ever seen. And believe me…I've seen a lot."

He was about to go on, but this time Sebastian reigned him in with another question. "Um…sorry…forgive me for asking but…why can't I read you?"

"What do you mean?"

"I mean, I can usually feel people's energy. Yet, for whatever reason, I can't feel yours."

"That's strange, has that ever happened to you before?"

"Yes, it has actually. It occurs when I am around other people who share my gift. They usually know how to turn it on and off."

"Sebastian, I can assure you that if I did have your kind of gifts, I certainly would not be trying to conceal them. I would give anything to experience just an ounce of what you partake in. To be able to read people the way you can. Well, you're very…lucky."

Margaret looked at Sebastian to see if he was finished with his probe. He gave her a quick nod of assurance that he was done.

"Mr. Church, could you give us a couple of moments alone?"

"Of course, take your time."

As soon as he left, Margaret spoke up. "Listen, I have seven other showings lined up for us today. I say we go check them out and see which one fits us best. If this is the right option for us, then I can always call him back and get the lease agreement." They both agreed that was the best way to go.

So they took off and spent the day viewing all the different locations she arranged. There were a couple that came really close to what they were looking for, but they had some cons as well. The first office was designed with an open space concept. They would definitely have to make changes to the room in order to make it work. Still, it was something to consider because they really felt a good vibe going on there.

The other location they liked was also inviting. However, it would be a pretty tight space to handle all their needs if they grew.

On their last showing, they gathered around outside to make a final decision. Margaret looked toward Sophia. "What are your thoughts?"

"Well, although I loved the one where we felt it had such an uplifting vibe, I think Mr. Church's house would still be the better choice."

"Sebastian…?"

"I gotta say I definitely feel better now that we've seen all our options. I think Sophia is right, though. His house will work best for us and it will also give us space to grow as we need."

Margaret's face began to light up. "Great, then we are all in agreeance. We will go with Christopher's location. I feel like we need to celebrate!"

However, noticing the dark shadows underneath Sebastian's eyes, she changed her tune. "Perhaps another time though. It's been a long day. Why don't you guys go home? I need time to finalize the lease terms anyway. Let's wait till everything is signed and then we'll celebrate. I'll contact you guys soon with the updates."

"Alright…thank you for understanding." He gave her a hug and Sophia followed suit. "Goodbye, for now then. We'll be looking forward to hearing back from you soon." They turned and walked away.

As they both got closer to his car, she gently stopped him and took a moment to observe his face. "Sebastian, you really do need some rest. Let me drive us home, okay?"

"I guess you're right. I don't want to get us into an accident."

The ride home was quiet, both in their own thoughts. When they reached his apartment, they quickly got changed and went to bed. Sebastian put his arm around her waist and softly kissed her shoulder. "I love you, Sophia."

"I love you too." He gave her another tender kiss and then laid his head back down on his pillow.

Although he would have rather stayed up and celebrated with her in his own way, he knew he needed sleep. His eyes grew heavier by the second. "Goodnight, my love."

"Goodnight…" Soon enough, they both feel asleep.

At some point in the middle of the night, a dream started to form in his head. At first, he saw just a vision of Sophia standing by herself. But not long after…the dream manifested. He began to visualize her in a store. She was talking to a guy. Eventually, Sebastian showed up and became part of the dream as well. He was so close to them he could actually hear their conversation. However, they didn't notice him listening in on their chat.

"Sophia?" The guy was surprised but happy to have run into her. Damn, she looks hotter than ever.

"My goodness, Jacob? It's been years since I have seen you." A smile formed on her face.

"I know! How the heck have you been?"

"I've been good, actually... You?"

"Yeah, things are going great right now." His eyes moved ever so slightly down to see if she had a ring on her finger.

"I would love to sit down and catch up with you sometime."

"Oh, actually, yeah I..." Suddenly Sebastian became enraged with the scene that was unfolding in front of him. He couldn't even wait for her to finish her sentence. He pushed his body inward and positioned himself between the two of them. Now they took notice of him.

"What the hell is going on here?"

"Sebastian, what are you doing? I thought you were supposed to be over at Clarissa's?"

"Don't change the subject, Sophia! This man obviously wants you!"

He turned around to look at the guy. "She's taken, GET IT!" He wanted to slam him to the ground so badly, but he held himself back. "Leave us...NOW!"

The guy took off as he turned around to face Sophia again. "Who do you think YOU ARE!" Then...out of nowhere, an entity with no face comes up from behind and grabs Sebastian's arm to pull him away from her.

After that, he abruptly woke up from the dream. Immediately he turned his body around to look for Sophia. She was right next to him, of course. *What was that all about?* He tried to calm himself down by reminding himself that it was just a dream. Still…it had felt so real.

He looked at his clock next to the bed. It read 5:38 am. Laying his head back down on the pillow he realized how tired he still was. Fifteen minutes later, he thankfully fell back into a deep sleep.

When he finally woke up, the sun was brightly shining through the window curtains. Memories of what he dreamt last night popped back into his head. *Just a dream, Sebastian. Just a dream.* A second later, Sophia walked into the room.

"Oh good, you're up. I was getting worried about you." Thank God, his thoughts got interrupted by her.

"What time is it?"

"Around 4 pm."

"Really? I haven't slept in that long since I was in college."

"Well, your body must have needed it. I'm glad you got in all that sleep. You look refreshed and ready to start your day. And for once, I have plans for us." That made him smile.

"Do you now?"

"Yes, so why don't you go take a shower and I'll finish preparing for the evening." He did as she asked and then came out to see what she was up to. He saw her sitting in the kitchen reading something from her phone when he spotted a picnic basket and blanket on the table.

"Looks like you have been busy."

"Yes, well, I hope you don't mind. I used your car to go home so I could grab my basket. Then I went to the grocery store so I could create a fabulous picnic for you."

"For me?"

"Yeah, after everything you've done for me. I wanted to do something nice for you. I know it pales in comparison to the great food extravaganza vacation you took me on. But because of that, I was able to pick up on a lot of your likes and dislikes. I'm going to really enjoy feeding you tonight." She looked at him with a playful smile.

Good God, he thought. She was so flirtatious with him. "Keep acting like that and we may never leave for this picnic you have planned."

She let out a small chuckle. "Okay then, let's go. I have the perfect place in mind."

She took off driving the car. "I'm taking you to a hidden gem that not many people know about. It's right up the street from here." When they arrived, he grabbed the picnic basket and she picked up the blanket. Then they took off walking.

Initially, all he could see was a mass amount of trees in front of him. But as they got closer, he began to witness what she had been boasting about. It was a picturesque portrait of nature working at its finest. There was a running stream. Some part of it was low enough that you could walk through it by foot. Other parts had water cascading down a series of mini waterfalls.

"Sebastian, come over here." She lifted up the blanket and spread it out on the ground. "Let's put our feet in the water. I swear it's the most calming feeling you'll ever experience." He did as she asked and took a moment to take in all the nature. *She's right, this really is soothing.* After a couple of minutes went by, he slipped his hand under hers and slowly lay his back down on the blanket. She followed his lead.

The energy surrounding him was so very light, it was almost as if the dark did not exist. Though last night, he had gotten a pretty good dose of it in his dream. But that was not what he wanted to be thinking about right now. He quickly shook off the unwanted thoughts.

"Sophia, this place is awesome; thank you for sharing it with me."

"I thought you would like it here." They stayed there for hours just talking and eating from the basket. She had made him Vietnamese spring rolls, curry beef skewers, and goat cheese beet salad with pistachio nuts. For dessert, chocolate beignets. It was a smorgasbord of food.

"I noticed you like to eat more international foods. I guess that comes from all your travels?"

"That's funny, I never looked at my eating habits in that way. But that seems to be the case, doesn't it." He looked at her lovingly. "It's thoughtful that you put so much effort into this basket."

"I wanted to…it made me happy to do this for you."

She looked at her watch. "It's getting late, are you ready to go back?"

"Actually, I'm having the time of my life out here with you. I really don't want the day to end."

"Okay, what do you want to do?"

"Well, it looks like there is a trail over there." He pointed his finger to the right. "You want to go walk off some of that delicious food we just ate?"

"Sounds like a plan."

When they finished walking the trail, they finally went home. "Thank you for a lovely evening."

"You're welcome, Sebastian." When the night ended, he felt a little apprehensive about going back to sleep.

"Sophia, I have a weird question."

"What?"

"Do I ever talk in my sleep?"

"No, not that I've heard. Course, I'm usually asleep whenever you are, so I guess there is a chance." Her mind lingered over that question for a moment…*that really was kind of a weird inquiry.* "Where did that come from, Sebastian?"

"I don't know…just wondering, that's all."

As they made their way to bed, Sebastian leaned over to hold Sophia. "Today was fun, love."

"Yeah, it really was." She was so tired after all the cooking and walking, she easily started dozing off. Her eyes were halfway closed when she said, "Until tomorrow then…my…" He got a quick chuckle on how she ended the night. Eventually, his eyes began to feel heavy as well. Not long after, he was asleep.

The next morning, he woke up, covered in sweat. *What the hell is going on here?* He just experienced the exact same dream as the night before. Taking a long deep breath, he got out of bed and went to the bathroom. He splashed cold water on his face hoping the images would go away. But it did zero to calm his nerves.

The next day was the same thing…and the next and the next. Four days had gone by and still the horrible nightmares would not stop. Why? The only thing different that transpired was when the dreams occurred. Some materialized in the middle of the night. While others took place in the morning.

He looked at this clock. It read 9:00 am. He got out of bed and went into the living room. He started pacing the floor to think it through when Thomas came to mind. *How in the world am I supposed to reach him?* Just then, his phone began to buzz with a text.

Margaret: My lawyer looked over the lease agreement and made a few changes. Mr. Church approved the minor alterations we asked for. So I signed the agreement today and faxed it in. We are now official tenants of 6158 Dickerson Road. Congratulations, my friends! Would you guys like to meet me for a drink later on this evening to celebrate?

That news finally changed his mood. He went over to see if Sophia was up yet. He came in the bedroom and saw her yawning. "Good morning."

She looked up at him. "Hey…"

"So I just got a message from Margaret. The lease agreement has been signed and she wants to go out and celebrate with us tonight. What do you think?"

"Yes, of course, I do. That's so awesome!"

"I know…this is the start of everything for us. Let me text her back real quick."

Sebastian: Yes, that sounds great! Where and what time do you want to meet?

Not long after she messaged him back.

Margaret: How about Brix…6 pm. Will that work for you?
Sebastian: Perfect, see you then.
Margaret: K.

After he finished texting her back, he looked up at Sophia. He could tell something was stirring around in her head. "Care to share your thoughts?"

"Oh, it's just that I haven't been home since our vacation, I need to take care of a few things." He came over and sat down on the bed next to her. "I'm glad we had a chance to spend so much time together. But to be honest, I have a few things to attend to here as well. So if it's alright with you, let's just get dressed and I'll take you home."

"Okay, sounds good."

Soon after they got ready, he drove her home. When he got back, he tackled the laundry first. It hadn't been handled since before the trip. So you can imagine that scene. And then there was the matter of the apartment. Plain and simply put, it was a mess. He swept the kitchen floor, vacuumed the carpet, washed the dishes, emptied the trash, made the bed and so on. That kept him busy throughout the rest of the day. Next thing he knew, it was almost time to pick her up again.

He took a shower and finished getting ready. Before long, he was on his way to her house. He arrived right at 5:30 pm.

"Hey there, beautiful."

"Hello."

"Did you get everything done that you wanted?"

"Yes, I did actually. How about you?"

"Yeah, I did." He came in a little closer and put his hand around her waist. "I missed you, though." Embracing the back of her neckline, he went in to kiss her lips. "I definitely missed these lips."

Moments later… "We are going to be late if we keep this up."

He let go of his hold on her. Both of them still breathing heavily. "Sorry, I got a little carried away there."

"So did I, don't feel bad." They both gave each other a grin.

"Come on, let's go celebrate." He gently grabbed her hand and they took off.

When they arrived at Brix, they found Margaret inside almost immediately. However, they were surprised to see her sitting with company. "Hello Margaret…"

She looked up at them with a huge smile on her face. "Hello guys. Christopher wanted to come down personally and hand us the keys himself."

"Oh, that was kind of you."

"It's my pleasure, Sophia." He reached into his coat pocket and took out three polished brass keys. Sebastian picked one up, examining its unique shape. "By luck, I found the original key that was made for the house over 100 years ago. I was able to replicate the top part of the key."

"That's a pretty cool looking design."

"I thought so too, Sebastian."

"Well, I'm afraid I have to go now." He looked at Margaret. "Thanks for the drink. It sounds like your business will be very successful."

"Thank you, Mr. Church."

He gazed over all three of them. "Now listen, call me if you need anything to be fixed. Per our agreement in the contract, I'm responsible for most of the repairs in the house minus certain things that I'm sure Margaret can fill you in on. Other than that, rent is due on the 1st of every month. I hope you will enjoy many happy years at this residence." Then he gave everyone a warm handshake and took off.

Sophia picked up her key. Then Margaret grabbed the last one and put it in her purse. "By the way, guys, I have a table reserved for us." She started to get up. "Let me just go find the waiter."

She came back a minute later and picked up her drink. "Come with me, guys." They followed her lead and sat down at a table located in the back of the restaurant.

"Thanks for reserving a table for us Margaret."

"It's no worries at all."

Seconds later, the waiter came by to take their orders and then left. “So, Margaret…how does it feel to follow your dreams?”

Her eyes got a little watery. “It feels like I’m walking on cloud nine. I’ve never felt so blessed and happy to be able to help people on this level.”

Sophia chimed in, “I know what she means. The way you have already helped us so much I can’t image what you can do for others. You really are amazing, Sebastian.” Just then the waiter came back with their drinks.

Margaret pulled her glass up to make a toast and they followed suit. “I never thought I would be at this place in my life, but I got to say…it feels damn good. My wish is for all of us to enjoy this journey together as we help heal the wounds of this earth one soul at a time.”

They all smiled and clanked there drinks together in unison. “That was the perfect toast.”

“Thank you, Sebastian.”

They spent the rest of their night laughing and talking. Henry’s name came up quite a bit actually. They were filling Sophia in with stories she hadn’t heard before. However, this time…they were able to laugh at his irrational behavior. Margaret also mentioned the idea of building the spiritual center again, but not much more detail formed as to what it will actual do for mankind. “I’m still waiting for more to come on that project.” Sophia commented further, “Still, if it is even an ounce of what you’re initially describing it to be, it sounds pretty amazing.” Sebastian nodded his head in agreeance. “It really does, Margaret.”

That night was a bonding moment for their relationship. A silent creed was being made to change the world in their own way. It felt good. But most of all…it felt so damn right.

Sebastian watched Sophia take her last sip of wine. “Love, I’m sorry…but I’m feeling tired. I think all the excitement of tonight has caught up with me.”

He glanced over at Margaret next and gave her an apologetic look.

“No worries at all…you guys should go. I’m going to get started on things tomorrow. I won’t need you to come in until all the furniture arrives. I’ll text you when that happens.”

“Okay, sounds great, we’ll be looking forward to your text.”

They said their goodbyes and left. By the time they got home, Sebastian was done. He went straight to bed. It took Sophia a little while longer to slow her mind down and fall asleep. But eventually, it happened.

It was quiet as could be in their bedroom. Both dreaming away the night.

He heard the doorbell ring. "Come in, love!"

She walked in, looking beautiful as ever. "What do you want to do today?"

He looked puzzled. "I thought we already discussed it in our text?" Out of nowhere, irritation started to rise over him. "You don't remember our chat?"

"What chat?"

"How many other guys do you chat with, Sophia, that you can't remember mine?"

Confusion aired through her face. "Sebastian, are you alright? You're not making any sense."

"So now I'm stupid?"

"No, that's not what I'm saying."

The rage he felt towards her just spurred him on further. "Don't belittle me, Sophia. I'm on to you. NOW...tell...me...your...wrong!"

She was so distraught with the turn of event that she didn't know what to do. She just started to cry.

"Please Sebastian, whatever I did to make you this upset at me, I'm sorry. Please don't be angry at me. PLEASE!" She was standing there, waiting for him to come to her. But he never did.

"I need time to get over what you did to me. I've never been with anyone like you who makes me so incensed. Why do you think that is, Sophia? Why do..."

But just then, he couldn't finish his rant as the faceless entity came and took him away from her ...yet again.

He woke up from the dream seconds later. Feeling more uneasy than ever. Not only was this dream different; but he also noticed there was someone else, lurking around in the background of all the chaos. That someone else was another version of him. He was simply standing on the side of the dream watching the scene unfold as an observer. Worst of all, he seemed to be thrilled with what he was viewing. The smug look on his face showed every indication of that.

His thoughts then shifted to the words he had shouted at her. The feeling of being ashamed of how he had treated her came crashing through him. He looked over to see his sweet Sophia lying peacefully asleep. He bent down and gave her a kiss on her forehead. *I love you, Sophia.*

He put his head back on the pillow and moved his arms around her body. That calmed him enough to fall back to sleep.

Chapter 13
Fork in the Road

Two weeks had gone by and Sebastian was beside himself on what to do about his nightmares. He tried every day to find a new method to reach Thomas, yet nothing panned out. He was however able to summon his other angels, only they did not have the same kind of wisdom that Thomas seemed to possess.

He was finding that he needed more and more distractions from his daily thoughts. The guilt of what he was doing to Sophia by night was starting to eat at him as well. He found that he was always trying to weigh out the bad from the good during the day with her. Today was no exception…he was taking her to a place he knew she would absolutely love.

He had just finished putting the dishes away when he realized the time. *Shoot, I'd better go get ready myself.* He walked into the room and saw her looking at herself in the mirror. She gazed back at him, "Is this outfit okay for where we are going? Since you won't tell me what you have planned, I'm not sure what to wear."

He examined her shoes. "Everything is great except the sandals. Do you have a pair of tennis shoes?"

"Yeah, I think I do, let me go check."

He went to go brush his teeth and change his clothes while she checked her bags. When he came back out of the bathroom, she was sitting on the edge of the bed with her legs crossed. On her feet were a pair of blue tennies with orange stripes along the rims.

"Those are perfect. Looks like you're ready."

She got up, excited. "Okay, let's go then." They made their way to the car and took off. The drive to their destination spot was a little over two hours.

When they finally arrived, she saw a sign that said, Earthjoy Treehouse Adventures. She gazed at him in wonderment. "I don't know about you,

Sophia, but when I was a little kid, I would have given anything to have been able to climb trees. This place makes it possible for adults to join in the fun as well." She got out of the car and viewed all the beautiful trees and nature around her.

"I tried to book us a treehouse for the night; however, they said they were booked solid for this evening. Even so, I think we will still have a blast." They went up to the main entrance to sign in and pay for the experience.

"Hello, my name is Sebastian Sinclair, I made a reservation for today."

The owner glanced up at him. "Oh, yes, I remember taking your call. I was just about to contact you actually. I had a last-minute cancellation. Are you still interested in staying the night?"

Sebastian was overjoyed with the news. He looked at Sophia. "I know we don't have anything packed, but who cares. It's just one night. We'll be home tomorrow within a couple of hours. What do you think?"

"Sounds amazing."

His grin turned wider. "Okay then…we will take it!"

"Great, you won't regret it. Janice will be your assistant today with the tree climbing experience. Enjoy, my friends!"

She put them into their harnesses and checked to make sure they were secure. "Okay, you guys are clear to let loose." They both headed up the tree at the same time. After about twenty-five minutes of climbing, they stopped for a breather.

Being so high up in the trees, they could see the creeks flow through the meadows. "Isn't that a view?"

"It certainly is, love." A couple of minutes later, he saw a unique opportunity come his way. "Sophia, look at what they put up here." She turned to see what he was talking about.

"It's a hammock?"

"Yeah, let's go hang out in it." They made their way over and Sebastian moved around to help her get on top. Eventually, he climbed his way into it as well.

"I really do feel like a little kid again."

This made him happy. "I figured you would like it here."

They lay in the hammock for a while just listening to their surroundings. "It's pretty cool that we get to sleep in a treehouse tonight."

"I know…I'm looking forward to it too." She gazed further up the tree. "You want to keep going?"

"Yeah, let's see what it feels like to be on top."

When they finally got as far as they could go, they found a branch to sit on. And they watched as a scene unfolded in front of them. People of all ages were in sync with one another and nature. Climbing trees with ropes…walking their way from branch to branch. Such a simple concept, taken to its highest level of perfection, he thought.

When it was finally time to go back, Janice told them how to descend their ropes while hanging upside down. "Oh my gosh, Sebastian…this is such a rush, you got to try it!"

"I'm very glad that you are enjoying your last encounter with the trees, love, however, I think I'll stick to doing it the old-fashioned way." He was happy to see her embrace the moment her own way.

When they got down, Janice helped them take off all the gear and equipment. "Okay guys, you are all taken care of, have a great rest of your day."

"We will; thank you."

They decided to go grab some groceries and campfire supplies at the local store in town. By the time they got back, they were fully ready to have the complete camping experience.

Before they knew it, they were making themselves at home in their cozy treehouse. They made a quick pasta dish and ate it outside on a little patio facing the woods. They could see a small campfire area set up just below their house. Sophia suggested they go do the campfire thing next.

"Sounds like a plan."

Moments later, a small grin began to form on his face as he took notice to the color of the furniture. "Sophia, does this furniture jog your memory of anything?"

She skimmed her eyes around. Suddenly…they both started rolling with laughter. The color of the furniture reminded them of the electric blue mustang they had rented on their drive to Chattanooga, Tennessee. It made her reflect back on all the memories he had given her from the trip.

At some point they made their way down to the campfire. Where they toasted marshmallows, talked, and laughed the rest of their day away. Though…as the moonlight lit up the sky, Sebastian's mood began to shift a little inside. These days, he was becoming more and more apprehensive of falling asleep.

An hour later, Sophia began to observe the dark lines forming underneath his eyes. "Sebastian, you look tired, let's start to head upstairs."

He knew darn well his body was ready for sleep. Yet, he still resisted.

"Um…if you don't mind, I'd rather stay out here with you."

She checked out his eyes again, and thought…*how could he not comprehend how tired he is?* She tried to reason with him again. "Listen, not to sound like a broken record, but your eyes are painting a very clear picture to me. You really do appear exhausted. And understandably…you drove over two hours just to get here. Then, afterwards we climbed trees for an hour and a half. Truth be told, I'm a little beat myself."

He let out a deep breath and put his head down in defeat. "Okay…you're right. Though it would be great if we could have just another five minutes more out here together? Then we can go back, I promise."

She nodded her head and put her back against his chest as he held his arms around her waist. They gazed their heads up to the sky and watched as the stars did their magic at night. When it was time to go in, Sebastian surrendered himself to what may come in his sleep.

That night he slept…and slept…and slept. For once…the nightmares ceased to exist. The next morning, he woke up to hummingbirds chiming away in the near distant trees. *Thank God!* he shouted in his head. *Finally, a break from the damn dreams!*

He peeked his head over to Sophia who was still sleeping. He didn't want to wake her up so he got out of bed and decided to make them something to eat. By the time he finished, she was awake. "I made us breakfast…eggs, bacon, and toast."

"I know…I could smell bacon from the room. It looks delish."

"Shall we take it outside?"

"We shall."

They both ate their meal in bliss. Sophia was having the time of her life with him. And Sebastian, was ecstatic that the dreams went away. At least…it did last night. He didn't want to think about tonight's possibility. He decided he was going to just live in the moment.

By the time they got home, it was already noon. They spent the rest of their day hanging out, relaxing in his apartment. That night, his sleep was the same as before. No nightmares came back to haunt him. He woke up relieved it had not been just a one-time occurrence.

Days and days went by and still nothing returned. He didn't want to think about why he had received them in the first place. He was just glad they were gone.

Today, Margaret asked them to swing by and check out what she had done with the office space. So after they were done eating, they got ready and drove right over.

When they got there, the first thing they observed was all the furniture she bought. "Wow, impressive, Margaret!"

"Thank you, Sophia."

It looked very professional, yet still keeping with the tone of the Victorian appeal. "Yes, what you have done with this place is amazing. I would love to see which room you are going to place me in."

"Oh, of course, Sebastian. I have you set up in the large bedroom on the first floor. Follow me." When Sebastian walked into the room, he was once again stunned at all the hard work she had put into it.

There were two matching chairs sitting across from each other in the center of the room. Then she had placed vintage couches against the walls directly behind the chairs. She had decorated them with beautiful pillows and throws. And above one of the couches was a rendition of the famous Van Gogh *Almond Blossom* painting. She had also brought in an electrician to put up a new candlelight-style empire chandelier. It was exquisite. The perfect setting, he felt.

She gave them a tour of the rest of the rooms. "As you can see, the first floor is completely furnished. However, there is nothing done on the second. Those will eventually become our offices."

"I can see how much effort you put into all of this, thank you, Margaret."

"Oh, I loved every minute of decorating this place. Now I believe we are ready for business. Which is good, because I have some news to tell you."

"What is it?"

"I have six clients lined up for you tomorrow."

"For Christ's sake, Margaret, how in the world did you pull that off?"

"Oh, it was easy, actually. I found them in holy places. You know churches, synagogues, Buddhist temples… It came to me that people who are dealing with this kind of hardship go to the places they feel most comforted. I didn't even need to speak to anyone at first. I just went and left my sign in an inconspicuous spot."

"Really? What message did you put in the sign?"

"It says…call me if you are looking for peace of mind from another outlet."

They gave out a little chuckle. "Well, Margaret…it's cryptic, but clever at the same time."

"Thanks, I thought so too. So, we shall open our doors for business tomorrow at 9 am."

"Okay, we will be here." They both got up to take another look around.

"Oh…before I forget, let me show you what Mr. Church gave us the other day. He said it was a gift for our grand opening." She opened up the box for them to see. It was a small elegantly designed jeweled elephant. "Apparently, it's supposed to bring good luck to our business."

Sebastian picked it up. "He told me to ask you specifically, Sebastian, to put your energy into it. The lights on the crystals are supposed to reflect your energy off to everyone else. Do you want to give it a try?"

"Sure."

Sophia glanced at Margaret. "I must say…this was a pretty thoughtful gift to give us."

"Yeah, it was." Sebastian closed his eyes and did his thing. A couple of minutes later, he reopened his eyes. "That should do it."

"Okay, great, I was thinking we could just put it over here on the living room mantel."

"You're the queen of decorating, Margaret. It should go wherever you think is best."

"Alright, then that's where I'll place it." She turned and walked towards the mantel. "Now you guys should go and enjoy the rest of your day. I'll see you first thing tomorrow."

"Okay." Sebastian held onto Sophia's hand. "Until then, Margaret, goodbye." They both left excited about Friday.

When they got home, he poured her a glass of wine and himself a bourbon. "Here's to new beginnings, Sophia."

"Yes, cheers…for what tomorrow will bring." They clanked their glasses together and took a drink.

"So, what should we do now?"

Turning her head, she gave him a mischievous grin. "I don't know Sebastian, do you have something in mind?"

He came over to her. "Yes, I actually do have something in mind." Putting his hand around the back of her neck, he began kissing her lips. His other hand made its way down the waistline of her pants, just below her belly button. He gently walked her back against the wall. Then he stopped and spread his arms around each side of her head.

He came in very close to her, yet purposely did not touch her. She was beside herself on how much she wanted him. Then, he slowly kissed her on the cheek…her ear…her neck. He began to work his way down to her shoulder.

She embraced him back by unbuttoning his shirt. By the time she got to the third button, Sebastian seized her hands…and softly kissed them.

"Are you sure you want to go there, love?" She was so enamored with him all she could say was yes. He kept his eyes on her while unbuttoning the rest of his shirt. Then, he tenderly lifted her up and lay her on the bed.

He proceeded to run his hand up and down her body. Then before he knew it he was on top of her, whispering in her ear, "I'll always love you, Sophia."

"Sebastian…"

They spent the rest of their afternoon sharing intimate encounters. Both lost in their own love for one another.

By the time nightfall came, they fell easily asleep.

"Why is he always around? You know how uncomfortable I am when he just shows up out of the blue. Hovering over you and sniffing you like a dog."

"Sebastian, it's not my fault he comes around."

"I don't care, Sophia! I just hate it! Do something ABOUT IT! Do you HEAR ME!"

Suddenly, he heard a demonic voice laughing in the background. He peeked his head up only to find the same headless black-shaped torso. 'What the fuck,' was the last thing Sebastian said before he was viciously picked up by his leg and brutally dragged along the floor.

He was scared to no end. Screaming at the top of its lungs. After a couple minutes of being thrashed around his apartment, the entity abruptly stopped and said, "GET OUT!" Then he threw him off a cliff and out of his dream.

He woke up…practically hyperventilating.

This caused Sophia to wake up. She rolled over and turned on the lamp next to her. "What's wrong, Sebastian?"

He quickly got up and paced the floor to calm himself down. "Sorry, I didn't mean to wake you, Sophia. It was just a nightmare."

"Sounds like a pretty bad one."

"Ah, yeah…you could say that. Listen, I'll be okay. Go back to sleep, love. I'm just gonna go to the kitchen to get some water." Still, she waited for him to come back.

Moments later, he re-entered the room and glanced at the clock. It read 3:35 in the morning. "Are you sure you are alright, Sebastian?"

"Yes, it was just a dream, I'm okay." Though he knew without a doubt that he was not.

He got back into bed and tried to relax himself. Sophia obviously had no idea what was going on inside his head. But he told her he was okay. After everything they went through together, she trusted him completely. She had no reason to think otherwise. So she went back to sleep.

Not long after, he began to feel a sharp pain located on the same side of the leg that the entity grabbed. He got up to evaluate it, but there was no redness or bruising. *How strange.* He laid back down on his pillow and took a deep breath.

He was beginning to feel like he was going insane. He turned around and laid on his back. His eyes stayed bulging open for what seemed like hours. The last thing he wanted to do was fall back asleep. Despite that fact, every human falls victim to exhaustion at some point. His eyes eventually gave way to the heaviness as he fell back asleep.

Hours later…

He looked unhinged. He was pacing the floor as he was speaking to her. "I'm afraid, Sophia."

"Of what? You can tell me anything."

It took him a moment to get the words out. "Of…hurting you." He felt ashamed, saying it out loud to her.

"You could never—"

He cut her off. "You don't understand, I've had dreams about you. Terrible dreams. I'm tearing you up, and saying unimaginable words to you."

"Sebastian, stop worrying yourself. They are only dreams."

"Sophia…I fear it is much more dangerous than that. I keep seeing them as if I'm a person in the audience, watching myself annihilate you. It's starting to become too real. I'm concerned this all has something to do with the darkness inside me."

"Sebastian—"

He cut her off again. "You don't know, SOPHIA!" Suddenly, he couldn't control his own words. He was turning into a mad man right before his very eyes with her.

"You're making me do things I don't want to do! You can't comprehend how FURIOUS I am with you right now. I hate feeling this way! This is YOUR fault why I am turning into this lunatic! Get the hell away from me." Then he violently pushed her to the ground.

That's when he heard that deranged laugh again. "Wow, coming back for seconds in the same night? You're very entertaining to play with. Be that as it may, you're going to wake up extremely wet from this one."

An hour later, he woke up breathing heavily and covered in sweat. The time was 7:22 am. He caught sight of Sophia and saw that she had not woken up this time. He was shocked by the turn of events…the dreams were not only returning, but they were coming back even stronger.

It was at that moment he found himself at a turning point. He hadn't really considered Sophia's perspective. So far, in his mind, they were just his dreams to bear. Yet she was the victim in them. Shouldn't she know what was going on with him?

He decided at that moment, he needed to tell Sophia everything. He glanced down at her and watched as she peacefully slept. How in the world was he going to explain these nightmares to her? He got out of bed and went to the living room to think things through.

Today was going to be a big day for him. There were going to be a lot of people relying on him to fix their issues. The idea of telling Sophia before going to work did not sit well with him. But what was more evident was the fact that there was not even enough time to divulge what he needed to say to her. His alarm was set to go off in a couple of minutes.

Although it was going to be a long night, he would have to wait and speak to her tonight. He sat there for a moment reflecting on how he treated her in his nightmares. There was only one thing he knew for sure…those dreams were coming from a very dark place. This might be what the angels were warning him about.

Realizing that, he decided he would have to disclose the impending obstacles they were bound to face as well. He could no longer wait for Clarissa to get back to him. The idea of revealing that information to her was overwhelming, to say the least. All the same, though…it was becoming necessary to share it with her at this point.

Just then, he heard his alarm go off. He went into the room to turn it off and saw that she had woken from it. “Good morning, Sophia.”

“Hey…morning.”

“If it’s okay with you, I’m going to go take a shower.”

“Of course, go ahead. I need a minute to wake myself up anyway.”

When he finished getting ready, he went into the kitchen and saw that she had beaten him to the punch on breakfast. “Wow, thank you, love.”

“No worries, I wanted to.” They sat down and ate their meal. Sophia could tell something was up with him. He wasn’t his usual talkative self. “What’s wrong, Sebastian?”

“Um…there is something I want to talk to you about. Obviously, now is not a good time as we have to leave soon. However, it would be great if we speak tonight?”

“Yes, of course.” She glided her hand over his cheek and smiled. “Let’s talk tonight.” They took off shortly after they finished eating. Arriving at the office right at 9:05 am.

As soon as they made their way through the doorway, they saw another car pull up. “Ah, just in time, guys.” She was excited to start the day. “Your first appointment is here.”

“Alright, just bring the person to my room when you’re ready, Margaret.”

“Will do.”

He took Sophia’s hand and brought her in the room with him. With everything that had happened last night, he had spent little time in getting himself prepared for what he was about to do today. He began to feel a little nervous.

She picked up on his vibe and looked into his eyes. “You can do this, Sebastian.”

“I just…don’t want to mess up.”

"That's not going to happen. Remember, you are gifted for a reason." Those words calmed him down enough to move forward.

He gave her a kiss on her forehead and then connected his head to hers. "Thank you for being here for me, Sophia."

"Always." Then she gave him a kiss on the cheek and left the room.

Shortly after, Margaret knocked on Sebastian's door and came in with a woman. "Sebastian, this is Ms. Annie Tulsan. Please take a seat right here, dear." After the introductions, she quietly left the room.

"Hello Annie. I just need a minute to see what comes up."

"Sure, take your time." He closed his eyes and held one of his hands up, then stretched his fingers out as much as he could. Recently, he had discovered he received energy best when his hand was in this position.

A moment later, he started to feel a faint presence in the air. Then it began to manifest. Not long after, a rather tall black man dressed up like he was ready to go to a fancy dinner or ball began to appear.

He said to Sebastian, "That pretty lady sitting in that chair is my wife." He gazed at her adoringly.

"What is it you would like to tell her?" He waited for him to convey his message. Then glanced back towards Annie.

"Your husband has come forward today. His name is Sunny, right?"

Chills ran through her entire body. "Sunny is my nickname for him, yes."

"He's standing beside you to your right." She naturally turned her head in that direction. "He wants to talk about his death. Is that okay with you?"

She slowly nodded her head.

"He said to tell you…it wasn't your fault why he died. It was your daughter's wedding day. You guys were running late. So to make up for lost time, he drove faster than he should have, especially in the rain."

Tears started making their way down her cheeks, as an important reckoning was brewing in her mind. "Sunny, listen to me…it was my fault why we were running late. I was trying to find the rosary I had worn on the day of our wedding. Cecilia asked me to bring it so she could wear it during her wedding. I thought I had enough time to look for it. I didn't realize how late it was getting."

"Sorry…hold on a second, Annie…he is gesturing he wants to respond."

A minute later, he spoke up, "He is saying…believe him when he says this to you…it was not your decision to drive fast that day. You guys were running behind by only 10 minutes. Surely, Cecilia and Tom would have been happy to have waited that small amount of time for you guys to have arrived."

He watched as his wife tried to grab some sort of understanding as to what he was trying to convey. After a while, he continued, "More importantly, Annie…he wants you to know that he came on earth to learn about family and how to make it all work. In this life, you taught him so much more than he could have ever asked for. You showed him how to be a better man and father.

"He wants to clarify that his upbringing was not the best. He realized early on that you knew what to do. He was just smart enough to follow your lead. And because of that…he got to feel the love and joy of a family that most people never experience in a lifetime."

She sat there taking everything in. "Oh, and one more thing…tell Cecilia to stop beating herself up as well. Nobody could have known that darn rosary would have caused so much heartache." He could see that his death had caused a domino effect with everyone who was close to him.

"At the end of the day, it was just his time to go. If it wasn't the car crash, shortly after he would have passed away from something else. He wants you to move on with your life now and be free of this…guilt."

A feeling of relief showered through her body as he said those words. "He wants you to know that he will always love you guys. But for now, he will just have to love you from above.

"He's starting to fade away now, Annie. Is there anything else you want to say to him?"

"Yes…" she said with great passion. "Thank you…Sunny, for all the great years you gave us. We'll always love you!"

"He is smiling at you right now. He says, 'Until we meet again, my sweet Annie'."

All she could do was cry…however for once, it was with tears of happiness. "Is my Sunny gone now?"

"Yes, he has left us."

She could not believe what had transpired. To be able to talk to him one last time was…well, she couldn't quite put it into words. A feeling of gratefulness went through her soul. She wiped her tears away and focused her eyes on Sebastian. "You have no idea what you have given to me. I could never thank you enough."

"It was my pleasure helping you today, Annie." Seconds later, she got up and walked out the door.

When she found Sophia and Margaret, she looked like a completely new person. "Margaret, you said that you only take donations, right?"

"Yes, Annie, only if you want to though, please don't feel obligated." She sat down and started to write out a check. When she was done, she ripped it out of her checkbook and laid it upside down on the table.

She peeked into her purse and pulled out a tiny white leathery pouch. She put it on the table next to the check. "Tell Sebastian I don't need this anymore." Then she walked out the door.

When she left, Margaret glanced at the check. It was written out to CASH in the amount of two thousand dollars. On the bottom left-hand corner of the check, it read…Donation for restored mental health. "And so it begins," she said to Sophia.

Soon after, Sebastian came out of the room. Sophia grabbed the pouch and went over to give him a hug. "She gave a donation of 2,000 dollars."

"Wow…that was generous of her."

"Yes, it was." Then she handed him the tiny pouch. "She told us to tell you that she didn't need this anymore."

A smile started to form on his lips, as she handed it over to him. He opened it up and found a yellow rosary made of crystals. He was about to explain the story behind it, only his next appointment just arrived. "Guess I'll have to tell you guys another time."

He grabbed Sophia's hand and gave it a soft squeeze, gesturing to her that he will talk to her soon. Then, he walked over and shook the young man's hand. "Hello, I'm Sebastian. I'll be working with you today. However, I believe Margaret has a few things to go over with you first. Then she'll send you back my way."

"Sounds good." He left to go back to his room.

The rest of the day was pretty much filled with the same kind of reactions. Some gave donations in the form of money, others in the way of jewelry. It was what Margaret had predicted would happen.

By the end of the day, Sebastian was extremely drained. He needed sleep. Before he left, he asked Margaret if she could tone it down a little on how many people she brought in a day. Obviously, she did not have a problem with that. In fact, she felt terrible it took such a toll on him.

"I'll text you soon when I get a new group of people, K?"

Sophia answered back for him. "Thanks Margaret, we'll see you soon." Then they turned around and left. He was so bone-tired, he fell asleep about a minute after she started the car.

All she could think about during the drive home was how incredible he was with everyone. *What is he not capable of doing?* When they got home, she woke him up and helped him to bed. He fell right back to sleep as soon as he hit the pillow.

She went out into the living room to look for a piece of paper and pen. Understandably, they weren't going to be able to have a talk tonight. And since he was probably going to sleep through the night, she decided it would be a good time to go home and take care of stuff.

When she was done, she put the note on the kitchen counter underneath his phone. She went back into his room to give him a goodnight kiss, then went on her way.

Time passed since she left…

He suddenly felt his elbow crunch into something. The pain was agonizing. It felt like he may have broken it. But that didn't matter. There wasn't enough pain in the world that could supersede this deep sense of fear he had.

"Good…I see you are all ramped up today? I'll let you go ahead and finish what you started this time."

Then, out of the blue, his mind went blank and the dream was gone.

Chapter 14
Cracked

He woke up hours later once again completely drenched from head to toe. *Damn it...it's just never going to stop!* He started to reflect on the details of the dream. For whatever reason, there wasn't much to recall this time.

He turned his body around and immediately felt a horrible pain on his right elbow. Naturally, he went to touch it and was surprised by its texture. It felt like an open wound.

This scared the living daylights out of him. He moved his hand over to where Sophia should have been laying, only to discover she was not there.

He got up to turn on the light switch and found his entire room ransacked. Somebody had punched large holes in the walls. Sophia's personal belongings were ripped to shreds and discarded everywhere. His television and cords had been ripped from their sockets and thrown to the floor.

Who could have possibly done this? But then a horrible thought came to mind... Maybe it was him. He pulled his arm up to evaluate his elbow. It was completely mutilated. Parts of his skin had been broken open and surrounding the wounds were massive bruises. Panic quickly washed through him as he was beginning to understand what had gone down.

He walked into the living room and saw the same horror scene unfold out there as well. Perhaps even worse than his bedroom. There were more holes on the walls only this time they were covered with blood...his blood.

A deep sense of fear for Sophia's life began to manifest within him. He searched his entire apartment. Yet, she was nowhere to be found. He started to hyperventilate. Last thing he remembered was getting in the car with her to go home.

He went to grab his phone in the kitchen to give her a call and found a note written underneath it.

Dear Sebastian,

I wish I could stay every day and night with you. However, I have things that I need to take care of. Since you were so tired, I figured you would sleep through the rest of the night. So, I decided it would be a good time to go home. Call me when you can.

I will miss you!

Love,
Sophia

Thank God...she's all right...thank God! His breathing finally began to calm down. After finding out where she was, the realization of what happened came slowly back to haunt him. He knew what needed to be done next. Though it was the last thing he wanted to do, he had to see for himself what really went down.

So he went over to the couch and sat down. Then he closed his eyes, and pulled up his life archives. He started to flip through it until he found the right one.

Taking a deep breath...he opened it up and watched.

He was running around like a crazy man. "Where is SHE! She wouldn't leave me! She knows how much I NEED HER!" He checked the living room. She was not there. "SOPHIA! WHERE THE HELL ARE YOU!"

Rage was not just within him, it had become him. "GODDAMN IT!" He brought his arm up and smashed his elbow into the wall. THIS IS WHAT YOU DO TO ME, SOPHIA! Before he knew it, there were holes everywhere.

He picked up the clothes she had lying around and tore them to pieces. Then he took a good gaze around the room. Why does she do this to me! I can't stand how she controls me! If she thinks she can just leave me this way...SHE HAS ANOTHER THING COMING!

There was no love left for her in his mind. And he liked that feeling. It spurred him on to become even more maddened. He picked up the lamp on her side of the bed and threw it against the wall. The pictures he had of them on his nightstand were now flung to the ground and smashed. He lifted up the television and ripped off the cords, then threw it onto the floor.

He wreaked havoc wherever he could find it, especially if it had something to do with her. When there was nothing left to break in the bedroom, he moved onto the living room.

Again…beating his elbow against the walls. That's when his skin began to fracture open. Blood was splattering everywhere at that point. Still, he did not care. Nothing was going to reign him back in.

He picked up a glass he remembered Sophia had been drinking from and thrashed it against the wall. "You will know my wrath tonight, YOU FUCKING…"

That was enough for him. He had to stop watching it for his own sanity. His whole body was ready to collapse into shock. But he stayed conscious.

Why in the world would he knowingly write such a devastating state of event in his life? He had gone fully dark in that dream. So much so that it completely took over his mind.

He was so thankful she left when she did. Then again, that just brought up an entirely new consideration… What if she hadn't left? He peeked another glance around the room as the significance of a new fear began to immerse… He could have very easily murdered her last night.

He reminded himself of the conversation he was supposed to have with her yesterday. He was going to tell her everything. For a while, he let his mind wonder. Contemplating the results if they would have had that discussion.

What he came up with was not in her favor. She would have insisted that everything was going to be okay and they would somehow find a way to work through it. Yet, no one could have predicted how evil the darkness could get. There would have been absolutely no warning to avoid her tragic fate.

The notion that was now crossing his mind was startling. Given all they had been through together, how could he not include her in finding a solution? It was just so wrong of him. Nevertheless, being fair was not his priority at this point. Her way of handling the problem would have gotten her killed.

Suddenly, the discussion he had with the angels came crashing back to him. *We can't disclose too much information. But what we can say is that you cannot serve your purpose on earth, if you do not fulfill a significant undertaking with Sophia. You will have to bear enormous obstacles with her. Things you could never imagine will take place between the two of you. It will require you to have…blind faith.*

Blind faith? What does that really mean anyways? He took a moment to meditate the meaning. And then it hit him.

...Even though the tunnel looks gruesomely dark. Having blind faith would require Sebastian to surrender to whatever the present moment brought him and tolerate whatever results may come from it.

He gazed his eyes at the bloodstains surrounding the walls and brought his head down in shame. It was in that moment, he made the decision that he could not consent to blind faith. At the end of the day, he believed her life was in too much danger. He would have to find another road.

He remembered a while back a conversation he had with Josephine about this very subject matter. She mentioned she may be able to help with the darkness if he needed further assistance.

But could he really stomach bringing her in on this? He reflected on how she was with him at the dinner. She was overly flirtatious and cocky. Yet, at the same time, very serious when it came time to speak about her gift. Her specialty was dealing with dark energy.

It would only make since to bring her in and at least hear what she has to say. He could handle her loud personality traits if she could bring a solution to the table.

He grabbed Josephine's number out from his wallet and dialed. After about four rings, she finally answered. "Having difficulties already, my friend?"

"Um...unfortunately yes, I am. I find myself in need of your services rather quickly actually. I created a regrettable scene in my apartment last night."

"Oh...I see. In that case, text me your address and I'll come over to see if I can remedy the situation."

"Thank you, I would greatly appreciate that."

"I'm sure you would, Sebastian."

When he hung up the phone, he promptly texted her his information. Thirty-five minutes later, she arrived.

"Jesus Sebastian, you have been a busy boy, haven't you?"

"As I told you, I had a difficult night."

"I see your dilemma...I take it this plight of rage was meant for Sophia?"

"Unfortunately, yes."

"Does she know what you are capable of doing to her?"

"No, she doesn't. And I prefer to keep it that way."

"Oh, well, that's one way to approach the problem."

"I have my reasons. She has already been through enough violence in her life. I don't want to push her over the edge."

"I get it...you're embarrassed of what you could have done to her last night. I mean, it's ironic actually. You of all people, the one with all the golden gifts, could impel so much darkness upon her."

"It's not like that, Josie." He was beginning to get worked up over her words. "I plan on telling her about my issues with the darkness, and that it has become stronger than I could handle. Which will explain why I need to bring you into the equation of my life. However, she doesn't need to know the gruesome details of what happened here last night."

"Okay, so you have justified your decision...I get the picture!"

He couldn't understand why she kept harping on the matter. "Josie, please...take a look around this room! She'll think I'm a raving lunatic."

"Aren't you though?"

"You're missing the point of why I called you. I need to protect her."

"Of course, you do...So then let's talk about what my fee will be."

"Yes, I was wondering how much it will cost."

"I don't crave regular monetary funds from you. No. I have a special job I need you to perform." That caught him off guard. He thought it would be a normal transaction and if need be, he could always ask Margaret for additional money.

"I've been waiting for someone like you to come around for a while now. You've got just the right qualities I need to fix my...affairs. The good news for you is that I won't need your help right away."

"What? I don't understand how that is good news. As you can see, I'm in need of your help immediately."

"No need to worry about that, Sebastian. I will still provide what you need from me...all the way up till I get what I want from you."

Huh... "Although that is very generous of you, I don't get why you would do such a thing for me."

"Oh, believe me...I'm not really doing you any favors. What I need from you is a pretty hefty deed, my friend. Especially for you." He started to get concerned as to the nature of the job.

"And what exactly would you require me to do?"

A small grin formed on her lips. "There is an acquaintance of mine that needs...motivating. You will be the carrot."

"Josie, please…could you stop talking in code?"

"Fine…I'll say it how you want it to be told. I need you to put on a sensual, intimate scene with me where my business partner Todd will see it. He likes me…I can feel it, but he needs the motivation to spur him further along in the process."

"Josephine…No… Please…don't ask me to betray her like this."

"Like it or not, Sebastian, that is what I require of you."

"Why in the world would you even need me to do this? You are an attractive woman in your own right…you could probably find 10 other guys who would even enjoy doing this for you."

Her tone turned menacing. "As I recall, you are the one that needs my services. Not the other way around. So I certainly don't need to explain my reasons to you. Get it!"

Sebastian was beside himself on what she was asking him to do. "How far would we need to go in this performance of yours?"

"As far as it needs to be taken. Because if it doesn't get the job done…no further services will be offered to you and you'll be owing me back a whole lot more than what you put into the deal."

"How could you put me in this position, Josephine? You know how much I love her."

She didn't answer him. Instead, she stood there with a smug face, watching him struggle internally. What she was asking him to do was outrageous. There was no absolute way he could do that to her. Without another hesitation, he shouted at her to forget it! "It's not going to happen!"

"Oh…okay, I guess my services are not as necessary as you originally portrayed them to be. Thanks for wasting my time…Sebastian." She grabbed her purse and started to leave. "Good luck on figuring out this mess."

However, as she got about five feet away from the door, she began to feel his change in thought. His ego was getting the best of him. Suddenly, all his fears came rushing back into his mind. His ability to make the right decision was becoming unhinged.

"WAIT! Josephine…wait!" His voice became gruff as he said his next words. "I'm desperate to fix this. Please, can we come up with some other form of payment? Surely there is something else you need? You mentioned you don't want money, but would you please reconsider? I know someone that could loan me a lot of it. Name your price."

"As I already told you before, I don't need money, Sebastian."

"Okay, fine!" He ran his hand through his hair. "I never thought I would be considering this…but worst case scenario is I will have to break up with her and never see her again. The pain will be enormous to bear on both our ends…still; at least she would be safe."

"Oh, Sebastian…you and I both know the answer to that. If you thought that was a choice, you would never have called me up in the first place."

"Well, I'm running out of options here, Josephine."

"Then I suggest you put mine back on the table."

"I told you, I can't do that."

"Look…it's better than the alternative. The scene you created here is proof of that. Besides, you may think if you stop seeing her, she will be out of danger. Unfortunately, you will be mistaken. Just like how your dream came true last night. Eventually, during the day, you will seek her out, and God knows what after that."

"Why is it just her that I am seeking out?"

"I'm afraid you are getting it wrong, my dear. It will not stop with her. You are targeting Sophia right now because you love her and the darkness doesn't like that. However, if you don't curb your temperament in some way, there will be other situations you will have to deal with in the future."

He rubbed his hands over his face in discouragement. "That's just fucking great!"

He got up and started pacing the floor to think of other possibilities. Josephine just stood there, watching in delight as he squirmed through this whole quandary. After a while, he came up with something else. "What if I simply throw my gifts away! I'll never use them again and keep it turned off for the rest of my life."

"For Christ sake, Sebastian…don't you realize that these powerful gifts you acquired have already become a part of you? You can't just dump them. Yes…many times during the day, you can turn it off. Except, what about when you are tired? Or worse…what about when you are sleeping? No…my friend, at this point you need me."

He held his head down again in frustration. Then one final image came to mind. "Clarissa, I need to find her…"

Josephine let out a shrewd laugh. "And how will she cleanse you, Sebastian? Her goodness can't fix what you need right now.

"Besides, that is another one of my stipulations. You cannot divulge any information about our agreement to her or anyone else for that matter. I forbid it! And let me be clear, if you so much as hint our deal to another soul…the arrangement will be over with. Do you understand me?"

All he could do was take in her words. "The only exception, of course, will be with Sophia. Obviously, I know how you are going to spill the beans with her."

Clearly he did not like this restriction. The idea of not being able to tell her or another single person was making him feel trapped and isolated. But he was not in a position to negotiate.

"Tell me… If I were to move forward with this arrangement, how do you intend to keep Sophia safe?"

"Aw…now you're starting to ask the right questions. You see, Sebastian, I possess abilities that unfortunately, you have not received. I hold the gift of transferring energy from one place to another. You will need to come see me whenever you need a cleansing. And in your case, quite often, I suspect.

"Let me show you how it works." She closed her eyes and within seconds, he began to feel lighter. Almost euphoric-like.

"How did you do that?"

"Same as you, Sebastian, it's just a gift."

He felt a tiny pinch of jealousy run through him. *Just a gift* was saving Sophia's life. Something he truly wished he had acquired himself.

The cost of what he was going to have to pay for it was something he never believed he'd be contemplating. He felt so conflicted inside. Yet, the agony of needing to accept this deal was painfully evident. She had left him with no other alternatives.

He rubbed his hand over his lips, not wanting to release the words that were about to escape his mouth. But they emerged anyway. "Okay Josephine…it appears there is no other way of getting out of this.

"So I'll give you what you want…in exchange for her safety from my unsightly wrath. Just please…promise me you will protect her at all costs."

Her voice turned harsh again. "Don't worry about my job, Sebastian! You just make sure you come see me when you need to be cleansed."

"Yes, of course, I'll make sure to do so."

"Good. Then we have an agreement. Now, I have other obligations that I need to attend to today." She looked in her purse and held out a card.

"Here…take this. If you call these people, they will know how to deal with this type of…problem."

She took another glimpse around the room and scoffed. "Be thankful you have me in your life now. It will serve you well to remember that." Then she turned around and walked away.

He let out a long breath as he watched her leave. When she closed the door, he collapsed onto the couch. The pressure of what he had signed up for weighed heavily on him. He was so pissed at Josephine for giving him such a horrific ultimatum. Why would she do this to him? How could his life take such a quick turn of fate? He sat there rethinking those thoughts over and over again.

Eventually, he realized he had to stop and deal with the hideous room situation. He got up and dialed the number on the card. A guy with a heavily Russian accent answered the phone. "Hello."

"Um, yeah, Josephine gave me your number—"

Without any further explanation, the guy abruptly cut him off. "Yes…yes…yes…just text me your address, and we will be over soon."

Then he hung up the phone on him. "Okay?" *Guess this isn't his first rodeo.*

He texted him the address and then tended to the wound on his elbow. Not long after, he saw a large truck pull up to his apartment. *That can't possibly be for me?*

Then he saw a team of five guys get out. They showed up at his doorstep with gloves, Clorox, and large garbage bags. *Jesus Christ! What kind of business was Josephine running?* But that question got squashed immediately as he realized he didn't really want to know how far her rabbit hole went.

After a while, things started to seem normal again. They fixed all the holes on the walls and even coated them with fresh paint similar to the initial color. The broken furniture was put into bags and thrown in the back of the truck.

At some point, the doorbell rang with deliveries. They were replacing all the things he had trashed during his episode. They ordered items closely matching their original appearances. By the time they were done, it looked as if nothing had occurred.

"So, how much do I owe you guys?"

"No, this one is on Josie. We already have something worked out with her."

Of course, you do. They all left without saying another word. Soon after, he heard his phone buzz.

Sophia: Hey there, how are you?

He took another panoramic view of the room. *This is as good as its going to get.*

Sebastian: I'm good, you?
Sophia: Same...
Sophia: I'm done with all the things I needed to do. Is it all right if I come on over?

He was going to have to talk to her about Josephine. A conversation he was frightened about having with her. Even so, things needed to be said, and there was no point in delaying the inevitable.

Sebastian: Yes, of course.
Sophia: Okay, I'll see you soon, then.
Sebastian: K.

Fifteen minutes later, she arrived. She came in and sat down on the couch. It didn't take her long to realize that his apartment looked slightly different. "Sebastian, your walls…they, um…they appear as if they've been painted?"

He had only seen her for a couple of minutes and she was already diving in. *Okay…it is what it is.* He let out a deep sigh and sat down on the couch next to her.

"Sophia I…ah…I need to talk to you about some troubles I've been having."

"Troubles?"

"Yes, well, the last thing I wanted to do was worry you, so I was trying to deal with it on my own."

"Deal with what?"

"You see, lately I've been experiencing a lot of nightmares. Unfortunately, as it turns out, these dreams were not your typical run of the mill nightmares."

"How do you mean?"

"Well, mine apparently manifested into very dark energy and somehow managed to take over my mind."

"Take over your mind? I'm sorry, I'm trying to understand you. What are these dreams even about?"

He hated what he was about to tell her. He was going to have to lie to her completely. "…There is this man in my dreams who comes up from behind and tries to kill me. It takes place in different ways yet it is always the same man. I have to defend myself over and over again. He never leaves me alone."

"That sounds horrible, Sebastian, really it does. But I still don't get the connection between your dreams and why the walls needed to be repainted?"

She was going to find out one way or another. So he slowly began to roll up the sleeve of his right arm and pull off the bandage coverings.

"My God!" She jumped out from the couch and pulled her hands up to her mouth. "Aww…what the hell is going on, Sebastian?"

"I get it, it looks pretty horrific. As I said, I constantly had to defend myself. Apparently, in my dreams, I really thought I was punching him. Only to find out when I woke up, I was punching the walls instead."

"So you were sleepwalking while you were punching the walls?"

"Yes, that's what I'm trying to say."

"Jesus Christ, Sebastian. This sounds incredibly dangerous. We need to find a way to get you help." She came back over to look at his wound. "There's got to be something we can do."

He began to feel sick about what he needed to tell her next. "Sophia, ah…listen, as I said to you earlier. I didn't want to worry you, so I found a solution on my own."

"What do you mean, you found a solution? Didn't this just happen last night?"

"Yes, it did. When I woke up this morning and saw what I did. I immediately thought of someone who could help remedy the situation."

"Who?"

"Do you remember meeting Josephine at Clarissa's party?"

The hair on the back of her neck crawled up in unison. "You mean the woman who kept asking us if we were together so she could have a shot at you? That's the person you got to help you get through this?"

"Sophia, I'm sorry, it's just that she handles dark energy for a living. She was able to make mine go away."

"Why in the world would you make such a rash decision without coming to me first? I thought we were closer than that."

"We are, Sophia, I swear to God! I've never been closer to anyone in my entire life."

"...I see. So you couldn't stop for a second to consult with the closest person in your life? That's pretty hard to believe."

"I wish you would not perceive it in that way. I made the decision based on the fact that this is where she is gifted."

She held her head down baffled by his admissions. After a while, she started to become curious about something else. "Tell me...how did she manage to help remedy your situation?"

"She used one of her gifts to grab the dark energy out of my body and released it back to the universe. I swear, Sophia, after she took the darkness out of me...I've never felt lighter."

More questions kept lurking in her head. "And how much is she charging you for her services?"

"I've already set up a payment arrangement with her. She was reasonable with me given my position." He was getting way in over his head with the lies.

Something else just occurred to her. "You needing her to take the darkness away...will this be a permanent thing between the two of you? I mean..."

"Sophia, let's not think about that right now. You never know...I may eventually receive her gift someday. Right now, she is my short-term solution, until I come up with something else."

She still couldn't shake the fact that Josephine was going to be in his life. Suddenly, her voice turned melancholy. "Why are you doing this to us, Sebastian? Josephine obviously likes you. How did you think this was going to make me feel?"

He got on his knees. "Sophia, I swear to you on my life that I don't like her in that way. I love you! Only you, love!"

"Then don't do this! Don't go back to her! Let's work together to find another solution. Please, Sebastian...something tells me she is bad news for us."

It broke his heart what he was about to say to her next. "...Sophia, that's the one thing I cannot do. Right now, she is the only person who can cleanse the darkness out of me. These gifts are a part of me now. Whether I like it or not...they come at a price. I hope you can understand."

“So that’s it then.” He sat there and watched as her head bent down in defeat. “I can see the decision has been made, and there is nothing I can do to change your mind. However, I hope you see that this will come with a price on our relationship.”

Alarm immediately took over. “Sophia, please don’t leave me because of this. Please!”

“I didn’t say I would, Sebastian. Even so, I want to make it clear that I would have chosen another path.”

Inside, Sebastian wanted to scream…*that is precisely why I could not come to you!*

“I guess there is nothing else to say for now.”

“Sophia…”

She put her hand up to stop any more words come out of his mouth. “I’m done for the night, Sebastian. I’ve got nothing left. Please, just let me go to sleep.” He realized she needed time to get over what he had done.

They walked into the bedroom and got ready for bed. He was beside himself over how heartbroken she looked. She got dressed quickly and went straight into bed. He turned off the light and lay in bed with his eyes wide open. “I love you, Sophia.” But all he received from her was silence.

Chapter 15
Discontent

The next morning, he woke up to the worst feeling. Flashbacks of last night's argument came rushing back to mind. He glanced over and watched her sleeping away. The pit of his stomach was eating away at him with all the lies he had told her.

He got out of bed and went to sit down on the couch in the living room. The thought of Thomas came to him again. He needed to try a new way of getting in touch with him.

Thinking back to their last meeting with Clarissa, he had learned something specific about the angels. They each had their own distinctiveness about them. Kind of like a human's DNA. However, the angel's identity could be found through their souls.

He reminded himself of what Thomas's energy felt like and decided to give it a shot. He held up his hand and stretched out his fingers to receive the highest amount of energy possible. Then began to put himself into a meditative state.

When his brain drew a blank canvass of nothingness, he started to feel tingles all over his body. His soul was in the middle of leaving the body. Next thing he knew, he was standing on a ledge. He bent down to touch what was keeping him up and discovered nothing was there. His hand went right through whatever was holding him up.

He got back up to look around and saw pitch black as far as the eye could see. Then suddenly, the atmosphere changed. It became alive with millions of souls streaming through an invisible tunnel. At least, it appeared as if something was keeping them aligned in a perfect cylinder passageway.

From what he sensed, he was among both angels and spirits from the other side. Each soul had its own aura light illuminating from its body. Sebastian looked down and saw that he too was now glowing with the color blue. *Guess I'm in the system now*.

He wondered if there were other humans migrating among the crowd. However, he could not detect a single one. It made him feel a little crazy knowing he was the only being existing in this dimension.

But then he heard a familiar voice. "*Might as well jump in, you have already located the realm.*" It was Thomas. He gazed his head up and down and saw there was no beginning or end to the tunnel. How would he find his way back? "*That should be the least of your concerns. Come find me...we need to talk.*"

Those words gave him the will to jump. A split second later, he found himself traveling with the other souls and took notice that something else had now transformed around him.

It was hard to comprehend what he was witnessing. Although it was pitch black, there was definitely another structure surrounding them. Within it were mass accumulations of tiny holes with light shining out from each one.

Somehow, he received the insight to view individual holes while still traveling within the tunnel. What was most peculiar was the energy he felt from each specific hole he passed by.

Out of curiosity, he went to closely observe a specific one. What he saw was a spirit from the other side visiting a loved one on earth. There was another human present as well. He had the ability to translate messages from spirit to human.

Peeking through another hole, he watched an entirely different scene play out. A human was driving a car. He was almost about to get hit by a drunk driver. But an angel stepped in and turned his steering wheel at the perfect time so as the drunk driver missed him by a hair. When the angel finished her job, she turned around and looked at Sebastian. "It wasn't his time to go."

Upon realizing what this place really was, he became spellbound for a second. This realm...was a mega portal for spirits to travel back and forth from heaven to earth. How fascinating to be able to experience this, he thought.

He continued to travel until he located Thomas's energy. He was finishing up with someone who was grieving the loss of a loved one. When he sensed Sebastian's presence, he messaged him telepathically to hold on for just another minute.

A short while later, Thomas turned around and teleported them to another hole for privacy. "I see you have the capability of finding me now."

"Yes, Thomas. The journey was quite astonishing. I don't understand why more humans are not allowed in on this unbelievable wonderment."

"When you are on the other side, you can travel through this place whenever you want. But when a soul decides to come down on earth, they are experiencing a human existence, not a supernatural one."

"Yet, I am allowed to see it?"

"It's because of what you needed to experience at this moment. However, I do see you have other pending matters to discuss with me."

"Yes, unfortunately, I do." Going through the tunnel gave him time away from thinking about all his troubles. It was a welcoming divergent.

He began to pace the room before he spoke. His tone of voice grew dark as his words came out. "My life has become shockingly terrible in a very short amount of time, Thomas. I worry about how to navigate my way through the many pitfalls I have put myself in."

"I know, Sebastian. I see you are going through a rough period. I am helping you when I am allowed to step in…unfortunately, I can only do so much. You are human, and the ego can sometimes take over. Regrettably, there is nothing I can do about that. It's your path to lead."

"So is there nothing you can do to help me?"

"Only if you are willing to follow my guidance as we go through this very important discussion."

"Okay."

"Now, I understand things don't add up to you right now. All the same, you chose such a difficult road to lead. One that most souls will not ever encounter, at least now for now. Nevertheless, as we told you before, you would be facing tremendous obstacles with Sophia. They are coming at you in this present moment."

He put his head down in shame. "I couldn't do it, Thomas. I could not tolerate her outcome."

"Possible outcome, Sebastian."

"If I had that conversation with her one day earlier, she definitely would have died."

"Speaking in absolutes tells me your ego is not living in the now. Life is not so black and white. Your mind has told yourself stories of a future that has not happened yet."

"The only way I could possibly entertain what you are saying is if you tell me that I won't ever harm her. That she will always be safe from my wrath?"

"I'm not allowed to tell you the answer to that question, Sebastian. You know that. What I can tell you with clarity is that your ego has become obsessed with trying to keep her safe. Because of that, you are going down the wrong path with Josephine."

"She is only in the picture because I need her protection for Sophia."

"Believe me when I express to you, I completely understand why she seems like the safer option to choose. But you need to keep your eye on the bigger picture. Remember you are not merely living this existence for her. Whether she gets hurt by you or not, you were meant to play out the course with her."

He shook his head in disagreement. "I love her too much to take that chance, Thomas! Don't you get that! Surely, when I was writing my chart, I would have taken some precautions, knowing that I could possibly go down the wrong road?"

"You did actually take the notion into account. Unfortunately, I cannot divulge any more information other than what I have already told you at this point."

"That's just perfect, Thomas!"

He rubbed his hands against his face in frustration. "Again, I ask…why it would be so necessary to go through something this horrific? As it is, I'm already helping people heal their wounds through my gifts. Is that not enough?"

"Sebastian, what you are trying to achieve is not simply about mending souls…The mission is to evolve mankind. One cannot do that unless he has evolved himself. This journey with Sophia would have allowed for that progression to happen."

He took a minute to digest everything Thomas disclosed to him. He weighed in on his words very seriously. His own angel was conveying without a doubt that he was moving down the wrong path. Even so, no matter which perspective he evaluated it from, he was not willing to take a chance that he could hurt her. He could not be swayed.

Thomas shook his head in disappointment. "So…I can see you are not going to change your mind for now."

Josephine's image popped into his head when he thought about the choices he'd made. "It's too late anyway to get out of the deal I made with her. She has already given me my first cleanse."

"Again, that is where you are wrong, Sebastian. It is never too late. Although I will admit, it will absolutely make your time here on earth a whole lot messier than it already is. All the same, it would at least put your life back on track."

He gave out a long sigh before replying. "That is just not an option for me right now, Thomas."

"Okay, then respectfully, I have said all I can communicate at this juncture. I want you to know I am always here for you, Sebastian…you know where to find me now. I'll see you when you need me next." Seconds later, he vanished.

He stood there for a while in silence with himself. Reflecting on Thomas's advice. It was an impossible undertaking he was wanting him to fulfill. When he finished wallowing in his own pity, he came back to reality. As it turned out, all he had to do to get back home was jump back into his soul.

When he opened his eyes, he saw it was nearly nine o'clock. He wondered if she was awake yet. As soon as he got up to check on her, she came walking out of the bedroom. Her demeanor was somber and she was carrying a bag around her shoulder. "I want to go home, Sebastian."

"Please, Sophia…don't go. I can't stand having you be mad at me."

"I don't think you understand the magnitude of how deeply upset I am at you right now. I need to leave before I say things I'll regret later." He could see the resentment in her eyes.

Wanting to respect the space she needed, he conceded to her wishes. The drive home was quiet. On her way out of the car, she told him she would text when she was ready to speak again.

Not wanting to leave things on such a bad note, he tried to utter a few words. "Sophia, I wish—"

But she interrupted him, "I know, Sebastian. You were very clear last night about everything. I don't need any more information. What I need is time to think things through." That was all she said to him before she left.

He watched as she walked up to her door and went inside. *If she only knew the full truth*, he thought. Driving away was not easy; nevertheless eventually, he left.

Days went by and still he did not hear from her. After another week and a half later, depressive thoughts began to prowl his head. He wondered if she would ever be able to get over it. He considered the fact that she might possibly even break up with him, although she said she wouldn't. This was what it would feel like if she really did call it off.

He couldn't take the negativity anymore. He needed a distraction. So he went out for some fresh air and found himself at one of the local bars in the neighborhood. "Can I have an Eagle Rare, please?"

"Sure, how do you want it?"

"Make it neat, will you."

"You got it, buddy."

The bartender poured him his drink and laid it on the counter. "Thanks." He gulped it down like water. Something he would never normally do with bourbon. He wasn't in the habit of getting drunk.

However, shortly after he took a swig of the drink, he asked the bartender for another…and then another. It seemed to take the edge off the nightmare he was swimming in. He was about ready to pound down his fourth one when someone lightly tapped him on the shoulder.

He turned around and was surprised to see who was there. "Christopher… What are you doing here?"

"I just had dinner with my girlfriend. Long story short, we took separate cars because she has plans to stay with her sister tonight. When I was coming out of the restroom, I noticed you sitting here."

He turned his head around to make sure no one was close enough to hear him. "Listen Sebastian, I hope I'm not overstepping my bounds here, but I have to say…you don't look so good. Is everything okay?"

Usually, he was a closed book to people he didn't know very well, still after drinking the bourbons as fast as he had, the effects were beginning to rub off. "To be honest, I've been better."

"Oh, well, that's not good. Do you want to talk about it?"

He looked over at the open seat next to him. "Guess I could use some company."

The bartender came over as soon as he sat down. "What's your poison?"

"Basil Hayden on the rocks."

Sebastian took note of his choice. "I see you are a fan of bourbon as well?"

"Yes, it's one of my favorites." The bartender came back over with his drink and then gave them their privacy.

"So, what's got you all eaten up?"

He put his head down for a moment. Then pulled it back up, taking a small sip of his drink. "You ever feel like no one is ever on your side? I mean I'm trying to do the right thing. Yet, nobody seems to understand the stakes? And even after everything we have been through, she just won't let me do the one thing to keep her sa…"

He had to watch what he said as a stipulation to one of Josephine's rules. No one can know about the arrangement they made. "I'm assuming you are talking about Sophia?"

"Yes, she feels one way and I feel another. It's driving me mad that I have not seen her since the argument."

"Well, how long has it been?"

"I haven't seen or heard from her in more than two weeks."

"Ouch, yeah that is a while. But what was the disagreement over?"

Sebastian grabbed his drink and took another swallow. "She is angry with me because of a choice I made without her consent. I did it because I was terrified that if certain precautions were not taken, something horrible could…"

"…Could what, man?" He didn't respond at first. He just sat there, gazing at his drink despondently for a while. Still it wasn't hard for Christopher to fill in the blanks. He leaned in a little closer, knowing that this might be a bit touchier subject than originally thought. "Are you saying that Sophia might be in some kind of danger?"

"Um…I'm not really at liberty to voice all the details." He brushed his hand through his hair and took another sip. "You see, in her past, she has already suffered unimaginable pain. She has finally been healed from all that. The last thing she needs is to bring on a whole new set of… issues."

"I think you will find that I can relate to that statement more than anyone you'll ever know."

Sebastian was surprised by his words. "Why do you say that?"

"Well, like you, I've been faced with certain difficult situations myself with Leslie." His face turned dark. "One of her own family members did some rather grotesque things to her when she was a young girl. Then a couple years ago, he came back into town to stir up new trouble with her."

"My God, Christopher…what did you do about it?"

He shrugged his shoulders and took a swig of his drink. "I did what needed to be done."

"I see. Did Leslie go along with how you…handled things?"

"No actually, she did not. We fought all the time over it. We even broke up a couple of times. But the thing is…I just knew the bastard wasn't going to stop screwing with her. She couldn't understand that it was the only way of keeping her safe from him."

Huh…perhaps he really does know where I'm coming from.

"How did you guys get through it? Obviously, you are still together."

"Naturally, it took some time, but eventually, she came around. Now she even thanks me for how I handled the circumstances. She realized how necessary it was."

"Well, I guess you got lucky then. I'm not sure Sophia will ever change her viewpoint."

"Make no mistake, Sebastian. It was not luck that got us through those times. It was our love for one another. And it will be the same for you as well. You'll see. I've seen the two of you together. Sophia loves you. That's the foundation right there. You guys will get through this obstacle in your life and then you will move on to greener pastures. Believe me…I of all people should know." He reached into his pocket and pulled out a tiny box. "Check it out." He unsnapped the top of the box and opened it up.

"You're going to propose to her? Wow, congrats, man!"

"Yes, well…as I said it has been a long time coming with all the issues we had to deal with. But we have finally gotten to that point where we are grounded again. And it will be that way for you too."

He took in his words and started to feel a little better about his plate. "Maybe you're right, man. Either way, thanks for the ear."

He took another glance at the ring and realized something that made him chuckle a little. "Quick question, Christopher…how long have you been carrying this around? I mean, most people don't normally carry engagement rings in their pocket unless they intend to propose."

He started to laugh.

"Okay, funny story, I've got the ring, I'm just not sure when I'm going to give her the ring. I keep thinking every time I see her that today is the day. Yet it never feels like the right time or place to do it."

"You know, what you need to do is simply plan it out. Not everything needs to be spontaneous."

Christopher gave out another laugh. "Yeah, I guess that is not such a bad idea, my friend."

When they finished their drinks, Christopher ordered another round on him. It felt so damn good to have someone validate where he was coming from. Who knew, maybe things would somehow work out with Sophia.

They continued to talk for hours after that. Spending the rest of the night chatting away as if they were long lost friends. They told more stories about how their relationships developed with Leslie and Sophia. It was exactly what he needed to keep him from having his own nervous breakdown.

The next couple of days, he dealt with Sophia's absence in a more rational way. He reminded himself to have patience. *She will come around*, he kept telling himself. Until one day, she did.

Sophia: I'm ready to talk. Can I come over?

Sebastian: It's good to hear from you, Sophia. You are always welcome to come over.

Sophia: K.

He got off the phone, overjoyed that she was ready to talk. As soon as he put his cell down, his phone buzzed again. He looked down to see who it was and a feeling of relief came through him. Finally, she had responded.

Clarissa: Sebastian, I'm sorry I could not get to you sooner. I've been dealing with the passing of both my mother and father. The day after we met with the angels, they died tragically in a car accident. I've been taking care of their affairs ever since. To be quite honest, I wasn't in the right mind frame to help anyone at the time I received your messages. I hope everything is okay with you and Sophia. I've been worried about you guys; however, as you can understand, I have been dealing with my own grievances. I'll text you guys when I get back in town. I still have a little left to follow up on. Talk to you soon.

All Sebastian could do was feel compassion for her. He knew what it was like to lose both parents in a close period of time. His mother had passed away of cancer. Then three months later, his father had died of a stroke.

Sebastian: My dear friend. I'm so sorry to hear the news of their passing. If there is anything I can do for you, let me know. Please make sure to take care of yourself, K.

It had been such a long time since they had last spoken. He was simply happy he even heard back from her. Twenty minutes later, Sophia arrived. Though she did not look as well as he had hoped. Obviously, the break had not given her enough time to get over the anger she felt for him.

"I came over to tell you something."

"Okay, what is it?"

"I need to see her. I want to make sure she is not fucking with us. It's the only way I'm going to get through this position you have put me in."

No…no…no…that would be a very bad mistake. There is no way these two should ever be put in the same room with each other. "Sophia, I…um…I don't think that is a good idea."

"You saying that to me… totally validates exactly why I need to see her. It makes me wonder why you don't want me to talk with her!"

Damn it, I'm only making this worse!

"I swear to you I'm not hiding anything, Sophia."

"Good, then make the appointment." He saw the resolve in her eyes…still, this was the last thing he wanted to do. How in the world was he going to get out of this?

"I'm not getting you, Sebastian. Don't you want to set my mind at ease?"

"Of course I do." He thought of a different way to approach the subject. "Listen to me…Josephine can sometimes be a little rough under the edges. I don't want her to voice anything to you that would hurt your feelings."

"So, my instincts were correct, she does taunt and flirt her way with you."

"I didn't mean it that way, Sophia. I just meant sometimes she can assert some pretty derogatory words to get under people's skin…that's all."

"Yet you seem to be able to handle her disparaging shenanigans. Are you insinuating I cannot?"

Okay, this isn't going anywhere. He took a moment to think things through. Resignation kicking in that she was not going to back down. How was Josephine going to react to this request? Even worse, he was going to have to beg Josie to be nice to her and possibly lie about their payment arrangement. Shit! This definitely wasn't going to be an easy request.

He took another glance back at Sophia's face. She looked like she was getting more pissed by the second. *I guess this is the way it's going to go down.* So without wasting anymore time, he gave into her demand.

"Although I don't think this is a good idea, I can understand where you're coming from. If this is what it will take to set your mind at ease then I will do it. I'll arrange a time for all of us to meet up, okay?"

She let out a sigh of relief. "Thank you, I'll feel much better after I have a little chat with her." She put down her bag and went over to the couch. Then gave him a half smile and gestured for him to come over.

He took her hand and gave it a kiss. "I'm glad you're back, love." She nodded in agreeance. "Is it all right if I hold you?"

"Yes, I would like that very much actually." She got up and put her back against his chest. They sat there together for a while, both in their own thoughts at first. Until Sebastian broke the silence.

He pulled her hair back and gave her a kiss on the neck. Then whispered in her ear, "*Tu seras toujours le seul pour moi, Sophia.* …You will always be the only one for me."

She brought her arm up to his head and lightly brushed her hand through his hair. "I love you, Sebastian."

"I love you too." They spent the rest of the afternoon intertwined with one another.

By the time nightfall came, they were starving. "Do you want me to order something for delivery?" He picked up his phone and saw he had a new text.

Margaret: Sebastian, I have people who are ready to see you. I have them booked for tomorrow starting at 9am. Let me know if that will not work for you? I can always reschedule.

Damn… It meant he would need a cleansing right after he finished. He was hoping to get more time with Sophia before he had to go talk with Josephine. However, getting the talk over with had some merit to it as well. He already had so much other stress weighing on his shoulders; it might not be a bad thing to take this problem off the table.

"Who texted you?" He needed to make a quick decision. So he went with his gut. "Um, yeah… It's Margaret. She is ready for us to come in tomorrow."

Good, she thought. "Guess that means you will need to see her after you finish, right?"

"Yes, it does."

"Perfect, let's just get this over with, shall we." Her level of enthusiasm for seeing Josephine was beginning to scare him a little. How harsh was she planning to be with her? He'd never known Sophia to be so smug. He definitely needed to prep Josephine. Avoiding her comment, he told her he needed a second to message Margaret back.

Sebastian: Sounds good, Margaret. Sophia and I will be there a little before 9 am?

Margaret: Great, see you then.

Sebastian: K.

He put his cell down and walked back over to her. "Sophia, love…if it's okay with you, can we not bring her name up anymore? I promise when I see her tomorrow, I will make an appointment for us to meet. But until then, I would love it if we could just focus on us. I have not seen you in weeks."

"I actually think that is a good idea."

That night they opted out on ordering food and landed up cooking dinner at home. Making food together had become somewhat of a thing for them. It always seemed to make them more at one with each other. Which set the tone for the rest of the night. They went to sleep both feeling closer than ever. *Please let it stay this way,* was the last thing he thought before closing his eyes to sleep.

Chapter 16
Pinched

The next morning they woke up early and got ready for work. By the time 8:40 am hit, they were out the door and arrived at the office a couple of minutes before 9:00 am.

As they came in, they saw Margaret working on a sketch.

"Hey there."

She peeked up from her paper. "Hello guys, long time no see." She got up and gave them both a hug.

Sebastian pointed to her drawing, "What's this about?"

"I'm trying to sketch out what I saw in my dream last night."

Sebastian studied it more intently. "It looks like some sort of a building."

"Yes, actually, I believe I saw a vision of what the spiritual center will look like in full color."

"Is that right?"

Sophia came in for a closer look as well. "Wow, that's amazing that you're getting full blown visions of it now. Did you get a glimpse of the inside as well?"

"No, I didn't. Hopefully, I'll dream of that next."

"We can't wait to see it when you're finished."

"I know; me too. I'll make sure to show you guys when it's done."

Seconds later, they heard a car pull up. It was a Mercedes-Benz SL Roadster. Sebastian glanced at Sophia. "Wow, that's a beaut." He quickly gave her a kiss and started walking towards his room. "Just send him in when you're ready, Margaret."

"Will do."

Shortly afterwards, Margaret opened the door and introduced him to a young man named Marcus. He could immediately feel his trepidation. "Thank you, Margaret, I can take it from here." She left quietly closing the door behind her. "Hello, Marcus, please…take a seat." He slowly sat down in his chair.

"So…I see it would ease your mind very much if you understood a little more how I operate, correct?"

"Yes."

"Fair enough, Marcus. It goes something like this. I have abilities that help me find the root of where your problems lie.

"One of them is the ability to see Spirit. What I mean by that is people who have already died and crossed over to the other side can sometimes come back and visit us. The other form of spirit I'm referring to is your personal angels. We all have them, it just so happens I can see them as well. Their job is to help us get through the challenging parts of our lifecycle.

"Another gift of mine is the ability to see your past history. I view it through your archives located on the other side. I know it's a little hard to understand, but you'll see once we get into the thick of it."

Marcus sat there for a moment utterly shocked by what he had learned. When he finally got his wits together, he asked Sebastian if he had the power to view his entire existence.

"Yes, I do if need be. However, that is usually not the case. I merely observe the parts where the pain lies deepest in your soul. The purpose in that is to mend the affliction you are having trouble releasing. It is why you are here today, right? To get it all…out." He nodded his head in agreeance.

Only internally, Sebastian could see he was battling with the idea of showing someone else his past. "Can you already see my history?"

"No, Marcus, I have not started the process of all that yet. You obviously have concerns about me doing that. In fact, even in this instance, you are deciding if you should stay or go."

"How could you know that?"

"I am able to feel your internal energy. But that is not important to discuss right now." He reached in a little closer to Marcus. "Let me tell you what is going on in your own pathway. Whatever you are holding onto is stopping you from achieving your true purpose. I can see a shift in your road that was already supposed to transpire. Which has put you off course a bit from the road you are meant to be on.

"I can tell you with clarity, when that shift finally takes place, it will ultimately lead to the happiness you are seeking."

His facial expression suddenly gravitated to a frown. “What if I don’t deserve happiness? What if it is justified that I live the rest of my life in despair and anguish?”

“Believe me when I say this, Marcus…we have all done things we are not proud of. I mean, painful, horrific things we sometimes cannot take back. That doesn’t mean you should live in punishment for the rest of your life.”

“You voice this now, Sebastian, but you have not yet seen my journey.”

“It doesn’t matter what I see, I will not judge you. Try to understand that the point of our existence is to make whatever mistakes you are going to make and then grow from them; otherwise, what is the point of living at all?”

“Still, I—”

Sebastian held his hand out, politely interrupting him. “Your mistakes, Marcus, are a piece of you, yes; however, they do not own you, and they certainly do not define who you are in your soul.”

He sat there, taking Sebastian’s remarks into account. After a couple of minutes, he finally conceded. “Where do we go from here?”

“Give me some time to find the point of your grief.” He closed his eyes and began the meditation process. Soon after, footprints of Marcus’s life began to scroll through his mind. He viewed his footprints for a very long time, until he finally got to the root of his pain. He had to pause for a second to think of how he was going to approach the subject matter. This was going to be a rough ride for him. Even so, there was no easy way to voice what needed to be said. He decided it would be best to just be straightforward with him.

“Listen, Marcus, first…I want to thank you for letting me into your life. I know how difficult it was for you. I see what has been eating at you.”

Immediately, Marcus got up and began to pace the room. “So you know then?”

“Yes, I know.” Sebastian felt his energy wanting to leave the room. He was freaking out!

“Please, don’t take off, Marcus, stay and hear me out.” He didn’t answer him, instead he continued to hold his head down and pace the floor. “Marcus…try to understand, sometimes we fall a certain way because of the circumstances we lived through.

“In your case you were not given the tools to live in a more humane way. When you were a child, your parents’ job was to mold you in the right direction. Despite that, they failed you epically in that area. The divorce got the best of them. You were only eight years old when all hell broke loose in their relationship.

"Unfortunately, you never got a chance to recover from their parting. The divorce had your parents venomously fighting over custody battles and finances. They continuously put you in the middle of their conflicts. It hurt you deeply to hear them degrade each other over and over again.

"They didn't realize the toll it was taking on your mental health. Being that young, you were still learning how to emotionally handle pain and conflict. In enough time of living in that environment, you learned saying unspeakable things to others is just a normal way to live. Because of that, it changed your heart and made you numb to humanity.

"Before you knew it, you started bullying kids at school. Picking on the ones you knew wouldn't fight back. I see that you were very popular in school. So rarely did anyone ever call you out on it. In fact, most of the time the crowd was in your favor, which egged you on even more to keep the behavior going. And you enjoyed the attention you got out of it.

"So the harassment continued to get worse as you got older and wiser. There was one particular kid in high school that stood out to you. His name was Oliver. He was the one you targeted most with your negative energy. Of course, there were others. But, you preferred to pick on him if he was around."

Marcus started to lose it again. "Sebastian, please…you need to stop…I can't do this."

"You can, Marcus. I promise you, it will begin the process of releasing some of the heartache. Besides, there is more to come than merely telling your story."

"What do you mean?"

"I don't know yet, I can just feel something coming."

Marcus lowered his head in thought for a moment. Eventually, he softly uttered, "Go on then, Sebastian."

"All right." Carefully easing his way back into the conversation, he continued, "One day, you noticed Oliver did not show up for school. You thought it was strange because he was the kind of kid who always had perfect attendance. However, not long after, you brushed the thought away. There were others to bully in his place anyway.

"A week went by and still no Oliver. Out of sheer curiosity, you went up to the school attendant and asked about him. Her facial expression appeared uneasy. She moved in closer to you and quietly whispered to you that Oliver had passed away. '…I was told he committed suicide.'"

"You couldn't believe he had killed himself."

"Sebastian, stop!…I need a moment!" Seeing that Marcus was about ready to lose it again, he gave him his space to free his grievances. He watched as he sat in his chair with his elbows propped over his knees and his hands wrapped across his face.

All Marcus could think about was the ending to his story. A deep feeling of sadness ran through his body. While at the same time, a rushing sense of urgency to get the ugliness out became a necessary thing to do. It was like he couldn't help himself. Internally, he kept repeatedly shouting to himself…*Get this out. Get this out! Get this out of me!*

He abruptly stood up and stared at Sebastian. It was a look of understanding that they both knew what needed to happen next. "I believe it's my turn to be the narrator of the story now. Don't you think?"

"It's what I have been waiting for, Marcus." He eyes started to water as he took a long deep breath before sitting back down in his chair.

"It was the day before graduation. The teacher told us it was time to clean out our lockers. I opened mine up and instead of going through all the paperwork and books…I grabbed everything and shoved it in my backpack.

"That night, I dumped everything out on my bed and started sifting through all my stuff. I was surprised to find a note. I got excited at first because I thought maybe a girl from school wrote me a letter and squeezed it through my locker vent."

He stopped for a second to grab a crumbled piece of paper out of his back pocket. Then he opened it up and after a few short moments, he began to read it out loud:

Dear Marcus,

I can't take the mental beatings you give me anymore. I'm crying out loud for you to please leave me alone! Because I'm telling you that if you don't, I won't make it to graduation.

Oliver

Tears began to stream down his face as the truth finally came out. "I didn't know, Sebastian! I didn't understand how much my words were affecting him. I swear to God! Why in the world could I not have found his letter before he killed himself? I know it would have been enough for me to have stopped. I can't stomach the pain of knowing I was the reason for his death." More tears began to wail out as he continued to think about the pain he inflicted on Oliver.

It was in that moment when Sebastian felt three presence enter the room. Two of them were angels. The other was Oliver. He didn't want to interrupt Marcus' admissions. So he spoke to them telepathically. *"It's nice to see you, Oliver. I'm sorry for the fate you have suffered."* Only he said nothing in return.

"Sorry," one of the angels spoke up, *"he is very weak in this realm. So he is saving all his strength for his conversation with Marcus."*

"Yes, I see he is not from any realm I recognize. Why is that?"

"He has been residing at a place where the dead go when they leave earth before it was their time to exit.

"All humans who leave before their lifecycle has been fulfilled go to this space. We have been assigned to watch over him while he goes through the process of pushing out the pain. Sadly, we have not made much progress with him yet. He keeps focusing on reliving his nightmare story over and over again in his head.

"At this point, since both of them are off their written path, we thought bringing them together might be beneficial."

"Why did you not bring him here earlier so he could have heard Marcus's acknowledgements?"

"Oh, believe me, he heard every word of his story. We were in between realms while you guys were going through the journey. As we said before, this realm is extremely fragile to him. It's why it's so rare that we ever bring a soul back on earth before they are fully healed. However, in this case, with Marcus being in the state that he is in, we felt otherwise."

"So you believe he is going to be able to handle interacting with Marcus?"

"Now that Oliver has heard his side of the story, he is ready to ask questions."

"Okay, let's see where this leads then. Give me a second to prep Marcus." They all nodded.

He was still quietly letting out tears. "Marcus, what you admitted today was brave. And I believe when we finish all this, the pain will finally unravel from your soul. But I need you to be brave one more time."

"What do you mean?" He took a deep breath before releasing what he needed to say.

"Marcus, two angels are present in this room right now. They also brought someone else with them as well."

Understanding quickly hit him. "Oh, shit, it's Oliver, isn't it? My God! Did he hear the whole thing?"

"It's going to be all right, Marcus. Give me a chance to explain. The angels felt it would be good for you to face him. You should consider this a miracle. From what they said, not many souls come back to earth if they have exited in the way he did.

"He has been stuck on a different realm all this time, trying to recover from the pain. Unfortunately, he has not been very successful. So when they saw the opportunity to put the two of you together, they made a rare decision to bring him back."

"He must absolutely be repulsed by me, Sebastian."

"We won't know how he feels until we do, right?"

He took a moment to absorb his circumstances. He was overwhelmed with emotion. The fact that Oliver was standing in the same room as him was a blessing in and of itself. All the same, he was terrified of the outcome. Of what he had to face now that the opportunity has presented itself. Still, at the end of the day, he came to the same conclusion…it was now or never.

"Okay…where is he positioned?"

"To the left of you. Except hold on a second, Marcus. I believe he has some questions for you first."

"Oh, I'm sorry, of course, he would want answers."

"Let me see what he has to express."

Sebastian glanced back towards Oliver. "Go ahead and begin whenever you are ready." He wasted no time revealing what was on his mind. "I want to know, what I ever did to make him hate me so much?" Sebastian brought his attention back over to Marcus and disclosed the question to him.

"No Oliver, no…you got it wrong. I mean, understandably I can see why you felt that way. Even so, I never hated you. Honestly, I didn't even know you well enough to hate you. Which makes it all the worse that I could torture another human being so hard that he would…that you would…" He took a moment to calm his nerves, before continuing.

"…When I learned that I was the person behind your death, it opened me to see a new reality about myself. A crushing reality, actually. An awareness came upon me that I am truly ugly inside. That I grew up to become the worst version of myself. And you had to suffer the wrath of my ugliness."

Sebastian turned towards Oliver, to receive his response. "He says…all this time, when he thought you had read his note and continued to torment him, it was because you put no value to his existence. He already thought so little of himself. For you to agree with his own verdict, it was his ruin."

Marcus slowly got down on his knees at that point. Tears running down the sides of his cheeks. "Oliver, please understand…" His voice started to raise an octave. "I'm sorry for all the misery I caused you. I'm sorry for the years you spent in that realm trying to get over the affliction I put upon you. I can never give you back your life, but I can tell you without a doubt that if I had read your letter in time, I would have stopped the harassment. I do value your life more than you could possibly imagine. I swear to you, I never wanted you to die!

"…Also, you need to know what a terrible mental state I was in myself. Anybody who enjoys bringing someone else down like I did is sick in their own head. That is where I was at, when I bullied you. I see the consequences of my actions left a deep wound in your soul. Again, I am truly sorry for that. But Oliver, I'm begging you to move on from that realm! You never deserved to be there in the first place!"

Marcus, brought his head down, feeling the shame of it all. "I completely understand if you can never forgive me. Regardless of that, leave from whatever hell you are living in and be free of the suffering I caused you. If I could, I would take the pain you are holding onto and place it upon my shoulders to carry with me for the rest of my time on earth."

After those words came out, he remained silent. Oliver, was speechless as well. He had never known Marcus in such a humbled state. It gave him…peace. It was in that moment he had made amends with the way his path turned out. His soul began the process of reconciling with the pain. Before he knew it, he felt a deep urge to start over again.

He turned to face to his angels. "I'm ready to start the process of seeking the light. He has given me what I needed to hear. Although before I leave, it would be great if you could leave Marcus with one last message."

Sebastian listened to what he said and then turned back towards Marcus.

"Your words have given him what he needed. He has begun the transformation of letting go. I can see it has almost been completely dissipated, merging back into the universe where it belongs. By the time I am finished translating his last message to you, it will be fully released. And he will be free to start a new life, if he chooses to do so."

"What is the message?"

"He says to tell you…as you get older and start to have children of your own, be conscious of how you raise them. Teach them to be strong and stand up for others who are beaten down by the heartless. We need a more powerful network of humans that will raise people's spirits, not break them down. As you can understand the most, it all starts with the parents. That is all he asks of you."

Marcus was so taken back by his request. Such a simple, yet important calling. "Yes, Oliver, although you ask very little after what I have put you through, I promise to honor your request. I will be a part of the solution of raising a new generation of kids to have a kinder more evolved state of mind. And I will advocate to always stand up for the weak against the bullies of this world. I see now that it starts with us leading the way. I can't ever thank you enough, Oliver, for giving me a chance to become a better human being."

With that, the angels turned to Oliver. "I believe Marcus knows his new purpose on earth, and now it is time for you to find out yours."

"Yes, let us go then." Seconds later, they all vanished.

Marcus sat there in awe of what took place. After taking a couple of minutes to let it all sink in, he was finally able to get up out of his chair. Sebastian followed suit. "Thank you so much for everything you have done for me. The weight has been lifted and I look forward to keeping Oliver's promise."

"Good, the world needs more people to follow down your road, my friend."

Then he shook Sebastian's hand and left.

Margaret came into the room not long after he left. "Sebastian, I don't know what occurred here today, but he left us a 10,000 dollar donation."

"That's great, Margaret. I can't believe he gave so much money."

"Frankly, I'm not surprised. I told you this would happen. On his way out, he asked me to thank you for your contribution to humanity and promised to be more like you."

"Wow, that was kind of him."

"Yes, well, I kind of have to agree with him."

"All right, enough about me, what time does the next appointment arrive?"

She checked her watch. "Oh, I'm afraid any minute. Marcus's meeting took longer than usual. Do you need more time?"

"No, I'm good, let me just step outside for a moment. Can you come get me when they arrive."

"Of course."

He sat outside, thinking about what had transpired between Oliver and Marcus. They were both truly handed a miracle and he was the person who gave it to them. His gifts were more extraordinary then he ever thought possible. It made him feel so good inside to help another human being on that level. While all at the same time, he was living through his own private hell.

It was difficult for him to flip flop back and forth from both realities. During the day, he was filled with only joyful outcomes. By nighttime, he would have to deal with Josephine and beg her to go along with his needs to keep Sophia satisfied. It would be difficult to pull that off. He stayed lost in those thoughts until Margaret stepped out on the back porch and lightly tapped him on the shoulders. "It's time." He gave out a deep sigh and told her he was coming.

Sebastian went through three more appointments before Margaret came back in and told him he was done for the day. "I booked more on Friday, if that is okay with you?"

"Sure, it's fine."

Sophia came into the room a couple of minutes later. He had just put his phone down from writing a text. "How are you?"

"I'm good."

"Sorry I couldn't check up on you earlier. Now that things have started to pick up around here, Margaret has been keeping me busy."

"No worries, love."

Then an awkward silence arose between the two of them knowing what needed to happen next. Eventually, Sebastian spoke up. "I wanted to let you know that as soon as I receive a text back from her, I'll be heading out. Did you ask Margaret if she could bring you home?"

"Yes, she said it would be no problem."

Seconds later, his phone buzzed.

"Is that her?"

He looked at his phone. "Yes."

"Can you call me when you finish with her?"

"Yeah, promise I will." He gave her a kiss on the lips and embraced her with his arms. "I'll see you soon."

"K." After giving her another hug, he grabbed his keys and left.

He arrived at her house in less than twenty minutes. Driving up to a black wrought iron gate, he rang the buzzer. It opened almost instantly. "That was fast." He drove in and parked his car next to a beautiful Greek cream-colored fountain. Walking up to the porch, he realized she did not have a doorbell like normal people. No, she had one of those loud iron doorknockers. *Figures...*

When she opened the door, he was immediately taken aback. She was wearing practically nothing apart from a short, tight black dress that was almost see-through. "Well, hello, Sebastian. Come on in."

He entered her doorway and passed by the dining room. The door to it was halfway open. From a quick glance, it looked like she was setting up some sort of party in there.

"Hope I'm not intruding, it seems like you have your hands busy."

"Yes, I am getting things set up for something special tonight." When they got to the living room, she sat down across from him. Then she slowly took one leg and folded it across the other. There wasn't much he didn't see in that exchange. "Ready for your cleanse?" Not wanting to go there with whatever she was trying to expose, he answered her with a nod.

She closed her eyes and once again, within seconds, he felt euphoric inside. "Thank you."

"No need to thank me, Sebastian. You will be earning every ounce of what you owe me in the future.

"So, now that your needs have been met, tell me how has life been treating you?"

He did not want to have this conversation with her. His anxiety level was running so high he thought he was going to start hyperventilating. However, he had promised Sophia he would make it happen.

His approach was to be as humble to whatever words she dished out to him. "Um…I am actually glad you asked. I have something I wanted to discuss with you."

"Wow, I actually thought you were simply going to make small talk and leave." *Jesus, this guy…* She grabbed her glass and took a sip. Then flung her other hand up in the air for him to start talking.

"Ah, yeah, I just have this tiny situation that I could really use your help with."

"Huh…more help? What a strange request." She moved her body in closer to his. "So what is it this time?"

"Well, you see, Sophia is not exactly happy with the fact that I came to you for assistance."

"And how is that my problem, Sebastian?"

"…It's not actually. I know that. Even so, it would mean a great deal to me if you could take a small twenty minutes of your time to meet up with us. If you could just answer a few of her questions, it would set her mind at ease and then this whole problem would go away."

She gave out the most wicked laugh. "You've got to be kidding me! Why in the world would I do something like that for her?"

"I know I'm asking a lot, Josie. But I've tried to alter her way of thinking and nothing is changing her mind. It's the only way she can tolerate our arrangement."

"Oh, you want to talk arrangement! Because I'm definitely dying to hear what kind of deal you told her we struck together. I'm sure you wouldn't want me to go behind her back and lie to her…right Sebastian!"

He pushed his hand through his hair. "I promise you, I would not be here begging you to do this for me if I had a choice in the matter. I know what an inconvenience this would be to you, at the very least. And you're right, I'm completely aware of what a hypocrite I am to you right now. Asking you to lie to her on my behalf is fucked up. Still, I had to give it a try with you."

She got up and started walking around the room. "I've got to admit it takes some kahunas to come ask me for a favor like this. I take it she will leave you if you do not come home with the news she wants to hear?"

"Eventually, she will, yes. She cannot live with the fact that you will be a part of my life now. The only way she can get past it is by having some control over the situation."

"So on top of showing up to this fucked up meeting of hers, she wants to piss all over me to let me know the pecking order of our relationship! Oh right, Sebastian, I absolutely understand why you felt you could come to me! It sounds exactly like something I would do out of the kindness of my heart!" She was all riled up at this point.

Suddenly, she picked up the glass next to her and through it against the wall. She was starting to completely lose it. "I need another drink!" She left the room, screaming incoherent words to him.

Holy Shit! This was exactly what he had feared. He sat there in total terror, waiting for her return.

Ten minutes later, she came back. This time, her demeanor had totally changed. She was calm again, almost too composed. *What the hell is going on with her?* She sat back down and put her drink to the side.

Then he watched as a small grin began to form on her lips. Unfortunately, he knew that smirk all too well. She was up to something. He knew in that split second that his agreement with her was about to get so much worse. He tried to swiftly backpedal his way out of it.

"Again, I was simply just asking, Josie. Obviously, it's not something you are willing to entertain. That's fine. It was stupid of me to even bring this up to you. I'll make my way out and you can go back to whatever you were doing."

"I don't think so, Sebastian. You need to finish what you started with me. Fortunate for you, I found a way to see an upside to this. However, it will be in exchange for a few new things we will be adding to our contract."

"No, Josephine, I told you…I'm all right. I should never have brought it up. My fault for doing that."

"Are you done yet, Sebastian?"

"Listen, I'll just see my way out." He got up and started to walk towards the hallway. Only to get yanked right back in with her words and tone of voice.

"If you walk out that door before we renegotiate, you will never receive a single cleanse from me again!"

Goddamn it! She wasn't even interested in helping me a hot minute ago. What changed her mind so quickly?

"So, these will be the new terms in our agreement. I'll go play nice with your little girlfriend and even make sure she knows my services came at a fair market rate. But you will owe me, honey. Oh, you will owe me big time!"

My God, this woman is going to be the death of me! "Josephine, please… please try to understand. I'm just trying to keep both strings of my life afloat. What else would you have me do for you?"

"All in due time, my friend."

"Making me wait is even worse than knowing!"

"I think it merely sets the tone for how annoyed you have made me tonight. Besides, I'm doing exactly what you asked me to do in the first place. Really, you should be thanking me."

He was desperate to get out of this new deal. However, he knew there was nothing he could do. He was about to get up and walk out with his tail between his legs when to his surprise, she continued on with more conditions.

"There will also be no more breakups at this point. So you better hope and pray she doesn't break up with you, because that will lead to the termination of our agreement as well."

"Josie, I cannot possibly predict if or when she might break up with me. Our relationship is extremely vulnerable right now. She didn't even speak to me for over two and a half weeks. How can you hold me accountable for the future?"

She walked over to him and brushed her hand through his hair, then rested it on the back of his neck. "I would stop right where you are at…Sebastian. You're not very good at this game." Then she leaned his head over to her lips and whispered in his ear, "I'm capable of way crueler things than these tiny little changes I am making to this contract."

Before he knew it, she gave him a long sensual kiss on his ear. *Shit…I'm so fucked!* Eventually, she slowly let go of his hair. "Now let's plan on meeting this Friday at 6 pm. I have not thought of a place yet. I'll get back with you on that."

Then she planted a quick kiss on his cheek and began to walk away. "I'm thinking you can find your way out?" His face turned pale as he thought about what she might expect him to do with her. Despite that, he could not do a thing about it. He should never have come in the first place.

Chapter 17
Tip Toe

The days that led up to Friday were difficult to get through. The new deal he was forced to take with Josephine definitely threw him for a loop. It made him more depressed than ever. In the meantime, he was busy nursing Sophia back to health. She had become very ill with a stomach virus.

Fortunately, it looked like the worst part was behind her. Although she was feeling much better, she still opted out on going to work with him today. She wanted to save her strength for tonight's meeting with Josephine.

"Hey love, I'll miss you today."

"Me too." He gave her a hug and kissed her on the forehead. "I'll be home around 5:30 pm to pick you up."

"Sounds good." He took off to work soon after.

When he arrived at the office, he noticed another car was already there. Strange, that was not what Margaret usually drove. He glanced down at his phone and saw he was 20 minutes early. He also realized he had missed a text.

Margaret: Mr. Church said he was coming this morning to do some repairs around the house. Obviously, he has his own key to get in so it's no big deal if he gets there before us. I merely wanted to give you a heads up in case you arrive ahead of me.

Sebastian: Yes, I believe he is already here. Thanks for letting me know. I'll see you soon!

He walked into the house and saw Christopher in the kitchen working on some pipes underneath the sink. "Hey man, what's up?" He moved his body out from where he was at.

"Hey there, good to see you. I was just thinking about you recently. I wanted to tell you that I finally proposed to Leslie!"

"That's awesome, congratulations!"

"Yeah, I'm only glad you suggested to plan things out or I might not ever have gotten engaged to her."

"Stop…you would have done it eventually." He got up from the floor and sat down on one of the chairs.

"So what is going on with you and Sophia?"

"Oh wow, a lot has happened since we last spoke. We are much better on one hand, but now there are new complications. She came over to my house a couple days after I saw you."

"Well, at least that's great news."

"Yeah, it definitely is great that she came back. However, understandably, in order for her to feel comfortable with the circumstances, she made me promise to do something that I should never have done."

"Oh man, sorry to hear that. Is there anything I can do?"

"I wish, but no, there is nothing anyone can do. I'll simply have to wait it out and see how things turn out."

"So it's a waiting game, huh?"

"Pretty much."

"Do you ever find yourself needing a distraction from the chaos in your head?"

"What do you mean?"

"It's just I can image what you must be going through right now. Waiting to see how the chessboard plays out. While at the same time, you can't stop thinking about all the worst case scenarios that could happen to everyone involved."

"You could say that sounds an awful lot like my life at this moment. The only thing that stops me from that sort of thought is when I'm busy helping people heal. However since we are merely at the beginning stage of our business, Margaret usually only has a couple days a week lined up for me."

"Huh, you know what…I honestly didn't expect you to say that. Nevertheless, if supernatural stuff works as a deterrent for you, then I might be able to help you out."

"What are you suggesting?"

"Well, as I told you before, I'm obsessed with the paranormal. It just so happens I rented out a time slot to do a hunt at the Waverly Hills Sanitarium. Do you want to come along for the ride?" He was taken aback by the invite.

"Frankly, you would really be helping me out. It would give me an opportunity to test my equipment against your knowledge to see how accurate it truly is. That should keep your mind pretty busy."

As he was finishing his last word, a thought began to register in Sebastian's mind as to where he wanted to conduct this hunt. It caused him to chuckle a little inside. "You know, Christopher, you don't have to go to one of the most haunted places in Louisville in order to track a ghost down. Hell, there's probably one right down the street from us."

"I know…I know…but throw me a bone, will ya. I've been told by more than a few people that I can be a bit eccentric with my ideas. This is merely how I roll. Thank God, Leslie is awesome enough to put up with my crazy antics."

"That's hilarious. Is she into the supernatural as much as you?"

"I'm afraid not…although she puts up with it, it doesn't necessarily mean she likes to be a part of it."

"That's too bad, I would have liked to have met her."

"So I take it that means you're in?"

"Yeah, it sounds like fun. Thanks for the invite."

"No problem, man."

A second later, Margaret walked into the kitchen. "Hey guys, what's going on?"

"Oh, you know…normal conversation. Christopher here just lured me into going on a ghost hunt with him at the Waverly."

She stared at them like they were crazy. "Okay, well, that's one you don't hear very often." They all laughed.

"Anyway, I only wanted to let you know that your appointment should be here soon."

"All right, guess it's time to go then." He looked back over to Christopher. "What date do you have it scheduled for?"

"Aw, yes, it's this Thursday from 4-6 pm."

"4 pm?"

"…What?"

"Well, you have to admit, if you're going for crazy scary, that time frame doesn't quite fit the mold."

"All right…all right, you got me on that one. But unfortunately, it was the only time they had left to rent."

"No, it's cool, man, I was just giving you a hard time. In my experience, ghosts are not particular as to what time they choose to climb out of the walls."

"You would know, buddy."

He glanced back down at his watch. "Shoot, I really do need to go."

"Okay, so listen, let's plan on meeting here first around 3:20 pm."

"Sounds good. I'll see you then."

"Later."

He quickly turned around and took off to his room. The first person who came to see him was seeking advice on a medical situation. He felt he had been diagnosed wrong, but his current doctor would not believe him. He was desperate for answers. Sebastian landed up confirming he was right about the wrong diagnosis. Ultimately, through the help of his angels they gave him the name of another doctor in town that could help sort things out.

As the day went by, he went through three more people. The last one was particularly difficult. He had to help a mother mourn the loss of her three children. They had died in a car accident. Thankfully, they were all able to come visit her. Having an opportunity to speak with them one last time was the medicine she needed in order to move on with her life. She could finally say goodbye to them in peace.

Margaret came in shortly after she left. "She told me to tell you she was more grateful then you could ever imagine and she left a pretty hefty donation as well."

"Oh, um, that's great, Margaret."

She could tell something was on his mind. "Are you okay?"

"Yes, there's just something I have to do tonight that's weighing on me."

"I hope whatever you are going through is not too troubling? I hate to see you or Sophia burdened about anything."

"Your words are kind, Margaret. Thank you for caring."

She gave him a smile in response. "Well, you better go now, you told me you need to leave by 5:10 pm. It's almost that time."

"Okay, when do you want me to come back to work?"

"If you can come in on Monday and Wednesday, that would be great."

"All right, I'll see you then."

She watched his body language as he left the room. *Whatever is going on with him, it is definitely taking a toll.* It made her sad to see him so upset. But she knew there was nothing she could do.

He got home at 5:30 pm, exactly as he said he would. "Hey love, you look beautiful. Are you ready to go?"

"Yes, let's do this." She grabbed her purse and they took off. Not wanting to bring up Josephine's name, they made small talk until they got there.

They walked into the restaurant holding hands. "Let me see if she is here yet." He went up to the host. "There should be a reservation under the name Josie."

"Yeah, she has already been seated, follow me."

He could tell Sophia was a little nervous by the way she was holding his hand. "It's going to be okay, love." He brought her hand up to his lips and gave it a kiss. She landed up taking them to one of their private booths.

"Aw…so you've finally arrived. It's good to see you again, Sophia." She gave off a smug smile.

"Thank you for meeting with us, Josephine."

"Well, I didn't really have a choice, did I, dear?"

"What do you mean by that?"

The waiter came over at that moment and interrupted their exchange. "What can I get you to drink?"

Josephine was the first to speak up. "I'll take a Manhattan."

Sebastian looked at Sophia and got a silent response. Glancing back towards the waiter, he told him they didn't want anything for now.

"So, I was simply saying that it seemed you were going to give Sebastian such a difficult time if I did not show up. Well, I couldn't have that now, could I."

"You know what, I'm not sure I like the tone of how you speak about him."

"Sophia, I'm confused…would you like me to not care for him? Because, when I don't care for someone, my wrath could be quite…excruciating."

Jesus Christ, this is already not going well. I thought she was going to play nice. I've got to somehow change the subject matter. "Josephine, maybe this would be a good time to give me a cleanse. I'm in need of one pretty badly right now. This will give Sophia a chance to see how you help me."

Just then, the waiter came back with her drink. "Thank you." Surprisingly, she grabbed all the menus and handed them back to him. "I don't think this is the kind of crowd that is going to eat today. But don't worry; you'll still make a handsome tip that I'll leave in exchange for our privacy." She gave him a devilish grin, which he appeared to enjoy very much so.

"Of course, whatever you say. If you change your mind, I'll be around."

"Thank you."

She watched him leave then started the conversation back up again. "So, as Sebastian was suggesting, would you like to see how I cleanse him?"

"Yes."

"Okay…Sebastian, go ahead and hold your hands out like you normally do."

What the fuck is she trying to pull here? Goddammit, Josephine! He took a deep breath before following her orders. Then laid them on the table to do God knows what.

"See Sophia, this is all I have to do." She gently caressed his hands for a while and then eventually gave him a cleanse. When she finished, Sebastian swiftly moved them away from her. "I don't recall him ever telling me that you need to touch hands in order for you to do your thing with him."

"Oh, that's such a small detail compared to the magnitude of the release I provide him. It's probably the last thing on his mind. Right, Sebastian?"

He glanced over at Sophia. She looked like she could throw daggers at them both. He needed to somehow calm the situation down. "Sophia, I'm sorry. It's just the darkness can get so intolerable, I swear having her touch my hands to give me what I need is necessary."

Why the fuck is she causing so much chaos!

"So let's move on then, shall we. Sebastian tells me you have a few questions to ask." She was about to bring one up, but Josephine simply kept on talking. "Yeah…he said if I could do this for him, it would set your mind at ease. I mean, how caring of him to respect you so much that he wants to set your mind at ease, even though he is the one in the desperate situation."

Sophia scoffed at that. "You are just talking out of your ass, Josephine. I don't need you to tell me how much he respects me…understood! Our relationship is our business. Your job is to cleanse, that is what he is paying you for right? You are nothing but a vendor to him."

Sebastian was starting to sweat this one out. He began to nervously brush his hand through his hair. That's when Josie let out a brisk bolt of laughter. "My, my… Sophia. So there is some spice in you after all! How…endearing. But it looks like you are starting to stress him out a bit. See how he just put his hand through his hair. Yeah, that's a tell-tale sign he's uncomfortable. Believe me, I should know."

"Are you freakin' kidding me, Josephine? Nobody knows Sebastian more than me! And if I make him uncomfortable, I'm close enough to him to know that he would put up with anything I dish out to him. There is a simple reason for that. He loves me! You can dance your way around this conversation all you want, but at the end of the day…know that he is simply using you for his fix. Are you picking up what I'm putting down now, Josephine!"

"Crystal clear on what you are putting down, Sophia." Just then, a grin began to blossom across her lips. *Oh no…please reign it back in, Josephine.* "What you are saying is that I need to watch how I speak to your lovely boyfriend. You think I treat him a little closer than I should. Is that right?" She arrogantly nodded in agreement.

"So I take it you are okay with our payment arrangement we have set up." *What in the world are you doing, she hasn't even brought that up*!

"What about the agreement?"

"It's just your jealous behavior is surprising today given the fact that you know how he intends to pay for my services."

She glanced over to Sebastian. "What is she talking about?"

"I'm entirely as much in the dark as you are, Sophia. Josephine, please tell her the truth, tell her about our financial arrangement."

"Financial? I thought I made it clear to you that I don't want money from this deal."

"Josephine, come on. What are you doing?"

"Sophia, listen to me dear…he's only agreed to give me one good go at him. That's it! After that, he's all yours again. I was under the impression that you wouldn't mind sharing him in order for him to receive what he needs…from me."

"Agreed to give you one good go at him? What the hell are you saying?"

"It's simple, really. He has consented to give me one sensual intimate performance with me in exchange for a cleanse whenever he desires one." Sophia was stunned to the core.

Josephine stared at her. "Oh dear." She turned her head back towards Sebastian. "Looks like you never let the cat out the bag, did you? I'm sorry if I messed things up for you. I only wanted to make sure we were all crystal clear on where the pecking order was at in our little triangle here."

"Get…up…and let me out of this booth right now, Sebastian!"

"Sophia, she is lying. I swear to you."

"Let me out or I swear to God, I'm going to scream at the top of my lungs for help!" All he could do was let her out at this point.

She ran out of the restaurant and he was about to follow her. But Josephine grabbed his arm and pushed him back down in his seat. "Where do you think you're going? I have some words to say to you. But hold on just a second, you're gonna need this." She saw their waiter through the corner of her eye and waved him over.

"Can I get you something else?"

"Yes, the gentleman will have one of your top shelf bourbons; I'm thinking he's the kind of guy who likes it straight up. Am I right, Sebastian?" He didn't say anything, he simply sat there waiting for the waiter to leave. "I take it that's a yes, and I'll have another Manhattan as well, thank you."

"Sure, I'll be back soon with your drinks."

"Why did you do that, Josephine…why! I thought we made a new agreement. You said you would play nice and make up a financial arrangement. How in the world am I going to get past this with her!"

"Looks like you have your work cut out for you."

"I can't lie to her anymore!"

"Then how will you convince her otherwise?"

He knew all too well, there was nothing he could do. Not long after, the waiter came back with their drinks. As soon he put it down, Sebastian picked it up and shoved the whole thing down. "See, told ya you would need it."

She took a small sip of her Manhattan and put it down. "Let me tell you something. You came to me for help, and then later asked me to degrade myself to your girlfriend so she will feel…more at ease. But what about my comfort? Did you ever think that would be an issue? I mean, the nerve of your request to ask me to lie to her solely for your benefit.

"Naturally, anyone would find that insulting. The punishment for doing such a thing to me required you to pay a price on your relationship. I know it was a rather harsh penalty, but you simply did not get the message the first time we negotiated our deal. So I will spell it out for you one more time. The pecking order will always have me on top. Then you. Then her. Do you get it!

"And if you ever pull another stunt like that again, believe me I can make things a lot worse." His stomach turned upside down at that moment. "Now listen to me very carefully. You best put your finest acting skills forward and get her back. Because my renegotiation of the deal still stands with you!"

The thought of not being able to get what he needed to keep Sophia safe from his wrath was daunting. However, there was a real chance she would not get back together with him. "You need to give me some time to get back into her good graces. Please, be reasonable for what you are asking me to do. You were pretty convincing with your words today."

She thought about it for a second. "Okay, fine…just don't take too long with my generosity of time. I will only be patient for so long. Do we have an understanding?" He held his head down as he told her yes. "Now, I think you should go and find your precious little Sophia. I'm getting rather bored of this particular subject matter with you."

He got up and left as she requested. When he got in his car, he texted her.

Sebastian: Where are you? I'm sorry I couldn't leave immediately after you. I had a few choice words for her after you left. Believe me when I say to you that she is lying!

Minutes later…

Sebastian: Please tell me where you are at? I'm worried sick about you! I love you!

Seconds later…

Sebastian: I would never do that to you! You know me! I told you she likes to get under people's skin!

Still, she did not respond. He started driving around the neighborhood searching for where she might be. He noticed when she had left the restaurant, she had her purse in hand. Maybe she had called an Uber to take her home. Eventually, that was where he went next. But she was nowhere to be seen.

Saturday and Sunday were much the same. He camped outside her house almost the whole time.

When Monday rolled around, he went to work. Making sure not to look somber when he walked through the office door. He didn't want Margaret to worry about him more then what she already was. Thank God, she only had a couple people for him that day, otherwise he would have been forced to get another cleanse.

Tuesday came and went slowly. There was still no word from her. He was starting to lose hope. When Wednesday rolled around, he went back to work…thank God! Anything to distract him from constantly thinking of her.

Once again, he put on a happy face for Margaret. "Hey Sebastian, I've got a full house for you today." Four was his limit and she gave it all to him. By the time he was finished, he definitely needed a release.

Sebastian: Where are you?
Josephine: 112 W. Washington Street.
Sebastian: I'll be there in 20.

As he was driving, he thought about tomorrow. He was starting to look forward to seeing Christopher. He seemed to be the only one who could cheer him up these days. They had an understanding about each other. He knew what it was like to live in Sebastian's shoes. *The diversion will be welcoming*, he thought.

When he arrived at the address, he thought it was strange that the entrance was located in the back of the building. He opened the door and walked into a room no bigger than a tiny hallway space. The walls were covered with brochures of places around town. Out of the blue, a door opens up on the other side of the wall with a woman walking through it.

"Hello there. Do you have a reservation?"

"I'm looking for somebody named Josie."

"Oh yeah, she said she was expecting you. Sebastian, right?"

"Yes."

"I'll take you to her room."

She took him down a long narrow stairway. *Jesus, what is this place?* It was like he had gone back in time and was now living in the 1920s. After a second he figured it out. It was an old speakeasy bar, but it had been completely refurbished. He heard people talk about these places around town, but had never been to one before.

Leave it to Josephine to bring him to this joint. They walked through the first floor and then back up the stairs to the second. "She rented our Boudoir room for the evening. Here we are, sir. Please enjoy."

"Thank you."

He walked up to where she was sitting. "Sorry to intrude on your party."

"That's okay, Sebastian. I'm actually getting quite used to you interrupting things around me. Why don't you sit down and have a drink with my friends."

The last thing he wanted to do was sit around with her friends and make small talk. "Josephine, I'm exhausted."

She didn't take to kindly to his rejection. "Sit down, Sebastian."

Without saying another word, he sat down in the chair next to her. Shortly after, a waiter came up to him. "What can I get you sir?" Josephine looked at him with a formidable face. It was her signal that he had better order something.

"Eagle Rare…neat."

"Yes sir, I'll be right back with that."

When the waiter walked away, Josephine introduced him to her group. "So guys, this is Sebastian."

That prompted one of them to speak up. "Good God, Josie, you're right, he's exactly how you described him." He glanced directly into Sebastian's eyes. "You really do look delicious."

Josie let out a mischievous laugh. "I don't think he swims on your side of the pool, Carlson…or do you, Sebastian?"

"No, I don't."

He gave him sensual stare down. "That's too bad. I bet you would be a lot of fun in the…" The waiter came by with his drink before he could finish his sentence. "Here you go sir. Anything else I can get for you?" "No, I'm good." Josephine leaned in close to his ear. "Go ahead and take a sip." Of course, he did as he was told.

The woman sitting across from him spoke up next. "Sebastian…Josephine here tells us you are going to help make her partner sing a different tune very soon."

"Did she?" He was taken back to hear those words come out of her mouth.

He glanced back over to Josephine. "I meant to tell you myself, but my friend beat me to the punch."

He had to hold himself back from hyperventilating. "I thought you said it wasn't going to happen for a while?"

"I'm afraid we have two different perceptions of timing, Sebastian. For me, it has already been a while.

"When is the date?"

"I don't have a specific one yet. I'm merely warning you that things are starting to align perfectly with him. He's almost ready to see you in action."

All he wanted to do was get out of there. But she wasn't quite finished with her questioning. "So how are things going with Sophia? Have you won her back yet?"

"I'm still working on it."

"I see, better get a move on it."

"Then you might want to release me from here so I can continue my search for her."

She thought about it for a second. "Okay fine, I guess you have entertained us enough. Let me give you what you came here for." She closed her eyes and did her thing. It felt so good every time she released him from the darkness.

"I'll see you soon, then." Without saying goodbye to anyone, he simply got up and left.

That night when he got home, he texted Sophia again.

Sebastian: It's been five days, Sophia. Can you please just message me back that you are all right? That's all I am asking.

Ten minutes later…

Sophia: I'm all right.

He couldn't believe he had finally gotten a response from her. He knew he had to tread lightly with his next message. He didn't want to scare her off.

Sebastian: Thank you, Sophia. I simply want to leave you with these words. Do you really believe in your heart that I could ever conceivably do something that hurtful to you? Think about all the times we've spent together. Think about how much I love you!

The lies he had to say to her was torturous for him. He hated it all. Josephine was cruel-hearted making him do this to her. But for better or worse, he had made his bed. All he could do now was play out her demands.

Chapter 18
The Hunt

He needed to catch a good night sleep with all the stress he was under. However, that was not what he received. Instead, he tossed and turned all night. He woke up the next day unrested. The only thing that helped him get out of bed was the fact that he was going to get a much-needed distraction from his everyday thoughts.

Course, up until this point…the day had gone by very slow. Due to the circumstances he was under, he found himself not very hungry lately. Today, he forced himself to eat something.

He dined at one of his favorite Vietnamese joints off of Barret Avenue, called Eatz. "I'll take a bowl of your Beef Pho."

"For here or to go?"

"For here."

Five minutes later, his soup was placed on the table. He grabbed some noodle and beef on his chopsticks and consumed it without the satisfaction of even enjoying the flavor. Though that was not surprising to him. He just needed to get something in his stomach that he could tolerate. Soup was the first thing he thought of.

When three o'clock finally rolled around, he was all too eager to get started on his diversion. He found himself driving a little too fast on the way to the office. The sound of sirens behind his car put a bump in his mood. "Shit…"

Meanwhile, Christopher arrived early at the office. Not wanting to be rude knowing that Margaret was there, he opted to ring the doorbell instead of just barging right in. "Mr. Church, hello…how can I help you?"

"Actually, I came by to meet up with Sebastian. Remember our little excursion we planned at the Waverly?"

"Oh, that's right, I remember now."

"Though as usual, I'm afraid I have arrived a little too early for the party."

"Oh, that's no problem, Mr. Church, come right in. You can keep me company until he gets here."

He followed her into the room where Sebastian usually met with his clients. "So is this the place where the magic happens?"

"As a matter of fact, it is." Christopher looked around the room and noticed a Van Gogh picture hanging on one of the walls. A kindhearted smile formed on his face.

"You know, Margaret…I have another Van Gogh that would go perfect on the other side of the wall, if you want it?"

"Really? What's the name?"

"It's the Vase with Daisies and Poppies one."

"Oh my goodness, that's one of my favorites."

"Well, it's yours if you want it."

"That's very thoughtful of you, Mr. Church. Though I would feel much more comfortable if you let me give you some money for it."

"Margaret, really…it's just a reproduction. I hardly paid anything for it. No worries."

She thought about it for a moment. "Well, since you put it that way."

"I am, actually."

"Okay then…thank you for the offering."

"Oh, and by the way, I put the order in for a new bulb to go in your outside lighting fixture. For whatever reason, it takes a special kind of bulb that I couldn't purchase at a regular store.

"Unfortunately, I'll be out of town for the next couple of weeks. So I won't be able to drop by and install it for you in person. However, if you want you can come by my office and pick it up while I'm gone, I can have my receptionist hold it and the picture for you at the front desk."

"Yes, that would work perfectly. I usually need to be here during the day, but I'm sure Sophia would not mind picking it up for me. Since I've been leaving later these days, the lighting would be much appreciated."

"No troubles…I'll let you know when it arrives. If you could just text me back what time she will be dropping by, that would be great."

"Of course, Mr. Church, I can do that."

Sebastian finally walked through the door as they were finishing up their conversation. "Hey there, ready to roll?"

"More than you know, buddy."

"Okay, let's take off then." They both said their goodbyes to Margaret and quickly drove away.

"So how has the engagement life been treating ya?"

"Actually, pretty damn good. Since she is a teacher, her first day off for summer break starts next week. I'm taking her on a surprise vacation to Canada. She has been wanting to travel there for some time now."

"Sounds awesome, man."

They continued to make small talk until they arrived at the sanitarium. They got out of the truck and were greeted by a tall man with a neatly trimmed beard and uniform. He shook both their hands. "I'm Ted Johnson, the 2nd shift security guard. I just wanted to go over a couple of guidelines with you."

"Sure."

"You will have approximately two hours from now to conduct your investigation. You can visit wherever you want as long as it is not roped off. We had to close down some parts of the building for safety purposes. Other than that, it's all yours; just make sure you watch your step. If you need me, I'll be in that building straight across from you."

"Sounds good, Ted, thank you."

He was about to turn around and walk away but out of curiosity, he found himself asking another question. "Mr. Church…I was just wondering something."

"Yeah?"

"It's just, in all my years of securing this place; I have never seen an investigation conducted without at least one tour guide."

"That's funny, when I spoke to the manager over the phone, he acted like it happens all the time."

"Huh…never on my watch it hasn't. Anyway, since no one will be with you guys today, I thought I should warn you."

"Warn us about what?"

"For whatever reason, the building has been particularly active today."

Sebastian took notice to his statement. "Say again?"

"Let's put it this way, I don't think you boys are going to have any trouble finding visitors today."

That got Christopher all fired up. "Well, guess there's no time to lose then." He went to the back of his truck and grabbed all his equipment.

Naturally, this would be the ideal climate for a paranormal investigator like Christopher. However, Sebastian was not in the same caliber as him. Something didn't sit right about the statement Ted had made. Nevertheless…he thought about the souls that might be trapped in the building. Helping them break free back to the other side might bring him some much needed joy he had been craving.

He walked over to the truck. "Do you want me to help with anything?"

"No, I got this. You just do your thing. I can't wait to see if my equipment matches up with your capabilities."

As they took their first steps into the sanitarium, he could immediately feel the energy. It was unforgivably heavy. "Let's start off this way."

Sebastian followed his lead. "Here, take this flashlight. I brought an extra one for you." He turned it on and they continued on their way.

"Let's go up the stairs." They walked up the fragile-looking steps and onto the second floor. Moving further to the left of the corridor, Sebastian heard a voice. It came out muddled at first. He couldn't figure out what it was saying. So he let it go for the moment.

As they kept walking, they noticed there were rooms on both sides of them. Christopher whispered to Sebastian, "This must have been one of their main sleeping quarters. I was going to wait until we got to the cafeteria, but this seems like as good a place as any to set up shop. What do you think?"

"Yeah, it's fine."

Christopher lowered his bags and began to place his equipment in various areas around that location. It was during that time when Sebastian started to feel drawn towards one particular room. At least, it used to be one. Currently, there was nothing left except some old stone walls.

As soon as he entered the room, the muddled voices started up again.

"We…ar…ppy…st!"

…I can't understand what you're saying? Instantly when those words broke free from his thought that was when the voices went from jumbled to extremely loud and coherent.

"Thought you were never going to arrive! Can't wait to get our guests all settled in!"

O...kay, I definitely heard that! Suddenly, a terrifying sense of ill will transcended through Sebastian's body. There was no doubt, he could feel where the voices were coming from. It was emerging from the mood within the walls of the place.

In an instant, he realized the distraction he was originally hoping to attain there, wasn't at all what they were about to receive. The best thing he could do at this point was pack up and leave.

"Christopher...listen to me very carefully. We need to get out of here as soon as possible."

"Why...what happened?"

"It doesn't matter right now. What's important is..."

But he never got to finish his sentence. Without warning, Sebastian simply stopped all communication with him. His body began to feel extraordinarily heavy. So much so, that within a few seconds, he could no longer move a single muscle.

Next thing he knew, a flashback of an incident that occurred there over 80 years ago began to play out in his head. *My God...* It was a horrifying scene! He tried to push it out of his mind, still it wouldn't go away. There was nothing he could do except stomach what he was forced to observe.

When it was finally over, he was able to instantly talk and move again. He turned around and began to run out of the room. Only to be slammed to the ground when he reached the edge of where the door should have been. Something was keeping him trapped in there.

He began banging against the invisible wall. "Christopher, can you hear me! I can't get out!" Gradually, his vision of Christopher slowly started to vanish and was simultaneously being replaced with a real wall.

What the hell is happening? Next thing he knew...the two side walls were starting to change as well. Slowly, he turned around and watched as the entire room was manifesting itself back to the exact same scene he was forced to view only minutes ago.

When the room eventually finished recreating itself, someone or something turned on the play button. It was now being acted out in real time as if he existed in the scene.

There was a nurse, attending to three patients in the room. She was busy extracting blood from one of them. But then, one of the other patient's behavior began to distract her attention.

He was sitting on his bed with drool hanging from his chin. His hands were lifted in the air moving to the tune of his own deranged voice.

"…Better be careful. They are gonna get ya when you're not looking. It's best just to stay low and mind your own business. Nobody likes a tattle teller…"

Suddenly he stopped short and glared directly at Sebastian with hostile flaring eyes. "Shut up…Just Shut Up! You see…look at her. She has that frown over her left eyebrow again. She is already starting to suspect. Remember what they do to people who talk." His breath was beginning to become erratic. "The last one they took from us never came back!"

The nurse couldn't help but take notice to his jabber. "YOU over there! Stop that horrific nonsensible chatter…you're driving me crazy!" Sebastian glanced down at his body and saw that he too was now wearing a hospital gown. *This can't be! How is this happening?*

Seconds later, the patient closest to her grabbed the syringe from her hand and jammed it into her arm. Then he proceeded to inject all the fluid into her body.

The third patient who was located in the corner of the room watched with delight as the entire scene unfolded. A wicked laugh came rumbling through his mouth. He was enjoying every second of watching tainted blood being injected into her arm.

"What have you done, you crazy fuck!" She started screaming at the top of her lungs. "My God, how could you do this to me? You have just given me your death sentence!"

At that moment, two male nurses came in through the door and saw the horror scene. Immediately, one of them grabbed the syringe out of her arm and took her out of the room.

While the other nurse took action on Sebastian. He grabbed the back of his head and threw him on the bed. "Please, I'm not a patient. Look at me, I'm not even sick!"

"Shut up or this is bound to get a whole lot more ruthless for you."

Suddenly, he realized why they were treating him that way. Originally, there had been a total of three patients in the room. Now he saw only two. *Oh shit!* He had somehow become the third patient. The one that had just struck the nurse with the syringe. *My God!* "No, no…I'm telling you! You've got the wrong guy. I'm not a patient!"

That just made the nurse all the more angry. He slapped Sebastian across the face, then grabbed a baton from his belt and began punching the living daylights out of him. When he finished, he had to wipe the sweat off his face from all the effort he had put into his attack.

"Now…don't move another inch, you hear me!" Sebastian was beside himself. There was nothing he could do but lay there like a dog playing dead. The nurse began to restrain his hands, then bent down to his feet and did the same thing. When he finished, he stuck a syringe in his leg. Immediately, he started to feel a sense of weariness.

When the other nurse came back in, he helped transport Sebastian onto a mobile stretcher. Then attached his restraints to the rail of the bed. As they were taking him down a long corridor, he was coming in and out of consciousness.

He was able to comprehend a little of their conversation. "So, where do they want us to put him now?"

"I was told to send him to the lab. The doctors are always taking in new stock to do experiments on. It's what he deserves after what he did to Nurse Lucy."

Hours later, he woke up in a room no bigger than a small bathroom. It smelled of human waste and there were over six patients in the room, not including himself. They all appeared like they had been through hell and back.

A long time went by when finally, a nurse came in with bread and water. "Just make sure you all keep to yourselves, got it!" Sebastian took his tray over to a corner and started to eat it as quickly as he could. However, when he took a second glance at the bread, he discovered it had mold all over it. He started shaking over the fact that he may never get out of this nightmare.

That was when a doctor came in and grabbed one of the patients. "This one will do. He doesn't look like he has much longer left anyway."

"NO…NO…you can't take me back there! Please, don't do this to me…please!"

Somehow, he broke loose of the doctor's grip. Making him lose his balance and fall back on top of Sebastian. "Here…take this guy. He's new! Perfect for new experiments!" Then he grabbed Sebastian's gown with both hands and gazed into his eyes. "Sorry…guy…nothing personal. But dying would be better than what they are going to put me through."

The doctor had enough by then. "Security, come help me!" Seconds later, two men came in and grabbed the patient. Before the doctor left, he looked back down towards Sebastian. "Don't worry; your treatment is coming after his. We are in need of lots of resources today."

Jesus Christ, I've got to get out of this archive! He closed his eyes and tried again to fight his way out through his mind. Still, there was a weird blockage he had never experienced before. It was as if he had surrendered complete control of his brain to someone else, yet he still was able to have his own separate thoughts.

He landed up falling asleep for a while. Only to be woken up to a completely new archive. Out of nowhere, the voices came back out of the walls.

"We wanted to make sure you received the full guest experience. Nobody likes to watch a bored visitor!"

This time, his narrators had put him into the role of a nurse. He was waiting outside of the bathroom for the patient to do his release. But he should have been more careful. Having his guard down was not something you ever did at this sanitarium. The door opened and the patient quietly came out with one of his hands wrapped around his back.

He glanced at Sebastian with an unhinged smirk. "You people disgust me…acting like you actually care about my well-being." Then, without warning…he viciously threw him to the ground and quickly wrapped a wire twice around his throat. "We all know you can't wait for us to die in here! Well, I'm not leaving first, asshole! Do you hear me…do you hear me…do you hear me!"

He had ripped the wire out of its socket from the bathroom. "There's always something you guys never think might be dangerous enough to use on you. However, you will always be mistaken."

As he continued to restrict the breath from Sebastian's airflow, he wondered if he could actually die in an archive.

But just as he was about to pass out to his death, he found himself in yet another footprint. Eventually, he lost track of how many archives the place made him take part in. He must have died at least five times and killed God knew how many people.

When the scenes finally started to die down, he found himself on the floor holding his body in a fetal position. Gradually, he began to hear the rumbling of voices speak up again.

"Oh we've been so amused with our special visitor today. And you are unique indeed. Coming with all the gifts that you have. It has been fun seeing how much we can break you. Wonder how long master will let us have our way with you…

"So far, we have only seen you play out our history here at the sanitarium. However, now that we've had the opportunity to see just how juicy your life is…we couldn't resist having a little pleasure with your own existence."

Then the collective voices of talk swiftly transitioned into one very sinister voice.

"It seems your precious Sophia doesn't stand a chance with you. She is going to die, you know…"

Suddenly, a new nightmare of Sophia emerged into his head. He was made to watch violent clips of him screaming at her, slapping her face, choking her neck, throwing her to the ground, and brutally kicking her. As much as he tried, he could not get the footage out of his head.

They made him relive the scene over and over again until it finally came to a halt. He was relieved for the short reprieve they gave him. Although, it did not last long. Minutes later, the evil voice made its presence known again.

"See…you will kill her…your darkness will see to that."

The malicious murky liveliness of the place seemed to grow even more intense as Sebastian pushed out the energy of his thoughts. It enjoyed the misery he was suffering through. A dark hideous laugh began to come through the walls as it felt its strength rise.

Not long after that, the entire gruesome nightmare started all over again. Only this time…they compelled him to put an ending to the story. They forced him to kill her, and then made him watch all the different ways he would do it.

The video in his head never stopped from that point on. He just had to lay there and take it. Continuously re-experiencing the horror scenes…until he eventually passed out.

Next thing he knew, he found himself lying down in the back seat of Christopher's truck. He immediately panicked, moving his whole body to the corner of the seat. He was shaking compulsively out of control. "Where am I?"

Christopher instantly turned around. "Sebastian! For Christ sake…you scared the ever living shit out of me! Thank God you finally woke up. I wasn't sure what I should do. Jesus…it doesn't matter now. I'm just so thankful you're awake!" He quickly pulled into the nearest gas station and stopped the truck.

"First of all…I need to make sure you are okay."

Sebastian took a second before replying. "I'm not sure how to answer that, Christopher. What I've experienced is like nothing I've ever witnessed before. That place had so much power over me."

Suddenly, he started to feel claustrophobic sitting in the back seat. Maybe it was from the memory of how that place constricted his mind. "Sorry …I need to get some fresh air." As he was getting out, he realized how incredibly weak he was. The sanitarium had drained the living life out of him.

Damn it! This meant he would have to tolerate seeing Josephine again. Unfortunately, there was no other choice. He needed to be cleansed of the all the darkness he had taken in tonight.

"Christopher, I hate to ask you this…"

"Go ahead, man, what do you need?"

"Can you drive me somewhere?"

"Of course, wherever you need to go."

"Let me just text someone first." After he sent his message, they both waited in silence for a response. Five minutes later, she replied.

Josephine: Home.
Sebastian: Will be there in 20.

Sebastian told him which area to drive towards. "When we get closer to her home, I'll give you more direction."

"All right, sounds good." Knowing whatever he went through must have been horrendous, Christopher treaded lightly with his next words.

"Is it okay if we talk about what happened to you tonight?"

"Where do you want to begin?"

"Well, from what I observed, you were totally fine and coherent until the moment you walked into that room. After that point, things got weird. You stopped mid-sentence and then you were completely comatose to the rest of the world."

"How long was I out for?"

"After about twenty minutes of you being in that state, I started to get extremely worried. So I decided to get the security guard for help. We had to physically drag you out of there. There was simply nothing else we could do."

"Oh wow, man…thank you for taking care of me."

"No need to thank me, Sebastian. Anyone would do the same."

"Even so, I am still grateful." Just then, he started to wonder what Christopher's experience must have been like. "What happened to you while I was in that room?"

"Nothing happened to me. In fact, I did not hear or feel a single thing the whole time I was in there. After you stopped talking in the middle of your sentence, I came right over to you. I tried everything to get you to respond, yet no matter what I did, nothing brought you back."

"I see." He put his head down and brushed his hands through his hair. "That place, Christopher, was not a hospital. It was more like a prison that people were sent to when they were diagnosed with Tuberculosis. Unfortunately, they did not run it in a humane way. If you stayed there long enough, you would most likely go insane by the conditions they lived in."

"What do you mean?"

"The original owner of the Waverly did not view that place as a hospital. All he cared about was making money. He had no concern over the welfare of the patients or the staff for that matter."

"How do you know that?"

"Because…I lived through the lives of the people who took residence there. The energy of that place forced me to be a part of its archives. That included making me inhabit the owner's footprint as well. It very much liked me to see the culprit behind its darkness."

"My God, Sebastian, how is that even possible?"

But he bypassed that question and moved onto what was even worse. "They were able to reach into my fears and turn them into my own personal nightmares." He brushed his hands through his hair again and let out a deep breath. "That's something I will never be able to let go of." He flinched when he thought about all the different ways he had killed Sophia. It felt so real to him.

"It's as if the energy in that building is so potent, it took on a life of its own. Yet, you said it didn't do anything to you. How strange is that? Maybe I'm more susceptible to it because of my gifts? Still, that place was so powerful; I believe it could pretty much do whatever it wanted to anyone. Why did it specifically target me?"

"I don't know, Sebastian. Never did I dream something like this could ever happen. I'm so sorry, man."

"It's okay, you could not have known. I'm just glad you got me out when you did."

He sat there in silence for a moment, looking like he was mulling something else over. "What are you thinking about?"

"It's just…normally, in order for me to see someone's archive I have to touch some part of that person's body. Yet not only was I able to see their footprints…I was forced to be a part of them. I've never undergone anything like that encounter."

Before he could respond, Sebastian noticed they were getting closer to her house. "Anyways, I'll have to analyze that matter at another time. Make a left here on Johnson Road. Then an immediate right on Landon Avenue. Her house will be right up the street from there."

When they arrived at the gate, she made them wait ten minutes before she finally buzzed them in. "Just hang out here in the car for me, this shouldn't take very long."

"Whatever you say."

He went up to her door and gave it a knock. "Sebastian." As she went to open the door further for him, she happened to glance outside. "That's interesting, so you are just going to leave your company in the car?"

"He's not company, Josie, he's my ride. I was too weak to drive here on my own. Besides, I thought you wanted me to keep my affairs private. No one is to know, right?"

"Sebastian, silly…those are my rules for you. I, on the other hand, can do whatever the hell I want. Go ahead and bring him in. I'll see you inside." She turned around and left before he could say another word. *Shit!* He had no choice but to go get him.

Christopher rolled his window down. "What's up?"

"Yeah, um…she wants you to come in. She thinks it's rude that I'm leaving you out here."

"Okay…no worries." He got out of the truck and closed the door.

"Sorry ahead of time for whatever comes out of her mouth. One might say she is a little unorthodox about her approach with people."

"Say no more, man, don't worry about it."

They walked through the doorway and into her living room. "Well, hello there…take a seat, boys. Can I get you anything?" They both politely told her no.

"So, Josephine…this is Christopher Church." He glanced back over to him. "She goes by the name Josie as well." He went over to shake her hand.

"You know, you look very familiar to me, Mr. Church."

"Do I?"

"Yes."

Judging by how Sebastian had spoken of her, he did not want to get her feathers all riled up. So he just made light of the subject matter. "You know…I hear that a lot from people."

"Do you now?"

"That's what I hear, yeah."

"Anyway…enough about that. Do you happen to know why our friend Sebastian here needs me so much?"

"No actually. He hasn't disclosed to me any of his business with you."

"I see. Well, it's sad really…with all the gifts he has acquired, he never received the one thing he needs to balance everything out. I, on the other hand, happen to possess such a gift."

She gazed back toward Sebastian. "Although, I have to say when I told you I'll give you a release whenever you need one, I never anticipated it would be so many in a row. I just saw you yesterday, for Christ's sake!"

Just get through her bullshit so you can go home! "I'm sorry, I didn't foresee tonight's event to have such a deep impact on my energy level. I would not have come here otherwise."

"Yes, you really should know better. In the future, you need to plan your events out more carefully."

"Yeah, you're right, I'm sorry. I'll be more mindful of how many times I pay you a visit in the future."

"That's right, Sebastian, and pay you will. Unfortunately for now, just the cleanse." She closed her eyes and gave him his release.

"Now you should probably go." She got up and walked over to Mr. Church. "It was a pleasure meeting you." Then she bent in closer and whispered something in his ear. After that, she walked away.

When they got in the truck and drove off, Sebastian could not help but ask what she had whispered in his ear. "Well, she said…she said that I am always welcome to come back anytime. Honestly, she is probably the most forward woman I have ever met."

"You're telling me."

"I got to say though…as your friend…there is no question that she is trouble. I take it there is no other resource you can find to release your situation?"

"Not at the moment, she is the only person I know of who has the gift."

"I see. Well, just try to watch your back with her."

"That I will, my friend."

"Are you ready to go back to the office to get your car?"

"Yeah, thanks for driving me around."

"No worries. I'm just sorry that our adventure did not work out the way I hoped it would." Ten minutes later, he dropped him off at his car. He drove himself home somber about how the night had ended. It was perhaps possibly the most terrorizing night of his life.

When he got home, he took a shower and went straight to bed. He woke the next morning thinking about Sophia. Days went by and still he did not hear back from her. All he could do was keep trying.

Sebastian: So are we over? You are not even going to give me a chance to tell you my side? After everything we have been through. This is how it ends with us?

An hour later…

Sophia: Come to my house.
Sebastian: I'll be there in 10.

Finally, she had agreed to meet with him. He had to prep himself for all the lies he was about to throw at her. But there was no way around it. Thinking about the new nightmares the sanitarium put into his head, was a crushing reminder of why he was doing this with Josephine in the first place.

He rang the bell a couple of times before she finally opened the door. He was stunned when he first saw her appearance. She looked like she had lost at least ten pounds. She had not been taking care of herself. "Come in." He looked around and noticed that nothing had been lived in. "Where have you been staying, Sophia?"

"I'm not sure that's any of your business right now, Sebastian. You said you wanted to tell me your side. I'm ready to hear it."

His hands began to sweat with what he was about to tell her. "Sophia…Josephine knew that was the one thing she could say that would cause you to break up with me. Truth is, she would rather see us apart. She hates that we are together. She hates that she does not have a man that would fight for her the way I am fighting for you. She hates that I love you and not her. I'm not sure why she has become so obsessed with me. Even so, at the end of the day, I did *not* make an agreement to give myself to her!

"You know me, Sophia! Are you really going to trust her words over mine? Please, I'm begging you…don't let her jealous words break us up! Don't let her win, Sophia!

"I swear to you…what we have is a financial arrangement only. It's as simple as $200.00 per cleanse…that's it! And yes, I do have to touch her hands when I receive one. Honestly, it is the only way she is able to release me from the dark.

"That is the truth, Sophia…and if I had known she was going to misrepresent the payment arrangement, I would have told you a long time ago. I'm sorry about that, really I am. But please understand… she has everything to gain by breaking us up. And we have everything to lose if you follow her desires."

She digested everything he had to say. It made her think about her history with him. All the times he helped her through the pain she had suffered from her past. He didn't have to do that. But what was more was all the people he had helped with Margaret. That can't all be for nothing, she thought.

It all came down to one thing. Was she to believe Josephine's words …or Sebastian's. It was that plain and simple.

In the end, she decided to trust him. Not having him around these last days had been devastating for her. She had grown so deeply in love with him. It was almost foolish of her not to believe him over that crazy woman. Obviously, she was not happy with the fact that he still needed Josephine for his needs. But that came with the difficulties of a having a relationship. This was there obstacle to bear, she told herself.

So without further contemplation, she surrendered to their road. Whatever may come of it.

"Okay, Sebastian." She took a deep breath. "I choose us. I've decided to believe you." A sigh of relief rang though his mind. It's what had to be done, he thought. The days moving forward were bittersweet. They were careful not to bring the subject of Josephine up. It was just easier to pretend she didn't exist in their lives.

When Monday finally rolled around, they went to work. He decided to let Margaret know he could only handle two clients a day. This would alleviate having to see…*her*.

It wasn't until Wednesday night came that the reality of his stormy life with Josephine came rushing back into full gear. It was 8:05 pm when he received her text.

Josephine: It's time. Meet me at 112 Jefferson Street. June 1st. I'll text you the time on the day of the event.

The hair on his back began to rise. It was time to do it. Internally, he wanted to cringe. Thank God, Sophia was in the middle of taking a bath when the news arrived. He needed time to catch his wits. Putting his phone down, he began to pace the floor.

I need to get away with her again. Go somewhere free from all the turmoil that was about to enter his life. He would only have a week left with Sophia before he would have to do the inevitable with Josephine. But he would take what he could get.

As soon as Sophia came out of the bathroom, he came right up to her. "I've been thinking, love. We've both been going through so much recently. How do you feel about going away with me for a week?"

She didn't even need to think twice about it. "I think that's a great idea." Truth be told, she needed a break too. "Where should we go?"

"I don't know. But I still have most of the money left over from what Margaret gave me. So there is plenty left to go wherever we want."

"Okay, let's look for something online then." They went over to his laptop and quickly pulled up a travel site. "All right, let's see here...there are deals to Los Angeles, San Francisco, Chicago, Miami, New York?"

A smile started to form across his face when he thought about New York. He loved traveling there. Yet, when he really thought about it, he realized he never did have an opportunity to enjoy it as a tourist. He had always gone there on business.

"Sophia, I know I've told you I've been to New York many times over; still, I really think we could have a lot of fun there. I've never been able to enjoy the city for leisure."

"Really? So you are telling me in all the times you've been there you have never taken in a Broadway show?"

"Nope."

"Okay, how about the Statue of Liberty?"

"Never."

"Shopping in Soho?"

He started to laugh. "I'm telling you, love. Back then...climbing the top of the corporate ladder was all I cared about. So if we go to New York this time, it will be like I was going for the first time. What do you think, are you interested?"

"Yes, of course, I am!"

"Okay, great...then let's find a hotel!"

After about an hour, all the arrangements had been booked. Shortly after, Sophia left and went home to pack. Their flight left at 7 pm tonight. He only had two things left to do. The first was something he knew would bring them back to their past. Before all the mayhem had begun.

The second had to do with Sophia's father. She had not spoken with him for quite some time. He wanted to surprise her with a visit from him.

He went over to the couch and relaxed his mind from everything. This time, he found his way into the tunnel fairly quickly. After about ten minutes of searching, he found Thomas.

"Hey there."

"Sebastian…it's about time you paid me a visit."

"Yes, it's good to see you again too. Though I am not here to talk about my path right now."

"Yes, I am aware of that. But the fact that you are here making plans just in case things may go sour in your life, tells me you are having second thoughts about your decisions."

"My decisions have not changed, Thomas. I'm merely putting safety nets in place. As you know, the future can always unfold in ways we cannot predict. Unfortunately, working with Josephine does not offer me very much control over the outcome. She will need someone to be there for her, just in case I am not."

Thomas gave out a heavy sigh. "You know that nothing is ever set in stone, until it is. You are getting closer to that mark, Sebastian."

"Please, Thomas…don't make this choice more difficult for me than it already is."

"Yet it is my job to bring your choices to the forefront. You are messing up your life more than you can possibly imagine."

"It's a mess no matter which path I go. At least Sophia has a chance to live down the road I'm choosing."

"Okay, Sebastian…I can see where this is going. Let me just go get who you came for."

Not long after, he came back with her father. "Thank you for coming, Ray. I have a favor to ask of you."

"Yes, ask whatever you want."

"You know how much I love your daughter. I'm trying to protect her as much as I can from my unfortunate situation with her. However, if something should happen between us, I want to make sure she has someone there for her."

Sebastian glanced back at Thomas. "Is there a sign he can give her to let her know he is by her side?"

"In her circumstance, we will allow that to happen. Please understand though…this is not usually allowed. Unfortunately, this is not a normal time for her."

"Thank you, Thomas." He turned back toward Ray. "I'll leave it to you to come up with whatever symbol you want to give her. I'm taking her away this week. It will be a good time for you to visit her again."

"Okay…I'll be waiting." Seconds later, he vanished away.

"I guess I'll find you soon, Thomas. Thank you for the exceptions you are making with her. I know it will bring her much joy to have him back in her life in this way."

"Yes, I believe it will, Sebastian. I'll see you soon then." An instant later, he was gone.

Chapter 19
Bleeding Out

Sophia and Sebastian landed at LaGuardia Airport around 9 pm that night. Their travels were more than comfortable as they had paid for first-class tickets. "Sophia, I made reservations at a restaurant for tonight at 10 pm. So if it's okay with you, I can arrange for our luggage to be taken straight to the hotel. Then we can catch a cab for dinner."
"Yeah, that sounds great."

Sebastian took care of the luggage and came back five minutes later. "All right, we are all set." He hailed down a taxi and told the driver to take them to Chateau St. Louis. "I've eaten there only once, the food is superb, you'll love it."

"Not that I'm complaining but I thought you wanted a whole new experience on this trip?"

"I do, Sophia, it's just tonight I have something special planned for you and I needed a familiar place to do it." She wondered what he was up to. "Don't worry, love, I promise you'll be glad that I made this one exception by the end of our date."

That was enough for her. She gave him a soft kiss and put her arms around his chest as she laid her head against his shoulder. "Don't ever change, Sebastian."

Those words cut him deep with all the lies he had been pushing on her since the whole nightmare began. Despite that, he quickly squashed all those thoughts from his mind. He was in New York to get away from all that pandemonium, and that was what he intended to do.

Thirty minutes later, they arrived. "Ah, here we are, Sophia." He gave the driver his money and they left. "One of my favorite first dates with you was taking you to La Relais. I thought we could take that experience to another level here."

She had to admit. She liked what he was dishing out. It was the perfect way to start off the trip. As they walked into the restaurant, they were instantly greeted by the host. "Hello, do you have a reservation with us tonight?"

"Yes, it's under the name Sebastian Sinclair." He glanced down at his computer and noticed there were several provisions he requested.

He walked around his podium and quietly whispered into Sebastian's ear, "All the accommodations you requested have been made. We will simply just add it to your tab, if that is okay with you?"

"Yes, of course."

"*Parfait, monsieur*. So then, please follow me."

He took them up to the second floor and walked them outside to a private terrace. The whole scenery was exactly what he pictured it would be when he made the arrangements. When they sat down, he lightly grasped her hand and gave it a kiss. "I'm so glad we are here, Sophia."

"Me too." She looked around the small but beautifully decorated terrace. There were flowers everywhere and fairy lights hanging from the ceiling. "This is just for us?"

"Yes, actually. Last time I was here, I noticed a small party had rented this space. I thought it would be the perfect setting for what I had planned tonight." She smiled at him. "Well I'm excited to see where the night leads us then."

A waiter came by not long after to take their drink orders. When he left, Sebastian found himself gazing out into the stars. It reminded him of the spirit tunnel he had traveled through to find Thomas. Something he would eventually come to tell Sophia towards the end of their trip.

In the meantime, he had other words to share with her. He moved in closer so as to have a more intimate conversation with her.

"Sophia. Obviously, you know how much I love you. I'm sorry for all the crap I have put you through. Everything in our lives is so fragile these days." She thought about Josephine. How much she hated what she had put them through. "Yes, I agree. It does feel sometimes like we are walking on broken glass."

"I just wish I had met you when we were both younger, Sophia. We could have been childhood friends. And you would have steered me in the right direction in life. Well before I ever met my ex-wife. I would have married you instead of her and we would have had so much more time to spend together during this existence." She let out a hallow laugh. "Yeah, that would have been nice. But that was not the hand we were dealt was it."

"No, unfortunately not, love."

He put his hand over her cheek. "Just know, that I would do anything for you Sophia. I'm nothing without your love." His voice sounded so desperate as the words came out of his mouth. "Sebastian, listen to me. We are in this together. I already decided that I'm in this for the long haul. So no matter how bad things get with Josephine, as long as we are at one, she cannot deter us from our fate together."

If only she knew the risky road he was really taking their relationship on. But he could not share those grievances with her. He could not voice how scared to death he was of their future.

After a minute of pouring more negative thoughts into his head, he realized this conversation was not heading in the right direction. *For God's sake, this is becoming exactly the opposite of why you took her on this trip to begin with.*

Thank God, the waiter came back when he did to bring them their drinks and take their order. When he finished, the server bent down and whispered into his ear, "The entertainment will be here shortly per your request, sir."

"Thank you." It was a welcome reminder of what he had planned for her tonight.

They went on to eat three courses that night. Towards the end of the dessert, a man came over to a rather large-looking table and pulled the tablecloth off. A piano was underneath it. Three people followed behind him. One of them was a woman. She came out with a microphone and stood in front of the piano. Sophia glanced at Sebastian with a playful smile. "…And what's this about?"

The waiter gestured his hand toward Sebastian. "The gentleman ordered it for you, madam, please enjoy."

That was when the music started to play. She was so elated with his thoughtful gift she didn't know what to say. Sebastian got up and held his hand out for her to take it. She followed suit…and he embraced her body closer to his as he slowly wrapped his arm around her back. That's when the voice in the background began to sing…

Never before
Have I met someone like you
It's true
I've been captivated through and through

Now I know it's been rough for the taking lately
The moon has not shined so brightly I'm just saying
But listen to me just this once my sweet
I have a beautiful dream we both could touch you'll see

So come fly away with me
From the worries of the day
Way back before all the haze
And from winter to spring
We could always be
At peace to love and to be free

The dream is there for the making
If we want it bad enough we'll be able to take it
Break free from the glass jar we've been liven
All we have to do now is believe it

So come fly away with me
From the worries of the day
Way back before all the haze
And from winter to spring
We could always be
At peace to love and to be free

He moved his head in closer so she could hear him. "When I heard this song, I thought of you. Have you heard it before?"

"No, I haven't actually…but it's beautiful."

"I'm glad you like it. It's called, Free. If you want, this can be our song to dance to?" All she could do was nod in agreement, she was so overwhelmed with her love for him. They danced through the rest of the song in silence. Just taking it all in and enjoying themselves in their own little world. When the music finished, Sebastian kissed her on the lips. "You will always be my love, Sophia."

"Yes…always."

Minutes later, the waiter came back with the bill. He didn't even look at the price. He simply gave him his card. "Are you ready to go back to the hotel?"

"Honestly, I'm on cloud nine right now. The last thing I want to do is go back to the hotel. We're in New York for the first time together, and you have just swept me off my feet. Let's go a little crazy tonight, shall we?"

That caught him off guard. However, if painting the town was what she wanted, then he was all in. He hailed down another taxi and paid him to follow their trail for the next three hours. They danced and drank…then danced again. He had never seen this side of her before. He was happy to watch her be so carefree. Eventually, they made their way back to the hotel sometime after 3am.

The next morning, they woke up to breakfast in bed. During the day they went sightseeing. Visiting the Statue of Liberty and taking a carriage ride around Central Park. By nightfall, they found a quaint little pizzeria to eat at in Little Italy.

They were making the most of the time they had together in New York. Taking in several Broadway shows, sailing at sunset along the Hudson River, and shopping along Madison Square Garden. They even navigated their way through Chinatown where they ate Peking Duck, Dim Sum and some sort of questionable Chinese liquor. They both laughed at their stupidity for gulping that down.

They were having the time of their lives. All the challenges they had been dealing with in the past seemed to have melted away as if they never existed. The last night they were there, Sebastian gave her his last surprise.

"Sophia, come over here and sit on the couch with me. There is something I would like to give you before we leave tomorrow. "

She walked over and did as he asked. "In all the turmoil we've been going through, I forgot to tell you about a new gift I received."

"You got a new gift?"

"Yes, remember a while back I was telling you about an angel named Thomas?"

"Ah…yeah I remember."

"Well, I first met him at Clarissa's house. He told me if I wanted to personally seek him out, I would have to find him in the tunnel."

"What's that?"

"It's hard to explain really. However, probably the best way to describe it is to view it as an invisible subway system. It's what the spirits and angels use to travel back and forth from earth. It's the most amazing sight I've ever witnessed."

"Wow, you're gifts are growing to heights I never thought possible."

"I know and I gotta say that this one is pretty special. Let me show you what I mean. I just need a second to get into the right mind frame."

He closed his eyes and drew a blank canvass in his head. Less than a minute later, he was in. "Okay, so at this moment, I'm somewhere outside the tunnel. It is completely pitch black out here. I mean I cannot see a single thing. However, I know for a fact that I am standing on something. Yet when I try to touch what is holding me up, I feel nothing there. It's the most bizarre thing.

"Sounds scary."

"When I first found this realm, I was a bit terrified. However, I know what to expect now. So I feel safe."

"When are you going to reach the tunnel?"

"Soon, love…it will just appear before me."

After waiting a couple more minutes, it slowly started to emerge. "Oh… here it is, Sophia. Now imagine what an ocean current would look like in water. Then take that vision and put it in a space-like atmosphere. That's what it looks like to me.

"Wow, I'm imagining it in my head. It sounds so cool."

"Yes, it really is stunning. I'm about to jump in it right now." As soon as he let his body fall off the ledge, he immediately found himself in the tunnel. "My body is simply floating through the atmosphere now with countless of other souls.

"They all have different colors of light surrounding their bodies signifying their specific aura. Mine is blue. It's absolutely mind-blowing how this network operates. My brain just tells me where to go without putting any thought into it.

"At the moment, I'm trying to find Thomas's energy. This part is a little trickier to explain. You see, around the tunnel that I'm floating through, there is another circular structure that embodies the tunnel completely.

"If you can imagine what a honeycomb looks like. It's basically a mass amount of tiny cells with honey stored in each hole. However, instead of honey coming out of each cell, it is light. Millions upon millions of lights as far as the eye can see. I guess you could say it looks like a massive endless honeycomb hotel. At least, that is my perception of it.

"But what is really going to blow your mind is what is located within each cell of light."

"Good lord, Sebastian, don't keep me in suspense…you are putting on a pretty good show here." He was glad she was enjoying the experience.

"Okay… so each light represents the scene of a human life, being played out in real time. When a spirit or angel goes through one of those holes of light that is when they enter the human realm."

"Wow…that's just crazy. I can't believe you are actually able to see that."

"It is indeed, Sophia."

"Ah…hold on a second, I believe I just found Thomas. Let me go see if he is available to talk." When he walked through the light, he heard Thomas finishing up with someone. "Looks like I made perfect timing!" He turned around to look at Sebastian, though he already knew who was there.

"Hello there, I take it you are ready to unite Sophia with her father again?"

"Yes, I am…thank you for helping me out. You don't know how much I appreciate this."

"I do, Sebastian, and it's no problem at all. I'm happy to assist you with anything I am capable of doing. Give me a second while I go get him."

"Okay."

A few minutes later, he came back with Ray. Then without saying a thing, they were all transported to the human realm inside Sebastian's hotel suite. "Sophia, Thomas has now joined us. He says to tell you hello."

"Oh, um…tell him I said hello back."

"I will."

"I also have another visitor with us. It's your father."

She was so surprised with that news she could hardly talk. "Wh…really? He's here?"

"Yes, he says hello as well."

"Dad? Where are you?"

"He's right beside you on your left-hand side."

"I'm so glad you could come. I wasn't sure when I would be able to see you again. This is such a pleasant gift."

"For him too, he says. He is here to discuss something with you, if that is okay?"

"Yes, of course, what is it, Dad?"

"After you spoke last, he made a decision to stay on the other side and watch over you for the rest of your life on earth. He won't come down and live another life until he reunites with you in heaven. He felt it was the least he could do for you.

"Up until this point, he has been visiting you often without you knowing about it. However, recently, the angels have granted him a very rare gift. He has been given the ability to show you a sign whenever he is around, to let you know he is visiting." Hearing that news brought her so much joy.

Yet at the same time, she got a nagging feeling in the pit of her stomach that something was off. It made her think about the timing of it all. "Um…Dad, I'm sorry, I don't mean to sound like I'm ungrateful, but I don't understand why this gift has been granted to you at this moment of time, and why am I the rare exception?" Ray looked to Sebastian to answer that question.

"Sophia, it was my idea actually to ask the angels for this request. I already knew of Ray's plans on staying back and watching over you until you cross over. Unfortunately, whenever he has visited you, I have not been around to let you know he is there. It got me thinking, it would have been nice for you to know he was visiting you."

"Sebastian, I…I can't believe you thought of this for me." She once again was taken aback by his gesture. "I don't know what to say."

"You don't need to say anything. It makes your father happy as well that he can do this for you.

"He says his sign will come in the form of a red and orange butterfly with a very specific hint of purple on the right-hand side of the wing. Whether you see it in a dream, picture, nature, or any other form…know that it is your father visiting you at that very moment."

Tears began to shed out of her eyes for the love she felt. "Thank you so much for giving me this gift. And dad…thank you for staying back and watching over me. It means the world to me."

"He says no need to thank him, he's grateful to have a chance to finally be there for you."

"I love you, Dad!"

"He loves you too."

"He has to go now, Sophia. He says he will visit you soon and don't forget to look for the butterfly."

"I won't forget, Dad. Thank you again!" Seconds later, he was gone.

They spent the rest of the night together in their room, never leaving each other's sight. The next day he woke up still wrapped around her body. He lay there just watching her sleep for a while.

A half hour later, she woke up. "I can't believe we have to leave today. It really has been a dream vacation."

"Yes, it has." Packing their bags to go back home was bittersweet. Even so, it was exactly how he hoped the trip would turn out.

The airplane back to Louisville was not so smooth. After all, it was May 31st and that meant tomorrow he would have to pay off his debt with Josephine. His anxiety level was at an all-time high. He found himself in the bathroom vomiting several times before finally landing. Of course, he told Sophia that he had probably just caught the same stomach virus she had contracted a couple of weeks ago.

When they got home, she took him straight to bed. After she got him settled in, she was about to leave to the kitchen to get him some water, but he couldn't stand not having her by his side. "Please Sophia, lay with me, will you?" She felt so bad for him, she agreed to whatever would make him happy. That night he fell asleep in her arms.

He woke up the next day late…11:46 am to be precise. The first thing he did was look at his phone.

Josephine: 4 pm sharp. Dress sexy…lover.

Back to the bathroom he went. Sophia could hear him vomiting from the kitchen. She felt so bad for him. When she heard the door open, she came over to see him and put a large bowl by his side. "I just finished making you some chicken soup. Although nothing probably sounds good to you right now. I just thought…"

Suddenly, she was distracted by his body movement. *Huh…why is he shaking?* She immediately thought he must have a temperature. However, when she touched her hand on his forehead, he seemed completely fine. *That's Strange.*

Regardless, she went to go grab a blanket and put it over his covers. "I'm supposed to go in and help Margaret today with some errands, but I'm thinking maybe I should take you to the doctors instead."

"No Sophia, I'll be alright. You go and help her out. I'll just probably be sleeping all day anyway."

"Are you sure? I mean, for Christ sake, you're shaking, Sebastian."

"I'm shaking because I'm cold. You put an extra blanket on me. I'll be fine now…promise, love."

"Okay, I'll trust your judgement then." He just wanted to scream off the top of his lungs that he was not to be trusted! That he had been lying to her for days and weeks on end! Yet in the end, his fear for her safety always crawled right back into his head and overruled the right thing to do…again!

She left soon after their conversation ended. He set his phone alarm to alert him when it was time to get ready to go. After that, all he wanted to do was sleep. Anything to get his mind off the inevitable. Fortunately, he was so depressed he did actually manage to fall asleep.

He slept all the way until his phone alarm buzzed him awake. Purposefully, he got ready like a robot. Completely deranged of emotion. He was tired of thinking about it. At this point, he just wanted to get it over with. When he finished getting dressed, he looked at his watch. It read 3:30 pm. But just as he was about to grab his keys and head out, he received another unpleasant text from…her.

Josephine: Looks like we are going to have to change the time to 6 pm. There was an unfortunate delay in his scheduling.

Sebastian: Fine.

Great… He had finally gotten the nerve to get the job done and now he would have to wait another two hours! *Fuck me!* As he was going through his own rant in his head, he received another text.

Sophia: Hey love, I wanted to let you know that I ran into some delays this afternoon. I got a flat tire. I called the towing company but as luck would have it, they are really backed up and won't be able to get here for a while. Once I get it fixed, I have one more errand to do and then I'll be home. Just wanted to keep you in the loop. Love you!

Sebastian: Thank you for letting me know. Be safe…K.

Hearing from her made waiting around all that much worse. Knowing she was out there with a flat tire and there was nothing he could do to help her…drove him nuts. It would have been such an easy fix for him. Nevertheless, she is under the impression that he is terribly ill. He knew she would never allow him to get out of bed.

At some point, he decided to go to a local bar down the street and grab a drink. The bartender came over to him. "Just pull whatever bourbon you get your hands on first and pour."

"Sure thing." A minute later, he came over with his drink. "It's Old Forester."

"Thank you." He took his time with this one. Getting drunk would just mess things up even more. Still, it was enough distraction to calm him from his thoughts.

When it was time to go he settled his tab and left. By the time he arrived at the location it was 5:50 pm. He caught a glimpse of Josephine outside a restaurant. She was waiting for him. It was at that moment, he felt compelled to message Sophia.

Sebastian: I will always love you. Don't ever forget that.

Sophia had already fixed her tire by then and was on her way up the elevator to Christopher's floor when she received his text. *What an off message*, she thought. When she made it up to the top floor, she sat down in the lobby area and texted him back.

Sophia: Is everything all right with you? Please message me back as soon as you get this.

However, he had no plans on waiting for her response. As soon as he sent his text to her, he took off and deliberately did not look at his phone when it started to buzz. He was ready to do what he needed to do.

After Sophia waited about five minutes in the lobby, a woman finally came walking up to the front desk. "Oh I'm so sorry; I didn't hear anyone come in. Can I help you?"

"Yes, I'm here to pick up a Van Gogh picture and lightbulb. Mr. Church was supposed to have someone leave it at the front desk for me."

The woman looked around and didn't see anything. "Tell you what, let me go look in his office and see if it is in there. I'll be right back."

"Okay, thanks." *What a day this has been*, she thought.

Sebastian nervously walked up to Josephine. "So where do you intend on doing this?" He looked around and observed how much traffic was on this street. *She can't possibly want to do this here?* That was when she grabbed his hand and took him down several blocks before they hung a right around the corner.

It was a quieter street located away from all the hustle and bustle of heavy traffic. She walked him into an alleyway no bigger then maybe 6 feet apart from one building to the next. "Remember, we only get one shot at this! So don't fuck this up for me, Sebastian."

She took a quick glance at the sidewalk on the other side of the street. "He could come by any moment, so I suggest you start now giving me what you owe me."

He took a long deep breath before pounding on her like she was a piece of meat. He put one of his hands around the back of her neck and locked onto some of her hair. Then tugged it back, so her face could be lifted to his mouth. After going in hard with a kiss, he was able to gauge what turned her on.

She liked it rough. His hands slowly made their way down to her breasts. He quickly discovered she was not wearing a bra underneath her dress. She started to quietly moan as he caressed them. Eventually, his hands moved to her waist abruptly turning her around so her back was now facing his chest. He moved her hair out of the way and began kissing her neck.

Then he proceeded to move his hands back over her breasts. After a while, one of his hands gradually moved further down past her belly button. He thought this interaction would be good enough for her. But with Josie, you never quite knew what you were going to get.

"Is this how you would treat Sophia…rough and dirty in an alleyway?"

"Leave her out of this, Josephine. This is between you and me. I'm trying to make sure I satisfy your thirst. That is…unless I'm wrong." Bending down into her ear, he whispered, "Tell me I'm wrong."

She thoroughly enjoyed his dirty talk. But she wasn't about to give away that little piece of information. She wanted more of whatever he was giving her. "If you want your debt to be paid with me, you're going to have to do a hell of a lot better than this to satisfy me."

He was beside himself on how far she wanted him to go. This infuriated him to no bounds. But there was no turning back now. He just needed to get the job done.

Instantly, he turned her back around. Then grabbed both her arms and tossed them up above her head, holding them tightly in place with one hand. While his other hand formidably cradled her ass. That led him to sliding his hand around her thigh and hoisting her leg over his. This only brought their bodies more intensely closer to one another. He gripped her hair again and began kissing her lips and neck. Then leisurely, his hand made his way down to her breasts again. "That's right Sebastian, now you're getting it."

Eventually, he let go of her arms allowing him the ability to grab both her hips, and lifting her up forcefully and blatantly against the wall. With all the chemistry going on, he couldn't help but start to get lost in his own sensual moment with her. As much as he didn't want it to happen, he was getting turned on by the scene that was unfolding. In the heat of it all, he turned her around and backed her up against the other side of the building.

While they were busy going at it, the woman finally returned with the lightbulb and picture frame in hand. "Here you go, sorry for the delay."

"It's no problem." It was getting so late she hurriedly picked up the items and left.

Back down the elevator she went. The guard standing post said goodnight to her as she opened the door to leave. All she could think about was coming home to see how Sebastian was doing. Especially since he hadn't texted her back, she was getting a weird vibe about the message he had left for her.

She made her way down the stairs onto the sidewalk. Her car was just across the street. She moved her head up to brush the hair out of her face when she suddenly stopped. Her eyes blazed out in front her watching something going on in the alleyway.

Sebastian was getting more worked up by the second with Josephine. She leaned in and whispered in his ear, "I just knew you couldn't resist me." But he did not stop to respond to her banter. He was too into the act.

It can't be... She had to take a double look with her eyes. *He's supposed to be at home sick!* Her stomach began to turn into knots. *Please God, please, don't let this be happening.* But the more she watched, the more understanding came through to her. He'd been lying to her this whole time.

She remembered his words like it was yesterday. *You know me, Sophia! Are you really going to trust her words over mine? Please, I'm begging you...don't let her jealous words break us up! Don't let her win, Sophia!* Yet, there he was, practically banging Josephine right in front of her.

She was so startled by the scene she was witnessing, she did not realize she had walked into the street. The screeching of a car finally broke his affection towards Josephine. He turned his head around to find out where the noise was coming from.

Sebastian saw her almost instantaneously. There was a split second when their eyes locked together. He could barely get her name out he was so shocked. "Sophi..." He immediately threw Josephine down against the wall. She started to laugh in a frenzy as she saw Sophia hastily run away. Based on Josephine's reaction, he realized the stark truth of the situation. He had been set up...

However, there was no time to dive into that right now. His priority was to run after Sophia. But there was no way Josephine was going to let that happen. "Where the hell do you think you are going?"

He hastily stopped himself and fell to his knees at her mercy. He said to her in hoarse voice, "What else can you possibly do that could hurt me more than what you have already done."

"You'll find out soon enough, Sebastian."

"What do you mean by that?"

"Oh sorry, maybe I said too much."

"Why won't you just fucking tell me what is going on!"

"I'm not the authority in this matter anymore."

"Of course...now is the perfect time for you to talk in riddles with me." He brushed his hand over his mouth with distain. "...I guess this is what happens when you make a deal with the devil."

"Ha... you should take a strong look in the mirror yourself before you judge me. Everything you did was by choice."

"Because I had to, because you convinced me she would die otherwise!"

"Oh, how easily we turn the table when things don't always work out the way we hoped. At the end of the day, we both got what we wanted." She bent her head down to glance at the time. After muttering something to herself, she told him he could leave. As soon as he heard the words, he took off around the building where he last saw her running. However, by the time he turned the corner...she was nowhere to be seen. He was too late.

Even though he knew he would not find her, he kept searching. Running completely around the entire block making a full circle until he found himself right back where he started. He pushed his hands through his hair and glanced up around his surroundings. How did Josephine even get her to come here? And then he noticed the name on the front of the building. His face nearly turned white as he slowly read the sign out loud in disbelief. "Church Enterprises..."

Just then, Josephine came strolling back up to him. "Figured things out yet?"

His voice went so soft only he could hear his next words. "This can't be?" He put his hand over his head and sat down on the steps for fear he might just pass out right then and there. That's when questions started floating through this mind. He glanced over at Josephine with the most enraged look on his face.

"...Why are the two of you colluding with one another?"

Her lips rolled up in a menacing smile. "Well, Sebastian, like you...Mr. Church and I have an arrangement. And now, I just fulfilled my end of the bargain. If you want to get the full scoop of the situation, you'll have to pay him a visit."

"And what if I refuse to meet with him?"

"Well, I think you will find that to be a mistake. You see, besides me...he is the only other person that has acquired the gift you need to keep your mind from going insane from the dark."

Flashbacks of the moment Christopher and him were talking about Josephine being trouble. He remembered telling Christopher that she was the only one with that ability. *My God, he was playing me the whole time!*

"I wouldn't keep him waiting too much longer though; Mr. Church can be a rather cruel man if tempted."

He brought his head down in thought. *This guy has completely fucked me over. How could I have missed all the clues?* The more he thought about how much he had manipulated him, the more irate he became. Suddenly, speaking with Christopher was all he wanted to do!

He got up and walked through the glass door to security. "Who are you here to see?"

"Christopher Church."

He looked at his computer log. "Your name?"

"Sebastian Sinclair."

"Oh yes, I see you are on the list. Go straight up and make a right to the elevators. He takes the entire top floor." *Of course, he does...*

When he reached the 30th floor, the door opened to the penthouse. He walked through the double doors and saw that there was a woman waiting for him at the reception desk. "Mr. Sinclair?"

"Yes."

"Come with me, Mr. Church has been waiting for you to drop by." As they made their way to his office, he saw two security guards standing post in front of his door. They opened it for him and followed Sebastian inside.

"Mr. Church, do you need us to stay?"

Christopher turned around from his seat with the most sinister grin on his lips. "No, you can leave us for now. But...make sure to stay on your toes."

"Yes sir." After that exchange, they quietly left closing the doors behind them.

Chapter 20
Lay Down

"So…Christopher, obviously I had you mistaken for someone else. Clearly, I'm the idiot here."

"Yes, it appears you are. But I'll offer you a piece of advice." Without giving Sebastian a chance to respond, he solicited it anyway. "It will serve you well to remember that I will always be two steps ahead of you in this little game of ours."

"Oh I see, so you're telling me that you will always be superior in a game with rules I have not been given the privy to know? Hardly seems like a fair match!"

"As you get to know me better, you will realize that I'm not really interested in what is fair in this dog-eat-dog world we live in. All the same though, I think you were dealt a pretty good hand."

"How so?"

"Am I not to understand that you have been gifted with extraordinary abilities of your own? Gifts that some might say most humans couldn't possibly comprehend or conceive of possessing?"

"My gifts are meant to heal people, not to be played in a chess match with a Person I Don't Even Know Anymore! Goddamn it, Christopher!" He rubbed his hands against his face in frustration. But then silence suddenly took over him as scenes in his head began to protrude his mind.

Like you. I've been faced with certain difficult situations myself. I just knew the bastard wasn't going to stop screwing with her. So I did what needed to be done!

He looked back at Christopher. "You fucking told me exactly what I needed to hear to put my mind at ease. You saw how I was struggling internally with my choices. So you handled the situation!"

He gave out a snide chuckle. "Yeah, I have to admit you sank right into that one. I couldn't believe how gullible you were to the matter. I mean, you made it so easy for me. Still…it was entertaining to watch you grapple through the experience."

"So that's what my life has come down to for you…a circus act for your amusement? Does human life mean nothing to you?"

"Oh, don't start on that holier than thou shit with me, Sebastian. I wasn't the only one deceiving people in this show. How many lies have you managed to tell Sophia during the course of time you have been with her?"

"It's not the same and you know it!"

"I don't think reality has caught up with you, my friend. Let's face it, you got sucked into all this because deep down, your ego got attached to a fear of her death. It's that simple.

"But hey, listen…don't beat yourself up over it. You just got a little too over ambitious when you decided to create your human path on earth. It always happens that way. You got all riled up over this evolutionary change crap.

"Lucky for you, I see the dark side in you. Which is a blessing in disguise actually, because we hold all the cards. There is much more dark on this planet earth then light. It will take an extraordinary undertaking to balance it back out. At this point, there are ten dark humans for every light one.

"And I mean, listen…you are a perfect example of that equation. Someone who truly has all the gifts he needs at this fingertips to be a leader of the light. You have even experienced what it feels like to do good on a level that most people could never dream of reaching. Imagine how much greater you could have become in the years to come. Yet, here you are today, in quite the predicament. Still valuing ego over enlightenment."

"You speak as if I have already turned to the dark!"

"Well… I'd say you are on a pretty good start. I mean even the taste of light that you have been given doesn't supersede the attachment you have over her."

"I was told that her chances of survival were slim to none if I did not commit to utilizing Josephine's antidote."

"My God, Sebastian! You have managed to annoy me already...don't you have a particular angel on your side of the fence telling you the exact same shit that I'm saying to you right now? Jesus, I feel like I'm working for both sides here.

"At the end of the day, we are more alike than you think. It's just that you have somehow sugarcoated your ego with the word love. It's a classic human error. Just add that word love to any situation and somehow, it gets special treatment. Unfortunately, the universe doesn't look at it that way.

"Mark my words, Sebastian...continue to use the word love for your own satisfaction, and you will eventually see where that leads. Take me for example; I embrace the fact that I love power above all things. You see, how we both love something... The universe doesn't see either one of our loves differently from the next. They are both driven by the same negative thought. The darkness in you will continue to use the association of love you have for her to its advantage. Until eventually, you will become the same as me."

"Stop saying that! I will never be in the dark with you. Even more so, I would never conceive of doing to another human being what you have done to me. You make me sick trying to rationalize your behavior by manipulating my actions to be the same as yours!"

"All right, Sebastian...calm down. No need to get all hyped up. I'm merely pointing out some simple facts about your life. As of today, you are still going down the wrong path from what you originally created in your life chart...am I wrong?"

How does he know so much information about my personal road?

"Look, Christopher...you got me up here to talk. It seems you have clearly done a good job of fucking me over. To what purpose...I still have no idea. Perhaps you can finally give me some insight as to why you have decided to play with my life and destroy it so carelessly."

"Oh, you couldn't be more wrong, Sebastian. I have yet to begin to destroy your life."

Alarms went off in his head. He could not understand why he was the target of so much suffering. "Just tell me where the stakes are at, Christopher!"

"Okay, then...I see you cannot be swayed for now. So I will just tell you what I want straight up. You have certain powers that I wish to possess. Unfortunately, I could not obtain your powers unless specific events unfolded first."

"You mean the need to crush Sophia's heart by having her watch that perfectly timed out exchange between Josephine and I."

"As I recall, Sebastian, at some point you seemed to be enjoying yourself, quite pleasurably."

"Whatever, Christopher, you know what pressure she was putting me under."

"To answer your question, yes, that was one of the events that needed to unfold."

"And what do you get out of all of this?"

"I told you already…I'm a greedy man, Sebastian. Your gifts will serve me well. And I would like to have them all to myself."

"So what do you suggest I do, just take them off and neatly leave them on the table for you? You can't just steal my gifts from me."

"On the contrary, I believe I can take them from you…if you let me."

Frustration was building inside of Sebastian as to how he planned to seize his abilities from him. Christopher couldn't help but grow a smirk of a smile on that observation. "I can feel your irritation for me, Sebastian. And I can honestly say it brings me so much pleasure upon how much I'm getting under your skin.

"But you will eventually need to tone the attitude down, once you become one of my servants. I don't tolerate insubordination within my network."

Sebastian was taken aback by his suggestion of being under him.

"You actually think I would ever consider serving you? For what? I don't have Sophia anymore. She'll never come back to me after what I just put her through."

Christopher cut him off right then and there. "I beg to differ, Sebastian…you have a couple of new snags in your life."

"Such as?"

His lips grew into an arrogant grin before saying his next words. "For one thing…you will need someone else to get rid of your 'temperament issues' now that Josephine is out of the picture. Secondly, and probably more importantly is the fact that I have Sophia now."

"What do you mean, you have Sophia?"

"Well…when she ran off, I made sure to have my men find a cozy place for her to mend her woes."

"You can't be serious?"

"Oh, I'm afraid I am, my friend. You see, she was so distraught over watching your intimate encounter with Josephine, she wasn't paying attention to the potential danger around her.

"It was all too easy to grab her from behind and throw her in the van. I was surprised to see that she didn't give much of a struggle at all. As soon as my men captured her, they drove off none the wiser."

Sebastian couldn't believe what he was hearing. He was in such a state of shock he could not move a single bone on his body. Christopher was really getting a rise out of that. So he continued on with his rant.

"Oh, I forgot the best part. Once they abducted her, they put tape over her mouth and shoved a mask over her head. Then they gripped her wrists and restrained them behind her back. Though I got to admit she suffered a tiny bit of pain during that interaction. They were pretty aggressive with the handling of her body. After that, things went relatively smooth. They gave her drugs through a syringe to calm her nerves, and then eventually, she passed out soon after."

That was when his adrenaline finally kicked in. He lost it! He came over and started immediately pounding on Christopher. Of course, his security quickly came in and took control over the situation. They caught hold of Sebastian and swiftly pulled him off Church.

He started laughing profusely at Sebastian's actions.

"You think you can just do something like that to me without consequences? Well, you are sadly mistaken. Unfortunately, Sophia will be the one to pay for your little outburst."

He picked up his cell phone and auto dialed a number. "Bracen, make sure within the next couple of days you give Sophia a little homecoming present of roughing her up a bit. You can use your imagination on how to handle that. She needs to know her place anyway. I think it will be a nice intro to her stay with us." Then he abruptly hung up the phone.

"See how this is going to go for you." At that moment, his security restrained Sebastian's hands behind his back and pushed him forward so he was kneeling before Christopher. "You know, I was really pushing for you to come over to my side the easy way. Somehow, I was hoping you would see the darkness as an attribute by the way you have been making your decisions lately.

"But no, I guess we will have to do it by force with you. I'm afraid you leave me no other option in the matter."

Sebastian brought his head down in thought as he was trying to digest the quick turn of events. Never did he think Church would ever kidnap Sophia.

Even so, Christopher wasn't about to watch him grieve on his turf. "Look at me when I'm talking to you, Sebastian."

Not wanting to upset him even further, he brought his head back up. "Please, I'm begging you. Don't hurt her!"

"Unfortunately, she is open to free range of my choosing at this point."

"Goddamn it, Christopher!" His guards didn't much care for his tone of voice with Church, so one of them kicked him hard straight in the gut to calm him down. Sebastian fell to the floor in pain.

Seconds later, they picked him up and placed him back down on his knees. "Again, Sebastian, you need to watch your temperament with me. I haven't even begun to punish you with my dark attributes yet."

"Haven't you though? All those times you put those nightmares in my head about Sophia. And what about the Waverly? Were those not your tricks?"

"Oh, that's right…I'm glad you brought that up actually. To answer your question, yes, I'm responsible for all those…tricks…as you call them. However, they did not come from my thoughts. They always derived from your fears, at least the ones about Sophia. I used the inevitable darkness that was already heading your way to my advantage.

"As far as the Waverly is concerned, I have to admit that was a rather fun night for me. To be around all that anger and watch you have to play out those scenes through their eyes was quite the spectacle. I had to manipulate the energy quite a bit to make that happen for you the way it did.

"But make no mistake…that is just the tip of the iceberg of what I can do to you if you don't follow my direction."

He completely bypassed his statement and went straight back to Sophia's welfare. "Is there nothing I can do to get you to release Sophia?"

"Sebastian…giving up Sophia would be like giving away a Ruby. That's just not something that I would ever do. However, I will promise you this. As long as you remain obedient…I will make sure she stays alive."

Sebastian began to go insane inside from the outcome of the situation.

"WHY, Christopher…why can't you just leave her out of this! I'll do whatever you want. Just please leave her alone. Let her be free to live out her life…peacefully. You can have all my powers if that's what you like to call them. In fact, I will do anything you want for the rest of my life. Just let her go!"

"Oh, so I see you have finally found yourself in such a desperate disposition that you have chosen to be beneath me after all. So that's…nice." Church then got up out of his seat and walked over to Sebastian. He put his hand under his chin and lifted it up so he could let Sebastian see how delighted he was that things were going his way.

"So…this is how our deal is going to go. You will change your tone with me from this moment on. And you will do as I command without question. In return…I will make sure that Sophia does not die. That is where we are at in this negotiation."

How did it get to this point? Once again, he was put into a position of needing to do the wrong thing. He had no ammunition to fight. All he could come up with was…for the moment, this is what he needed to do to keep her alive. A deep sadness began to mold over his soul as he sank his head down, mortified by what he was about to say next.

However, Christopher was not about to let it go under like that. "Oh no, Sebastian. This won't do. When you beg for her life, I prefer you to look directly at me while groveling. I'll enjoy it so much more that way."

So he let out a long deep breath and pulled his head up. "I'm yours, Christopher…to use as you please…as long as you do not kill my Sophia."

"Ah…now, that's perfect. We have finally struck a deal!" Elated that he had finally come around, he settled the details quickly.

"Now that we have reached an agreement, you can feel free to let me know anytime you need a cleanse. We won't need to see each other in person, I can do it telepathically. I'm a little more advanced than our beloved friend, Josephine. In the meantime, stay close by, I will text you with your first assignment soon." Then he glanced at his guards and told them to take off his restraints. Sebastian's stomach began double over in a throbbing ache with the decision he had just made with Church.

As soon as they released him, he left without another word. When he got outside of the building, he began to vomit uncontrollably. "Jesus…what have I done! I can't believe this is happening all over again!" The only thing he could think to do was find Thomas.

His hands were shaking when he got in his car. *I've just got to get home*, he told himself. Nothing could be done while he was driving. He thought about Sophia. The pain of not knowing what in the world he was going to do to her…it practically drove him mad.

When he finally got home, he immediately began meditating to get into the tunnel. Within minutes from the time he got in, he found Thomas. He was located in a church of all places. "I've been waiting for you to come, Sebastian."

"So you've been watching my life…yet you offered me no help today?"

"You may look at it that way. However, I cannot just stop you from making your own free-will decisions. Now you are in a rather large dilemma."

"Yes, it seems I am."

"Well, what's done is done. What matters now is what you intend to do with the choices you have left in front of you."

"Call me crazy, but I don't see many options to choose from."

"You are wrong again, Sebastian. You have the choice to not take his offer."

"Somehow I knew you were going to say that. So let me ask you a question. Now that her chances of dying have gotten increasingly higher in the hands of Church, that is still not a good enough reason for the universe to let me save her?"

"You're missing the point. Although I agree your circumstances have now taken on an entirely new range of substantial problems, it is not too late for you to learn how to be egoless. You must not focus on what happened in the past or what will happen in the future. All that matters is that at this moment, she is still alive.

"As far as the future goes, I don't know what it holds for her. It might very well be gruesome, but again, it is how she wanted her life to be played out."

"So she said in her chart that she would be willing to die for the cause? Is that what you're telling me?"

"Not necessarily, Sebastian. Everything you see is so black and white in your canvas. You need to look at the bigger picture of why you both came down here in the first place.

"Otherwise, I'm afraid things may get so much worse for you if you don't."

"What are you insinuating, Thomas?"

"Only that you are at an important crossroads in your life. Change to your rightful path or suffer the consequences of an alternate life."

"Alternate life…what does that mean for me?"

"Do you remember the last time we spoke about what will happen if you possibly go down the wrong road?"

"Yes, as I recall you said I took that possibility into account. However, that was all you were able to say at the time."

"I was hoping to never have to breach the subject matter with you, but as it stands, you are at that moment in which it must be discussed." He started to pace the room in anticipation of what Thomas was about to divulge. "You wrote in your alternate life that you would go to the path of the darkness."

His heart nearly broke in two. "No, Thomas, what kind of life is that to live?"

"I know, Sebastian…it is not what you wanted to hear. I'm sorry I could not offer you better news."

"I don't understand, what I signed up for. I came down here to do good. To lead humankind to light. Yet, I myself could fall to the dark. It's ironic actually, Christopher told me I would end up just like him. Apparently, he was right. I'll be doomed to live under his wing for the rest of my existence."

"It's not over with, Sebastian. You still have time to change your course of action."

"Thomas, listen to me. All I need to do is work with Christopher on a short-term basis. I just need to bide my time until I find a way to get Sophia out of his hands."

"Do you understand the enormous risk factor you are putting yourself into, Sebastian!

"The darkness you have felt towards Sophia is not the only kind of negative energy out there. Other layers exist, one of which is particularly potent to the human soul. It is what turned both Christopher and Josephine away from the light.

"If you stay in that kind of darkness long enough, you will get trapped in the ugliness of it all. In fact, turning you over to the hands of Christopher was Josephine's last encounter, before she completely left the light. The moment she sought you out at Clarissa's party as a candidate for Church to seize as an acquisition, was the moment she decided her fate.

"So you see…every time you sign up to do an immoral act for Christopher, it will set you on the path to your alternate road."

"I'm hearing you, Thomas, but I won't let it get that far. I just need to get her out of danger from him and then I'll never do another single act for him again."

"Please grasp what I am saying here, Sebastian, there is no science as to when you will turn to the dark. It just happens if you stay in it long enough. Again, I caution…if you do this, you will be putting yourself in massive jeopardy by taking your chances down this road."

"Thomas, do you not understand that Sophia is in Christopher's hands because of me. Solely due to the choices that I made. No…I must do this for her! I will just have to hope and pray that I get her out before it is too late for me. It is the price I am willing to pay for her freedom."

"Have you considered all the things that Christopher will be asking you to do? It will be on a much grander scale than anything you could ever imagine. His mind has been dark for a very long time."

"I know, Thomas. It is not a decision I am taking lightly. I'll find a way to get her out as soon as possible. Then that will be the end of it."

"For your sake, I hope you are right."

He didn't respond to his comment. He just held his head down in reflection.

"So…Sebastian, if there is nothing else, I'm afraid I need to go for now."

"I know. I just wanted to say I'm sorry for the comment I made earlier about you offering me no help. Clearly, you are here for me."

"And I always will be, unless the day comes when the darkness shuts me out of your life forever."

"Let's hope that day never comes, Thomas."

"Yes, agreed." With that, he vanished and he was left with one last impending thought.

What if he's wrong…

CPSIA information can be obtained
at www.ICGtesting.com
Printed in the USA
BVHW010945230622
640288BV00022B/146